To my elders

A CLEVER *Girl*

Book One

JEANNIE TROLL

PAGE PUBLISHING, INC.
New York, NY

First originally published by Page Publishing, Inc. 2017

ISBN 978-1-63568-044-7 (Paperback)
ISBN 978-1-63568-045-4 (Digital)

Printed in the United States of America

The Warring Queens of the Frankish Kingdom

Fredegund (549-597) was a slave girl who became the wife of the Frankish emperor, Chilperic. Brunhild (567-613) was the wife of Chilperic's younger brother, Sigebert. Brunhild managed to survive Fredegund's unscrupulous and ruthless attacks for almost forty years. The war between the Frankish camps continued even after Fredegund's death. Brunhild lived to old age, when she was betrayed and brutally tortured. She died in 613. T

From A History of the Franks by Gregory of Tours

Chapter 1

AD 603

In the meadows, she liked to imagine the archways and porticoes, the statue lined loggias of the ruined world. There, eager minds read Pythagoras and Plato. Ladies with tumulous hair strolled the courtyards, tittering at Ovid's indecorous couplets, the ring of their laughter like silver coins. On street corners, sages touted discoveries-lost now, forever, to the learned world. And everywhere, in bathhouses, markets, and synagogues, there would be discussion. Strangers would accost one another in the libraries to share ideas and to argue on didactic points.

Someday, she would like to visit such cities, or what remained of them far to the east. True, she had been warned of their dangers: the precipitous rioting which could lead to massacres, the lawless streets, and marketplace thievery. The particular dangers to girls. Although she might well be safe from these, for she was unlike other girls in this way—a fact which left her often disinclined to leave the forest and her reveries of a forgotten age.

She turned her gaze now from the clearing and unto herself, to her own body and time, which could not disappear. God had put her here for His purposes, the yoke must be borne. There was no way to forgo it, her mistake of a body, the essential wrongness of the current world.

Of course, what she most longed to amend was herself. A smooth gait, a right hand that opened easily, an untwisted right foot which matched its mate and allowed her to run—to date, these remained only fantasies. In her child's mind, she could still believe in miracles; but though she'd tried, she had found no resultful magic. Other children, waxen angels on vigorous legs, flew across the fields like sparrows. Even the least of them had companions. Most had mothers who idolized them. Warriors smiled, maidens cooed when these cherubs passed by. Heedless, they ran about in raucous hordes by which it was inadvisable to be caught.

She also wished to fix the men. Some were humane and led uneventful lives. But others were a constant source of calamity. Usually drunken and smelling of rot, at small provocation, they could maim and kill one another, at even less, beat their wives or children to senselessness. The next morning, they would roam bewildered about the town. By afternoon, they were warming again to their habits.

Such things would never happen in her perfect world. But why could they not be corrected here? Kindness was not such a hard lesson. But Tahto said it was pointless to expect such things. Man had lived with cruelty for millennia. Lifetimes of effort might be expended on such an attempt.

Nevertheless, she was certain adults could reform things. They were able to predict harvests, weather, the birthways of women and animals. Their tacit comprehension of town events bespoke a studied canniness of the human soul. If progress was possible, which it must be, were they not the ones to make it? But Tahto said that change was slow, and that her mind was not, running always ahead, leaving the long settled, and rushing on into the impossible.

Not only ahead but back to the past, her refurbishing imagination sought—like her broom straws into corners, her fingers under the rumps of hens. How it could have been different. How her mother would not have left her, certain the child she'd borne was an imprecation. She could have taught her mother to see a future in which that babe would grow not only useful, but born for scholarship, as Tahto said. A child who could learn and remember things in a way that astonished her teachers, who could say things, although she was not always sure which ones, that caused them to tilt back their heads and laugh, and to regard her with a combination of appreciation and surprise. But her mother had never foreseen this for her daughter.

8

Had never even named her. This was left to Tahto who had found the red-faced bundle in his alley, days old and screaming with hunger.

Actually, it was the wet nurse, a local Frankish girl, who'd named her. But when she was returned, eight months old and round as a poppy, Tahto had revised this. Her original name was Agoberthe, but he had not liked the sound of that. For he could see in her infant face all the promise her mother had not. So he named her after an angel and called her Achtriel.

With the thought of Tahto, her mind returned to the present, specifically to the waning light. She was expected home before sundown. Tonight was Sabbath, and the day Tahto's *chevara* came for dinner. The berries and mushrooms she carried were awaited, and no less so her insightful comments. Raising the pail in her stronger left arm, she resumed her trundling pace through the woods.

Naturally, it was a source of much amusement to the normal girls that she should be reckoned angelic. There was nothing less celestial than her labored gait. But she had perfected what grace she could and, with her usual aptitude, had ameliorated her hobble to a useful roll. She was strong despite her infirmities, and it was a source of internal pride to travel, if not as fast as her peers, at least for as long a distance. In fact, her wanderings had far exceeded theirs, for they never strayed far from the walls of town.

Achtriel, like her namesake, frequented outlying realms. She had explored more forest than all but the swineherds. Here, the only murmuring was the wind's. Tree trunks, clothed a jolly pea green by the climbing moss, stood by like sentries. Sometimes, an animal would peek at her, a wolf howl in the distance, or a fierce boar snarl. She gladly risked these dangers for the gift of solitude.

The angel Achtriel was one of the protectors of YHWH, but initially, it was the baby Achtriel who had needed help. She was, because of her infirmities, slow to grasp and easy to topple. And because she was by nature a *berrieh*, a doer, she would become enraged and would scream and kick. That was why Tahto had hired Macha.

Macha had been in her second pregnancy. The first had produced a sturdy lad of four who had already outgrown her. So she cheerfully trailed the infant girl and helped her to hold things, mitigated her stumblings, and dried her tears. Macha was also a *berrieh* and so went to work on the coiled muscles of Achtriel's right arm and leg, the ones that had been damaged by her birth. Gradually, Achtriel's bent fingers had gained strength and her foot, once curled in abnormally, had been able to bear her weight. So that by the time of her first birthday, she could use both hands and pull herself to standing on whatever would hold, a workbench, a chopping block, Tahto's footstool or his trousered leg. She distinctly remembered the pride in his first surprised smile and the wonder it had engendered in her. She remembered also how she'd resolved that day to find new ways to delight him, to feel again that sense of joy.

Because of that decision, she had begun, almost immediately, to talk. Tahto still liked to tell how she would sit among his students, for all the world like a visiting dignitary. And how, with remarkable facility, would repeat the words she heard, so that the students would turn and stare, the lesson forgotten, in their awe at her precipitant vocabulary.

How in a few months she could form sentences and by age three was able to both read and write in Latin, Greek, and Hebrew. Oh, yes, she was bright as a cricket and a good thing too, they all agreed, because she would most certainly not wed. Now she was employable, and thus saved the beggary that befell most unfortunates who shared her lot.

But their sympathy, and the certainty that this defined her, was also what had driven her to the woods. There was no one here to abhor or pity her. She could construct her own world. A hollow tree blackened by ancient fires was her village. An acorn-headed pinecone was Seigneur and a stick his dog, who never would obey. Lady Sec was made of burdock root, her coif a strand of violet heather. She had three daughters who thought highly of themselves. The youngest was beautiful and many suitors, formed of branch tips, bowed before her.

A wyvern also lived nearby. But unlike those feared by townsmen, this beast, a log, was gentle. He guarded the wood folk and communed with fairies. Tahto said that fairies weren't real, but she had heard folk tell of meeting them. She would not be frightened if sprites came upon her. Like her, they were separated from the world of men by an innate and irrevocable divide.

She was sure, for instance, that no one possessed a head as full of questions as her own. Wonderings stirred her mind like eddies. If there were heavens, what hid them? And how did men learn of them to spread the tale with such conviction? Could she, in fact, be sure that other folk were real, not crops of her imagination like Lady Sec? What fashioned the realm of dreams, did animals walk upright in their own phantasms? Did they reflect on death? Questions nagged at her all day till, as evening neared, they could turn caustic. Then she must admit they circled in her mind about a hole, a central lack of something that she could not name. It lay in the past, buried like last winter's leaves.

And what was the past? How could Time form invincible walls yet be made, at last, of nothing? Why chop itself into days, unremarkable till dusk dissolved them to reveal the naked reaches of the sky? And what was Now?

This was Now, this moment in the woods when she was eight and a half, stopping to imagine things in the coppice. She could see the sky beginning to color, softening toward dusk. And there, the woods' leafed canopy lifted in wind, as if to the eternal *Ruach,* the breath of worlds. Now was the air, scented by bark and the molder of leaves, the furze at her ankles, the lush moss cradling her feet.

Now held also herself, what she could see of it, her rumpled kirtle, ash from the oven muting its dye. Her small shod feet turned inward, the ends of her awkward braids, studded with twigs. This was Now, this parcel of time, with her mind alive and aware in the midst of it. But her restless thoughts, not sufficiently impressed, raced on and did not care that this momentous Now was passing, past, and in the light of an instant, gone.

Time was something even Tahto could not well explain. He would admit at that juncture that he must veer into cosmology. Time as the *ha mahut,* the giver of form. And yet he was discomfited by religion, though he loved to discuss it, because he had been choked by worship, as he said. But Achtriel found it hopeful. Especially since the world of man did not offer her much standing. She loved to picture heavens and the many eyed angels who disported there. She liked to believe that since she had an angel's name, the Seraphim might, even now, be watching.

And yet if they beheld her, they would know what she knew—that an angel she was not. When Macha, jesting, called her *Chayot*, Achtriel laughed but felt an inward shame. Of course, she behaved well in front of others, as a foundling she had no other choice. But when she was alone, she entertained much evil. She would take the wool doll, Rael, that Macha made, and pinch its face, too smug with its dimpled grin. And Achtriel's own ugliness would burn into her daily thoughts and fill her sight like cinders.

At these times, her deformity enraged her. It was unthinkable, her twisted hand and foot like chicken claws. Why could not time be construed to undo her fate and make her look like other girls? When she was most unhappy, she yearned to cut the affected limbs and thus become only injured, not misshapen. With difficulty, she would pull herself back from such extremes; and soon, her mood would shift to one of gloomy resignation. This she could transform into a serviceable acceptance.

No one, she knew, suspected her struggles for she hid them well. They thought her wryness cheering and her wit a strength. What they could not see was that these were ramparts, all the more impregnable for their invisibility. Only Tahto sometimes seemed to guess her grief in his quiet way. He would come to her room and ask her to read to him.

Once, she had explored the subject. She'd asked him if she had been a boy, would matchmakers have ignored her infirmities, painted them perhaps as a *kavid*, an obstacle she'd surmounted with humility and holiness to gain her rich scholastic standing?

He had looked uncomfortable, even angry. He said that her infirmities were minor, a common condition he'd read of in Greek texts, an accident of birth. He said the local souls were ignorant of medical wisdom, how could they not be? If their custom were not to present each newborn to the Pater for acceptance, there would be many more like she was. Instead, they chose to kill those helpless infants for their differences, a murderous crime yet one endorsed for centuries.

As it was obvious there was no wrong with her mind, the worst effect of such conditions; and since she had, with her humility and holiness, improved her limbs so that they worked almost as well as anyone's, no one had a right to belittle them or see her as an oddity. Although he had a practical and jesting tone, his eyes were sad, and she decided not to talk of this again. She knew he did not understand. She was a cripple in the eyes of all mankind and always would be.

The only one who knew how black her spirit grew was Rael. She beat and berated the doll for its clumsiness. But soon again, Rael became her playmate and slept beside her. They were kindred and imperfect souls.

Yes, there was darkness in Rael and in Achtriel too. One that made her hate other girls even when, on a Sabbath, they might act kindly to her. She dreaded them as a sinner feared holiness and shielded her eyes from their shapely limbs and dark beauty. They could belong here. They would marry, have families, be happy. They would be able to mention, offhandedly, their husbands and children, to wag heads with mock perturbation and relate, like a small thing just recalled, their family's impressive accomplishments. They would be accepted even as their beauty faded, and they grew old. They were of the fabric of the town. This she could never be. So she felt she had no place beside them and banished their existence from her own.

But why then did she feel an even greater venom for Sorgen, the little slave who cowered when she walked the street, errand basket clutched to chest, biddy head practically tucked between protruding scapulae? How dared she, Achtriel the cripple, bear such hatred for a fellow unfortunate? But scold herself as she might, she could not befriend Sorgen. She smiled at her when she gave her alms but was always relieved when the girl hurried off to her duties.

The *chevara* encouraged her to seek playmates, but such friendships seemed as reachless as the stars. She dreaded her own tremulous overtures, and the self-contempt that would inevitably follow, more than the children's taunting. And she remembered all too well her experiences when, as a younger and less cautious child, she had accepted the local girls' invitations.

She would follow the chattering mob, insinuating herself on its fringes. The girls would tolerate her for a time, perhaps as long as a morning. But then some disagreement would arise and their tempers sour. Soon, she would be swarmed by their intrusive questions.

"What games can we play with you? Do you not see that we have rightly shaped hands, see mine, see Astruc's, and you," lifting her beaklike fist, "I think you are part twit." The rest would laugh. "Can you then fly, Achtriel? For you are an angel and should surely try." And they would chase her till, exhausted, she stumbled about like a broken-winged bird.

Once, after they had gone, some Gentiles came, whose faces were so dirty you could not tell the features; and they pushed her off a stone wall. On another day, those children, or some equally filthy ones, threw manure on her. Soon, before the girls could ask, she would hurry to the forest, then come home at dusk and tell Tahto she'd had a fine rest day.

Her times in the woods were indeed pleasant. Only swineherds and hunters entered there and were easy to evade. The problem was that when she did appear in town on some necessary errand, her unwonted presence was notable. The children and even impolite adults would point and stare and bring their faces close to whisper.

Things were probably not improved, she could admit, by her style of dress. Each Rosh Hashonah a sack would appear on her doorstep, the gift of some matron, priding herself on her *mitzvah*. It held the cast-off finery of merchant girls, the loving handiwork of some mother or skillful slave.

Perhaps because of the embarrassing irony, she had no regard for the clothing. She would tie embroidered kirtles round her waist or wind their sleeves about each leg like workmen's pants. She wore whatever lay at hand and kept it on for weeks with little attention to its state of cleanliness.

The clothing lay in scattered piles about her room in which she played or sometimes slept. Periodically, Tahto would hire a woman, Macha had long since given up, to launder them and put them in a trunk. This reform, however, proved ephemeral. The clothes soon returned to her floor, to form what Tahto called her nest.

Since no one had taught her the niceties of dress, nor did it matter as she was not to marry, she only thought of what felt soft or fit the temperature. Occasionally, she'd choose with interest an ensemble and wear it on an errand into town. There, however, folk would laugh out loud and point at her. But as they did this often, it was not instructive.

She stopped to put down the bucket. The church bell, signaling day's end, echoed through the wood. Here, at the forest's edge, she began to pick up village scents, dinner fires advertising their ware. The smoke was more fragrant today when both Jews and Gentiles would be serving special meals. Those who could afford it would be eating fish; the rest, maslin or barley bread. In the synagogue, a board would be set for the poor by the elected elders. Everywhere, folk would be more cheerful, for their plates were full.

Spotting a patch of mint, she bent to gather some as she resumed her pace. The bush spilled its fragrance, piquing her hunger. She knew she was fortunate that, unlike many in her village, she had never famished. There was no need to share the proceeds of her garden or their purchased food. No sisters, brothers, aunts or uncles, slaves or apprentices lived in her house. Only herself and Tahto. So they managed on his small but adequate income to sustain themselves.

"Why," she had asked him once, "do so many babes and old ones die each winter? Could not the families plan better and save food to strengthen them against the cold?"

"The synagogue offers a group each month to the public." He sighed. "We try to teach them planning and healthful habits. But even so, they wait until someone is dying before they come to us. By then, it is quite hard to doctor them."

"Why cannot the synagogue bring food to them all?"

"Alas, we are a small *Beth Din*," he said, "and often struggle simply to fill the poor table."

"But there are so many wealthy merchants here, among Jews and Gentiles both!"

"It is a curious fact that the richer a man grows, the less he shares with his neighbors."

"Why?"

"I cannot say." He frowned. "I only know that I have observed it so wherever I have lived."

"Will we ever be rich, Tahto?" she asked.

"I doubt it."

"But if we were, we would eat well and also help feed the village."

"Indeed. But as we are not, we had best be satisfied with our monthly contributions and our simple fare."

And simple it was. Vegetables, cheese, milk, and grain. And the fruits of the earth in the spring and summer.

Sometimes, knowing Tahto would accept no more than he was owed, his students' gave Macha eggs or butter for his dinner. He would ask her how she had afforded these. She would reply that her son had got them—believable enough for he was known to be *balmalucha*. These treats and the occasional wine Tahto's friends provided marked the only changes to their Sabbath feast. What made the evenings piquant was the conversation.

Lately, the *chevara* was considering the nature of the Self: of what material consciousness was formed and what defined it. A Greek manuscript, come by in Paris, held that the Self was an actual organ, secreting emissions in the form of thoughts.

Some held attractive properties, which gathered similar thought substance to them. Repellent ones made diseases like spiritual sloth and madness. The book had a diagram with samples of ideas and their corresponding properties. Tahto's circle found this inane and joked about the passing of spiritual wind. Nonetheless, they felt privileged to have the text which was Alexandrian and very old.

One of Tahto's friends, Fagim, held that the Self was but one's birthright. She said that we are born as ready Selves and that the purest expression of Self is the child. She was always interested in children and paid attention to Achtriel's comments, probing her sometimes to the point of discomfort. Samiel Meyr insisted that the Self was God's joke, put here to entertain both Himself and us. Tahto pronounced Self the great mystery and said few would decipher it. Most people spent their earthly days in ignorance of its enormity.

Tonight, Achtriel planned to explain to them the obvious: that Self was made of the same thing as Now. You could approach, within your mind, a flavor of it and know, even as you did, that to hold it was as hard as touching Time. Also, like Time, Self's weight could change. When laden with unspoken thoughts, it clogged one's head. The tangle could be painful, but sometimes another Self could soothe it and make that go away. So Self was no different from the soul of an animal or any living entity who wanted its way; to follow its curiosity, to be loved, not to become too bored or be in excessive pain. She had explained this already to Tahto, who had liked her ideas and smiled, but she felt nonetheless that he had dismissed them. He was sure from his readings that the Self was a concept as deep as Eternity. But Achtriel knew human selves were not that grand. You had only to watch them to discover that. And observing people was her incessant occupation; the field of inquiry from which her most effective knowledge came.

She stopped again to push moist hair from her forehead. She had emerged from the woods and stood atop the promontory overlooking the town. Outside the village walls lay the communal plots, green with ripening corn. Beside them, near the fallow fields, stood the enclave of those Jews who would not neighbor with non-Jews. Oddly, although she and Tahto were deemed Jews by the townsfolk, these reclusive members of her own faith often seemed more foreign to her than the Gentiles. She remembered when, some years past, and likely due to reproaches from the synagogue, Tahto had invited some of the more educated of these Jews to his Sabbath.

One was a newly arrived scholar from Pumbedita who had brought along his wife and three children. After dinner, the man's family stood stiffly in the kitchen while he joined the disputants in Tahto's study. They had remained so, the mother mumbling discreet instructions to her brood for nearly an hour. Finally, she had given doubtful permission for the twin boys and a plump older girl to play in Achtriel's room.

Achtriel had been initially delighted with the prospect of play-mates. But the boys, although her same age, could only kneel in prim disapproval and not think of a single game. At last the girl, who had begun to fold and straighten Achtriel's clothing piles, suggested a reciting competition.

Achtriel tired of this quickly, but the boys only grew more emphatic, trying to catch her in mistakes and arguing over abstruse interpretations of the Torah. Finally, she cried that she did not care, and this shocked them into momentary silence. Then the girl, who at ten had already developed horizontal and rather forlorn-looking breasts, declared Achtriel to be ungodly.

"How can that be?" she demanded.

"You are a Jew who does not follow the teachings of the law."

"The law is to honor God in all things. Nothing can be ungodly because everything is God," she responded.

"So you think He lives in rocks and trees and in the slaughter beasts?"

"Tahto has seen God looking out of the eyes of cows."

"Is that why you serve no meat or fish at your Sabbath?" One boy smirked.

"Yes, because He lives most vividly in flesh."

"Most vividly." The girl snickered. "God is not vivid. He is just. It says nowhere in our scriptures that meat is wrong. Animals are sacrificed to honor Him."

"What kind of honor is a killing?" Achtriel asked her. "Even that their souls transmigrate, they must die in fear and suffering. But Tahto says we all observe in ways that suit us. If that is your faith, we will not quarrel."

"Our faith? Are you not of our faith?" The other boy laughed.

"Yes, but..."

"But you have never eaten flesh, neither fowl nor fish?" the first pressed.

"Not that I know. Once I was sick and had some soup that Macha made. It tasted odd, and she admitted she had put some fowl in it."

"And was her grandfather enraged?" all three had asked. "Had he fired the cook woman?"

"Of course not," Achtriel replied; he and Macha were old friends, and he had simply reminded her that they chose to forebear flesh, as his Eastern texts commanded. Macha had muttered that "the child" would surely weaken, but when Achtriel returned to her usual robust health, the matter had been dropped.

"And do you," questioned the first twin, "ever work on the Sabbath?"

"Sometimes," she admitted, "the garden must be tended and the housework done."

"Then what scripture," they demanded, "did she and Tahto follow if, in fact, they were Jews at all?" The one that Tahto kept in his study, she told them, which was thousands of years old and came from Alexandria. The sister stopped her folding, and her face went white.

"You are worse than ungodly then," she gasped. "You are *apikorsim!*" Then she proceeded to tell Achtriel of the seventh hell to which she would descend at death, and the manner of demons for whom her eternal torture would be all delight. And the twins described to her the *Seirjim, shedim* or demons clothed with scales and hair with one pale eye in their middle chest that rolls like a ball and told her how one who sees them falls instantly upon his face and dies. They said the *Seirjim* roamed the streets at night looking for ungodly weakened souls to murder. That night, she had awoken Tahto three times with her nightmares. The scholar and his family were not invited back.

In that part of town also lived Priscus, another Jew with an ancient text of the Pentateuch. As he was highly educated, Tahto had invited him to one Sabbath. Priscus had emigrated to Briga from Rome where he had lost a son to conversion and a daughter to disease. He had come with his last child, a thin-lipped woman, and her husband, a dyer. Although the pair had born him two granddaughters, he continued to bemoan the loss of his boy. That evening at Sabbath, he had drunk over much and begun to cry for him.

"What," Tahto gently asked, "is the point of religion if not to help men love one another and their families?"

"You are suggesting I forgive him then?" the scholar sputtered.

"On which side lies the smallest suffering?" Tahto shrugged. But the man had become furious and had gone about the next day telling whoever would listen that Tahto was no Jew but a heretic. Since most of his audience had long ago formed this opinion, the event caused little disruption to their social life.

Tahto's *chevara* included Samiel Mayr the butcher, whose son, a prodigy, had been sent to study in Lunel. Samiel was familiar not only with Jewish books but those of Greece and Persia, Babylon, and Rome. He owned and had copied many manuscripts from the great Alexandrian library. Samiel was one of the most educated men around, but more importantly, he was funny. He could mimic anyone in town with droll precision and loved to repeat the silly things they said. He also imitated Tahto to the delight of the circle, which made Tahto laugh out loud.

Profait, the tailor, was also well read and, like his profession, precise and reliable. He could be counted on to know exact quotations and passages of scripture, and on one occasion had even corrected Tahto. This gave him immense standing in the group and made them hesitate to contradict him. But Achtriel's favorite guest was Mosse, a retired merchant and scholar from a genealogy of scholars.

Mosse was also droll. His humor was darker than the butcher's, but Achtriel enjoyed it more. He would mutter some wry comment beneath his breath, as his thick eyebrows rose and his beard emitted a deep "heh heh." His jokes were the kind that took everyone a few moments to understand, and when they did, they laughed with a kind of delighted pride.

Then there were the sisters, Fagim and Esther. They were from Austrasia and had come to Briga because of their husbands. Not, like most Jewish women, because they had followed them there, but because they hated them. Fagim's husband was a wealthy merchant who spent all day conferring with traders and the local gentry. He traveled a good part of the year and had women and children in many towns but, because of his wealth, was accepted in the synagogue.

When Fagim had born their first child, a deaf boy, he accused her of having got him by another man. He behaved cruelly toward the son. Fagim left when the boy was three to go and live with her sister. Once there, she discovered that Esther's husband was worse than her own.

That husband would fly into rages and even broke the arm of the boy when he had tried to shield his aunt. Fagim was knowledgeable in medicine and had reset the arm so that it was now strong, and the boy, Natan, a handsome fourteen-year-old. Esther had divorced her husband. At twenty, she was young enough to remarry. Fagim was always mentioning eligible men, but Esther said she had grown happy in her solitude and could not abide a husband to treat her like a slave.

The sisters were witty and lively and very bright. They sold and imported cloth, dye, and spices and often found manuscripts in their travels which they brought back to share. Remembering that they had just returned from Rodom and might have books and other treasures, Achtriel lifted her pail and hastened down the hill toward home. When she arrived, however, she heard, from within, someone crying.

Pushing open the door, she glanced at the lighted common room. It was cleaned and swept, the long table set for guests. From Tahto's chamber came the animated sounds of discussion. But when she entered the house, she heard a sniffle coming from the kitchen. There, Macha stood by the counter, drying her eyes on a dishcloth.

"What is the matter?" Achtriel asked, coming in and depositing her pail on the kitchen floor.

"Aah, a wicked, wicked boy," Macha emitted by way of answer.

"Who?" Achtriel asked, though she well knew.

"Who else?"

"Elies?" Her twelve-year-old, "But he is not extremely wicked."

"What else can you call a son who thinks only of himself, nothing for his family?"

"You could call him…"

"Phoo, Achtriel. You know what I mean. He goes thinking nothing of my wishes nor the good of his brother. Nothing!"

"What has he done?" Achtriel asked, sitting on the paring stool. She liked Elies. He did not show a bent for study, but he was quick

21

minded, and he made her laugh. Also he did not treat her as an odd-ity. He teased her, but only as he would anyone else, and for this, she was quite grateful.

"Here I have found him the perfect match." Macha lamented. "The daughter of a nabob from Rodom."

"Does he like her?"

"Like! She is a respectable girl. A beauty even, well not so bad—who can tell at her age, but good and capable. Too good for him."

"Maybe he does not want to wed." Achtriel reached for the fruit bowl on the counter and took an apple.

"He does not want. He does not *want*, Achtriel, to think of anyone or anything but his adventures. And his high-blown theories. Slavery is evil he tells me."

"Is the merchant a slaver?" she asked, biting the fruit.

"Who can tell? He is a Jew and would not advertise it if he were. But he is so wealthy that he heads the Jewish council and collects its taxes. And supports the local *schul*. If Elies married him, then his brother could afford to study."

"But he would not be marrying *him*, Macha…"

"Psh! You know what I mean to say! And don't talk with your mouth full!" She wiped the counter in silence. "Marrying into that family would be our salvation," she continued. "Elies is no scholar nor ever will be, but Eliazer shows the makings of one. They might take him in and raise him to the life of study that befits him. But Elies can only fret over the man's ill gains and such nonsense."

"Perhaps he means that his own enslavement is unappealing."

"You!" Macha swiped at her with the dishcloth, "What do you know? Marriage is marriage. It is a fact of life."

"But what does Elies want to do?"

"To prance around town like an *amhaaretz*, selling Oriental trinkets to merchants. He imagines himself a businessman. He wants to build a boat!"

"That could be useful."

"Where is he going to get the money I ask you?"

"But, Macha, if this is what he wants, he'll find a way. Tahto says children are not cows to be bartered."

"Ah. That old man can fill your head with his ideals, for you it does not matter. You will…" She stopped herself.

"Never marry?"

"What do you mean? Of course you will, someday. Maybe not to…maybe not in the way of most but…"

"You mean none will seek me. Nor will I command any great price."

"Well, but these things are…Listen, Achtriel! Don't turn me around with your clever arguments. I know where you are leaning. It is a blessing to make a marriage match."

"I wonder if cows feel that way too when they are sold."

"Get out! Get out of my kitchen!" Macha shouted, but her mouth crooked into a rueful smile. "And go wash your face and hands you are filthy as a Gentile!" Achtriel rose and went out the kitchen door to the washhouse.

"And when you are clean, come and help me set dinner," Macha called. "I'll not have you hiding in your nest. You will serve like a proper girl."

"But if I am not to marry, why do I need to?"

"Because you will not like your food very well if you cannot sit down."

Achtriel chuckled. She knew Macha would never hit her, as she did her boys, but it was a comical thought. She tossed the apple core into the garden and went to wash herself. The water was cold and smelled slightly of decay. She emptied the bowl outside and refilled it at the well. When she returned to the kitchen, Macha seemed more cheerful. She was tasting the soup. Then she removed her duster and wiped her hands on it.

"This is ready." She nodded. "You can serve it when the *tzaddik* comes from his chambers. Oil and season the mushrooms. Wash the berries and serve them for dessert. There are parsnips and carrots in the pot. Also, there's rye loaf in the oven door. When the soup is done, you can ladle it into those trenchers I made with last week's bread. The loaf will finish soon. Do not let it burn."

"Yes, Macha,"

"If you hear that I have run away with a traveling poet, tell my son it is his fault. Let *him* find work to care for his brother."

"Yes, Macha."

"And if you burn my cooking, I will come back from my travels and haunt you like the *shedim*."

"Yes, Macha."

"I am going." She kissed Achtriel on the top of her head.

"Have a good Sabbath." Achtriel smiled. Macha made an exasperated face at her as she went out the door.

Chapter 2

Achtriel removed the bread and brought it, steaming, to the table. She could hear Tahto's laughter from the study. Then came a new voice, clear in tone and speaking the unaccented Latin of the gentry. Such a guest merited a special course, so she found her basket and went out to the garden. Although it was almost September, some lettuce still grew. She gathered it with some mustard and radishes. These she washed and dressed for a fresh salad. When she returned, the group had emerged from Tahto's annex. Behind and at least a head taller than all of them stood a blond man.

She was surprised, not only by his shaven face and long hair, but because his coloring so matched her own. Tahto noticed her astonishment and smiled. "Antonus, this is my young ward. Achtriel, meet our guest, Antonus de Capitestano."

The man seemed startled when he noticed her. "How came such a child to your house?" he inquired.

"Ah, we stole her for our dinner," Fagim said, coming from behind him and straightening the serving dishes on the table. "Achtriel, jump in the stewpot!"

"I had not seen a Jewish child before with such light hair," the stranger said abashedly to Esther.

"Not all of us are dark, sir," she replied, "For we come from every corner of the world. In fact, a Jew moved here last month from Burgundium who is as yellow haired as she."

"I thank you for the information," the man said, pulling out a chair for her. "I will enter it into the store of ignorances I harbor concerning your people. It will stand there in good company for this evening have I added a new column to the account of my illiteracy. In truth, I had thought myself well prepared to discuss those texts with you. I was bred, you know, in the finest schools of law and letters."

"Breadth of study is hard-won in these days," Esther agreed, sitting, with some delicacy, in the proffered seat. "It is because we love our learning that we rake the cities for its remnants."

"Yet, we are but townsfolk," Fagim said, sitting across from her sister. "Our civilized kin can no doubt best us."

"I do not think so, for I have met with many of them." The man sat next to Esther, trying to appear as if this was unintentional. "Too often, they boast themselves better learned than they are. I myself can dispute them. But I think I have met my match this evening. Thank you again for inviting me, good lady." He kissed Esther's hand, and she bowed her head gracefully in acknowledgement.

"And now you shall taste the legendary elegance of our cooking," Mosse remarked slyly, dislodging the bench beneath the far side of the table.

"I fear we stand as ignorant of culinary elegance in this house as you assess yourself in the world of letters," added Samiel, behind him, sotto voce. Nonetheless, the two men sat happily and surveyed the simple fare.

"Oh, I have dined on swan's tongue and hummingbird at the tables of kings." The blond man smiled. "But I think I shall enjoy me this meal tonight as none before." He produced a wineskin from his satchel and offered it to Mosse.

Tahto came from the kitchen, carrying the soup pot. "Macha will be pleased to know she's served a connoisseur," he said. Achtriel followed him with the ladle and spooned soup into the trenchers which the guests then passed about the table. Then she brought her salad and presented it to the stranger. She saw him eye her pronate hand and felt unbidden redness rising to her cheeks.

Profait had taken the chair on the stranger's vacant side. "So," he said now, taking the salad from Achtriel and surreptitiously inspecting it for insects, "Tell us of your courts." He served a spoonful of salad to Antonus and one to himself. "Are they as fallen as ours? We had hope that, with the death of dear Fredegund, our Brunhild might be some assuaged. But, no doubt she shall continue to rile her grandsons and she has their elders."

"We have heard much of your warring queens," Antonus smiled. "Our humorists are greatly indebted to them."

"They are less amusing to us, "Fagim frowned. "They have done nothing but bring us near-continuous war. As yet it remains too distant to affect us. I would hate to think what would happen if it does not."

"Brunhild, no doubt esteems herself a modern Theodora," Esther said, accepting the bread from Samiel.

"Compared to Brunhild, Theodora looks a most able states-woman," Samiel observed.

"Compared to Brunhild," Mosse said, "Her clodpate spouse seems a Belisarius."

Later, as Achtriel cleared the table, the stranger beckoned her to his chair. "For such a child, I have a gift," he said winking and searched in his satchel. Then he drew out a roll of vellum, an ink-pot, and a long quill pen. Achtriel's mouth fell open and rendered her speechless. The stranger laughed. "No need to thank me, little scholar." He smiled. "Your face has already done so."

Still astonished, she took his gifts and slipped with them into a corner of the kitchen. The vellum was much smoother than the rough leather she normally used. The quill pen bent slightly as she dipped it in the ink and again when it touched the surface of the vel-lum. Its flexibility allowed her to make lines as eloquent and sinuous as a river.

"So this fear of the Jews will harm us all eventually," the stranger was saying as the dinner conversation waned. He turned to notice Achtriel, at his elbow." What have you…" he began, and his face became pale.

"Why that is something!" Tahto said.

"It is us to the life!" Mosse exclaimed, rising from his chair to see, "And Antonus! You have captured him utterly. Well done!"

"Does the portrait offend you, Antonus?" Esther asked, seeing the furrows that lined his brow.

"No, no! Thank you, Achtriel. Your work is astonishing. It is so like me that I…have you made others with me in them?"

"No, sir," Achtriel told him, "Just this one."

"Ah, well then, may I keep it?"

"Of course," she said, "I had thought only that I might like to have it to remember your kindness."

"But such a work metes recognition in the wider world." He laughed, somewhat nervously. He took the portrait from her and rolled it quickly. It was not until he left that Fagim offered an explanation.

"He is concerned that folk would see it here," she said to Achtriel.

"Is he a brigand?"

"Not at all." Esther bristled. "He's an honorable Christian."

Fagim let her eyes linger on her sister's face for a moment before she spoke. "He is that. However, he has endangered himself this night due to the enticement of my sister."

"He begged to be invited!" Esther insisted.

"Wait! Please. I don't understand," Achtriel interrupted. "Did I offend him? I would not like to think I…"

"No, no, do not worry," Fagim consoled her, "You need not reproach yourself."

"Then why was he discomfited by my portrait?"

"It was not your drawing, child, that was at fault but its accuracy," Tahto said kindly.

"There are some who feel it is wrong for Christians to dine with Jews," Esther explained. "We told him such a trifling offense is negligible here, but he was nervous nonetheless."

"I am sure he was only being cautious." Tahto sighed. "Yet how are we to know if he has enemies to make much of such a minor breach. The world of the courts is unending treachery."

"And how would you be so familiar with it?" Fagim asked. But he would say no more.

The next morning, Tahto came to Achtriel's bedroom. She had allowed herself one corner of vellum to draw on, saving the rest, and had filled it entirely. She was now using charcoal to decorate her walls with pictures. The drawings were of trees and animals. They bore them all as good a likeness as the stranger had his portrait. Unfortunately, the coal's residue now covered her face, hands, and several items of clothing on her crowded floor.

"You have found a new talent." Tahto smiled. "These are wonderful. But perhaps Macha will not like the mess." Achtriel glanced absently at her blackened walls and at her skirt, now filled with handprints. "Ah, well, it was time to have the cleaning woman back again. It has been several months," he said.

"What is wrong with idols, Tahto?" she asked, finishing the outline of a cow.

"I am really not sure. Let's think. Well… you know that in the time of Moses, there were many faiths. Some people held to very ancient ones. In some of them, cows and bulls were sacred; their seed was said to have engendered life. So people made art about them, much as you are doing now. It gave them courage."

"Then why did Moses say idols are evil?"

"Probably he wished the people to unite under one God and so become a nation."

"Why couldn't they all worship cows then?"

"Why a formless god and not a cow, eh? Hmm. Perhaps the cow worshipers were unruly. They were purported to do evil things. Like killing children."

"Sacrificing them?"

"It is rumored."

"But God told Abraham to murder Isaac, Tahto."

"True."

"And in the lands of the Canaanites, God said to kill and not to spare the babes and women. And why is it better to eat baby lambs for Pascal rites? Why did God want that?"

"Who decided that the heavenly ones like the savor of burnt flesh, you ask. A good question." He lowered himself onto her bed and picked up her woolen doll. She was quiet for a time as she finished her drawing.

"I think I would rather have a cow for God," she said at last.

"Cows are not known to plot against their sisters and make war," he agreed. "You do not hear of cattle armies."

"Let's start a religion of worshipping cows."

"I'm afraid in these times we might both be sacrificed for that," he said. They were chuckling at this when they were interrupted by a banging at the front door.

Tahto turned his head toward the sound with some consternation. It was unusual for him to have Sabbath visitors. Few Jews went out on Sabbath, and the Gentiles who sometimes came to his school would assume he would rest on a holy day.

"Shall we answer it, Tahto?" she prompted.

"I suppose we must," he said and rose with some difficulty from her low bed.

They were an odd pair as they approached the door, the old man stepping carefully on his bare feet, the child peering from behind him like a terrier. "Who is it?" Tahto asked politely. "I am a poor Jew and do no business on the Sabbath."

"I've not come to rob you, old man," a rough voice said. "Open your door."

Tahto moved the latch and pulled the door back. A tall man with the smell of damp stood shivering in the rain.

"How can I be of help?" Tahto asked him.

"Well, ye can have me in," he said, "I've rode all night to deliver this of me master."

"Of course, of course, come in, sir." Tahto backed away so that the man could bend under the door frame. "We shall make you something hot. Achtriel have we more soup on hand?"

"Yes," she replied but remained staring at the craggy man who stood stamping his boots on the doormat.

"Come into the kitchen," Tahto offered. "We have not stirred the fire today but shall do so at once. I can see you are in need of it."

"Thankee kindly," the man said and followed them to the kitchen.

"Please sit," Tahto gestured toward the paring stool. The man smiled gratefully and sank onto it as if he had had no rest in days. Achtriel could not turn her eyes from him but, at Tahto's nod, she hurried to the pantry and returned with the soup pot. She stirred the fire absently, her gaze scarcely departing from the stranger's face.

"I've been on road since midweek coming here," he said, "Master bid me ride by night for the brigands about. But the only 'ns I met was indoor. I've been from home here for three years, the roads have bettered."

"The local gentry have set up patrols on the coast road," Tahto said. "It is safer now. It doesn't further business to have the thorough-fares troubled. You are from these parts then?"

"From Lexovia. There is an Irish monastery there now and folk have come to settle beside it, my wife and son among them. I shall see them soon God willing."

"Where have you been for the three years?" Achtriel asked as she offered him the remains of the rye loaf. "I've been at sea, young miss. I thank ye." He took the bread and hungrily bit into it. Tahto's eyes told her to ask no more till he had eaten. When he had devoured the bread, he told them, "First meal I've had in two days. My master sent me with provisions, but I stayed in a roadhouse and woke robbed. Would have fared better in the wood."

"We will be happy to provide you food for your remaining jour-ney," Tahto offered.

"Thank ye', sir." The man nodded. He accepted a trencher of cold soup from Achtriel and drank it like a tankard. Then he wiped his mouth on his hand and belched. "Ah. It grows warm in here," he said, "I'll drop asleep ere long." He gave Achtriel a sly look out of the corner of his eyes.

"Please, sir, give us your message first," she begged.

"Ah, ye can wait a day more, never even knew I was coming till now, a few hours won't be the death of you," he yawned widely. But then he wrinkled his nose at her and reached into his shirt. "Yea'd like to know what this is would you, miss? But I've strict instructions to hand it to none but this gentleman."

"Then please hand it him, sir. Please?"

"Ah she's an impatient mite like all of them. My lad will be as eager for the treat I've brought him."

"I must confess to monstrous curiosity as well," Tahto said, taking the parcel the stranger handed him. "I cannot think what your man has for me."

"Well, here you have it. My master sent it with none but me, knowing I'd have the best keeping of it. It was I told him of your local port at the coast. Else he'd have sailed to Quentovic and paid half his profit to Frankish tax. Made my journey short as well. He's rewarded me, you see, with my freedom."

"I am most pleased for you, and so shall be your wife and son. Tahto removed the oil string from the leathern packet."

"What is it? What does it say?" Achtriel asked.

"Well, he might know if he'd a chance to open it now, would he or no?" the man chided.

"Tahto, you are taking so long that winter will come sooner!" she complained, rushing to his side to see the package opened. Inside it was a letter. "You are to travel to the coast and meet my ship the Shahbaz before we sail in two weeks' time," it said. "I bear a missive for you from the East. Captain Trovus."

"He has a letter for me," Tahto said, astonished. "Where was it given him, do you know?"

"Our last port was Marcellus where he took on your missive with a cargo of ivory carvings. Don't worry, he will not leave ere you come. He will not be paid the second of his fees till you have signed for it, and he has returned that to the broker."

"Who could it be from Tahto, who?"

Tahto seemed distracted. "The one thing I can think is that is from my brother. I have not seen him for many, many years."

"My master's ship lies docked at Ormaris. Have you the means to get there?" the man inquired.

"Yes, I can rent a cart," Tahto answered vaguely. "It will be some day's journey…"

"And the young miss here will tend to things at home. Seems a fine capable girl." The stranger poked her heartily. "Don't fret! He'll be back in a week or so, maybe a bit more."

"Tahto!" Achtriel protested loudly. Tahto's attention reverted to the room and her distress. "Ah, no. I must have a road companion," he said. "Macha can look after things." Achtriel exploded with such glee that both Tahto and the stranger could not help but laugh.

On the following day, they rented an oxcart and Bridey, the cooper's mule. They gathered their provisions and sent word to Tahto's students and friends. That evening, she had bedded in fresh straw on the cart's wood floor and was rocked to sleep by its motion. In the morning, she awoke to the smell of hay, the dray's good-natured lurching, and a sky blue as cornflowers. Her gaze lingered on it till she recalled where she was. Then she wanted to suspend this moment for she knew she never had been happier.

Tahto was singing a Persian song, mournful and lovely in the maiden light. Bridey nickered at every chorus, as if she knew the tune. Stuffy town odors and minds were absent here on the Roman road, where blackbirds trilled to mark their passage, and the air smelled of wildwood.

How clean the world was at this hour. How simple in purpose. Why men felt the need to trouble themselves with all they did— besting and cheating one another, arguing, fighting, creating wars with their harvest of grief—seemed incomprehensible. The clop of Bridey's hooves and the raw creak of cartwheels was all that dawn required of man for complement.

Tahto glanced back at her and saw that she was awake. He must have shared her thoughts for he smiled gently and began his second verse. Bridey chuffed and the birds, raucous in the new day, briefly stopped their chatter to approve the song. Achtriel could catch most of the words, a princess and a prince who left their kingdoms to seek justice. They brought with them a dog whose eyes espied a magic fire. She would have joined in the refrain but did not want to break the moment's perfection.

The sky itself seemed to be listening. She wondered again how human beings, beneath such beauty, could stir at all unless in reverence or ignore the edict of such heavens to forbear below them anything less holy. If kings and courts and fighting men but studied dawn, how could they again be roused to war? She decided that if she were king, her first proclamation would be to make men worship daybreak and perceive its wisdom.

They rode on like this as the sun rose and neither made a sound until Bridey halted and brayed uncomfortably. Across the road loped a covey of wolves. The leader glanced at them briefly then disappeared into the bordering trees. However, one wolf, a red one, looked up and, seeing Achtriel, halted. For a moment, its lucid gaze held her own. It was as if it knew her. Then it turned to follow its fellows.

"And to think men hunt that lovely beast." Tahto sighed and clicked his tongue at Bridey who had stopped.

"He had a wise courageous face," she said, "As noble as a lord's."

"Oh, far more so, at least of those I've known"

"Have you known court men, Tahto?" she asked and came to sit by him on the wooden plank.

"I have known a few, and that is plenty," he replied. She could tell from the set of his bearded mouth that he would say no more.

"Was your brother of the company of kings?" she inquired, hoping to approach the subject sidelong.

"My brother? Well, I suppose it's possible. In the countries near where we lived a Jew, a merchant say, a lawyer or doctor could consort with royalty. I suppose my brother might have climbed to such estate. When I knew him, he was hardly that well-off."

"Are we well-off?"

"We live a life so free that monetary riches could not buy it."

"But we are not rich."

"Not if you count worldly loot."

"What's loot?"

"The spoils robbed of our natural world and given human value by our greed."

"Like fox's fur?"

"And mead and gold, the meat of lambs and calves cooked still alive."

"And animal pelts on doorposts for a hunter's pride."

"Yes, and see how here, where the wolf is unopposed, he heeds us not, and his fur, which looks so bleak in death, shines more luxuriantly than silk."

"But could your brother have dined with kings? Could he be like our guest Antonus, a man who knew court life well?"

"Little sparrow pecking at the grain."

"But could he?"

"He may have done so," Tahto said, and his distant look returned.

"Were you a child then when you saw him last?"

"I was a boy of ten, and he was four."

"Did you go to the academy or were you..."

"I see you mean to have the tale of me." He sighed and pursed his mouth at her. "And so I must start at the beginning and leave out naught, or you will make me tell it all again." Achtriel sat still so she could savor every word.

"My brother and I were born on Ghirba, an island off the coast of North Africa. My father was of a merchant caste which went back, some claimed, to the founding of Carthage. The Jews on that island led privileged lives, not so much in riches, for our goods were communally shared. But we lived in equal standing with our neighbors and in a friendly peace. We were left almost undisturbed by mainland laws and those who maintained them."

"Because of the purple dye?"

"How did you know of...?"

"I heard you speak of it once, to Macha. She wanted to know how it was made. You said snails."

"Indeed, my little Archimedes, from snails which lived on our coastline. The Jews had found a process of extracting the dye from living snails, rather than crushed ones. This required patience, but it led to reliable and less expensive dye production, and gave us a strong advantage with those who produced the cloth. But when the mainland Vandals were defeated..."

"By General Belisarius."

"Yes. The Byzantine emperor, Justinian, or more likely his wife, Theodora, who ruled from behind the throne, decided to punish those who had profited from his enemies. Belisarius' soldiers besieged our island. Jews and Gentiles fought as one to overthrow them, but starvation became the fate of many, including my good father and his wife."

"Was she then…?"

"Not my blood. My mother was from Egypt. She came to our island, to escape an unwanted marriage, and loved my father. She died giving birth to me. My father remarried and that wife bore my brother."

"So he is your half-brother."

"I have trouble with the way my vision paints that term, but yes, he was. I loved him as a brother though, he was my joy. After our parents died, we were adopted by the synagogue. We grew our own food there, and though we shared it with the poor, we managed to hold out. We passed our days in study and were much cosseted. My brother and I were happy and would have spent our lives there."

"Why didn't you?"

"Due to the siege, the elders of the synagogue were forced to look for funds simply to stay alive."

"But what…"

"An offer came from Alexandria to have me wed."

"But you were poor!"

"Yet a renowned boy scholar whose fame was vaunted abroad by avaricious merchants."

"You were loot."

"Indeed. But as I had been so kindly cared for by the synagogue, I could not refuse them this chance for reimbursement. Besides, I needed to provide for my young brother. So I accepted the offer. I agreed to go off to some mainland stranger's house and wed."

"Like a cow."

"Like a cow, like a cow." He clicked the rope at Bridey and looked unhappy.

"Was the family mean then?"

"Well, they were…they were ordinary I suppose. Doing things the way they felt they should be done."

"Did you like your bride at least?"

"Oh, she was fair enough, too fair for me I was an ugly lad. But she was… I did not understand her, and she frightened me."

"Tahto, you afraid?"

"Oh, yes, I was! She was four years older than I was and very spoilt."

"What's spoilt?"

"Like some of the merchant's girls in town. Accustomed to getting everything the way they like."

"I see."

"She had little use for me at first. She tolerated me much like a dog. In the early years, she did confine herself to insults, but a healthy dose of those. I woke to them, ate them for breakfast…"

"And slept on a pallaster of them."

"Precisely. But she grew older and demanded more of me. I was a boy and she a woman. I was…I did not know how to give her what she asked."

"What happened?"

"Her spitefulness grew, and she began to torment me."

"How awful!"

"Yes. She woke me in the night and threatened me with knives. Once she killed a rooster and splashed its blood on me and when I woke, she told me she had cut my hands off. She hid my books and canceled all my students, my only freedom in the day. She hurled things at me, pans of scalding water, I bear a scar…" he raised his sleeve and pointed to a patch of skin that still looked melted.

"Then finally, she told her father she had quit of me and planned to sell me for a slave."

"Did he let her?"

"I did not wait to see. I packed my books that night and fled. I caught a ship at Thessalonica and went to sea."

"Did you see your brother after that?"

"I tried to. I went back to Ghirba when I could get passage. I had to travel stealthily because my wife had offered a reward for my capture. I could not write to him, or he would be arrested in my place. But once, I managed to visit our synagogue to look for him.

37

They told me he had disappeared. I tried to learn of him for many years and inquire still when I meet folk from the East."

"How sad. Poor Tahto, how lonely for you."

"Yes, I missed him. But I hoped he had found the same freedom as I. I was not altogether sad. I was quite happy to be free, I had no one to answer to, and went where and when I pleased. I sailed for a time with the Mauritanians, an interesting lot, more civilized than we."

"And so you never married nor had children?"

"Not for many years. How could I? I was legally wed. But then when I was thirty-five, I learned from a seaman that my wife had wed again and lived in Cyprus. So I felt myself a free man and… fell in love, I suppose you'd say." There was a silence then, which she did not interrupt. "I see," he said at last, "that I was a poor judge of character. What did I know of women? The only ones I'd known were dead or cruel. But there was a woman, Ruth, I met in Paris. She appealed to me."

"Why?"

"Well, perhaps that she was bright like you, full of ideas."

"Did you have children then?"

"Not that I know. She left me after seven months. She'd met a furrier in Perpignon and found my simple scholar's life too dull."

"And you never saw her afterwards?"

"No, nor have had word of her in all these years. I still live in the house we built so she could find me if she chose, but she has not done so."

"Poor Tahto."

"Now, don't grieve for me." He laughed. "I am happy as a bird." But she did so, nonetheless, and made a fuss of him all morning, fixing him a meal and handling Bridey while he slept.

Chapter 3

The next four days were ones of quiet wonder. At the smells and colors in the woods, how these changed perceptibly with the terrain. At the different bird calls with their lucid timbres. How time itself grew bolder, naked, here. Without the day's events to hem it in, time swelled and blossomed like a lea. There were moods to it, the sweetness of morning, the stout noonday, the unhurried ease of afternoon, the clemency of dusk. And night that spread above them like a jeweler's till, ablaze with splendor.

She had never been so long away from town, but Tahto had, and she delighted in his tutelage. He knew about the plants and trees and animals and even spoke the tribal languages of haulers that they met along the road. At midday on the fourth day, they passed a village, ringed by fields with children running through them to scare the birds. She would have like to visit it, so different from her own with its long common house and tiny thatch roofed huts. But Tahto said that it was not a market day, and strangers there might not be welcomed. So she watched reluctantly as it disappeared beyond a bend.

But by late afternoon, the town was long forgotten as they neared the coast. Tahto told her to watch for ocean signs, and she had no trouble doing so. Everything foretold the sea's proximity, seemed swathed and faded by it. Even ordinary things, like leaves, were muted by the ocean's touch and mystified. Then there came a smell of distance, of cold, and the lovely wrack of brine. The wind got in one's head and freshened it, so clean it seemed it could clear every sorrow from the mind, and air each thought like a shaken out sheet.

"I can see why you were happy at sea," she said happily to Tahto.

"Yes." He smiled. "Civilization disappears with the shoreline. Then there is only nature, wild and pure."

At the top of the next ridge, she spotted blue beyond the hills. She could barely sit still as they descended, past grassy fields whose yellow sprigs tipped sweetly in the wind. Everything seemed made of mist. Even the prosperous small town they passed was toy like, its ramshackle huts strewn gaily on the hills. The rosy faced inhabitants looked up and smiled as they waved them past.

Below the town lay a flotilla of ships, the tree lines of their masts tilting like dancers. Beyond them stretched a great dark plane. Away and away out it went, broken only by the frilly crests of waves, or the mull of lesser ones whose round backs rose among the blue. In all directions, to the corners of the world, the ocean spanned, till far away it thinned out into sky. How bold were these tiny boats to cross such distances. Beneath it, she knew, great creatures dwelt. How would it feel to be that beast, to roam this wild demesne so borderless and free of man?

The road came to an end before a yellow desert, bordering the shore. She scrambled from the cart and found herself up to her ankles in its pliant surface. She could walk easily on it for the soft sand buoyed her so that her less useful foot became more serviceable. She moved faster and found, to her astonishment, that she could almost run. This seemed truly now to be the realm of magic.

She danced across the beach to the lip of the sea. It surged across her toes with chilly delight. Wave sounds filled her ears, a great boom that fell and echoed, even as the next crescendo rose. She watched the swells fall, one upon the other to the shore, where they spent themselves and died as whispers.

The tide left curving trails of things, pickled-looking viney plants, luminous stones, and branches gnarled in artful shapes and blunted by the sea. She walked beside them, gathering keepsakes, in air so fresh it seemed that time itself could set sail on its breeze and not return. At last, she turned to gaze out at the sun, now becoming orange in the west.

What could it mean—this endless motion? What could it mean but that things must live, continuing, although they may not always wish it, trying again forever for it was the law. She came back and found Tahto, who was watching Bridey forage in the grass. She said as much to him, and he nodded sagely in assent. They sat together on a fallen tree and watched as purple gathered in the crescents between waves. Soon, the sky itself took on this color. Crimson bled into the nearby clouds and dyed them like madder in a vat of cloth.

"Does this happen every evening?" she asked him once.

"Most nights, yes."

"How?"

"The sea and sky ignite the setting sun."

"But how?"

"There are many theories, but no one really knows."

"There are so many things that no one knows." She sighed. "Why aren't there more answers?"

He laughed. "If persistence is the road to knowledge, then I have no doubt you shall find them," he said, "But now we must sleep for we will rise with daybreak."

"And solve the great mystery!"

"The sunset?"

"No! The letter!"

They slept on the sand, and all night, in her dreams, she heard the sea. When she awoke, to her surprise, it had retreated, its great waves shrunk, their roars now tiny splashes in the distance. Crowds of seabirds bustled on the strand, scuffling occasionally but generally tolerant, although of differing species. Some had beaks that angled down like Samiel's famous nose, while in others, the curve went upward. There were white ones, gray ones, brown ones. Large ones bobbed or waded in the sea while tiny deft ones raced along its edges. Others hovered above the waves then folded their wings and plummeted like stones, only to recoup and rise again, a wet fish dangling in their beaks. She watched them as the sun came up and warmed the air.

The bird sounds were soon joined by others, the knock and scrape of heavy things, the call of a workman early at his post. Tahto woke, sat up, and scratched his chest. His face looked rested. In it, she could see the young man he once had been, the one who had fallen in love. She walked to the ocean and washed beside it in a river that emptied there. When she returned, he had risen and was eating biscuits.

"Will you go to see the captain now?" she asked, taking the biscuit he held out for her.

"I can find no reason to avoid it," he replied.

"Are you afraid to go?"

"Ah, well. Perhaps I am." He brushed crumbs off of his chest and onto his stomach. "It seems like opening old wounds."

"Maybe something wonderful will happen," she proposed and went and leaned on him and kissed his fuzzy cheek.

"Something wonderful," he mused and patted her hand. "You are the only wonderful thing to happen to me."

"Can I come with you?"

"I would not attempt it otherwise."

Never having seen a ship, only some drawings Elies had showed her, she found she had a ravenous curiosity to see one now. She wished she had not left her parchment roll at home. She could have made sketches now and kept them to remember. But there was no time for regret. They gathered up their things and paid a boy to watch the cart and Bridey. Then they straightened their clothes and headed to the village.

The lowest part of the town, mostly a jumble of graying huts, sat close to the shore. The huts were strung with twine on which hung intriguing implements, oars and poles, bunches of netting. She loved the colors of the sea-worn walls, a gray born of fog. A squat browned man emerged from one of the huts and squinted at the sea as if deciphering a codex. Farther on the houses were encircled by heaps that turned out to be sleeping men.

"Why do they lie about, Tahto?" she inquired.

"Hum. They mayhap made their way here and fell down."

"Were they drunk?"

"Most likely."

She stepped more closely to him then, for she had seen men when they woke from drink.

As they turned a corner, past the street of drunkards, they were accosted by an ancient wretch who waved her hand at them as if at apparitions in the mist.

"Who goes there, I do not know thee," she demanded, squinting at them with her rheumy eyes. Before Tahto could reply, she reached inside her cloak and held an object up at them. "Who will buy it?" she cried. "Who will own the wind?"

"We have no need for…" Tahto said politely, but she turned her nose toward Achtriel.

"You. You have need, I say. You must buy my charming."

"What is it?" Achtriel inquired, looking at the limp thing shaking in her hand.

"The wind, I say! He who holds this will be safe from harm on these forsaken waters. You will need it. Look, here, look." She motioned Achtriel close and bade her take the wet thing she was holding. It was a curious lump, a frayed and decorated rag. "See you these knots?" The woman pointed. "Lo, there are four. Are there not?"

"Yes…"

"And what think you they command?"

"I do not know."

"Well, where have ye grown child? Not at sea edge I knew that. And I am blind as moles. But I can see that you have need of my device."

"What does it do?"

"Look here," the woman took the rag and held it reverently. "Four knots, here see, each one holds the wind, one for each, north…" she fingered the farthest knot, "east, south, here west. He who holds this in his hand controls the winds. Do not think to travel on these seas without one!"

"So if your wind is from the east…"

"Precisely! And it bodes unwell, you loosen this knot a bit, and soon, the wind abates and a kinder one ensues. You are traveling now, are you not?" she asked Achtriel.

"No, madam. I am only here on errand."

"Hm. I felt for sure… Ah, well. Take it, you will have need of it I say."

"I do not have any money."

"Ah. Well, perhaps you have a thing to trade?"

"Here," Tahto gave the old woman a nummus. "We will buy it. You find a pleasant breakfast."

"Why, thank you, sir," the woman gaped. "I shall do that, sir, and right away." She squinted once more at Achtriel then hobbled off with more alacrity than her slight frame might suggest. Achtriel examined the device as they resumed their pace. There were drawings on it, shakily embroidered. She longed to unravel it and see them whole, but she feared the magic would be lost.

"You had best put that in your pocket." Tahto smiled. "You will have need of it I say."

"Did she mean I was going on a journey?"

"So it seemed."

"But then I would have to leave you, and I never want to do that."

"You have a long life ahead of you." He smiled. "Who can tell where you will travel in it."

"Nowhere that is far away from you," she told him.

Soon, she spotted hulls between the huts and ran ahead to have a view of them. They lay at the end of a wooden causeway that led out into the sea. The ships were of diverse sizes, some as high as houses, others simple leathern coracles tied in tandem and stocked with corded bales. The largest had curving prows adorned with fanciful figures: legendary beasts, she-gods and demons. Rows of oars, like insect legs, sprouted from their flanks. Tall masts rose from the decks where rolled sails hung like branches.

It looked as if a crew of men could room on board. The thought of living on a ship did seem exciting. Thus preoccupied, she bumped into a scar-faced man who stared at her with eyes still dim from sleep.

"Good, sir," Tahto said, accosting him. "Do you know the whereabouts of Captain Trovus' ship, the Shahbaz?"

"I might," the man said, scanning him with an exploratory glance. "Who wants to know?"

"I am a Jew from Briga. He has a missive for me."

"Ah, you're the Jew. He'll want to see you. Look for the cedar wherry with a yellow dragon at her prow. He'll be within her at this hour."

Tahto thanked him. The man nodded, and his eyes lit briefly upon Achtriel.

"He's not a slaver." The man picked at his teeth. "I can point you to one if you wish."

"I do not!" Tahto replied, and his face went white. He was still scowling when they neared the ship. A boy in foreign vest and cap appeared over its railing top. "Are ye the Jew?" he called.

"I am," Tahto replied.

"Hold on, sir, I will tell master."

In moments more, a man had jumped atop the deck rail, clad in the caparison of Easterners. He was not as old as Tahto, but more weather beaten. His hair was not yet gray, however, and he had it tied in a topknot. His earlobes sported golden hoops, and below his pointed beard, a silver pendant gleamed. Beneath his robe, he wore fine leggings with a silken sash, but his makeshift shoes seemed formed of rope.

"You are my man then. Thank the gods!" he said. "We can set sail when my sentry returns. Boy, go tell the others to leave off their drink." The boy nodded, jumped off the ship, and ran down the causeway to disappear among the huts.

"I am much obliged to your man for bringing me the letter," Tahto said, "I am sorry to have delayed you. I came as soon..."

"No need, sir, please no need." The man shook his head and reached down with his gold-ringed hand. "My envoy was reliable. He made good time and so have you."

"I hear you have a missive for me."

"That I do," the captain said and beckoned with his outstretched palm. "Please come up, and your missy also if you wish."

The missy did not hesitate but scaled the closest piling column, took the captain's hand, and scrambled aboard. "You're a ready shipmate, child," he said. "Have you been on decks before?"

"No, sir," she said, discovering planking, tar-sealed barrels, cabinets, and tidy benches fastened to the walls. At the ship's far end stood a barrack, whose door and roof were framed with colored tiles.

The tiles, designed with patterns, ringed the shipboard rails. They were interrupted, at even intervals, by metal tackles from which strung high wires to the central mast. At the foot of the mast, a huge sail, tied and rolled, spanned the length of decking. Besides the sea smells, to which she was now accustomed, there were aromas that she recognized: woolens, furs, dates, oils, wine, and leather. Other unfamiliar scents lent the odor an exotic air.

"Let me give you a hand, sir," the captain said and reached down to help Tahto aboard. "Your young friend's set to sail with us." He winked when Tahto was on board the ship.

"Ah, I do not doubt it," Tahto said. "She has a yearning for adventure, just as I had at her age. And what more intriguing place to find it than at sea."

As if to underscore this remark, three of the oddest looking men that Achtriel had seen came out of the barrack door. The first was thin, with amber skin, and a white cloth wrapped about his head. The next was huge, freckled like an Eyerlander with a red beard to his waist. The third was even taller, with wiry hair and skin as black as onyx. This last one smiled, revealing teeth so white she would have gasped, had she not been preempted by the roar of laughter that exploded out of them. Her startlement set the others laughing too, and soon she could not help but join them.

Chapter 4

"Don't be afeared, miss, by my crew," the captain said. "They only take delight in your acquaintance."

"They call me Zurvan, gracious lady," the black man said and came to bow before her.

"I am Achtriel," she told him. The men laughed loudly, but Zurvan hushed them, waving his large hand.

"Miss Achtriel, we laugh for joy. You are the sweetest sight these seadog eyes have met in many months."

The Eyrish man knelt close to her and stroked her hair. "Me sis had locks like this, the hue of moonlight," he said softly.

"Perhaps the child would like to see our ship?" the amber man suggested.

"Yes, please!" she cried, before either Tahto or the captain, could object.

"Then so she shall," Zurvan declared and lifting her up, set her on his shoulders. The world looked different at this height. Zurvan chuckled and began to run. He pretended to lose his balance near the rail and tipped her toward the sea. She shrieked with merriment, but this caused him to return her to the deck.

"You are not frightened," he asked, looking worried.

"No, sir, do it again," she begged.

"Ah, you are braver than these two." He stretched his great smile. "We hit a squall last winter had them crying in their bunks."

"It must have been a bad one then," she said, "for they do not look cowardly."

"Well, this one's a damn sight brighter than yourself for seeing that." The redbeard told Zurvan. "My name is Firchus by the way, and this puny pecker is Sateem."

"See to your words around the girl," Sateem admonished.

"I've heard them before," she said.

"How's that?" Firchus asked, amused.

"Well, you're a stout-born sailor then," Zurvan affirmed. "Perhaps you'll ride with us! We've need for a ready hand. Come, let's go inspect the ship and see if it's to your liking."

He took her hand and led her round the decking. "These are our nets, and here, we repair them and clean our catch." He pointed out a wooden trough. "We cook on this turve stove here when it's not too rough or inside if we need to. A sailor must eat ocean's bounty, or the sea gods make us ill. And here's the place we stash the rigging. This here, he hoisted her above it, is our main sail. She lets us outrun pirates and the law alike." Sateem ahem'd, but Zurvan winked at her and beamed down at the sail. "When out full, she's more beautiful than heavenly gods, like what you'd call an angel with her white wings spread in the wind."

"Why do you need her to outrun the law?" Achtriel asked.

"Ah, the law's another privateer, miss, with bigger guns is all," Firchus said. "Every country's greedy for our wares and would take all they could for nothing if we let them."

"You see, mem, we have families and villages to feed at home; we've left our loved ones far behind, and to make the loss worthwhile, we must return with good remuneration," Sateem said, somewhat unconvincingly.

"We ply the coast," Zurvan explained, "except when we make crossings to the isles or return east, and every port from here to there would rob us blind. It's a fair negotiation to traverse in trade. Our captain's done it all his life and even he must oft be wary. That's why he's happy for the trade with Jews. They will strike a hard bargain but never cheat nor rob you."

"It is in your scriptures, is it not?" Sateem inquired.

"Yes, but some ignore it," Achtriel said.

"Ah, the same is true of any," Firchus said. "But by and large, a Jew's a trusted businessman."

"And woman," Sateem added, "I know a female captain trades from her own vessel along these shores."

"That might become your future!" Zurvan smiled.

"Where do you go next?" she asked, half wishing Tahto would permit her to go with them.

"Around the coast out to Hibernia," Firchus said. "We've a load of gold for them and liquor from the East. We'll buy their wool and mayhap port a monk out to Ionia. But better yet, I'll see my love or, if not, find another."

"Who lives there?" she inquired.

"A lot of crazy men," Zurvan replied.

"And lively women." Sateem did a little dance.

"Are you from the Celtic isles?" she asked Firchus.

"That I am. And would be there still if mother fate had let me."

"Why did she not?"

"I had a falling out, let's say, with one of her great chieftains." He twirled a strand of beard. "You cannot stay on land in such a case or…"

"Hush, you large pork, don't frighten her with that," Sateem reproached.

"Ah, so right, my friend. The child has no need to learn these things. Come on, let's go inside."

They led her through the barrack door. Behind it was a little room with stacked plank beds beside a sturdy table. Sun came in through round glassed holes which lit the disarray with comfortable warmth. The bed covers smelled as if they'd not been washed in years, but the damp wool odor was not unpleasant, simply rough and natural like the ocean. Only the table's surface lay uncluttered and suspiciously clean.

"Down there is the galley where we row her when the winds asleep," Sateem said, pointing to a stairway, "and under it's the hold for storing cargo."

She turned back to the empty table and saw his face take on its nervous look. "Do I interrupt your lunch then?" she asked them, "I am sorry."

"That's not what you have interrupted but no matter." Firchus laughed. "But you must try our vigands...if you can stand his cooking." He jerked his head toward Sateem.

"You weaklings have the palates of babes." Sateem returned. "I wager she will like my dahl."

The two men looked down at her then, and Firchus stroked his beard. "They say the Jews eat strange fare," he mused. "But your fireslop is another thing."

"Let her try it," Zurvan said. "She has a brave look to her. I wager she will like it."

"Alright then." Sateem smiled and gestured to the table. "You sit here, and I will serve it up."

"And you must say honest what you think," Firchus insisted.

"What is the wager?" Zurvan asked, placing his great hands upon the board to sit beside her.

"A dinar for each, and I say she will spit it out," Firchus said and smacked his hand down letting go a small brown coin. Sateem brought out a wooden plate and on it was a pile of lentils.

"Be careful not to take too much," Zurvan admonished, handing her a spoon. "It can be very..."

"Spicy!" she exclaimed as she tasted it." I like it very much!"

"Hah," said Zurvan, as Firchus shook his head. "You are no mainland lass, I say, but born to sail the world." He took the coin and put it in his shoe.

"But if she is to sail, she needs to learn our sport," Sateem said wryly, watching happily as she devoured his dish.

"I will," she offered finishing the last of it. "What is it?"

"Well, we would not want your grandfather..."

"He will not mind."

"Oh, hah!" Sateem guffawed and took a lumpy satchel from his pocket. "If you say so, I will believe you. This is our game, it keeps us occupied you see, but it is not for everyone."

50

"What is it?" she asked curiously as he shook from the bag some stoneware pieces.

They were exquisite little idols with different shapes, half of them black and the others white. Some were simple mounds with rounded tops, but there were fine shaped ones as well. Large manlike figures, two with crosses on their heads, two with crowns, and four things turreted like alcazars, and four with horse's heads. The cleverest ones, to which her hands were instantly enticed, were two pairs of plump chimeric animals. They had huge ears between which a long nose reached down to their feet.

"Pick them up then if you wish." Sateem encouraged and she did so, taking the chimera and tracing its round contours with her touch. It had a tiny string like tail and curved horns in its cheeks that flanked the tube like nose. "What is it?" she inquired. "A dragon?"

"Ah no. That is a real animal; I have one in my courtyard at my home."

"Where is that?" she asked him, fascinated.

"A faraway place that few from here will ever see. It is a vast land beyond the shores of Egypt and the lower countries where Zurvan hails from."

"Are there more strange creatures there like this one?"

"Oh, many more. My favorites are some little manlike ones who live in trees. They are much like us with our hands and feet and have as well our curious habits. I had one as a pet when I was young. He slept with me and made much mischief in my rooms."

"I wish I could see one! What is this long-nosed creature like?"

"This one." Sateem lifted the identical idol and held it lovingly. "She is fearfully strong but the kindest animal the gods have made. The mothers care so sweetly for their young, and all live as a group with very little fighting. Unless they are wronged. Then they are fiercer than a musk ox and three times bigger. In my country, they are trained to carry people on their backs."

"Like mules."

"Yes, but they are bigger than the biggest mule. If you were standing on her back, you'd reach our mast top!"

Her eyes opened so wide that the others laughed.

"You would come only up to here on her." He smiled and pointed to below the sculpted creature's knee.

"I wish you'd brought one with you!" she exclaimed.

"Ah, these ignorant countrymen of yours." He shrugged. "They would have taken it for devil craft, who knows what other foolishness. I would not subject my noble beast to their brutality."

"But I would love it; I could ride upon its back." She held the idol for a moment more, wishing they would let her keep it.

"Do you want to see our game then?" Firchus asked.

"Oh yes, I had forgotten." She handed back the piece and watched them lift a game board from beneath the table.

"Although you want to learn it," Zurvan said," I would not want your grandpa to get mad; it is a gambling game."

"I will not tell him then," she said.

Zurvan looked at her for a moment. Then he smiled. "Now listen closely, this will take your full attention. The game is Chaturanga. There are sixteen pieces, eight of black and eight white. Each kind moves differently along the board and captures others also with its singular maneuver. We set the board like so." He lay it on the table. "Along this back row go the royals, king here, counselor beside him. Next comes the elephant..."

"What's that?"

"Your favorite." He smiled placing the chimeric beast upon the board. "Beside her goes the steed, and last the alcazar. These are the peons, fighting men whose lives are little valued. They can move only ahead, one step at a time, poor things, unless they reach the other side, and then they can exchange for the piece that lives in that place."

He placed the eight round peons down to form a row in front. The board had little sharpened nails that each piece anchored onto. "They capture on the diagonal if a piece stands next to them. The king can only move one square in each direction."

"Why so if he's the king..."

"Ah, kings have very little power in this world, despite what you and I may think. The king is hemmed in by his counselors and court men and the state, just as you see. To be a king is not so great a boon."

52

"In my land," Firchus said, "live kings who pass their whole lives with their feet upon a maiden's lap. They dare not move to touch the ground unless it is to die."

"Your country is a most unusual one, as I've observed before," Zurvan said dryly. "Now the counselor," he held the cross head piece up next, "has not much greater freedom. He goes one square to the diagonal and takes his captors there. Next your friend…"

"The elephant," she said, even its name was round and kind.

"She moves like this, two squares diagonally, but she can jump if something's standing in her way."

"How can she if she's taller than a house?'

"I will tell you," Sateem said," if I saw one now prepare to jump, I would get quickly out of way!"

"This," Zurvan said, smiling, "is the steed. And he can go two squares and over one, a very useful man. The chariot…"

"Why a chariot? It looks more like a castle."

"That I do not know, perhaps because a castle cannot move."

"If eeliephants can jump, I'd wager palaces can dance," Firchus remarked, and Zurvan gave him an irritated glance over his shoulder.

"The chariot," he continued," can move on any way along a straight line. He has the greatest breadth and can be used as scout or bait. Now you know the rules, my friend. Would you care to try?"

"Of course!' she said, "but I don't have anything to bet. Except for this…" she said, remembering her cloth and pulling it from her shirt sleeve.

"Ah, a windrag lady found you." Firchus chuckled. "Never tire, those ones. I will wager you for that."

"Alright then," Achtriel replied. "Shall you be white or black?"

"We decide like this," Zurvan said, placing a peon in his hand. He put his hands behind his back then brought them out. "Miss Achtriel, you make a choice." She hesitated and then pointed to his right. It held only thin air.

"Aha!" Firchus rejoiced. "I am white then. Let's begin."

"Notice how he brightens at the thought of besting one whom he can," Zurvan said slyly to Sateem.

But to Achtriel, the game was most intriguing and delightful. She was disappointed when Sateem, after she had won from each of them a silver coin, declared it over.

"You will beggar us." Zurvan laughed as he gathered up the pieces

"Oh. I did not mean to keep your money," she protested, "It was only for the sport." She handed Zurvan back the coins but he shook his head.

"No, you've won them. They are yours."

"I couldn't take them from you," she insisted.

"I'll tell you what then," Firchus said, retrieving the coins. "You shall have a better treasure."

He reached into the pouch tied to his shirtwaist and fished around. When his hand emerged, it was holding a misshapen coin. "This is the emperor Hadrian." He pointed out the profile on the coin. "He was master on the western isles more than a hundred year ago. Isn't worth a nummus today, but it's a lovely thing. You take it."

"Are you sure?" she asked him. "I would not take it from you."

"It's worthless," he said, "I only liked to look at it. But it will make me glad to know that you will keep it. And think of me."

"And think of us as well," Sateem insisted. "For you will have a long and interesting life, I think, and this will be only the first of your treasures." She thanked them and gave each a kiss. When she and Tahto left the ship, the three men stood and waved to her until she could no longer see them.

Chapter 5

Walking back through town, Tahto seemed distracted. Although he had been jolly on the boat and had laughed when they told him of her astonishing victories at Chaturanga, once back on land, he fell into a silence. She did not disturb his thoughts but walked beside him, looking at her coin and planning its enshrinement in her room. When they reached the edge of town and turned back toward the shore, he stopped and seemed confused.

"Would you like to rest here, Tahto?" she asked warily.

"Yes, I think I would," he mumbled vaguely and sat down on a small promontory that overlooked the sea.

"I'll go see to the cart then," she informed him.

"Here, please pay the boy..." he reached into his bag and handed her two nummi.

"I will." She smiled and left him, knowing this was what he wished.

She paid the boy and fed some oats to Bridey, then let her off the tether to explore. She gathered up their things and arranged the cart for travel, making sure her beachcombed treasures would be safe. Then she spotted Tahto coming. There seemed to be a change in his demeanor. His step was firmer, and his face was tilted upward. He waved when he got closer, and she saw he wore a gentle smile.

"Everything is ready," she reported as he approached the cart. "I think we can be home by midweek."

"No need to hurry," he replied. His face bore tear streaks, but it looked refreshed. "In fact, I thought to celebrate. I saw an inn in town. Perhaps we'll stop in for a meal, and they will curry Bridey."

"An inn? An inn, Tahto!" she was astonished. "Would they...do you think that they would serve us?"

"Well, why not? It seems the whole town has been talking of my letter now for weeks. I imagine they would let us sup if only for a chance to learn the details."

"Let's hurry then!" she cried. *Before you change your mind,* she added in her own.

Tahto had never eaten inn food, or for that matter, as far as she could tell, been through the door of one. She, of course, had peaked inside a few. They seemed the dark and smelly haunts of grogged men and women. But despite this or perhaps because of it, she was most anxious to go in.

"Bridey, love," Tahto addressed the mule. "Come along, and you shall have a brushing and a tasty meal." Bridey looked up from her foraging and, as if she understood him, ambled closer. Achtriel tied her to the cart, and they drove into town.

The seaport alleys, built for barrows and sledges and long ago for Roman vehicles, were wider by far than Briga streets. Tahto let her take the reins and she found it easy to navigate. She wished the children, who stared enviously from the streets, were the ones she knew. She imagined her own villagers watching, shocked and impressed. If they could see her now, they certainly would treat her differently.

The townsfolk waved at them as they passed. Their avid stares and whispers made her feel important. This is what it must be like to be a courtier, she thought. She pretended that she was a queen, and her mule cart a chariot, turreted like the Chaturanga one.

The inn was called the Booby and had a carven drinking horn on its doorway. She pulled up beside it and made Bridey stop. A boy came out from the stables, and she handed him the cart reins. Tahto gave him a coin and the boy clucked to Bridey and led her next door to the stalls. Then she and Tahto got down and ventured to the inn door. Tahto did not knock but walked right in, and she followed, somewhat nervously, in his footsteps.

"Hallo!" he called, "Would you serve a Jew a meal?"

From behind the bar, a man looked up. It took a moment for him to respond, but then he did so heartily.

"Ay, I would, good master Jew. But I do not know if my poor food would suit you."

"Have you some bread and cheese and glass of cow's milk?"

"I do. And I've sweet porridge for the child, if you desire."

"Yes, indeed," he beamed and sat down at the long front table at which several men, not all awake, were present.

"So!" Tahto announced and pulled the letter from his sack. "Shall I read this to you?" His words were meant for Achtriel, but at them, every patron turned to look. The commotion even woke the sleepers.

"Yes, please, Tahto," she replied.

"Or better yet," he said, "you read it on your own and tell me what you think."

"Yes, Tahto," she said and reached eagerly for the packet.

"The child can read?" a nearby man exclaimed.

"That I don't believe," the inn keep said.

"Nor I," another man slapped money on the board.

"The Jew must make her read it out aloud," another said, "and I will wager this that she knows naught of it."

"Now, now," Tahto demurred, his eyes amused, "I will not have my pupil a display. The child can read and so could you and yours if you would study it."

"There's none to teach us, Mr. Jew. Or I would have learned such a handy thing ere now."

"You must come to Briga then where we have a school. This young one here will teach you."

"Well, sir, that I might one day. But for now, I think you'd better read it."

"Well, I must, I see I must," Tahto replied then in his gentle way. He spread the leather out to flatten it. "My dearest brother...," he began. The nearby men leaned in and were soon shoved by another group that had gathered from the inn or rushed in, summoned, from the street. They watched him form words from the marks of text.

"Those aren't letters from around here," one observed.

"Nor the ones of Hebrews, I have seen those," said another.

"That is right. The script is Aramaic. A language they use where I hail from. It is much quicker on the pen and easier to write."

"Is that the land with houses like churches with indoor pools and water coming from the walls?" the inn keep asked.

"There are many places in the East with such accommodations. There are great cities, larger than Paris, with cathedrals, palaces, and squares. The wealthy fancy that they live like the Romans."

"Them's what built the streets, I heard of them," the inn keep said. "Now the churchmen fancy themselves Romans, I believe, and strut about in gaudery." The others chuckled wryly.

"The East is a wealthy place, my friends," Tahto confirmed, "but I am happier here."

"How's that?"

"Where there is empire, the common man becomes a slave."

"Is that why your brother has written you?" a young man elbowed closer through the crowd.

"What does he say then?" a fellow near his shoulder asked.

"Ah, yes, let's see… 'my dearest brother'…"

"You have read that part."

"So I have. Let me see now. 'It is many years since we have spoken. I was but a child when you were taken from me, but I have never once forgotten you. I became a wealthy man through marriage and through trade and have lived well in the Roman East—although my wife and I have not been blessed with children. Recently through circumstances, I shall explain when I see you, my business was taken from me and my house destroyed."

The watchers shook their heads in disapproval. "A good Jew should not be molested," one remarked.

"Our living is precarious," Tahto told them, "no matter where we set it. But I thank you for your good opinions.

"Read on then if you would, Sir Jew," another begged.

"I find myself now stripped of my possessions and in need of aid. Do not think that I have not earlier searched to find you. 'I have inquired with every seaman, but none had heard of you, save one who said you had retired from shipping and been wed…"

"You were a sailor?" a man inquired.

"Stop your questions, we want to hear the letter," his mates demanded. One struck him roughly and raised a cloud of dust.

"'Finally, I met a man who knew a trader who had heard of you. He said you ran a *heder* in Briga. I sent this letter then and hope it finds you. I must leave these parts, and as I do not have the resources I once did, I must come to you as soon as possible. I am arranging passage now and may be there by the new year, if the powers of this world permit. There are but three of us, my wife Berthe, her aide, and myself. I hope to see you soon, my brother, as I have hoped for little else in my long life. May YHWH oversee your days and bring us soon together. Your brother, Nimrode.'"

A commotion then erupted at the table, the men discussing shipping lanes, well-known captains and the routes of travel from the East. Some disagreements led to shouting and the need for intervention by the landlord. But of all this, Achtriel was only dimly cognizant. Her mind was teeming with speculations of her own.

What would he look like, this Nimrode? What treasury of learning would he carry? Another *chachem* in their midst—the school would surely be renowned for that and summon other scholars to their town. And what keepsakes of Eastern life would his household bring, what tales of the old world with its abundance and its intrigue. She hardly paid attention when her porridge came and barely tasted it. She was only half aware of Tahto's fond good-byes and thanks and their departure from the inn.

Due to their late start, they camped that night beside the village they had passed on their way out. It was dark when they stopped by its walls and slept. Achtriel woke before dawn and found herself ablaze with curiosity to see it. Tahto lay asleep and even Bridey dozed, her head nodding upon her chest. Surely, no one would be risen at this hour. If she entered as quietly as she knew how, even the hounds would not awaken.

She crept down from the cart and stepped out on the roadway. She could see crows in the fields, which meant the children sent to frighten them were still asleep. Emboldened, she made her way to the log gates and found they could be opened with a push. She slipped between them, barely breathing, and tiptoed forward into the village. The gates swung closed behind her with soft thunk.

Ahead of her lay the main square. It was quite small with stables for the animals and fodder stores bound up in sheaths. Beyond it, over the roofs of huts, she could see the larger central building, a barrow-shaped enclosure with a pike staved roof. She remembered Tahto saying that the village slept and ate together there. She advanced a bit more confidently then, for no one seemed astir yet in the predawn gloom. The ground was swept and free of stones. A tidy people these, who should not mind a visitor to view their labors with esteem. She was startled when a pig grunted nearby, but then its snorts grew fainter and fell silent. A dog's howl in the empty air caused her to crouch and look for cover, but as nothing followed, she crept on ahead.

To her left lay thatch-roofed huts encircling the central barrow. Here and there, a higher roof stood out above the low ones, drying sheds or foundries, ateliers, perhaps for artisans or dyers. No smoke rose from the spileholes. The only signs the buildings were in use were the slops dumped by their doors. She skirted them and headed to an open tract beside the fields. There she came to a small well, ringed by wooden buckets and a stack of washtubs. Farther ahead, in the morning fog, she could make out a lean-to.

She could not fully see its contents, but they struck her as unusual. She approached the structure slowly. It was a shrine, she realized, to some kind of idol. It was not a cow, to her disappointment, but the statue of a goddess.

The figure was wooden and carved in the shape of a circular cross. It had three heads, one at the top and two where her hands would have been. Below, in her womb area, a rudimentary infant had been fashioned. Strewn about the lean-to were offerings, pottery, a leather cradle, fruit, and eggs. In some piles of seed grain, mice were feeding. The tribute had begun to rot. Its fetor lent the shrine a doleful quality.

She left the shrine and wandered, less vigilantly now for she seemed to be unnoticed. Rows of gravesites, marked by smaller crosses with the same three-headed woman at their top, covered a nearby mound. On its far side lay some low constructions. Storehouses she guessed, for the crows atop them strode with a proprietary air. Behind the storerooms rose a steep hill, strewn with boulders.

As she approached the hill, she noticed that its nearest rock was freshly carved. The artist was attempting yet other tripart cross, for the rock face bore the contours of three simple heads. She had never thought to carve a stone. She went to touch it. The rough quoin had been burnished smooth. Below it, iron chisels rested, honed to a flat scraping edge. She bent and took one in her hand and rubbed it softly on the stone.

Suddenly, behind her, came a rush of wind. Something sharp and painful hit her shoulder and threw her forward. She fell, dropping the chisel, and landed in the dirt. She looked up to see a group of children moving toward her in a phalanx, armed with slingshots.

"Hello," she said and tried to sound unthreatening. This was difficult, for in her fear she could not think what language they were used to. "Do you speak Frankish?" she asked.

They did not seem impressed with her politeness. The largest one advanced toward her and threw a rock. It hit her in the leg, and she guessed then, from the pain, that this was what had struck her shoulder. She would have yelled, but that might wake the village—an even bigger problem. This group, an odd contingent she could see for, unlike the tidy town, they were bedraggled and as thin as twigs— seemed out of place. They were the lost, the foundlings like herself, she gathered. Otherwise, they would have called the elders from the village.

Before she could devise a strategy, they had surrounded her, muttering in some guttural tongue. She tried to hear words that might spark some recognition, but they spoke too quickly in menacing tones broken by derisive laughter. With difficulty, she recalled the Rhinish word for friend and said it loudly. Hearing it, the largest boy just laughed.

The others watched as he approached her. He eyed her curled right hand with knowing and disgust. Then he spat on her. He grabbed her arm and shook her. To her horror, her coin fell from her sleeve and rolled before him. He laughed again and bent to pick it up. She moved to stop him, but he shoved her to the ground. She could not afterward recall what happened next.

She remembered fear, but as if from a long distance. What she did feel, through and through, was anger. She had earned that coin. Moreover, it was all she had or ever would have of the Shahbaz. They would not take it from her.

Before the boy could claim the coin, she kicked him. In his startled pause, she reached behind her for the chisel and, like David, hurled it at his head. He swayed, collapsed, and fell. The others seemed astonished by this. One said a word she recognized as "witch" and they left him there and ran.

Trembling, she crawled forward to retrieve her coin. The boy lay like a crumpled doll. She leaned over him to see that he was breathing. Then she stood and put her coin back in her sleeve. She knelt again and turned his head to ensure that his wound was not severe. As she did, his eyelids fluttered open. Assuming this was proof enough, she scrambled to her feet and hurried off.

She glanced back as she passed the shrine and saw him stand and rub his temple. At that she took off speeding, weaker leg and all, out the town gates and, rattling Bridey, up into the cart. Tahto awoke briefly as she took the reins. She smiled at him as if there were no cause for concern, and he went back to sleep.

Then she exhorted Bridey to her swiftest trot and jostled the cart into the roadway. Fortunately, no one came to follow them. When the town was a safe distance behind them, she breathed a prayer of thanks. Later, when she was no longer scared, she found herself possessed of a sensation new to her. It was a kind of pride, a gloating of revenge and spite; and though she knew it would not sit well in the eyes of God, she did not mind it.

Chapter 6

"How old a man is your brother?" Fagim asked at the following Sabbath.

"He is married," Tahto said.

"Did I ask if he were married? I inquired as to his age."

"I am older than him by six years."

"A young man then," Samiel said dryly.

"Indeed," Mosse observed. "More importantly, a man of learning, availed, unlike ourselves, of the storehouses of the learned world. He no doubt brings us treasure for our *cheder*."

"It seems he had to leave in haste. I do not know what he can carry."

"He is a Jew," Esther remarked. "He will bring gold and other portable assets. And of course, his scholarly memory."

"I can't wait till he comes," Achtriel joined in. "How old will be his wife and serving woman?"

"I wish I had the gift of second sight so I could answer you," Tahto replied, "as it is I only know what is in the letter."

"I imagine they are both quite old," Fagim said, guessing her intention. "A pity that they have no child. One would be a welcome playmate for you."

Achtriel, who ordinarily would bristle at this allusion to her loneliness, found, for once, that Fagim's prying did not bother her. She had noticed, too, that she felt less slighted now by the staring townsfolk. Since the journey, in fact, she had discovered a newfound self-confidence. While it did not lead her to seek playmates—she knew too well the character of the local children—the thought seemed somehow to have grown less odious.

"Perhaps he'll draw scholastic families to Briga," Esther offered brightly.

"That would be welcome," Samiel said. "I hear the traveling scholars have resumed this year. One visited the Rodom synagogue last week. He was from Paris and came with texts and missives sent from Babylon. If we were a larger more scholastic center, they would come to us."

"Besides your brother, I have news of persons likely to enlarge interest in our little town," Profait informed them. He took a sip of wine before continuing.

"Well?" Fagim demanded.

"Well, indeed," the tailor said, "It may be well or may be ill, we will have to judge that as the time unfolds." He took a mouthful of soup and swallowed it before continuing. "A duke, the nephew of the mayor of a Frankish court, is coming. He inherited the manse on the hill and has decided to inhabit it."

"How did you learn this?" Esther asked avidly.

"The gentry want new clothing for the banquet. Some lesser folk also want fine outfits for a pageant that the town will throw him. In fact, if any of you has the time, there is much work to do. I have that diamond twill I bought from you last spring, and with the ribbon and eastern embroidery you brought back from Paris…"

"Yes, of course, we'll help you sew. But what else have you learned of him?" Fagim pressed, "Is he wed? What of his household?"

"A single man, I hear. A lad of thirty. He styles himself a sort of scholar I presume, for they say he claims a library among his riches."

"Indeed!"

"He keeps about him several friends who like to hunt and fight, the usual aristocratic pastimes."

"Best keep the maidens close to home," said Mosse.

"I hope his friends are not the type who go about demanding tribute from the ignorant for monsters they have slain or claim lurk just about the town." Fagim sighed.

"One would hope our folk are too sophisticated for that now," said Profait.

"Are they?" Fagim raised an eyebrow. "It was only several years ago that Burgundian mercenary stirred them up with similar tales. Many sold their field lots and were lost to slavery."

"But that is all you know about the man?" Esther broke in, "The gentry surely have learned more than that."

"There is talk of his needing to leave Paris quickly. Perhaps a quarrel or some other fuss."

"It does seem odd that a young courtier would move down to Briga," Fagim mused. "He cannot be that rich, nor so availed of choices."

"You must learn everything you can," Esther commanded.

"You can learn it yourself, if you wish. The Hildebards are the clients who seem best informed. I have some work at the shop but after that you may take their measures and assist me with the tailoring for their new clothes."

"I shall," she announced. "And Achtriel will help me."

"I cannot sew well..." Achtriel protested.

"Of course you can. And you can hold a box of pins, I'm sure."

"But..."

"Nothing but..." Fagim admonished. "It is time you came in from the woods."

At dawn the next day, Esther came and led Achtriel to the wash house. She washed her head with vinegar and ash soap and scrubbed her face and ears and knees and teased the snarls from her wet hair with an ivory comb. She cleaned her teeth with peppermint paste and soaked her fingernails in oil. Esther silenced all complaints with a firm "Tsh." Then she marched her to her room and found an outfit not too soiled or wrinkled to be worn. She made her dress and braid her hair correctly, then stood back to appraise her work.

"Quite nice," she complimented. She crooked her arm for Achtriel to hold. "We are off," she said and whisked her out the door.

The sun was rising, and as Achtriel hurried to keep up with Esther, she watched, a little sadly, as it lit the canopy above her woods. Birds churled in their morning rites, and the clouds around the thin moon were parting.

"It will be a lovely day," Esther said, "Don't you agree?"

"I must, or you will see I do."

"That is correct," Esther replied and laughed.

Profait lived in the merchant's part of town, a row of streets the townsfolk called the street of Jews—although the merchants were of many nationalities. His shop was in the front part of his house, and it had a workroom and a measuring salon, complete with silvered glass. His wife, Ardith, sewed too, but as she was a bit unfriendly, she often left the customers to him. Usually, she stayed behind the curtain which divided their small rooms. Now she was pregnant and seemed to be using this as an excuse to be completely idle.

Profait once told them Ardith was unhappy even when he met her several years ago. Nevertheless, they seemed content enough and often smiled when they conversed. Today, Ardith met them at the door. She told them that Profait had gone to the great house of the Hildebards, and that they were to sort the fabrics and match threading. Then she disappeared behind her curtain.

"Do you want to join us?" Esther called but heard a mumble of dissent. "Something odd about that one," she remarked conspiratorially.

They spent the morning looking at supplies. There were many kinds of linen, each woven in a way that identified its region. Wools in various shades of red and blue, and one of expensive purple which only the wealthiest could wear, were stacked along the wall. There were decorative materials too, exotic embroidery, small gems, and gold threading. All were to be handled with utmost care and required different methods of stitching.

"How are your sewing skills then, Achtriel?" Esther handed her a needle and a thread.

"I mended Tahto's cape once and patched up his leggings."

"That's a start. Let me see how you do." And all morning, Esther scrutinized her work until the rows were small and tight, and the thread stopped catching up in tangles.

At noon, Profait returned. A rain had come despite Esther's prediction, and he shook some wetness from his cloak before he hung it on the hook.

"Hello, hello," he said with what passed for cheerfulness with him. "The townsfolk are like rabid dogs today. I could not cross the street without one stopping me to set up an appointment. Thank you both for helping us, you know how hard it is for Ardith."

"She's in back," Esther informed him.

"Good, I'll just go see to her."

They watched him part the curtain and call out, "Ardith!" in a honeyed voice. This contrast with his normal dour demeanor threatened to incite a fit of giggling in Achtriel. Striving for propriety, she looked at Esther; but then, they both were smothering laughter. When Profait returned, they had just managed to compose themselves.

"I wish Tahto had told me he was going to the coast," Profait said, frowning. "I would have had him talk that captain out of a load of ermine cheap."

"Tahto cannot bargain," Esther said. "He is hopeless as a businessman. I don't know how he has survived."

"We cannot all possess these skills," Profait conceded. "I would trade mine, I often think, for his scholastic prowess. His mind is like a library. He forgets nothing."

"He forgot to tell you we were going to the ocean," Achtriel reminded him.

"He did not forget," Esther said.

"You mean he knew he'd be pestered to bargain, and he..."

"Correct," she answered, imitating Tahto's voice. Even Profait laughed at this as he unlocked his door for business.

All afternoon, a stream of townsfolk, mostly women but some men as well, came into the shop and asked for fittings. Many of them eyed Achtriel uncomfortably, seeing her bent hand and looking past it quickly as if they had seen a corpse. But she enjoyed the day in spite of this. Grownups were comical though they seldom knew it.

The women chattered as they turned from side to side before the glass, reminding Achtriel of ducks. She half expected them to quack with the pride of accomplishment such fowl displayed. The men, however, stood quite still as if their fitting were a serious matter. One self-important burgher named Geon of Dorestad farted as Profait measured his leggings. Achtriel rose quietly and hastened to the outhouse to contain her laughter. She did not think she could return and remain sober, but luckily, he'd left before she did so. Esther smiled at her when she came in.

"Profait's profession has its abjurations," she observed.

"A tailor rarely goes to hell." He sighed. "Our sufferings on earth absolve us."

That evening, Profait informed them that tomorrow, he had pledged them to the Hildebards. "An interesting lot," he muttered as he let them out the door. Achtriel wished to ask him why, but he was hurrying to close his shop. Esther would not tell her either. She said she'd tired of shop talk and wanted to reserve her mind for thinking. At the footbridge, she stopped and made arrangements for their next meeting. "Good work you did today," she commented, as they went separate ways, and Achtriel recalled this with a begrudging pleasure as she walked home.

They met the next morning, as planned, to walk to the Hildebard's. As before, Esther spoke little but looked about with interest at the morning sky. Once out of town, the footpath began to rise more steeply, and she slowed her pace for Achtriel.

The path continued uphill, nearly overgrown in places by the encroaching woods. Higher up the trees had been cut back, and they could spot, at the hilltop, the villa built from a Roman fort which people called the castell.

"That is where this duke shall be living," Esther said. "Though why he would want to is another question."

On the hills below the castell lay the villas of the wealthy and, below these, the neighborhood of the merchant class. Achtriel had had no reason to visit these neighborhoods. They were interesting, she observed, as they came closer.

Unlike the lodging of the common folk, the merchant's houses boasted several stories, some with balconies with hanging plants or rooftop promenades. Most were made of brick on which faux Roman illustrations had been painted. Angel children, birds, and goddesses lounged amid exotic greenery, although the artist's inexperience rendered them often indecipherable.

Although it was well past sunrise, there were few people in the merchant's plaza. Apparently, the wealthy, unlike Jews and peasants, could lie abed. Occasionally, one of them could be seen strolling the streets, arrayed in costly garments. A young man idled on his mount as if he had no cause for speed. Only the merchant's children, it seemed, were about, accompanied by nursemaids or at times a black robed cleric.

Esther said these families did not need to work for they owned many slaves who lived in stalls beside the animals. These slaves undertook the management of house and land as they had done, no doubt, since Roman days. The merchant women, gleaned from peasant stock, were eager to appear well heeled and made a steady market for the Jews who traded foreign luxuries. They would do better, she remarked, to bathe themselves more often and see to their teeth. Proper gentry, like the Hildebards, descended from the Roman dynasties and had what Esther called distinction.

The slope of the footpath grew more even and better kept, as they left the merchant quarter. It wound through fields and vineyards, populated by busy slaves and tired-looking animals. Finally, they came to an open tract, which looked as if it had been, at one time, a formal garden. Between rose bushes, the woodland plants were growing, and it was overrun with weeds. On the other side of the field, a stone wall, broken by a wooden stile, marked the far border of the field.

As they approached it, a guard slipped out from behind the stile and asked their business.

"We've come to tailor for the Madam Hildebards," Esther informed him.

"They will be at breakfast," he said, "But the gatekeep yon will show you to the house."

Esther thanked him and climbed over the stile, ignoring his assisting arm.

"Can the child...?" he began, eying Achtriel's twisted foot.

"Yes," Achtriel replied, climbing the stile and swinging her good leg over it to clamber down.

"The madames are particular..." he murmured to Esther. "Do they know she is a cripple?"

"Yes, they know," she answered, taking Achtriel's hand.

"The manse lies at the far end of the orchards," he said doubtfully. "Servants go to the back."

"Thank you," Esther told him as they walked away.

The house was so tall that they soon caught sight of it. Fronted by a peristyle, it rose majestically to the treetops. As they grew closer, though, one could see that the peristyle and the structure itself had seen better days. Smaller, more recent constructions lined the pathway, undoubtedly the dwellings of the slaves. As they passed one, Achtriel glanced inside, for it had no door. There were only blankets on the floor and a table not unlike the one aboard the Shahbaz. At it she espied Sorgen, the slave girl, her head bent over some endeavor. Achtriel wished the girl would look up now and watch with envy her admittance to the mansion. She soon reproached herself for such base pride. She had best become a tailor, she decided, or she certainly would go to hell.

"She seems a lonely child, the little slave," Esther prompted.

"Yes," said Achtriel and let the matter drop.

Chapter 7

As instructed, they followed the path to the back of the house. There they found workrooms, stables, and a kitchen garden. Rows of bushes framed a courtyard through which a paved footway led to the servants' door. Above it drooped the family standard, a winged beast crushing a serpent. Esther stepped up to the door and knocked.

They heard measured footsteps. Soon, a servant opened the door and asked them who they were. As she and Esther talked, Achtriel looked past them at the rear entry hall. Its walls were hung with weavings flanked by silver candle rods. Between these, heads of deer and bears stared blankly.

The ceilings were so high it was like looking at treetops, except that leaves let in some light and here there was none. Although it was full morning now, the tapers were all lit. Without them, it would have been too dim to navigate. The floor was strewn with matted pelts on one of which two dogs were lying. Behind them rose a wide stairway, which, no doubt, accessed the higher floors.

The woman instructed them to go up the stairs and find the leftward walkway. Esther bowed and entered, and Achtriel followed, copying her lowered head and shuffling walk. This attitude, besides conveying their humility, served to alert them to the scattered bones and rubbish on the floor.

Incongruously festive, sprigs of mint and holly lent the bleak floors an air of elegance as well as some olfactory respite. As they neared the foot of the stairs, the dogs looked up expectantly, but soon resumed their bored expressions. This house was gloomy, she decided. Although it was still summer, its walls had stored the winter's chill.

The second story seemed better designed. Windows, set high in the walls, had been added to let in the light. These, however, were obscured by adjacent trees, so the atmosphere remained dim. At the end of the left hall, they saw an open door which revealed a large room. A goose, which had been resting in its doorway, rose and charged with a proprietary hiss. When it pecked at Achtriel, she stroked its head and patted it gently. This seemed to appease the animal and it followed them affably into the room. Unlike the rest of the house, this room was well-lit, pleasantly outfitted and contained a glowing brazier. They were warming their hands at it when the Madams Hildebard swept in.

The mother was plump and wore a cap over her gray curls. Her outer tunic was striped and edged with fur. In her hands she held an embroidery kit. The younger madam, renamed since her recent marriage Lady Isobel de Scal, had small features in an oval face. She was what Achtriel supposed men found attractive with her neck and chin uplifted like a swan's and her thin pale hair wound round her head in braids. To Achtriel, she seemed merely uninteresting.

The mother reclined heavily on a chaise and took up her embroidery. The daughter dropped her outer robe and tunic as Esther took her measurements. Achtriel stayed at their side writing notes and numbers on a small square of calfskin. When the measuring was done, the younger madam donned a kirtle Profait had made for her that needed to be altered. She complained that since her marriage she'd grown thin, recounting in profound detail the contents of her diet of that day, the day before it and the day before. Behind her, out the window, apple tree boughs blew in wind. Achtriel had never been inside a many storied house and watched as the wind shook fruit from stems and sent it toppling. It seemed more rain was due, unusual this early in the year.

"A pity that the child was born deformed," a voice broke through her thoughts. "Now that you've cleaned her, I can see her face is sweet and with that lovely coloring, so unlike most of you dark Jews..."

"Not all share your coloring tastes, Mother," said the younger madam, eyeing Esther who was stooped below her measuring a hem. "They say Miss Esther here commands a following."

"Is that so, Esther? Do the men about consider you seductive?" the mother raised her eyebrows.

"I would not know, madam," Esther replied, intent upon her work.

"I have it from my husband," the young one said. "Your name is mentioned favorably among his friends."

"I would hope not," Esther said.

"Why is that?" both women asked.

"It is not meet or wise to stir ungodly thoughts in men."

"Oh, tosh. I don't believe you are so pious," opined the elder, "for I see it in your eyes. You simply tell us that, like all you Jews, so we will be chagrined. You are no holier than we."

"Well, if you would know, I am not holy. Simply cautious," Esther told them, pulling down the hem to even it.

"I suppose you have a point." The younger lady sighed, appraising her kirtle in the mirror. She lowered its neckline and turned to analyze the look. "An unwed woman should convey an air of chastity. That is, of course, till she is settled. That is when the fun begins."

"You had better watch your fun, my daughter, there is talk already of your exploits."

"Rumors simply, Mother," the daughter let the kirtle go and stuck a stray hair back into its braid. "It never hurts to stir up some excitement. Otherwise, we all should be so bored. Don't you agree?"

Esther continued working but mentioned nonchalantly moments later, "They say the one who comes to claim the castell brings us some excitement."

"Do they really?" said both madams. "What have you learned?"

"A customer alluded to it briefly. They said he had to leave Paris in haste."

"I heard that too," the mother said and raised her forehead as if to catch the memory. "It was a fight, I think, yes... A man was killed, and there was an expensive settlement. Such a fuss. That is the way in Paris. Thank God our local men are not so wild."

"Let's hope that they will calm him then, and not the other way around," Esther remarked.

"Oh, a little wildness could amuse," the younger Madam smiled. "I for one should welcome it. Life is so completely weary here. And I hate this mantle. Profait has no imagination."

"You have been to Paris, Esther. How does fashion differ there?" the mother asked.

"Yes, tell us, please. And we shall pay you more. What of these tunics, they are so shapeless.

"Well," Esther set her pin and rose to have a look, "it's true this style of sleeve is no longer worn, not even in Rodom—that is Rouen. They prefer it flared with a hanging placket to hide the lining. The outer robe is gathered at the waist to go with the tighter lines."

"Flared sleeves? How do they hang it? I must imagine it," Isobel said, squeezing her eyes small.

"I know a way," Esther said. "Do you have a wax tablet and stylus?" The older woman reached behind her to a desk and brought out the desired items. "Achtriel, come and do a rendering for us." The madams watched with astonishment as Achtriel took the writing implements. Esther described the sleeves and made Achtriel draw them.

"Oh, pray do mine like that," said Isobel, when the drawing was finished, "I want to be in fashion. How much more will you charge me to redo both sleeves and gather the waist?"

"Well, if we do that, we should pull in the kirtle too." Esther pinched the sheath beneath the outer dress, "These fuller lines aren't worn this year."

"You must do mine as well," the mother said, rising from her couche and coming to inspect the drawing. "I'm not so old that I can look old fashioned."

"This will take some work. I will need help."

"Can't the child sew? She seems to use her... fingers rather well," the younger madam said.

"Yes, she can," Esther said pointedly to Achtriel who had returned her gaze to the window.

"Look here, child, what is outside there that can interest you?" the mother called imperiously. "I have a slave your age, and she adores to sew. You will have to earn your living somehow; you'd best get started."

"Yes, madam."

"Actually, the girl is learned," Esther told them bending to resume her basting.

"Really!" said the mother, "And a renderer as well. Well, I have more work for you then when you've finished. My little sons will soon lose their tutor. You can begin them on their Latin when we have seen the last of him. Would you like that?

"Yes, madam," she replied, and this time meant it.

For the next few weeks, she bathed and dressed herself in the clothes which Esther had laid out for her. She looked forward to the mornings with the madames, although they still intimidated her. But she must allow the younger madame's observations were correct. The only liveliness that house contained was in the women's conversation. Perhaps that was why the old monsieur, affecting to surprise them at their talk, would creep up to their room and step in as if he merely had been passing.

They listened for him though, she had discovered. She and Esther also learned to catch the shuffled steps that marked his approach and to shift the conversation before his entrance. One day, they were discussing some fresh news the younger madam had got from her husband.

"They say the young duke is related to Chilperic," she told them, "on his mother's side. He is only a natural son but stands to come into a lot of favor if the older brother dies. If only I had not been wed last spring. My luck is awful."

"Do not give up," her mother said. "We've but to scour some dim but lovely maiden to attach him, and then when he is set in our midst...voila."

"What do you mean?" asked Achtriel, curiosity overcoming her instructions to be silent. Esther shot her a warning look.

"What do we mean?" the mother said. "Simply that we shall all be friends. Surely there's no wrong in that."

"What mother means," said Isobel, "is that with Esther's able costuming augmenting all my wit and charm, I shall entice the count to look my way."

"But…"

"Achtriel, how goes your seam?" Esther asked pointedly.

"It is almost done." She sighed.

"A woman never will go far who is unwilling to be bold," Isobel pronounced. "Even you, little cripple, should remember that. A day will come when you may have the chance to take your destiny in your two hands. And on that day, you may remind yourself of Isobel's advice."

"What advice is that, my dear?" asked Monsieur Hildebard, for once surprising them.

"That a woman must think well upon her actions," Isobel said, smiling.

"Indeed, I would hope that you espoused such wisdom," he remarked. "But let me ask the girl. A Jew, I've heard, must never tell a lie. What did my stepdaughter advise you?" His face was set in an attempt at jollity, but there was darkness in his eyes. Achtriel looked at the women. Esther's face was nervous, and the Hieldebards were studiously calm. The elder madam was intent upon her stitching.

"She told me that a woman must choose wisely and think always of what is best."

"A good sermon." He smiled mirthlessly. "Perhaps you have been listening in church, daughter, although your conduct there would not lend one to think it."

"Yes, Papa. And now I'm working to convert the heathen."

He left at last after examining the clothes and questioning Esther as to the pricing of each feature. He was continually reassured by madame senior that the style would mark them as leaders of the town. When his steps were of sufficient distance, the madames giggled with relief. That day, when they went home, Isobel gave Achtriel a sugar candy shaped like cupid.

The next day, as Esther stopped to gossip with the gatekeep, an odd thing happened. Sorgen came out of the slave house and beckoned Achtriel. Determined to be as kind as possible, Achtriel went to her.

"Hello." She smiled. "You live here, I see. It seems a nice place."

Before the pleasantries had left her lips Sorgen had punched her on the jaw. Achtriel was too surprised to think.

"You will not take mine job, I see to it," the slave girl hissed. And checking to make sure Esther was not observing them, she pinched Achtriel's arm. "This just a warning, you be gone."

"I…I'm only helping Esther, for the pageant," Achtriel managed to stammer.

"Leave!" the pale girl threatened and was set to strike another blow when she saw Esther coming and hurried back inside. Achtriel rubbed her face surreptitiously as she followed Esther to the great house. She did not feel much pain but rather a curious relief. That girl was not one to befriend in spite of Esther's hints, and Achtriel was glad.

When the day arrived to leave the Hildebards, some weeks later than they'd planned, she was truly sorry. The lively atmosphere about the madames had become her prime amusement. When she and Esther bid them farewell, the younger Madame hugged them. "I will see you at the pageant soon." She promised as she paid their coin and placed it in a leather purse.

"Don't forget, child, you're to teach my boys," reminded Madame elder. "I will send you word this winter when their tutor quits. The silly man decides to leave the world and join the monks in Lexovia. I do not think the monks will like him any more than we do."

"He is too thin and priggish to attach a mate. He may as well be holy," Isobel said. "I did some hope he would persuade my husband into holy orders, but Radolph would miss his meals. Ah, well, the old tup mayhap will come down with gout and lay abed. Until that day, I must avoid him. If the Jews have remedies for loutishness, please send one my way. I will pay well."

Esther laughed. "If anyone could concoct that brew, they'd make a fortune I suppose."

"Indeed they would." The older Madame sighed. "Every woman hereabouts would prize them."

"Perhaps I shall devise it then," Esther told them as she left.

"I will miss them," Achtriel said as they were let out of the mansion.

"Yes, they are quick minded. A rarity in this small town. A pity they were never taught to read and write; their lives would have been less boring."

"Perhaps they will attend my classes with the boys."

"Perhaps. You have been a fine assistant. How do you like to sew?"

"It is a useful skill," she answered vaguely.

"You do not like it."

"It goes on too long and is too much the same."

"Well, do I know it? That's why I drafted you to do the seaming."

"Does Profait require us more?"

"He has sent word for tailors from Rodom. I think we may be let free soon."

But at the Sabbath meal that week, they learned that their salvation was postponed.

"Do you know who is Bonda de Cresques?" Profait asked Achtriel.

"No," she answered.

"Then you are the only soul in Briga to boast such ignorance."

"Who is she?"

"The local beauty, is she not?" Samiel asked, "The family's had a stream of suitors every week since she became thirteen. The cook has told me of the meals they must prepare. I've sent my buyers all the way to Lillebon for cranes and swans and other costly fare."

"Not only is she beautiful as Helen, so they say," Fagim said, "her father is a friend of the Duke of Aulercorum."

"Why does this concern me?" Achtriel inquired.

"Because you are to go with Esther to design her wedding dress."

"I? But why?"

"Because the Hildebards have told them how you render, and that you and Esther make the best clothes in Briga. Don't look as if you've been condemned. They'll pay you well."

"But..." She looked at Esther for a sign of hope, but Esther sighed.

"When do they want us?"

"All week next," Fagim said. "I am taking Elies and Natan to Rodom as you are otherwise employed."

Esther muttered an expletive beneath her breath and Fagim chuckled. "The boys are thrilled. They recommend that you become a seamstress permanently and let them take your business."

"How kind of them," Esther said sardonically. "I am glad for the boys that they will go with you, although I wish it were for other reasons. Elies is a merchant born, despite his mother's wishes."

"Oh yes, quite true," Fagim agreed. "Our Macha had some words with me when I invited him, but I insisted. She does not like me well right now."

"Macha angers quickly, but she soon cools," Achtriel said. "But why cannot I be the one to go to Rodom and someone else become a tailor?"

"A tailor? I will not stand for such a thing," Tahto said. "My scholar shall not waste her talents long at such tedium."

"Thank you, Tahto," she replied. "But until the Hildebard's tutor leaves, I will not be hired for scholarship, so I must be useful."

"I think I know a remedy," Tahto said. "I have some younger students now, enough to form a class. When you have finished with the Cresques child, I shall speak with their parents about your teaching Latin grammar. I cannot lose my scholar to the trades."

"Oh, truly? Tahto, thank you!" she said happily. "Now, I'll have the fortitude to stand my work, knowing that my sentence nears an end."

When the new week came, she found her curiosity to see the beauty outweighed her loathing of the task ahead. Esther said that she had seen the girl when she was just a child and that, even then, her face made one astonished with its radiance.

They had learned the girl had been sent to a conservatoire in Paris, the local priest having advised her parents that she'd be better married so. The family had practiced some Rhinish hierology but had gladly traded their unfashionable gods for Jesus to further her career. In Paris, word had got about concerning the beauty, and since her return to Briga, the family had done nothing but evaluate her suitors. Esther confessed that she too was interested to observe the girl.

The Cresques house was hardly as large or well situated as the Hildebards'. It was in the merchant's quarter, and although its outside had been recently redaubed, the roof supports were sagging and the walls atilt. A thin slave opened up the door as they approached and led them to a street-front room. There, the girl's mother sat on a couche surrounded by her children. One child was nursing at her breast while yet another crawled over her lap. Two older ones, so close in age as to be twins, played noisily beside them.

"Oh, you are here. And very early too!" the woman said when Esther bowed and introduced herself. "I'll have the children taken soon and call for Bonda. She is in the garden. She spends her days there since she returned home, the quiet aids in her tranquility. Come!" she called the slave who took the children, detaching the infant in mid suck to its surprise and loud displeasure.

"I've gotten several vellum scrolls for you to render on, and some pen and ink," the mother told them, glancing once at Achtriel's hand and quickly looking elsewhere. "We've never had a renderer. I know they have them sometimes in Paris. We were told to have a portrait made of Bonda, but there was no need. Her reputation was established." The woman adjusted her kirtle and stood up. "I shall come back with Bonda now. You may arrange your workplace. I think beside this window will afford the clearest light."

When she had gone, they looked around the room. It was made of rough planed planks, which served as both exterior and inside walls. Nothing ornamented them as in the Hieldebards', and they looked as if they had not once been cleaned. Food stuffs lay about the packed earth floor and flies and other insects swarmed about. It smelled like dirty babes and unwashed fabric. Esther sighed and gazed up at the ceiling. "A whole solidus," she muttered, "and a hen and chicks."

"One week more," Achtriel echoed.

"Then I will go to Rouen myself and leave Fagim the minding of the stall. I must consult with my suppliers there, perhaps I'll stay a month. By then, one of those Rodom tailors will have usurped our business. A pity."

"And I shall be teaching. Our poor clothing customers."

"Ah, yes."

Presently, they heard the sound of footsteps in the back, and then a door opened behind them. "Here is Bonda," the mother announced as if the queen had entered.

Achtriel's first sight of her was one she would not soon forget. The girl was indeed lovely as a nymph. Her eyes were wide and clear as fox's and seemed sylvan and sly. The skin of her face and graceful neck was white and smooth and shone with the reflection of her honey-colored hair. She stood, inclining her head slightly as if modesty demanded that she thus avert her own awareness from the admiration she inspired.

"Here are the tailors which the Hildebard's commended," her mother said by way of introduction. "The silk she has on now is a good length, so I bade her wear it." Taking Bonda by the shoulder, she propelled her toward them. The girl moved as if stirred by gentle winds and looked up briefly with her vixen's eyes.

"You may remove your undertunic now, dear," the mother told her, "so that they may take your measurements."

It was impossible for Achtriel to turn away as Bonda let the garment slide from her shoulders. Even Esther, though she politely bent her head away, was stealing glances at the girl. Her body was so shaped as to remind the world of YHWH's intention in designing human forms. Such ones at least were earthly coinage of his elegance and glory.

"Step forward, dear, into the light," the mother urged. "Let's have the renderer devise a sketch of you to see how the dress will look." Esther beckoned Achtriel to come closer.

She had never worried, drawing in her room or even with the dress designs for Isobel. But now with everyone observing, with that creature watching, Achtriel was frozen. "I… I must get back a bit to see the form," she said, retreating. For the first time, she doubted her own skills as she attempted to catch the flow of Bonda's arms and shoulders. She reminded herself that there were no renderers in town and likely no one here had seen a drawing. With that to calm her, she made an adequate attempt.

"Magnificent!" the mother exclaimed in a sham Parisian accent when the sketch was finished. "You have caught her pose and features. Look, the form is perfect! Now how shall you design the kirtle?"

"Well," said Esther, glancing from the drawing to its subject, "I think we want to make the inner garment simple but with a hint of ornament. I have some rosette twill with embroidered threading at the neck and arms and with a small amount of silk brocade … simplicity will serve her well."

"Let me see a drawing of the outfit now," bade the mother, and to Achtriel's discomfort, stood at her shoulder as she drew a design of the ensemble she and Esther had planned that morning.

"Yes, that will be lovely, very nice indeed. And since your girl is so handy, I should like a portrait of my daughter for her future husband. He is so very savorous of her beauty." She smiled indulgently at Bonda who bowed sweetly. The mother then sat down upon the couche in no hurry, it seemed, to rejoin her children. She began to sew but looked up frequently to watch the progress of their measuring. Bonda, who until now had not spoken, yawned. "I am tiring, Mother, may I go back to the garden till they need me more?"

"Yes, of course, child." Her mother nodded. "But take with you the renderer. The garden is a perfect setting for a portrait." Bonda glanced at Achtriel. Then without looking back, she floated through the rooms and out the garden door.

The rear yard was, unlike the house, enchanting. It had arbors, climbing plants and shrubs in winding paths. Achtriel, following the beauty, remembered townsfolk's tales of magic beasts who came to lie with virgins in such idylls. But Bonda's loveliness tarnished as they passed the sightfall of the house. When she glanced back at the open window, her features had gone dull and waxen.

She stopped and picked a rose and smelled it. Then she crushed its petals with her fingernails. She quickened her pace, a bit ungracefully, and vanished down an arbored trail. Unsure what her subject intended, but following instructions, Achtriel trailed the girl into the shrubbery. She finally found her at a garden seat beside a pond.

Chapter 8

"You may draw me," Bonda said flatly. "But be quick about it." Achtriel began the sketch and managed to capture the soft slope of Bonda's back. But when she looked up to sketch the head, she discovered it was upside down, below the bench seat. When the head resumed the pose, its lips were swallowing enthusiastically from a flask of wine. Achtriel had never seen wine drunk except at Sabbath and never in the morning. Thus she was unsure how to reply when the girl proffered the flask in her direction and inquired, "Want some?"

"Thank you but I…I do not like the taste."

The girl coughed strangely. "You do not drink it for the taste," she said. Then she took another drink and placed the bottle on the bench beside her. "Are you drawing me?" she asked with marked disinterest.

"Yes, madamoiselle." Achtriel resumed her work.

"Why do they do it?" the beauty mumbled. When Achtriel did not respond, she raised her voice, "You are a Jew, you are so wise, they say. What is the answer to my question?"

"I'm sorry, Miss, I do not…"

"You heard my question, did you not?"

"Yes."

"Well?"

"Why do who do what, Miss?"

"You do not know the answer, clearly. That is because you are as stupid as a cow. But why, I want to know, do they always and forever do that." She plucked at the skin of her hands but then, as if she had been warned of this behavior, folded them upon her lap.

"Perhaps if I knew…"

But the girl continued as if unaware of Achtriel's existence. "From the time I was a babe, the nurses and the aunts, the women everywhere, they were the ones. What could they possibly have meant for me to think?"

"What did they…" Achtriel began but realized the girl was neither talking to her nor expecting a reply.

"They made it sound as if the heavens opened, and the angels walked among us." She laughed at that and took another drink of wine. "Why do they tell us that? What is the purpose to it, pray? So that we do not run away, so that we do not make ourselves as ugly as a Jew? A stupid, crippled, ugly Jew." She turned her head to Achtriel. "Do you know what I am talking about, you stupid girl?"

"No, ma'am."

"Look at you. You are deformed and twisted. No one will marry you. You have a limp and see, your arm all twisted up, ugh, you are disgusting. But you, I wonder do they tell even the likes of you? Do they spin for you their tales of love?" Her face contorted as she formed the word. "Oh, how they made me long for it, how alluringly they painted it. When you are in love, they said, and giggled and made eyes. When your husband comes to you at night and mother hushed them, but their faces told me love was…something oh so wonderful, divine. Yes, they hinted, how it would transform me. Such a one, so lucky a one as I to be blessed with such a face they said. Oh, they praised me always, always, how they loved my skin, my hair, my dimples, and my…" She glanced down at her chest then looked away. "I don't. I really don't conceive the reason." Sighing, she shook her head. "When in the end, you are… they know you are only to be handed over to a man—an old, old man—whose face is fat and full of red marks and who smells like…" She grimaced and fell silent.

"Your affianced…?"

The girl looked up as if surprised that anyone was there, but then she took another gulp of wine and said, "My betrothed. My future husband. Do you know how old he is? He is forty-eight. Oh, he thinks himself a young man still. He struts and waves his arms about and brags about his riches. And when he is alone with me he…

He has no hair... here... on the top of his head, his forehead. And his nose is flecked with buboes, and his teeth, and he touches me..." Her face grew bitter then enraged. "I will not stand it!"

"I... I am sorry for you. Cannot you tell your mother? Or ..."

"You stupid, stupid girl. I've told them all. Told them and told them and told them. And the priest and my mother and my dear, dear father, they all lie to me, just like the fables they all told me about love as light as bluebirds, ah love. And when you meet your husband, your true love, how the world will then become a heaven that all your life you've waited for. The gargoyles! Did they know? Of course! They knew it all along. That in the end, you're handled by some pig who must become your husband. Pig. Pig of a man. Unsightly great ox, who snorts like an ox, and his skin is rough and waxy and...and cold."

She sat in a long silence then till Achtriel said shyly, "I'd help you, you could run away. I know the woods. You could escape through them and go to..."

"You are an idiot! Ugly, crippled, and an idiot. I thought they told me Jews were wise. But you are as stupid as a...a stupid Jew." She looked down at her flask and raised it but then seemed to reconsider. Then she turned away and laughed until the tears came from her eyes.

"The woods," she said at last. "Do you know what is in the woods? Brigands who would sell me as slave when they had done with me. I cannot run anywhere. Oh, do not think I haven't thought of it. I thought I'd rather whore in Paris. Do not think I haven't thought it out. You see those women, the gigglers, the snakes, they would betray me. My father would come find me, and he'd kill me. Do not doubt it. He would pretend to Mother that I had been slain by bears or robbers in the woods, but he would strangle me, I've seen him do it. Do not think to disobey, he's said it every day since darling husband signed the marriage contract. Do not hazard me, my girl. Oh no, there is no escape. If there were a way some other one would have contrived it. It is a useless thought." She sat still for a while, to Achtriel's relief, and seemed to drift into her thoughts. Then her eyes cleared briefly, and she turned and reached her hand out and said, "Let me see the drawing."

Achtriel had had a difficult time with such an active subject. She would have liked to throw away the sketch. But the jeweled hand waved angrily, and so she had no choice but to obey it. The girl glanced briefly at it then returned it. "You didn't finish my hair. It has these ruby pins on top; you need to show them. He will want to see that." She was silent for a while and then continued. "The drawing looks like me. Let mother have it to remember. When I get big and sag with child, after child, and look like her in four years' time, she can remember. Tss. Love!"

She inclined her head so Achtriel could draw her jewels. Then her voice floated above them both as if she had already gone. "The irony." She gave a hollow laugh. "Here you are…crippled and plain and poor. Who will ever find you beautiful? You will never marry nor have children nor be mistress of a home. Your grandpapa will die, and you will slave away making the clothes of ladies, or if not, you'll beg and wither on the streets, growing only older and more crippled, more detestable. And I will be a great dame in my town with gold and fine things everywhere. But you—you stupid, ugly, crippled Jew—you are luckier than me."

"Perhaps you will find happiness."

"Perhaps I'll take a lover that would be all right. Perhaps I will be happy for a while. But if they find me out, I will be hanged. How can one be happy with a fate like that to fear? No, no." She laughed lightly as if at a game of cards. "You have the luck. Yes, a crippled ugly orphan Jew is more fortunate than me."

She fell silent after that and seemed to turn as stony as the bench she sat on. Achtriel had finished her first drawing and as the girl was now so still began another one. This time, she made the picture truer to the life, rendering the slump of her back and the slack eloquence of her tilted head. The girl's insults had made her very angry and though she wished to draw a scathing portrait of her unbeautiful soul, she feared to do it. Also, though she hated Bonda for her cruelty, in almost equal measure, she felt sorry for her. The drawing was nearly finished when the mother leaned out of the window to call them.

"Bonda dear! The renderer must start her sewing now. Just come in for a moment, darling, so that we may check the length." Bonda turned and gave a warning look to Achtriel, which made it clear that any mention of their conversation would equal doom. "Coming, Mother," she called in dulcet tones and hid her flask beneath the bench.

When they came inside, she pushed past Achtriel and faced her mother. "I tell you, Mother, that I will not have that cripple sewing anything for me. I do not care if the dress takes two months. I cannot stand the thought of that claw hand upon my clothing. Get her out of here."

"Oh my! Oh well, dear, if that is what you wish..." the mother stammered.

"Give me the rendering then and be gone," Bonda commanded Achtriel.

"Yes, of course," she said, complying. Esther's eyes asked silently if she felt injured by these cruel words. But Achtriel's face, when it looked up from bowing, bore the relief of a cage freed lark.

When the servant let her out the door, she hurried away. She hobbled through the street of merchants, down the road to town. Avoiding the market stalls, where curious eyes might too easily divine her mood, she hurried past Profait's shop, praying he would not see her and find her some alternate drudgery. Climbing the forest road, she stopped to catch her breath and view the town beneath her.

It was the world she had been born into, its familiar sights and landmarks just as they had always been. She wanted to see it now as she had always seen it, unchanging, eternal in its way. But Bonda's words had followed her. Like beasts from *sitra ahra,* they scratched at the surface of her vision, marring it. "Your grandfather will die," she had said with horrid ease, "and you will be alone."

The thought was not a new one but had been avoidable. Now it filled her ears like a swarm of flies. It was impossible for Tahto to not be here; he was her world. And yet she knew that it was possible and, even worse, inevitable. The years would progress as they always did, and he would grow older. How old was Tahto now, she wondered.

He had no use for such questions and said he did not count his life in numbers but as monks noted time, as functional units for certain tasks. He said only that he lived now in his golden years, and that they were the happiest of his life. That his dear face and voice might leave her, that he should suffer illness and disease; she could not bear the thought. She sank down on a rock and cried for him, his sweetness, his lonely life, and the unspoken longings she knew he hid from her. She wept for herself also. Her wretched form, which Bonda had detested with such vehemence. She would be left alone when Tahto died; no one would see or comprehend her as he did. She would have no children and no family and be forced into a life of slavery. Her future stretched cruel and bleak before her, and although the sun shone, her heart lay in a barren winter.

But the sunshine cheered the birds, whose job it was to celebrate each moment. Their voices roused her from her tears, and soon, she was able to dry them. The very fact of birds was proof that God did not wish man unhappiness, as some Christians claimed. No, the Blessed One was clearly joyous in His plan. He had made a world so full of beauty that it beckoned like a warm embrace.

The trees rustled their leaves and sent their smells her way. She remembered she had not been in the woods for weeks now, and that their balm awaited her. So she gathered herself up and went to seek the comfort she had long relied on, hoping it would serve to banish further thoughts of gloom.

Once there, she was enlivened by her familiar haunts. She visited her dragon and picked flowers in the clearing. Only now she pictured Bonda's face where earlier she had construed imaginary beauties. Perhaps beauty itself was no more than the cruelest form of loot.

The thought was interesting. Yet even as she played with Lady Sec, a restlessness distracted her. She admitted now to a sharp regret for the loss of income which Bonda had denied her. She had wanted to buy Tahto eggs and cheese and milk; he was looking thin since their journey. She wished Bonda a horrid fate but quickly scolded herself to a firm repentance.

Bonda had a hideous destiny. Achtriel would not exchange with her for all the admiration which the beauty now engendered. This made her think again of Tahto and the misery of his own early marriage. She vowed that in whatever time remained him, she would devote herself entirely to his happiness.

Chapter 9

The preparations for the duke's arrival commenced in earnest the following week. The village was abuzz with news of mendicants and craftsmen, arriving from such distances that one could only marvel at the speed news traveled. Celebrants from distant territories had already set up tents and covered wagons on the fallow fields. Performing jongleurs roamed the streets. At night, the fires of storymen attracted listeners to tales of love and battle.

Every kind of local vendor was busy doing trade, plying visitors with merchandise the locals had rejected. One smart fellow, influenced by Elies the rumor went, had minted clay coins with a portrait of the duke, although none in town had seen him. The coins were good for entrance to the revelries, and for the services of certain sectors of the populace—an explanation which Esther would elucidate no further.

The excitement tempted Achtriel as well to venture from her forest haven. She found a job collecting tickets for a group of puppeteers. Between events, she helped them with their lines. They were so impressed with her abilities of recall that they offered her a permanent position. She told them that she must stay here to care for Tahto but offered them her writing skills so that, should they have a member who could read, they might have scripts of all they had transported in their memories.

One afternoon, she saw an amber man pass by whose head was wound with a white cloth. "Sateem!" she cried, delighted, and gave her task over to an actor's son. She hurried after the tall, slim figure, imagining scenarios which might have brought him here—had the ship foundered? Did he bear an urgent message for Tahto? But when she reached the man and pulled his sleeve, she realized it was not her friend but another of his countrymen who, nonetheless, smiled as sweetly as Sateem himself.

"Hello," he said with a curious inflection. "How may I be of service?"

"I… I'm sorry, sir. I thought you were my friend."

"You have a friend from my country? How unusual! How did you meet?"

"He was a sailor on a boat we visited. They had a message for my grandfather."

"Indeed! Well, you are the first person in this country to show any familiarity with mine. Most of the folk about here take me for an African."

"How silly. There are many Africans about and they look nothing like you."

"Quite true. Young lady, you seem very bright. I wonder if you might be helpful to a foreign guest."

"Of course!" she offered happily.

"I am a performer. So I must make a mongering, you see. Something that will attract those here with musical interests."

"You are a musician?"

"Yes, I am."

"Oh, can you teach me? But I cannot pay you…yes, I can! I get a coin a week from helping out the puppeteers. Oh, but…I shouldn't."

"You need the money, do you? Well, if you've an interest in music, I will teach you for free. After all, you're to be my publicity." He laughed at that then instructed Achtriel how to find his tent, amid the other campsites in the fields. He said that if she came by on the morrow, she should have her first lesson. She said good-bye and returned to her post as if on wings.

She told Tahto that night of the musician's offer; and he, too, was delighted. "Ah, the sound of instruments about my house!" He smiled. "I have not had that since my boyhood. My brother and I loved to sing, and he would play on the p'samterion. That is a kind of long box with many strings. You play it with sticks, and it is as if beside you stood a choir of angels.

My stepmother would dance and weave about us. She had been an entertainer in her court and taught us songs from all the foreign dancing girls who lived there. She could play a Taare, a hand drum with small bangles and a kind of reed as well. How lovely it sounded."

"I will learn to work each instrument he has so I can play and sing for you," she promised, coming to his side.

"Well, I shall look forward to it." He smiled, patting her hand, and went off to his study.

She might have regretted her promise when she came next morning to the musician's campsite. He had so many instruments within his tent that it would have taken many years to learn them all. But her determination was undaunted.

The man came into the room then, pushing aside a tapestry that had been hung from the tent pole to form an additional quarter. He had her examine each instrument, and as he described them, she listened to his words as if it were the *Ahunwar of Zoroaster.*

He told her that his father was a famous singer at the court of Prabhakar Vardhan. Before that, father and son had lived with a guru named Matanga who had written many books on music theory. But the musician-son had disappointed both father and guru by being inspired only by the "vulgar music of the streets." "That is where the life is!" he said avidly and to prove it burst into a song the like of which she never had heard.

His voice rose and curved with cries and semitones that seemed to find the spaces between notes and curl around them. Achtriel could only sit enraptured by the range and pattern of the sounds. They bespoke both rage and fervent longing, jollity and anguish.

As he sang, he did a lusty dance in which his entire torso snaked and then stood still. Then each limb danced by itself to show its virtuosity. All the while, his eyes were flashing, and his face conveyed the meaning of the song, although she could not understand it. When he was done, she stood and clapped as best she could with her weak hand, and he bowed before her, smiling broadly.

"Now let me have a look at you," he said and took her hands in his. "Well, well." He raised his eyebrows. "You have got the soul of a musician. I can read it in your palm." He lifted each finger and watched it fall then turned her hands back on themselves and looked at them from underneath. "Ah hah." He nodded finally. "You have a little problem here I see with pirni, but you have overcome it well, your fingers have the flexibility they need, and…" He lifted her wrists and let her arms fall. "Yes. We may even make a creditable drummer out of you."

"Thank you," she said. "But what is pirni?"

"Eh? Oh, that is the condition of your hand and foot. It is a common problem evident in childhood. Your case is mild and should present no problem."

"You know others with…who have this?" Her voice was trembling.

"Oh, goodness, yes. In fact, there is a clinic in my city where they do nothing but treat those with problems of the limbs. They come from all about the kingdoms."

"My grandfather was right," she said, abashed, "And I did not believe him."

"Your case is minor. With diligence, you'll quickly work around it. And someone clearly has done well when you were small. Exercise the limbs in infancy, they say, that is the key."

"Macha," she said.

"Well, you must thank her then. And so must I! For I have found a pupil. She has trained your hands to work on fundamental levels, so now I can begin to show them how to dance. Come, let us begin."

"I have traveled much," he continued, as he held the tapestry aside and bade her enter the adjoining room. It contained a bed-chamber and several large trunks. "I have set myself about to learn the music of the common people there. Courtly music is so stilted everywhere, you see. They take the heat, the spice from it, and make it dull. Of course, it has its beauty, but a mournful and somewhat hollow kind. Have you heard the monks chant? It is like that. A solitary, empty sound, a song of deprivation, I feel. But not so the music of the streets. Why, I have learned tunes from whores which date to prehistoric times and from countries which have vanished from the earth."

"How do you remember them?"

"Ah, that is the gift of training. In my country, and in the lands of Africa, even in Hibernia and Brython, there are bards who start at your age; and by the time they are as old as me, have memorized thousands of songs. The mind can hold much more if it is set to tune, you see. A song you have befriended stays always in the memory."

"They say I have a good recall."

"Yes, I can see that in your hands. So," he lifted the lid of one of the trunks and took from it a tear shaped drum, "now we begin by teaching these fingers to tickle music from a skin."

He bade her sit cross-legged on the floor. Then he placed the drum between her knees. He showed her how to hit it using different combinations of her hands and fingers to make the many words with which the drum voice spoke.

It was not hard to modify the right hand strokes for her less able fingers there. He said, to her profound and secret exaltation, that her bent hand was really an advantage for a drummer. Many pupils work to get that shape, he told her, and she came by it naturally! By the end of her first hour, she had command of several strokes, and he was quite astounded with her progress. "You are a very rapid learner, Miss," he beamed.

"Thank you," she replied. "My grandfather says that is why I am to be a scholar, but I don't know."

"What is it that you do not know?" he asked, taking the drum and placing it back in its trunk.

"Well... most of the texts I've read are the words of old, dead men who seem so certain of their points of view, as if there could be no discourse or argument upon it. And I think..."

"Yes?"

"I think they should have to prove their arguments. We are supposed to agree with them just because they were renowned in educated times. But what do they know of what is happening now? Besides, they have all been dead for hundreds of years."

"Or thousands, in my country, thousands." He pulled out of his box a hoop with hide stretched over it.

"I like best the arcane texts, the ones that speak of spells and ventures of the magic world."

"You have texts like this?"

"A few. Tahto collects them, not that he believes in them just…"

"Who is Tahto?"

"He is my grandfather. Well, not really…"

"Not really your grandfather?"

"Well, he is my only family; he found me when I was a tiny babe."

"I see. Well, he sounds an interesting man. I would like to meet him."

"Oh, he would love to meet you too!" she cried. "We have a Sabbath dinner every week, you must come."

"This Friday then?"

"Oh yes. Except… I am ashamed to ask you this, but I do not know your name."

"You see? We are fast friends; it seems as if we've known one other for many years, and yet I also do not know yours."

"I am Achtriel."

"I love the sound. And I am Naadasya."

"Naadasya," she repeated. "I love your sound as well.

"Well, let us hope your grandfather is appreciative of sounds. You may not make such pleasant ones until you learn to ply the drum head. But once you do so, it will sing. Here is a training hoop for you. Come back in two days and show me you have mastered the strokes I've shown you. If you do them well, I shall reveal to you a very secret thing."

All the way home, she fingered the drum hoop and all that afternoon, despite Macha's vexation, she practiced on it. In the early morning, before she went to work, she made the strokes again till each one sang as when Naadasya played it. Macha came to her room exasperated.

"You will wake the dead!" she exclaimed. "And God forbid my mother-in-law be among them for she will come at me straightway to malign my housekeeping. And her *nayfish* son, whom I won't bless and not only because I do not know if he lives or lies at sea, may also adorn my doorstep, and I shall be forced to again feed and clothe him. So for God's love, be quiet."

"I cannot, Macha. Naadasya bade me learn my strokes. If I do not do them perfectly, he will be disappointed."

"And who is this Naadasya that his disappointment should mean so much to you?"

"He is my music teacher."

"I see. I suppose he is that dark handsome fellow I've seen performing in the market."

"That is him," she confirmed and resumed her banging.

"Well, he shall hear from me soon if this racket endures. Why can't he teach you a quieter instrument?"

"The drum is the oldest and purest accompaniment to the charm of the human voice."

"This he told you?"

"Yes."

"Hmph. The human voice can be also unpleasant. As he shall soon learn. Tahto has a headache too, you know. He refuses to tell you but at least have a care for him."

"I will, Macha," she promised and took her hoop to the far end of the garden where only the woodchucks need be charmed by it.

The following day after work, she hurried to Naadasya's tent. He was rummaging around in his trunks and did not see her. She took up her hoop and began to play it, and he turned around with a radiant smile.

"Ah, such a pupil! You have not only made the drum head sing, her voice is dancing! Come, I will teach you the syllable songs. Your surprise will approach us by and by."

He showed her how to take each sound and assign it a syllable. Then the syllables together made singsongy sentences.

"Create the different combinations in your mind," he instructed, "Now close your eyes. Do you see them writ across your thoughts?"

"Yes."

"Now make your hands say them," he whispered. She tried and found that although haltingly, her hands could utter rhythmic words. This was intriguing. She concentrated so hard on the exercise that she did not notice Naadasya go to the rear of his tent and come back to sit near her. "You have played so well that the souls of the netherworld have come forth to hear you," he said. "Take a look."

She opened her eyes and to her amazement, a tiny imp now stood before her. He wore a round cap full of buttons and a little vest of the same material. He cocked his head to one side then the other, examining her with a child's curiosity.

"Oh! Where did he come from? What is he?" she cried, dropping her hoop.

"He is a she, and her name is Sruthi."

"Is she...Macha told me I would call forth the spirits. Is she..."

"Macha did, did she now?" He chuckled. "Well, she is wrong. Sruthi is only my pet."

"Oh! Yes! Sateem told me of such creatures. The man I met on the boat."

"They are as numerous in my land as the birds in yours. They live in the trees and will come down to pester you. Sruthi is well behaved, though. She is a monkey."

"Can I touch her?"

"You can do more than that," he exclaimed. "In fact, I think she has plans of her own." He spoke some instructions in his language, and the monkey approached her and proffered its palm.

"She wants to take your hand," Naadasya explained. Achtriel touched the creature's tiny furred fingers that were human in almost every way. Then Sruthi grasped Achtriel's arm and jumped onto her shoulder, and she could only sit open mouthed as the little animal climbed onto her head then down to her lap and began to pick dirt from her clothing.

"She is very fastidious. Would you like to feed her?" Naadasya offered.

"Yes, please.

He handed her an apple slice, and she held it out for the monkey. Sruthi took the fruit in her hands and examined it carefully, turning it over. Then she began to take dainty bites from it like a well-behaved child.

"Now we must complete today's lesson," Naadasya insisted. "For if you make as much progress as you are capable of, we shall perform together at the pageant next week."

"Play...next...in front of people?"

"Oh yes. The musician's art demands a listening ear, many if possible."

"But what if...the folk near here are...what if they do not admire it?"

"They concern us not. Our job is to play for them as well as we can. Even if they throw manure at us, we will have succeeded in our duty and may rest content." He retrieved her hoop and presented it to her with a grand flourish. She took it with such a doubtful expression that he burst into laughter.

That Sabbath she prepared a feast, creamed peas and carrots, peppers black roasted to be peeled apart for their sweet insides, onion soup, a round of cheese she had bought with her earnings, buttermilk, and sour bread pudding. She was so excited, fussing about to set out the meal out right, that Tahto joked with her.

"Perhaps you are in love with your new friend?"

"Oh, Tahto, no," she said but blushed. "He is too old."

"As old as I?"

"No, not that old. But he is a grown man."

"Ah, so he will not steal you away from me, I hope."

"Tahto, don't be silly. I am eight years old."

"Well, I am glad of it," he said and hugged her close. "I get to keep you for a few more years."

"Many, many more," she assured him and went to pick the lettuce for a salad.

That dinner was the liveliest in years. Naadasya regaled them with tales of his travels. Tahto recalled adventures from his seaman's days and Mosse, it turned out, had sailed on three attempts to find a faster route to Orient.

"It all sounds so adventurous," Esther remarked. "It makes me want to pack my things and embark tonight. Alas! I am enslaved yet to Bonda."

"And who is Bonda?" Naadasya inquired.

"A local beauty with an ill-formed soul," said Achtriel. "She did not want my crippled hands on her wedding clothes."

"Well, good for her! For else those clever hands would not have found their true calling."

"I wish she'd objected to my hands." Esther sighed. "She is so cross in the afternoons that she hurls insults at me. Her mother sits there as if nothing has been said."

"Her poor betrothed." Naadasya laughed.

"She is the poor one, I believe," Fagim remarked. "Her slave tells me she much detests the fiancée."

"Well, I feel pity for her then," Tahto said.

They sat in silence for a while till Naadasya, seeing that the meal was done, leapt to his feet and bade them all learn a song. It was about a man named Mahomet, a businessman in Arabia who was much admired for his virtue. But this song was a silly one in which the man's servant pretended to be as wise as his master and got everything wrong. The verses rhymed and several of them Fagim refused to translate for Achtriel. They must have been quite funny for the adults who understood them laughed heartily. Although she did not know what she was saying, Achtriel learned the words and sang along, causing Naadasya to giggle hysterically.

After dinner, Achtriel saw him talking quietly to Esther. She felt a pang of jealousy and realized that some of Tahto's teasing had been near the truth. She did find an unfamiliar excitement in the presence of her teacher. She admired the way his dark eyes flashed and his black hair framed his handsome face. As he looked at Esther now, with a shy and cautious warmth, she found herself wishing he would look at her that way. But for her, such glances would be always impossible. Perhaps in his land, girls with pirni could attract a mate, but such was not the case in this one.

She bent to clear the table with a weary air, but Tahto came to help her and began a song they both knew. Naadasya followed them and, after listening once, had learned both words and tune. Then he sang it loudly, lifting Achtriel from her chore and dancing round the room with her. Soon, she was singing it too, even dancing on her hobbled foot. The others took it up as well and clapped and stomped until the room was filled with happiness.

Chapter 10

All day, crowds had thickened in the merchant street, now awash with entertainments for the passersby. Joining the players and magicians, comic troupes from far-flung hamlets had now arrived. They could be seen about the town attired in strange costumes.

A man in a black-and-white striped outfit shouted unintelligibly and waved a cane of similar design. A fat woman adorned with flowers dangled vegetation as she walked. Several maidens, their long tresses wound about them to hide their nakedness, rode about on donkeys, small rabbits in their tattooed arms.

There was a contest of strength among a crowd of large men. One held up a table with three women on it. Another lifted a cow above his head. Near them was drawn a circle in the dirt in which two men were fighting. When one had been held down by the other for a count of three, a new man would come in to fight the victor. There was much shouting and obscenity, but the women, who watched also, did not seem to mind.

In another part of the square performers did feats of superhuman bravery and skill. Some jumped over fires or landed in the flames and did not seem to notice. A Pict with dyed blue arms stood impassive as a woman pierced his skin with spikes and barbs.

A man from Vasconia had a huge bear and put his own head inside the creature's mouth. And of course, the soothsayers, astrologers, and herbalists were out in force, accosting passersby. From her post at the puppeteer's, Achtriel could watch it all.

Frenzy overcame the children. Running through the streets; they collided with adults who cursed them ineffectually. Arguments, which led to fights, broke out with ever greater frequency as folk imbibed the beer being sold on every corner. Roving men in boots and long woolen capes traded lustful converse with the passing girls. Matrons shouted oaths and threatened them with crooks.

The pageant was to last three days, beginning with the shows at dusk and the processional. Since only the oldest townsfolk could recall such an event, no one knew how raucous it might finally become. Speculative rumor filled the air. Some believed the pagans from outlying parts would enact the rites saved usually for harvest time. These included man-eating and all manner of unspeakable behavior.

Most insisted that they could not do such things in plain sight of the church and governors, but others disagreed, claiming every governor would be too drunk to notice. Already the bear had broken loose and killed a huntsman's hounds, and no official could be found to settle things.

She left her post at midday to bring Tahto his noon meal, for he had caught a cold. After serving him, she asked him what he thought might happen by that evening.

"It will be a rare thing, that much is certain," he said. "If I were feeling better, I would not miss it, but in such events, a Jew is often made the brunt of drunkards. Esther will stay close with you, however. I will not insist you stay at home. Keep beside her, and you may look about and tell me of it. Only take care for your safety."

"I will wear my capuchon and seem invisible," she promised.

"And if things turn dangerous, come home at once."

"Yes, Tahto," she said. When he went back to his study, she set out his evening meal. Then she packed bread for herself and Esther who was to come and get her when they finished work.

The expectancy in town heightened with each passing hour. It blazed in the eyes of celebrants. Stray dogs were riled by it and barked incessantly. Even the idiot, who usually dozed in the street, was running here and there accosting strangers. In the rampant oddity, he seemed somehow comforting. At least he represented a familiar abnormality with which the town had long grown comfortable.

At one point in late afternoon, when it had begun to seem as if nothing more surprising could appear, an odd large-headed boy came pushing through the crowd toward her. "Pardon Mademoiselle," he said, his crackling voice alerting her that, despite his childlike size, he was closer in age to Elias. "Can you tell me the direction of the castell?"

"Yes, of course, sir," she replied. "Go through this street and past the footbridge at the base of town. You will see it as you climb eastward up the hill."

"Ah, thank you much." He bowed. "I have asked a dozen of your neighbors here, and none would deign to speak to me. Thank God for those of liberal mind."

"My mind is liberal for I am unlike them as well. They only barely speak to me, and I have lived here all my life."

"One could wish for them to live inside our bodies for a while to see how they annoy us."

"There are some about of larger mind who do not quail at human difference. However, they are not the rule. Will you be in Briga long?"

"That I do not know. I was hired to present a poem for the courtiers. I am a performer by profession. I go where there is work."

"Well, I hope it fares well for you then. Welcome to our town." She held her hand out to him. He did not respond at first and then grasped her palm with such warmth of feeling that she knew this act of human touch was rarely offered him. Then he nodded and went off without a word.

As dusk approached, the revelry began in earnest. Soon, it was so noisy in the street that the puppeteers counted their coins and packed up. They gave her a semissis for her hard work and told her not to spend it all tonight. She laughed politely though she knew she would not waste a nummus on frivolity. Tahto had seemed tired of late and now he had a cold. The semissis would go for food. So Achtriel remained at her abandoned post worrying that Esther might not find her. By the time she did, it had begun to seem that the evening was going to be more frightening than fun.

"We must wear our hoods once night falls," Esther told her, out of breath. "The rowdies have assumed that every woman who goes bareheaded is for sale."

"Even children?" Achtriel gasped and pulled on her cloak.

"I have no doubt. But we will have a man with us so they will leave us be."

"A man? Who?" she asked but quickly guessed the answer.

"Why your friend, Naadasya. He quite graciously has offered to accompany us. Besides, you two are to perform at sundown on the green."

"I hoped he had forgotten that."

"Oh no. He's been preparing all day."

"You have seen him then?"

"Why yes, we met as I was leaving work. He was going home to fetch his instruments."

"Oh, dear."

"Now don't be shy, miss. You are a special girl; it's time more people knew it. Besides, I want to hear you play. What will your piece be?"

"I do not know the name. I am just to beat the drum the way he showed me."

"I can hardly wait." She smiled. Indeed, her eyes were sparkling in a way which Achtriel suspected was not due solely to her musical expectations.

At the green, they made their way through prone and seated folk to the platform erected for the entertainments. The performers were to gather there to learn their order in the festive program. Crowds filled the green like an animate sea, through which darted children, pigs, goats and dogs, shoo'd at with equivalent disdain. Trafficking through this, came sweetmeat vendors, acrobats, and clowns. The beggars who normally attended town events had been banished by thugs, hired for such purpose by the local church. All hoped the duke would find favor with Briga. Such wealth and influence in their small village would certainly improve it.

Her piece, it seemed, was to be among the first. For that, she was thankful. The nervousness she harbored was too dire to be born for long. She focused on Naadasya's words, repeating the rhythmic syllables he'd taught her, so that she hardly noticed when Esther made her sit beside the platform. Of the first two events, a recitation in mangled Latin by the Hildebard children, and a dour invective by the local priest, she was equally insensible. The din of the audience behind her, however, proved that in this, she was not alone.

The following performances were somewhat better. A jokester in a pigherd's togs told a comic tale about a chicken. Then two tumblers walked on their hands and spun themselves in summersaults and tumbled backward through the air. Achtriel heard the crowd's approval of these acts and feared her own must come as an unwelcome successor. But to her relief, a simpering girl went next. She sang about an elf and danced so badly that the listeners, politely for she was the mayor's child, began conversing halfway through her song. Afterward her sister or someone like enough to have been recited passages from the Bible. When they exited to mild applause, Naadasya took the stage.

He called out loudly in the local Frankish, "Men and ladies, please pay close attention. What you are about to hear is music from the East where all the trees are green and the fruits of music stir the loins and hearts of pleasant folk. I will sing you now a tale of war, of bravery and fierceness, and a bad king's trickery." He beckoned Achtriel, and she felt the world recede into her pounding heart. She floated up the wooden stairs and stood beside him on the stage.

His syllables served her well now for by repeating them, she found she could ignore the stares as well as the shouts of the crowd's more inebriated members. Naadasya raised his eyebrows. She struck the drum. The rhythmic sentences flew from her thoughts to her hands. "Yes!" she heard him say, and she turned to see him nod and smile at her. Then the drum began to play itself and all else receded.

Naadasya lifted his head and sang. His voice rang so true that, though none understood his words, they listened as if enchanted. Between each verse, he stopped to translate. It was a familiar tale, an evil lord, a prince who'd come to free his daughter from a spell. The king set tests of beasts and giants to be overcome, and with the help of magic tools the prince succeeded.

Achtriel was to show the various monsters with her rhythms, and it was such fun that she began to imitate the creatures too. The audience laughed at this, so she did it more and saw Naadasya smiling as he sang. Then he pulled a flute from his belt and played it, dancing round the stage. She followed him and even did a little caper. When they faced the audience again, she saw that folk had stood to dance and clap. At the end, she bowed, and there was cheering from the people. Such pride filled her then she thought she never could again be sad.

As they came off the stage, many young women ran to meet them. Ignoring her, they surrounded Naadasya like a flock of magpies. Achtriel glanced at Esther who seemed studiously unperturbed. She went to sit beside her leaving Naadasya to his admirers.

"That was wonderful!" Esther said and squeezed her arm.

"Did I play with regularity?" she asked. "He told me not to go too fast or slow but keep the rhythm even."

"You did so perfectly," Esther pronounced. "And I will say as much to Tahto. He will be so proud of you." Then Esther hugged her close and widened her cloak so that they both could fit inside it.

Now Achtriel could watch the program. She found herself laughing at a play about an ogre and the fool who comes upon its cave. The story seemed amusing despite her usual boredom with these common tales. Later, two clowns dressed as man and wife began an argument which led to pratfalls and a lot of comic brawling. Toward the end of the program came a jongleur. He juggled eggs and never broke one, though he threw them high and caught them without looking. Then he sang a bawdy song and a boy dressed as a woman danced and took his clothes off wiggling. The jongleur chased the boy around the stage much to the throng's delight. When he caught him, the boy took two eggs and broke them on the man's tall hat.

Then the jongleur offered a prize to anyone who could solve his riddles. The first of them went like this:

In a house sat a holy man with his two wives, his two sons, and his two daughters. The uncle and nephew were there as well but in all there were only five in the house. Who was he?

A young man, who had been one of Tahto's students, cried, "Lot who fathered two sons upon his own daughters." Then the man stepped up to take his prize. He was jeered at by others who shouted, "Such a family you have yourself." The man answered them with an obscene gesture and put on his prize, a colorful crown made of dyed feathers.

The second riddle was somewhat harder. It told of an object which swelled in the warmth under the kneading hands of a woman. When with fiery heat, it attained its most ripened state it threw up a crust which the woman swallowed. A proper old wife took to the stage with its answer, much to the raucous delight of the crowd. "Why it's but bread, you lecherous fools!" she yelled heartily and made off with her treasure, a leathern pouch. The third puzzled everyone but Achtriel. It asked the identity of a thing which walked on four legs in the morning, two in the day, and three at night.

"I know," Achtriel whispered to Esther. "It comes from a Greek tale which Tahto told me."

"Well, go claim your prize then!" Esther said and pushed her.

"I cannot. You do it," she begged and whispered the riddle's solution. So Esther went up on the stage.

"Well, she is pretty and smart as well!" cried the jongleur. "Pray tell me your answer, sweet raven hair."

"It is man," Esther told him, "who walks on all fours as an infant on two legs in his youth and hobbles about with a cane in his dotage."

"Why you are correct! Very few know this answer. And here is your prize." He handed her something too small to see. When she returned to her seat, she showed Achtriel. It was a ring made entirely of wildflowers.

The final act was long and dull, the priest again reciting psalms. Somehow, he managed to make even her favorite verses sound lifeless. During it, Naadasya came to sit behind them. "Well done," he said proudly to Esther.

"It was not I, but your pupil who knew the answer."

"And what was the prize?"

"It's a ring," Achtriel said, and Esther showed him.

"Why that is lovely," he said admiring it.

"It is yours," Esther told Achtriel.

"No, you keep it," she answered. "I could never have gone up to claim it."

"But you were so brave in our act, and you played well too!" said Naadasya.

"That was because I was lost in the music."

"Well, I shall keep you lost in it forever if it so strengthens you," he promised.

At last, the priest stopped his droning. The crowd rose as one, cheering. The priest smiled and bowed, not realizing their enthusiasm was in response his cessation. Also, it heralded the start of the processional. Now they would see the duke!

Chapter 11

The royal equipage was to be the finale of the procession. The duke and his courtiers would show themselves before ascending to a private feast with the local gentry. Esther, Naadasya, and Achtriel rushed with the others to get a place where they could see. They were shoved and pushed at by rougher folk but Naadasya, who was taller than most, guided them forward. People bowed and stepped aside for him. Soon, they were able to find a place to peer over the rows of heads. Naadasya lifted Achtriel onto his shoulders.

Fifers and lyremen began the processional, followed by girls bearing festive flags. Behind them the bear, on its hind legs, was trailed at safe distance by a troupe of mummers. Then came a warrior who jumped about, swinging his pike at the audience. He wore a horned helmet upon his head and was dressed only in oak leaves. Beside him the fat flower lady walked, blessing him with petals.

On a chariot pulled by oxen came a gigantic roaring man. He was clad in a breastplate, a golden toque around his neck. He brandished a sword with huge gems at its hilt. His other hand shook a beast-headed club of etched bronze. His chariot was an even greater spectacle. Two dead deer were tied to its front, and four tethered swans flapped above it. A cart rolled behind him bearing a cauldron.

A man on the cart paced, extolling, in nearly unintelligible dialect, the wonders of man, sword and pot. Then the cart stopped. Five men costumed as naked women emerged from behind it. They ran in front of the chariot man and waved their behinds at him. The man hid his eyes. The celebrants roared with delight at this, no longer caring if they understood the narration.

From the cauldron rose a giant beast. The spectators gasped although, if one looked, it was clear that the beast was only a man in a furry costume. The creature, however, could howl terrifically. It leapt from the cart and charged at the sidelines, causing audience members to scream. But the giant man jumped from his chariot and struck at the beast with his sword. They fought theatrically in the street as the cart moved along and eventually blocked them from sight. People pressed forward to follow the battle till the hero jumped back on the cart, bearing the beast's severed head above his own.

Then the men dressed as women rushed forward again. They took the cauldron and poured it on the hero. But at this, he said loudly in broken Frankish, "See how it boils at the touch of my skin!" And indeed steam arose from his back and arms. Then they moved on to reenact the play at a further point on the route.

Now a new narrator stepped from the crowd. Fortunately, he spoke local Frankish so his tale could be understood. He said we would now see, acted out, the tale of a king. He was out hunting and spied the most beautiful girl he had ever seen. At this, a man stepped from the crowd, a fat man on a hobby horse. Then from the crowd stepped the maiden. She was wearing a garment of green silk with a green pointed cap on her head.

"It is Bonda!" cried Achtriel.

"Indeed it is," Esther said.

Her attire was, by local standards, not proper for women. It showed every considerable curve of her form, at the sight of which the crowd fell silent. Then they cheered as Bonda, smiling, turned round to show them her every side. The king knelt before her. The crowd hissed at him as he implored. "Stay but one night with me, maiden, and you shall have from me anything you desire!"

Bonda turned away and began to sing. Her voice, so different than the one she had used in the garden, was lovely and clear. The sentiments, however, were all Bonda. "I would that your wife and children be banished and that you disarm every soldier and courtier," she sang. "Twelve hundred horses and cattle shall be forfeit to me, and a fourth of the gold of your kingdom." The king sang too, asking

111

what race of mortal she was, if in fact she was one. "I am of the race of Adam," she replied, "and yet I can do wonders."

The king sang by himself, asking the audience what he should do. Shouted remarks from young men suggested obscenities to perform on himself. The king at last acquiesced to the maid's demands. Then he tried to kiss Bonda. But an army of green men jumped from the crowd. They overcame and chained the king and lifted Bonda atop their shoulders. As the play moved down the street, the men's gazes went with it.

"Did you know of this?" Naadasya asked Esther.

"Oh yes. I had to make all the costumes. They kept me busy all week."

Suddenly from the crowd jumped a man with a hoop. He put a tinder to it, and it burst into flame. Then he whistled, and a dog ran and jumped through the fiery ring. A goat came behind it and jumped through as well. Then the dog leapt on the goat's back, and they pranced around. The man cried loudly, "Behold, my friends! A creature the likes of which you never again shall see!" From his jacket, to the crowd's astonishment, leapt Sruthi. She pounced on the man's shoulder and twirled three times.

"Naadasya, did you lend him your monkey?" Achtriel asked.

"Well no, not exactly." He glanced at Esther.

"What then, did he steal her?" Esther exclaimed.

"No, not that either. You see, I sold her. I thought I might stay here in town for a while. This gives me the means to do so."

Achtriel shouted, "Hurray!" and watched Esther's cheeks turn a shade of rose they had never worn.

"But will he be kind to her?" Achtriel asked, suddenly fearful.

"Oh yes, he is a very good man. He loves his creatures as if they were children. Sruthi liked him at once, and she does not make mistakes about people."

"I see," Esther said.

"That is why she liked you," he said, smiling at Esther.

"I see," she repeated.

Then to the performance space strode a long bearded man. He spoke in a dialect which was more Gothic than Frankish. He told

of a time when his people, then called the Winniles, were fighting
Ambri and Assi, leaders of the Vandal tribes. Both tribes approached
the God Wodan and asked him to give their side victory. Then the
narrator waved his arm, and a man on stilts stepped from the crowd.

"I am Woden. God of war!" he attested and showed them his
giant spear and gold-leafed shield. Two men representing the warring
leaders ran and knelt by his side.

"Great Woden," they shouted, "Help my tribe to defeat its
enemies!"

"I shall render victory," the God proclaimed," to whomsoever I
first look upon when the sun shall rise." The tribesmen ran off, and
a woman came forward.

"I am Gambara!" she cried. "Mother of Ibor and Aio, chiefs of
the Winniles. I cry to the goddess, Fria, protector of women!"

A large gray-haired woman on stilts stomped forward. "I am
Fria, wife of Woden!" she cried. "Because you have called me, the
protector of mothers, I shall bring you victory. Hear me, Mother, and
take my words to your women that we shall have conquest." Then
Fria bent and whispered in the ear of Gambara who ran away.

Woden came near his wife.

"Let us to bed, wife, for I am tired," he said and stretched his
great arms.

"Husband," the goddess said, "I come with you gladly."

Some helpers brought out then a golden palette and raised it
up to impersonate a vertical bed. The god and goddess pretended
to lie on it, and Woden snored. When Fria heard this, she rose from
her slumber. With the help of several young men, she turned the bed
onto its side as Woden, still asleep, turned on his stilts. He now lay
on the opposite side of the bed. Then when the sun rose, acted by a
child in yellow costume, Fria turned Woden's head to face it. Next to
the sun ran the Winnile mothers with their long hair brushed over
their faces.

"Who are these long beards?" Woden asked, yawning.

"As thou hast given them a name give them also victory!" cried
Fria.

"And so," the narrator explained as the wild-haired women danced, "our tribes were henceforth named the Langobardi, and we claim the right of victory from Woden."

"A very good story," Naadasya remarked.

"You approve of women outsmarting the men?" Esther laughed.

"That is not usually a difficult trick," he observed.

"Do you know how to walk on stilts?" Achtriel asked them. "I want to learn."

"Child, you are already a giant among men." Naadasya gave her legs a tug. "Why do you need two sticks to prove it?"

The sun was growing orange in the west. Encroaching darkness claimed the sky, and the mood of the crowd began to change. Folk seemed to grow restless and to seek excitement. Young men yelled disrespectfully at each other and the entertainers. The foreign performers spoke roughly too as arguments arose in a score of dialects. All this stopped suddenly as, turning the corner, came the party of the duke.

Chapter 12

His open tumbrel was drawn by a horse dressed in purple silks. The cart itself was laid out with finery. Embroidered pillows served as its seats, and felted wool lined the cart and spilled over its sides. The courtiers lay in languor, the duke among them. He waved to the crowd, and a roar swelled from it. The townsmen bowed their heads and the maidens, glancing up coyly, tossed flowers.

The men who accompanied him were dazzling in brocaded surcoats and gold-threaded leggings. Despite their indolent postures, they scanned the crowds with some interest. They seemed to find it amusing, as they nodded and laughed to each other. One called out mockingly to the duke, but his words were erased by the cheering. The others laughed, and the duke turned to give them a withering look. This only provoked more teasing, which he sourly ignored. He appeared to enjoy the crowd's adulation, however, especially that of the maidens. Then he seated himself by his friends and laughed with them at some private amusement. His cart rumbled past, and the excited throng broke lines and followed it.

When the entourage departed up the castell hill, people called out hearty wishes for good mead, wine, and feasting. Then they broke into smaller groups and headed back toward the center of town. The moon was high now, full and round. The smell of ripening apples filled the air. A nearby woman muttered that "they" would be at it on such a night. Achtriel wanted to ask them who "they" were, but the women, speaking hurriedly, had moved away.

"How long will the gentlemen be at their feast?" Naadasya inquired.

"We have not had a local duke in my years here," Esther replied. "And the habits of such folk I do not follow."

"I would suppose until the mead runs out," he guessed, "or until they quarrel and kill one another."

"I would hope that didn't happen." Esther laughed. "The town holds such excitement at the prospect of royal patronage."

"Look!" cried Achtriel, interrupting them. In the fallowed fields beyond the tents, bright lights were forming.

"Bonfires," Naadasya said, "Shall we go see?"

"We must not overtax out young charge," Esther admonished, taking Achtriel's arm.

"Oh, please! I want to go!" she begged them.

"Come then." Naadasya smiled and hoisted her upon his back. "Let's run, so we can get a place in front." He took hold of Esther's hand and began to run down the road, her laughter surrounding them like a zephyr.

Closer to the fires, they could make out silhouettes, some piling wood on the flames, some dancing. Music came from several bonfires and, with it, the noises of gaiety.

"Over there I think," Naadasya said as they reached the open field. Turning to the left, he took them to one of the larger fires. In its ruddy light, the faces of those nearby seemed like specters from the dawn of time. Youthful jollity rang from the fire's dark perimeter. Even the old men seemed greedy with expectancy. Then, from the blackness, stepped a figure dressed in feathers.

He paced the ring of firelight, hands behind his back. Abruptly, with a gaze that seemed to pierce the souls of all he saw, he spoke.

"Listen to my tale good brethren," he advised. His voice was crackly, like the fire, but strangely resonant. He raised his finger and pointed to the sky. "Under a moon such as this, my tale confers a magic. He who hears it shall find no ill fortune for three years hence, claim those from whom I learnt it."

He beckoned all to draw nigh him and seat themselves upon the grass. Young folk held each other close. Families gathered into comfortable piles. Achtriel slipped off of Naadasya's back and sat as close to the man as she could. Naadasya and Esther came to join her.

"Now listen well, good friends, and you shall have a tale which, older than the dusts of time, has traveled with our ancestors to reach us here. Yea, as waves fall, one upon the next, upon the sands, so swell my words to fill the corners of the thoughts of men. And as fell every wave in every land, from day present to day before, unto the first days of the earth, so long ago was my tale born unto the bardic script. In truth, there are two tales in one for those who can unknot the secret. So listen close, and you shall learn of many things. Of the early days and how our forebears came to live upon this ground.

In early days, there lived a people here. These folk were of the race of giants and had traveled here in mighty boats. On each boat rode fifty men and thrice fifty women in four ships companies. Those ships were built of cedar trees, which grew upon the mountains of the gods. Long before the Franks and Goths and Lombardi from here about, before Burgundians, and Frisians, and the sons of Meroweg, these people ruled the land. Of their dwellings, few are left upon these shores. But on the islands to the west of here, great circling stones bemark their presence. Each man and woman of that race could lift a mountain and as well fiercest magic do.

The leader of that folk was called Lotte, and she was grim to look upon. She had four eyes upon her back, and her hideous mouth was in her breast. She had but one arm and one leg, and her breath smelled like the rotted body of a whale. In fact, she was so fearsome that no one might look on her face and live, for they would turn at once to stone."

At this the man paused briefly to assess his tale's effect upon the audience. All sat as if entranced. It was as if he told a story they had known before but forgotten until he spoke.

"Now Lotte had a son who led his race in battle," he continued. "His name was Cichol Gricenchos. He was as big and high as fifty trees piled each upon the other. His hair was green as wild wood and his back all brown and ridged like hummocks. He alone could look his mother in the eye. The tribes of Lotte had conquered all the land they came from, and their people had spread out over the world. Having heard of our fair countries from the gods, they came hence to own it.

As you might imagine, there were none could challenge them. And so they built their giant villas on the land and forced the poor folk round to slave for them. One day, Cichol Gricenchos was striding in his villa, seeing to his honey and his crops; when glancing up into the sky, he saw a huge black boiling cloud. As he watched, the cloud grew larger. Lo, it grew and grew until it blotted out the sun.

Such blackness reigned for three whole days and nights that none could see his nose before his face. The giants huddled in their villas for they knew not what it meant. But Lotte, with her many eyes, went up into the mountains. She stood and roared upon the peaks. Of course, she had to look behind her, like this, because that is where her eyes were. She watched and watched with those grisly orbs whose very balefulness was her best weapon. But still she could not tell what caused the cloud. So she turned and looked to what had been behind her. There she saw a wondrous unexpected thing.

Raindrops were falling from the clouds and where each raindrop fell a soul sprang up. Each drop became the body of a man or woman, smaller than the giants yes but so precise and lovely that they made Lotte turn green. They were beings of the fairest face but more frightening to her by far was this: in their eyes lived ingenuity, cunning, and the grace of art. At once, the creatures mounted steeds and flew into the air. As soon as they had disappeared, the sun began to rise.

Lotte hurried her great self down from the mountain and called her son to her, and she cried. "A foreign race has come to challenge us! Go and gather all the warriors, let every man and woman meet us at the mountain top well-armed, and we will battle with these monsters!"

That very day, as the sun rose, but dimmed as through a strange mist, the giants all arrayed themselves for war. When they came to the battleground, they numbered fifty thousand. Each was fitted with a sword and shield of burnished gold and wore a horned helmet with iron spikes. They stood ringed about in battle form, and thus they waited. But the sun only rose higher in the sky, and none appeared to challenge them. Finally, at noon, Cichol Grincenchos could stand no more, and he cried out:

"Come and fight me, or I shall set fire to the land and all who live herein shall perish in the flames."

Then came a voice from the wind itself and, laughing, it replied, "What would that avail you?"

At that, Cichol was angered more and turned to espy his enemy but found only the empty air.

"Come and fight, or I'll unleash the sea, and it will crush the land for miles around and drown you." Again, the wind replied; but this time, it had many voices. "What would that avail you?" the voices asked.

At this, Cichol grew hotter still, and he cried out," Come and fight, or I shall send a plague upon the land, and all will die in agony."

"What would that avail you?" the voices asked again, and neither Cichol nor his mother Lotte could find an answer.

Enraged, Cichol commanded that his troops prepare for war. All raised their swords and shook themselves with savage battle rage. Fiercest of all was Cichol Grincenchos who could turn himself into a whirlwind till his face peered out his back, and his single arm became a mass of whirling weaponry. He commanded all his troops to charge!"

Next to Achtriel, a woman shrieked involuntarily as the man leapt, whirling, in the air. Other listeners drew close to one another as the man, impersonating a great giant, ran at them.

"The giants rushed about with battle screams and slashing swords. But still no one appeared to fight them. Then the voices came again, more numerous this time. And they said, "Doubt not that we could conquer you, for your swords and shields are useless against us."

"Step forward to fight and let us see then!" cried Gricenchos.

But instead of an enemy, there appeared a great white cow, ten times larger than the largest giants. She stepped between the mountains as if they were her fecal mounds. Lotte took up her massive sword. "I will slay you singlehandedly!" she screamed and rushed forward to attack the cow. Her troops, assembled by her side, hurled their swords like javelins toward the beast's great distant heart. But just as suddenly as it had appeared, the beast became an owl and flew away.

So Lotte, who could conjure well herself, brought forth a giant goat. This goat could reach the treetops where the owl had landed. But when the goat grasped the bird in its foul-bearded mouth, the owl became a host of bees and swarmed.

"Aeiiii!" the goat cried out. He turned to run away, but then the bees fell down as grains of barley. To these the goat bent with delight and nibbled humbly. Then from the errant wind a woman's voice was heard.

"Oh, Lotte," she said, "hear me well. We both are skilled in magic and the arts of war. If we fight, our sons and daughters shall be killed, and we will mourn them. If we fight, the land will burn, and the beasts and birds who live here all will die. If we fight, we shall be weakening two noble races who have grown to mightiness upon the earth. Let us meet and talk about a way in which to share this land in peace." Since the voice addressed her well, Lotte ceased her fury and began to think.

"I will meet with you," she said. "But I must know to whom I speak. Who are you and who your people who so threaten the mighty tribes of Lotte?"

"We are the daughters of Danu, child of Cotys who mated with the great snake of the sky. She who brought forth barley and who brought forth fruit, whose honey makes men mad with joy, who lay with ponies and lions on the isles of Mag, who is honored by bulls, and whose son is born to teach men peace and to sustain the priest-esses of Hathor."

"Then show yourself so that we may see you," thundered Lotte. "Unless you are too ugly for the light of day."

At that, the clouds began to tremble and the winds to roar. The mighty giants, though they made a show of bravery, were sore afraid. Just when the din had reached its peak and the mountains themselves roared and belched forth smoky ash, the noises stopped.

On the ground before them stood a lady. She was so beautiful to look upon that the breath of every giant caught in his throat. Her hair was yellow as the sun and curled about her naked body to her hips. Her skin was whiter than spring clouds, and from her face with its hooked nose, shone eyes as blue as morning. In her arms, she held a baby boy.

The babe was singing. Its voice held the melody of comfort after rain, of kisses from a lover's mouth, of children's laughter. And in its sound lived essences which the tongue cannot describe.

But Lotte only laughed. "You may be all you claim," she scoffed, "but I see only weakness." And at that, she raised her horny foot and crushed the white-skinned lady into dirt.

Then from the air came swarms of bees. Each bee became a warrior who let forth a stream of arrows. The arrows never missed their marks and flew into the eyes and hearts and viscera of every giant. The giants raged at their opponents, but the warriors were swift and tiny and the giant's swords too thick. By the dawn of the next day, the field was strewn with blood and gore. There was no giant left alive upon the mountain top."

The audience was silent now. The man waited a long while before his words continued.

"But as the sun rose in the sky, a strange thing happened. The gore began to form itself back into living things. And so by noon, the giants, reassembled, stood as they had stood the day before. Beside them sat the lady.

"I have given you a second chance, old mother," she said slowly. "Do you now wish to destroy your race?"

Lotte, waking from the sleep of death, recalled the battle and that, in it, she had seen her own son killed. She turned to look for him. He was alive, brushing blood from his knees and looking much confused. At that she made a howl of joy and fell upon her knees.

"Oh lady," she promised, "I see now your power. No more will we do battle. Therefore, our children and our children's children may be spared the pain of war."

"Giantess," the lady said, "I will accept your offer. We shall share this land in peace. But you must do one thing for me, or I shall return your souls to death and this field to charnel. You must free your slaves to return to their livelihoods. For only a free people may know me and live in my protection."

The giantess agreed, and the island folk whom they had captured were let go. The slaves rejoiced and held great celebrations. They sang songs, which the lady and her people taught them. They danced and feasted and pledged to honor her forever with their lives. Thus, the giants and their former subjects lived for many years. Over time, the giants became smaller and more peaceful. They entered into marriages and partnerships with those who were their former slaves, the race of men. After many generations, it was hard to tell which had been masters and which bondsmen.

All the while, the lady and her fairy folk remained invisible. The people, busy with farming and husbandry, forgot the meaning of her songs whose words had once held magic. Soon, their children, and their children's children, although they sang her songs, did not remember what they meant. Only in dreams or spells could she visit them, and often they mistook her for a shade. At last, only the poets knew her name. But the masters of the art of words, who are more alert than ordinary folk, remained loyal to her. They knew that, without her help, the world would sink into belligerence. So they kept her alive with the ring of their verse and their reverence for her beauty. And that is why until this day, my friends, the bards are honored still and go about the world to tell her tales."

"Hurrah!" Naadasya roared and clapped his hands. Others followed suit, but all too soon, the small man tipped his feathered hat and stepped back into darkness.

Chapter 13

They sat for a while, enjoying the warm fire and pleasant company. But as the storyteller did not reappear, they stood up and looked about. There were scores of bonfires in the field now, radiating sounds of revelry.

"Shall we see what other entertainments lie about?" Naadasya asked. Esther and Achtriel agreed. But as they made their way toward an adjacent fire, a woman stepped in front of them.

She was not beautiful like Bonda or Esther. Her dark skin was sorely pocked, and her thick hair was flat and dirty. She was four or five months pregnant. But in spite of this, the woman was alluring, her wide green eyes commanded theirs with bold tenacity. She began to make soft movements with her hips and moving backward this way beckoned them to follow. Esther was intrigued, but Naadasya seemed unsure. He glanced at Achtriel and moved to leave, but the woman grabbed him by the forearm.

"Do not go, musician," she cajoled. "Bring your friends to share our festive cup." She lifted a stone goblet to his lips and made as if to pour its contents into them.

"No, no." Naadasya pushed her hand away. The woman turned to Esther and addressed her.

"Do you let the man speak for you, maiden? Or will you of my cup?"

"No, thank you." Esther smiled politely.

"The child then?" the woman waved the goblet under Achtriel's nose. It smelled like rotten fungus.

"Certainly not," Esther said, and pulling Achtriel, began to walk away. But Achtriel was frozen to the spot. For behind the woman, standing in the glow of her small fire, was a scene she would remember all her life.

There were three other women. One was robed in scarlet, and her lips were carmine red. Her face defied the eyes to look away as she moved her body like liquid. Next to her another woman, dressed in white, was also dancing. Her white hair blew about like chaff, and yet she moved her hips in ways which older women of their town would never dare. Over her neck and coiling on her arms were several snakes. The third woman, in a black cowled robe, was older still; yet her withered face was fierce, as if inside her aged form a torrent raged. But the most arresting thing, upon which Achtriel's gaze was frozen, was on the ground beside them. It was Sorgen, a wreath of mistletoe around her forehead, riding on a pig.

Sorgen was clearly drunk, and she was laughing with abandon. She played on a stringed instrument and jangled little cymbals with her wrists. Then she jumped off of the pig and whirled about. She raised her arms and sang out in an odd high voice:

> Sky devours the moon,
> Babe devours the womb,
> Who shall we devour
> Sisters of the moon?
> Owl and eagle be her eyes
> Vagina, mare and sow her guise
> Through the opening she flies
> Sisters of the moon.

A crowd had gathered, and at the sight of it, Sorgen laughed louder and slapped the pig so that it charged the spectators. Then she squealed at them herself. She began to spin, and taking the arm of a nearby man, she pulled him toward their fire. The three women circled him as well and, stroking him, intoned, "Heed her, feed her."

The man seemed to enjoy the attention and began to do a clumsy imitation of their dance. Others joined him, one a woman with a baby tied behind her in a shawl. Sorgen, dancing, moved behind her and touched the child who began to cry. The father of the child stopped dancing then and pulled the baby from his wife and cursed Sorgen. But the dancing women only laughed at this. Coming close, the red one held the chalice out for him. She rolled her hips against his and placed her arm about his neck. As if entranced, he moved with her; and as he did, the oldest woman took the baby from his arms and danced about with it.

Just then, a blaze of torch light lit the scene. From behind it came the priest who, panting from his run, cried out, "Begone!"

"Who are you to so command us?" the white-clothed woman laughed. She stepped before the priest and spat at him.

"Heed the words of Rome and of Christ the Savior," he shouted, looking past her. "Go elsewhere tonight, good friends, and leave these women be."

"You be elsewhere!" Sorgen shrieked and slapped the pig, which ran at the priest and bit him. At this, the crowd laughed giddily and watched the women with renewed enthusiasm.

"Be gone from this place now!" he repeated. "These festivities are not condoned. Be on your way."

Sorgen began again to play her instruments. The four women, silky as snakes, danced up to the priest. The red one played with his hair, and the green-eyed one taunted him with her hips. When he pushed her away, she hurled the contents of her chalice in his face. He wiped the liquid off, as if it burned him, but he licked his lips.

"You have no authority to make us leave," she said, "You are but a mewling worm who would make the women of the world your slaves."

"I am a man, and furthermore, I have the law behind me," he replied.

"What law, which law?" The snake woman laughed. "The one you think will frighten us. It does not!" She made as if to let her snake crawl on his back, but he ducked away.

"The law of Rome!" he said.

"Where?" The green-eyed woman challenged him.

125

"I will no longer talk with you," the priest said, as the women began laughing at him. "Citizens begone from here, the law commands you!"

"Come, let's go," Naadasya whispered; and Esther, taking hold of Achtriel's arm, led her away. But the vision of Sorgen, self-confident, claimed by a people who clearly knew her, would not leave her inner sight. The slave girl was a child of that clan despite her present servitude. She possessed a home and kin. When she grew up, she would marry and be part of a community.

Achtriel, aware now of a chill the night wind harbored, told herself she must confront this fact. She was truly the lowest person in this town, the only soul with no real kin or blood relations. Naadasya saw her downturned face and ruffled her fair hair. "They are interesting, no doubt, but we have other things to see," he said.

"Were you frightened?" Esther asked her.

"Of course not," she replied.

"Let us go and have a bite to eat," Naadasya offered. "They are selling pulse cakes and such things beside the square."

"Achtriel?" Esther asked again, and to Naadasya, she confided. "I've never known this girl to refuse food."

"I am saving my money for Tahto," Achtriel said, but Naadasya interrupted her.

"But you have much more! I owe you your fee for a fine performance."

"I'm to be paid for that?"

"And why not? You played admirably, and you put in many hours of practice."

"But..."

"You will earn much money at your art in future. I am happy to be the one to first remunerate you. Here!" He handed her a follis.

"I... oh, thank you. But...I have never had so much money."

"You have earned it."

"I only played on the drum."

"That is a valuable skill. It is how I earned my livelihood for many years. And so might you if you so choose. But here I think it will not pay so well as in my country."

"But...I shouldn't spend it, Tahto has a cold, and I must buy good food for him."

"Well, I will treat you all. Unless the lady will refuse me?"

"I would be honored," Esther said and smiled. It seemed to take him several moments to escape that smile, whose radiance outshone the moonlight.

"Come along then," he said merrily; and plucking a branch from a nearby fire, he lit their way across the fields to town.

There was strangeness in this night, a smell of distance carried by the wind. Like the scent of wildlands, it seemed freer, more mysterious than the common air. It rang with the shouts and increasingly loud laughter of the celebrants. As Achtriel passed these groups of men and women, with their flasks of liquor, she stepped closer to her escorts.

She realized that this was a new side of village life, one she had not witnessed because she was at home by nightfall. But these same folk, the ones who seemed so tired or ill-tempered in the day, were now jocular and animated. They even waved at her as she walked past, as if they welcomed her. This should have been comforting but, instead, felt eerie. Perhaps their souls had been possessed by other, more loquacious ones, who later would attack hers, like the *Seirjim* or the *Succubi*.

"How long will all this last, do you suppose?" Esther inquired.

"At least three days I'm sure," Naadasya told her. "Many of your visitors are regular habitués of such events. I dare say some of them do nothing but go about to territories with celebrations in the offing."

Just then, a large man brushed past them and looking down at Esther made to kiss her.

"Be gone," she said and pushed at him, but he just laughed and put his arms round her waist.

"The lady tells you to begone," Naadasya said and stepped between her and the man.

"Who are you, black demon, to insult me?" the man said.

"A black demon who can make short work of you," Naadasya told him and stood at his full height. Something in his quiet tone must have convinced the man. He stumbled on and waved them away.

"Are you all right?" Naadasya asked, taking Esther's arm protectively.

"Of course," she said, "But that was gallant of you nonetheless."

"Drink makes fools grow bolder. Perhaps you two had better pull your capuchons about your heads."

"Oh yes, I'd quite forgotten, for I felt so safe with you," she said.

"Would you have beaten him?" Achtriel asked, pulling on her hood.

"I do not like to do such things unless I must," he said. "I have seen too much the aftermath of brutality."

"But you could have if you'd wanted to?"

"With ease," he said, releasing Esther's arms and waiting till her head was covered.

In town, several long tables had been set out. They offered for sale a quantity of foods. There were pear conserves on honeyed buns, quince pies, dried nuts mixed with raisins, currant jam on barley bread, baked apples in cream and dried crab apple tarts, prune cakes, figs, and acorn pudding. Achtriel had never seen such an array of treats. Naadasya told her she could choose as many as she wished. She would have loved to taste them all but, as was polite, chose only one, a decision that took several minutes. At last she settled on the apple tarts and turned to tell Naadasya.

He was at the tables' other end with Esther. They were laughing with some townsmen. As Achtriel awaited them, a woman pushed her way up to the table. She was plump with large round breasts and wore a tight pulled kirtle to define them.

"Out of my way, you idle lot," she said and shoved at several men who stood about.

"You aren't so tonight, I'll wager," one of the men laughed and slapped her on the rump.

"I must be sustained," she told them saucily. "And as you've put your hands on me, buy me some cakes." The man who'd slapped her looked surprised, and his friends laughed loudly at him.

"Your betrothed will hear of it," one told the man, "and break that new clay pot atop your head."

"And so she should. And will do more if I have words with her," the woman said. "Now, I want pie."

"Anything else, your ladyship?" the man muttered and took a tremissis from his purse.

"Look at his wealth!" she cried to all assembled. "Why you have been plying MY trade tonight in truth."

At this, his friends guffawed and whooped and made the sign of horns at him.

"Never in my life," he stammered. "I have sold a mule to one itinerant, and he has paid me..."

"You have sold your ass," she said and took the tremissis from his fingers. His friends laughed louder as she turned to the woman selling pies and bought a plate of them.

"Where is my change?" wailed the man.

"Take this, Vitalis; and from now on, keep your hands beside your belt." The pie seller chuckled, handing him a few coins.

"But you have robbed me!" he protested.

"As you have robbed and cheated every man from here to Caen," the plump woman called back and slipped into the night.

"You cow! You pocketed far more than those pies cost!" the man said, angry now, and banged his fist upon the table.

"Raise a ruckus, and your fiancée shall hear the sordid tale." The woman called back to him.

"I'll have it back!" the man cried, pulling a small dagger from his belt.

"You'll have my fist!" the pie seller declared and made to jump across the table at him.

"Come on lad, you'll well afford the loss," his friends said, still amused, and took his knife from him and led him off.

"I've a family to feed, and he is coddled by his merchant clan," the pie woman told Achtriel, for lack of other audience. "But for you, the price is five to a penta. I'm feeling generous right now. You'd better take advantage."

"Five pies then!" Naadasya said, coming up and plunking a coin before her.

"Ah, for you, bright eyes, I'll throw in some of hers!" The lady laughed and stole an apple tart from the young seller beside her. The girl made, playfully, as if to hit the first; and they tousled with each other to the amusement of the folk nearby.

"A feast!" Naadasya said and handed Achtriel a pie and the extra tart. She could not think of a reply and followed him and Esther to a corner of the square where they consumed the sweets with gusto.

"What now?" Naadasya asked. "I feel much like dancing."

"We passed a group of music makers on the road. Perhaps they have set up somewhere," Esther said.

"Let's find them then!" He cried and took her hand and, looking back for Achtriel, twirled Esther to imaginary tunes.

"Don't lose us!" Esther called behind her and held her hand for Achtriel. She caught up and danced with them as best she could, down the road into the night.

Chapter 14

Near the footbridge, a group of musicians had indeed assembled. One held a kithara and one a harp, there was a trumpeter and a flutist, a tambour player, and a chorus of singers. In the arena of firelight in front of them, several jongleurs were doing acrobatics. Naadasya could hardly contain his excitement and pushed his way through the gathering crowd.

The harpist raised his arm, and the musicians commenced. Their sprightly rhythms aroused an instantaneous response. People swayed and clapped, and soon, the lighted circle filled with dancers. Naadasya held out his arms for Esther, and she took them, laughing. Then they were spinning and swaying and skipping like children. Achtriel watched as they became engulfed by other couples and soon were lost within the lively crowd. The harpist began to sing.

The song's verses were long and complex. It told of a soldier who falls in love with a goddess. The regional dialect was unfamiliar, and she could not tell if she were understanding it correctly. It seemed the soldier did something with his male parts, perhaps that he cut them off. The crowd appeared to ignore the song's words so intent were they on dancing.

She looked at the sky. The moon was aloft now, like the lamp of Diogenes. It seemed very late. She yawned as a wave of sleepiness came over her. She had begun to feel somewhat uncomfortable in the crowd, whose level of drunkenness continued to increase. Perhaps Esther would take her home soon. Then from behind, she felt somebody pinch her arm. She turned to see Sorgen.

"Why you don't dance with them?" Sorgen asked, sneering. "Most be afraid to be clumsy." Sorgen's breath smelled rotten, and her pupils were round as moons.

"I...I don't really know how..." Achtriel mumbled.

"You don't really know how," Sorgen mimicked her, "to sew! You only know how to take mine place with the ladies. I make you dance now." Then Sorgen took her by the arm and pulled her away.

"No! I need to wait here for them!" Achtriel protested, but Sorgen only yanked at her so roughly that her fingernails cut into Achtriel's arm.

"They ant need you. They going to cuck soon."

"I don't know what that means," Achtriel said, trying to loosen herself from Sorgen.

"Nor ever will." Sorgen laughed cruelly and quickened her pace. She was headed back to the place where her people were, their shapes blackening the firelight. Strange sounds came from their bonfire, shrieks, howls, and laments. Achtriel did not want to find out what was causing them.

"Look out!" Achtriel cried with a terrified expression, gaping back toward the musicians. When Sorgen turned to see what had so frightened her, Achtriel pulled free and jumped away. Slipping between large adults, she ran into the darkness.

She could hear Sorgen running behind her, shouting curses in her alien tongue. Achtriel turned in the opposite direction. As long as she continued moving, she was safe. She knew well how to be silent. But she must stay away from fires till her pursuer lost interest. She could hear her yelling, "Cripple girl!" but she seemed to have stopped running. Achtriel touched her arm where Sorgen had grasped it. It felt scraped and sore.

She slowed her pace. In the night, voices passed her like owls, swooping close then vanishing. Some rang with laughter and others with a kind of frenzy. It was odd to hear adults behave so childishly. Nearby a crowd of young men sniggered at some joke and hollered brazenly. Someone launched a snatch of song about a girl named Brighe. By her ear, a man belched coarsely. She glanced back at the musicians' fire where Esther and Naadasya were, plan-

ning to go back to it as soon as it felt safe. Meanwhile she mean-
dered, bumping into bodies, which were unaware of her. When
it seemed that enough time had passed, she turned back toward
the way she'd come. Then to the left, she spied something truly
horrifying.

Before a nearby fire, irregular shapes were outlined. She did not
trust her eyes at first, the figures seemed unnatural yet living, though
hunched in listless postures. Around them bobbed a jeering crowd.
Walking closer, she could see that the figures were just people, but
unusual ones. Several were small with enlarged heads like the boy
she'd met. Others had tiny heads with pointed skulls while others
were immensely tall with long faces and jaws. Two children seemed
to share one body, although each had her own head. All of them were
tethered to a rope loosely attached to the cage.

Beside the strange people, a line had formed. There was a boy
who took money from the people in the line. A man approached the
two-headed child and lifted her to the catcalls and of his companions. Achtriel got close enough to see the look of misery and terror in
the children's eyes. Then a man came with a large wheeled cage and
whipped the captives till they staggered into it.

A voice spoke near her. "He will make more money tonight
than all the whores in town," it said. Achtriel turned to see the poet
boy. He had a harp strung on his shoulder.

"Who are they?" she asked quietly.

"Souls like you and I. Unusually formed. Bought to be used
unmercifully." She could think of no reply. The chill she'd noticed
earlier had settled in her stomach.

"How was your performance?" she asked him finally.

"It went quite well. I was given this by a court bard. An honor
they tell me." He used his head to indicate the harp.

"Can you play it?"

"A little. I will have to improve. In these parts accompaniment
is oft demanded."

"Where are you from?" she asked, realizing that she could not
place his accent.

"Everywhere," he said. "I have even spent time with wretched souls such as those," he turned away from them. "We must thank the Gods that our paths are not so grim."

She thought of Tahto and began to feel she should go home. She had saved two of her pies for him. "I know someone who can teach you to play your harp," she told the boy. "He is here in Briga."

"Good. I may be here a while," he said, "Your duke, it seems, enjoyed my singing and may hire me at his court. That is, if he remembers on the morrow."

"Well, if I see the teacher, I will introduce you to him. His name is Naadasya."

"You are off then?"

"Yes, I must go. My grandfather is home, and I must tend him."

"I will walk you home," the boy offered, "It is not a good night for a girl to be alone."

"Oh, thank you," she said, "But I must find Esther first and tell her."

"Will you be safe in this crowd?" he asked.

"I will be fine," she assured him, "It is dark now. If I stay away from the firelight, no one will see me."

"I shall await your return," he said, bowing, as she slipped into the crowd.

The image of those captive souls would not leave her mind. Their attitudes of bestial resignation repelled her. She could not forget their vacant eyes as she made her way among the crowds, bumped by hurrying bodies, and once only narrowly avoiding being trampled. A man stepped on her foot and did not stop to heed her cries of pain.

"Think that hurt?" Sorgen's voice came from her right ear. "I show you better." Before Achtriel could run, she found herself dragged by Sorgen, whose stick like limbs commanded fearsome power.

"Leave me be!" Achtriel demanded, using her fingernails in an attempt to dislodge Sorgen's hand.

"You no good," Sorgen said, slapping her. "You think you a lady but you like me. I show you where you real belong."

"I know I'm just like you. I don't think I'm different."

"Quit talking," Sorgen said and hit her again, this time in the face.

"Let me go!" Achtriel said and tried to dig her heels into the earth. But her strength was no match for Sorgen's, and she found herself stumbling behind the slave girl.

As they neared Sorgen's fire, Achtriel could see that throngs of people had been drawn to it. To one side, the duke's cart was leaning. Some of his guests were seated in the cart, but now, the women dancers sat with them. As she watched a dancer rose and danced around the cart before the men.

Then one of the men, to shouts of loud encouragement from his fellows, stood and danced with her. Others jumped from the cart and made their way up to the fireside. There was so much noise and shouting, Achtriel could not make sense of things. Besides, Sorgen was yelling curses, which, mercifully, were drowned out by the din. But suddenly, Achtriel was thrust so close to the fire that she barely managed to prevent herself from falling in.

"You make we slaves," Sorgen growled in her ear, "but you the weak ones, watch and see."

The heat was searing, but despite this, crowds of people danced wildly, holding chalices and flasks of wine and mead. Many girls had followed the red dancer's suit and were attempting her alluring dance. Pushing them aside, the white-haired lady with the snake cried out.

"Blood, blood and fire," she roared, and the snakes on her arms hissed and showed their tongues.

Sorgen had loosened her grip on Achtriel's arm. Still, she knew the girl was waiting for her in the dark, watching like some vile bird of prey. The only hope, she reasoned, was to move close to the dancers.

In that sea of heat, bodies were bathing. Despite the Babel of sensation, fear, disgust, contempt, and curiosity, and a feeling she could not begin to name; she was sure of one thing. She would not let Sorgen defeat her. She pushed her way between the writhing forms, catching sight of things her mind refused to fathom. A hand grabbed her, belonging to a fat man, with two brown crumbling teeth and knotted fingers. She gripped his thumb in her teeth, as he attempted to cover her mouth, and bit it until he screamed and let go. Then she ran, not fearing for Sorgen, caring now for nothing but to be gone from this abomination.

She raced, her good foot pulling her weaker one in an uneven hop. Dodging between bodies and changing direction to confuse Sorgen, she could smell the dancers' acrid sweat, feel their skin and hair against her face. But soon, the shouts and noise grew quieter. She began to think herself freed from that fire's influence. Then suddenly, she tumbled and fell down, her legs arrested by a pile of bodies. She could not tell what they were all attempting. Men and women reenacting scenes from the church wall, demons drowning in their trespasses and hurtling toward hell. To add to the queerness, the priest was with them, dancing with the green-eyed pregnant woman he had tried to banish.

Achtriel got up and continued running. Not bothering to look for Esther, she knew only that she needed to go home. Down the footbridge road and past the fields she hurried, her lame foot gamely holding its own, as if willing to forego the present pain to get away. At last she reached her door and pushed it open.

Chapter 15

At first, she could hear only her own loud breathing. Then she was aware of odder sounds. She noticed that the turf brazier was lit, unusual for August. The fire in the hearth was burning too. Beside them, a strange labored aspiration came and stepping closer she saw Tahto, lying on the floor. She knelt by him and touched his forehead. It was hot.

"Tahto!" she cried. "Are you ill?"

"Eh?" he asked as if he had only now noted her presence, "Oh. Yes. I seem to be. A little. Is there..." then he coughed and could not stop, "is there a bit of water?" he asked sweetly.

"Tahto, you are sick!" she said and tears sprang to her eyes. As she went to get him water, her mind was whirling,

"Yes, I think perhaps I am," he said when she had brought him drink.

"You are very sick," she cried. "What should I do?"

"Find Fagim," he said. "Although I hate to bother her."

"Tahto, don't be silly. You are ill. She'd want to know."

"She has medicines and such," he wheezed.

"But I cannot leave you here!"

"Nonsense. I will be just fine. I've built the fires and kept myself quite warm. But you protect yourself from mad folk. I've been lying here imagining the worst. All this noise..." He coughed again.

"Here," she placed a pillow underneath his head and fetched a blanket to lay over him. "I will go to Fagim's house and be back in an instant." But before she rose to go, the door swung open and a breathless Esther ran inside.

"Where did you go?" she cried. "I was so worried..."

"Sorgen, the Hildebard's slave girl, pulled me off. I tried to get away but…Tahto…he's ill."

Esther stepped forward and seeing his prone body rushed to kneel beside him on the floor.

"I'm afraid I'm…"

"Hush, Tahto," she said and put her head down on his chest.

"Is he…?"

"Hush," Esther commanded both of them and listened to his breathing. "It's gone into the lungs. Not good," she pronounced finally. "Achtriel go for Fagim. Tell her his chest is filled with fluid. Go," she said again, "and stay away from everyone!"

Back into the night she went. This time, however, she seemed to be running not away from her fear but into it. A thousand black thoughts whirled like *shedim* in her mind. Was this the end of everything? Would Tahto die and leave her to her destiny? Those misshapen souls in dull captivity—would that now become her fate? Never, she vowed, running up the narrow street that led to Fagim's dwelling. Even if she had to be a tailor, she would not succumb to that.

Fagim's door was open, and Achtriel ran through it. "Help!" she cried into the darkness and went to the room where Fagim and Natan slept. No one rose to greet her. Pushing past a curtain, she peered into the gloom. Natan lay sleeping on the bed. She went to him and shook him. He woke with a start.

"Where is Fagim?" she cried, making sure to form the sounds out with her lips so he could understand. He looked around and shook his head. Then he made a gesture of a large Semitic nose and raised his eyebrows.

"She's at Mosse's?" Achtriel gasped. "But…" Natan rolled his eyes as if to say it was his mother's business. Then he asked her with his face what was the matter.

"Tahto's very sick!" she said, and despite her stern resolve began to cry. Natan rose quickly and grabbed a cloak. He cocked his head to indicate that she should follow him and hurried out the door.

Their alleyway wound past the fronts and backs of crooked houses. Most were dark, but in some, firelight escaped the windows. Everything seemed strange. How could this village, where she'd lived all her life, seem suddenly so foreign? She realized she viewed it now as if it were a distant place, which it might become if Tahto died and she left it to seek elsewhere for employment. At last, they came to an oaken door, and Natan banged on it.

Soon, a rumpled Mosse came outside. Seeing Achtriel, he did not ask her what was wrong but hurried back into his house and got Fagim.

"Tahto?" Fagim asked worriedly.

"Yes, he's coughing. Fever. Esther's with him now, but she sent me for you."

"Natan, get my herbs and come to Tahto's," she commanded, "Mosse, find Samiel and meet me there. Come, Achtriel." She took her hand and hurried to the street.

"There's fluid in his chest," Achtriel told her.

"Yes, yes I see," she said. "Don't worry. We'll soon have him on the mend."

Achtriel could think of nothing more to say and let herself be pulled along the roadway by Fagim. Her knowing frown was reassuring. She had saved scores from the strange illness that had raged through town some years ago. Achtriel wished to ask her what might happen, but she could not form the words. Perhaps her fears were better kept in silence where they couldn't germinate. When they reached home, Fagim burst through the door.

"Over here," Esther called her from the hearthside. She had wrapped Tahto in blankets and was patting at his face with moistened cloths. Fagim knelt and listened to his chest.

"We must elevate his head," she said, "to help the fluid clear. Achtriel?" But she had gone already to bring pillows and soft clothing from the bedrooms.

"Good." Fagim nodded approvingly when Achtriel returned. "Now place them underneath his head and chest."

"You all are making such a fuss," Tahto protested weakly, but he let them raise him up and make him comfortable.

"Don't speak unless it's needed," Esther told him sternly. "You've got to save your strength."

"Nonsense, I'm..."

"Shush," Fagim commanded and fixed her eyes on him.

"We must make a broth for him. Esther, one of your chickens..."

"No, no..." Tahto waved his hands but Fagim outspoke him. "Tahto, you are very ill. I've seen this ague before, and it is serious. For once, you'll have to put your scruples by and take the broth."

"Take it, Tahto, please?" Achtriel begged him. Seeing her worried face, he nodded. "Yes, of course." He patted her hand. Then he smiled as best he could and rested on the pillows.

Soon, the door opened again; and Samiel, Natan, and Mosse hurried in. They gathered beside Tahto. Samiel took two folisses from his coat and laid them on the floor.

"He'll need fire and food for many weeks," Fagim said looking at the few remaining logs. "This will not be enough. Perhaps we should approach the synagogue."

"No," Achtriel told them, "I will get more money."

"We will need it tomorrow," Samiel said kindly, but his tone annoyed her.

"I can get it," she said.

"Come now. What will you do?" He smiled and shook his head.

"She's going to play her drum for money," Esther guessed.

"No, the streets are filled with skilled musicians now. I know a better way."

"What can you mean, child?" Mosse asked her.

"I will take my vellum and quill pen. Then I'll sit and draw the people. It's unusual to have a renderer, even wealthy folk will pay well for it."

"Indeed. I think you're right!" Mosse exclaimed.

"Yes," Esther agreed. "A worthy plan. But now you'll go to sleep. I will stay with Tahto till the morning."

"But..."

"Go." Esther said, pointing. "You'll need your strength to work all day. I have some good ink at my house, perhaps enough to keep you going till the pageant ends."

"We can't have you get sick as well," Fagim told her and gestured toward the bedroom.

"I will be fine," coughed Tahto, "such fierce doctors will frighten the ills."

"Those doctors told you not to talk," Esther reminded him. He wrinkled his nose at Achtriel, and seeing his familiar joviality, she felt somewhat relieved and went to bed.

But in the morning, he was worse. When she woke and went to him, he lay like a pale wraith on the pillows. Fagim had built the fire up to keep him warm.

"Esther's gone to get more wood," she said. "But she left this for you." Two bottles of ink lay on the table. Achtriel went to her room and found the pen and vellum that the blond man had given her. That day seemed very long ago and as if it had happened to another girl. To a child.

In the square, people were moving, even in the early dawn. They stumbled over sleeping bodies whose clothes were charcoal smudged and rumpled. Nonetheless, cheerful venders were laying out their wares.

"Break your fast?" offered the woman who had sold them pies last night.

"I cannot. My grandfather is sick, and I have come to work to buy him food."

"Is he, then? I am sorry to learn of it. You may sell beside me if you wish."

"I do not have things to sell. I plan to draw people for money."

"You can do that? What a rich idea. We'll be a team then, don't you see? They come for cakes, and I will send them by to you. Then a crowd will gather and stand nigh to watch and buy more of my goods. What think you?"

"Yes. I'll stand here by the road, so they will notice me."

"Now I've a better proposition for you. You draw me first, and we will set it here so folk will see it when they come."

"All right."

"So sit you here beside me, that way, I'll watch and see that no one steals your things. But first, I must pay you your fee. Alas, I've only food to offer."

Achtriel's stomach churned with longing for the hearty pies and moist-rich barley cakes. "I need to feed my grandfather..." she hesitated.

"We'll have him set right when you leave, don't worry. One must fill up for a day of higgling. Now take your breakfast."

"Thank you," Achtriel said and went up to the table.

"Here's three barley cakes for now. You may be able to afford the lot by lunch time," she winked. "I'll have to have my niece bring us more."

"Thank you," Achtriel repeated, accepting the cakes with pleasure. They were warm and steamy, redolent of honey.

After eating, she sat down near the baker's table. Unfurling the vellum roll, she placed some rocks on it to hold it open. She set her ink pots beside it and dipped her pen in one.

"You'll have to draw me while I work," the seller called, "I'm too busy to stand still. But make me lovely, nonetheless."

"I'll try," Achtriel promised. She sketched quickly, in outlines that caught traces of her subject's movements. Then she added deft but telling marks to define the facial features. When the woman stopped to look at it, she crowed, "The bloody saints! You've a gift for sure." She peered down at the strip of parchment. "It looks as if I'd jump off of that page and run about."

"What's that?" inquired the girl who'd given extra tarts to Naadasya. She set a basket filled with them on the table.

"She's made a manikin of me here, see, niece!" exclaimed the pie woman "Look at this, you lot of slumberers." Other venders looked up and took notice. Soon, a crowd of them stood about gazing at the portrait.

"How much for one?" an aleman asked and took two brass coins from his pocket.

"A deca for each," declared the pie seller.

"Oh no, that is too much!" said Achtriel before the woman silenced her.

"A deca for the small one and a follis for a large. She maunt waste her vellum for no less," the tart girl snapped.

"We'll leave the large ones for the wealthy folk," the aleman said, "but make me a small one and as lively. Better yet show me at dancing, as I was last night till early hours." He set his feet into a jig and clapped his hands.

"You'll have to do it slower," the niece chided, "She ant a wizard."

So Achtriel began to draw. She made the merchants' sketches first. By morning all along the row her portraits graced the sellers' tables. As revelers awakened she produced tiny tableaux of groups and couples who would save the gala in their memory. Working quickly, to accommodate her eager subjects she filled the vellum roll with clever forms. One by one she cut them off with the baker's knife and sold them.

She would have liked to keep the pictures all together. On a single page they would have made a pageant of their own. But seeing folk delighting in her portraits helped to ease the loss of them. One day, however, she would like to have the means to draw the scene in all its colorful detail and to keep it to look over, always.

"What is all this?" a voice inquired. The priest, slack faced now and with his robes unbuttoned, leaned his pointed nose into her work. "It's like nothing I've yet seen!" he mumbled, awed. "Of course this kind of art would never do for a church wall. Else you'd get a post with me."

"I can draw that way," she assured him. "I have seen the paintings there."

"It would simply not be right." He sighed. "To have a Jew construct them." Then he buttoned up his robe and walked away.

"Simply not be right," mimicked the tart girl. "As if he were the one to speak on that."

At noon, Achtriel hurried home to give Fagim her earnings.

"My god, child!" Fagim exclaimed. "You will make us rich!"

"Here are barley loaves, plum pies, and goat cheese," Achtriel said and laid them on the table, "Some merchants paid me out in kind."

"Well, Tahto, you had best eat well." Fagim called to him, spooning soup into a bowl. "Your ward has seen to it that you will live."

"Perhaps there is no need for broth," he proposed weakly.

"Indeed there is," she humphed, carrying the soup to his bedside. "But mayhap by morrow, if such a good supply of food keeps on, we may leave off it."

Tahto lay his head back on the pillow and said gratefully, "Thanks be to God."

"To Achtriel as well," Fagim said, "Now eat well, old man. And don't waste breath in countermanding me."

By afternoon, the square was filled with people, even more, if such a thing could be, than on the previous day. Clanmen she had never before seen stood squinting at the hubbub, like hedgehogs waking up from wintertime. Clothed in fur and skins, they stared at well-dressed folk and the occasional brocaded castell guest. The saucy woman, who'd got pies with her trickery the night before, now had a host of colleagues. They stood together laughing or paraded through the streets. The clanmen gaped at them as if they had descended from the skies.

When no one was hiring her, Achtriel amused herself by drawing what she saw. Guiltily, she saved a portion of the parchment for herself and filled it with such sketches. A man atop a swaybacked donkey, smiling with pride as if he were a king. Two young girls dancing, the hair billowing about their round heads. Three men arguing beside a well. The lecturing priest. But as the afternoon progressed and her work demand continued, she had to forego this private pleasure. By evening, she had used most of the vellum and was wondering what she would do on the morrow.

"Where's the renderer?" she heard someone inquire. He spoke Frankish but with a strange accent.

"Here she is, sir," the tart girl offered. "No finer one exists even in Paris." Through the shoppers stepped one of the duke's friends whom she recognized from the previous night. He was the one who'd danced with the red lady. Indeed, she was with him still, leaning on his side.

"A child?" he scoffed when he saw Achtriel. "A crippled one at that. How truly odd."

"A portrait, sir?" Achtriel offered.

"I have seen your drawings, girl. They're most unusual," he sniffed. "Do one of me and her together, and I shall pay you twice your fee."

"Thank you, sir," she said.

"Or you may have her do a large one," offered the tart girl, "So you can be the envy of your friends."

"Indeed. I think I must. Make us from head to foot and show her bosom," he said and pulling at the lady's kirtle to emphasize her bust.

Achtriel would normally have felt intimidated by such royal scrutiny, but after working under Bonda's hostile gaze and drawing all this afternoon, her hand felt confident. She sketched the couple carefully, making sure to emphasize his handsomeness and her curvaceous bosom.

"Well done," he said when he inspected it. "And now one of the lady only."

"I'm afraid I have no vellum left," she said reluctantly.

"Why not?"

"I had only some that a man gave to me…"

"How stupid of you. Well, we can remedy that. The duke must have some more about. I saw a deal of unpacked codexes in his library. He would have vellum for the copyists. 'Be here at noon tomorrow, and I'll bring you some. But mark its use for me alone, don't waste it on this rabble." Then he strode away, the lady seemingly attached to him.

When they had gone, the tart girl called out excitedly, "The girl is to draw nobles now!"

"Alas, they are not so interesting," Achtriel said. "They keep their faces very stiff."

"Never mind," consoled the pie seller. "They'll pay you better than we can. That's why you've come. My name is Duggan, by the way, and this chit is my niece, Margit."

"As I am interesting, you may draw me all you want." Margit struck a silly pose, and Duggan swatted at her playfully with a dish-cloth. At dusk, Achtriel thanked them for their help, then took her ink and pen and headed home. As she passed the fields, a voice called out her name. She turned to see the poet hurrying toward her.

"Hello." She smiled.

"Good day," he said. "I looked for you last night in vain."

"I'm sorry," she said, "There was a girl chasing me so I ran home. It is good that I did because my grandfather is ill."

"You seem more cheerful now than you were last night."

"I've made some money for my grandfather."

"I am glad to hear of it. Do you go to him now?"

"Yes."

"If you can get away this evening, I will be performing in the square," he told her. "I would be honored if you were to come."

"I'd love to, but I don't know if I will be able. I must ask Esther if she will go with me."

"Come if you can," he said and turned back toward the town.

Chapter 16

At dinnertime, Tahto's cough was worse, and the fever made his whole face red. Fagim and Esther bathed his arms and face with liquids and spooned foul-smelling herbs into his mouth.

"Don't look so pale, he will be fine," Esther told her. "It takes some days for fever to die down. Besides, it is always worst at night." But Achtriel sat stationed at his side, raw fear eating at her bones. Tahto's face did not look well, and he had lapsed into a kind of fervid sleep. It was terrible to see him lick his lips and moan, allowing Esther to wipe his sweat as if he were inert. Fagim came over and sat next to Achtriel. She did not speak but put her hand on Achtriel's back.

"What is happening tonight?" asked Esther. It took a while for Achtriel to realize that Esther had addressed her.

"I do not know. The poet will perform, he said…"

"Which poet?" Fagim asked.

"Oh. The boy, he's not a child but looks like one; I met him in the square."

"Where is he from?"

"I do not know. He said he'd been in many places. He performed for the castell guests last night, and they may hire him."

"He must be good then," Esther said.

"I will stay with Tahto if you want to go and see him," Achtriel offered.

"No. Not yet," Ester replied. "Perhaps by later in the week, he will be well enough. But now, I think we must stay by him."

"Why don't you go?" Fagim said to Achtriel. It was not a question.

"I can't leave Tahto."

"Yes, you can. That look of worry on your face is not helpful for him or you."

"It's dangerous to go out at night alone," she said.

"Natan will go with you," Fagim insisted. "He's been hiding in the house for days. Pining for that Violette. I will not have it."

"Perhaps he does not wish to."

"Of course he does. He needs someone to force him. Go to my house and tell him I said he must accompany you. Besides, we wish to know what's going on. You young ones must go for us and report."

"Absolutely," Esther said. So Achtriel agreed.

That evening, Natan came for her. He was dressed in clean clothes, and his hair was combed. Fagim eyed him with secret pleasure and remarked, "The maids will notice you tonight. Perhaps your Violette as well." Natan narrowed his eyes at her and made an exasperated face, but it was clear the complement had pleased him. Achtriel took her cloak and bent to say good-bye to Tahto.

"You will be asleep when I return, so I will kiss you now," she told him.

"Carefully, not near his mouth," Fagim warned. Achtriel touched her lips to his moist forehead. It felt wet but not as hot as it had been this morning.

"I think you are getting better," she said, smiling with relief.

"It was the soup, no doubt," said Esther, and Tahto made a grimace of such loathing that even Natan guffawed.

On the road, she did begin to feel a sense of intrigue. It was unusual to be treated with such dignity, going out with just a teenaged boy for chaperone. Having so many folk in town made it seem like a nobler place, one people might talk of to impress their friends. And now, she'd made the acquaintance of the pie seller, her niece, and many of the gentile tradesmen. Despite her worries, she felt a keen interest in the goings on.

As they neared the crowds, lit by ubiquitous torches, Natan's eyes widened and ardently surveyed the scene. His face, more expressive than anyone's, took in the unusualness of all he saw and reflected it like water. When they came to the square, he stopped and looked about as if trying to commit the scene to memory. Achtriel pulled his arm and pointed at some strolling courtiers. He nodded and then gestured at his clothes as if his hands could make them into silks. Then he donned a face of such hauteur that Achtriel could not stop laughing. He held his arm out like a duke, and joining in the mimicry, she simpered and curtsied for him. They paraded through the streets like this, he doffing his imaginary cap to ladies, and she holding an imaginary skirt out of the mud.

"Lord and lady pootpiffle," a voice addressed them, "how tres bon to encounteur you here." It was Naadasya who bowed with a flourish of his nonexistent hat. Natan pretended to speak back, and though no words came from his lips, the replica of lordly speech was unmistakable.

"You are a born comedian, my friend." Naadasya laughed, and they shook hands.

"This is Natan, Esther's nephew," Achtriel told him.

"Ah hah!" Naadasya said with interest. "She speaks of you." At Natan's curious look, Naadasya said, "Your aunt and I are friends."

Now it was Natan's turn at appraisal. He looked Naadasya up and down as a young man apprehends an older one. He appeared sanguine with the diagnosis if not overly impressed. "And how are you tonight, my peach?" Naadasya bowed to Achtriel. "Will the lovely Esther be accompanying you both?"

"No. She tends to Tahto. He is very ill with a feverish cough."

"Oh, dear." Naadasya frowned, but then he brightened." I am sorry to hear of his illness. But I know she will bring him about. And if I smile, it is not out of disregard for your worries but only because mine are somewhat eased. I am relieved to know why I have not heard from her. She left me suddenly last night. I thought I had offended her."

"It was my fault," Achtriel assured him. "She searched for me. I was waylaid by a girl I know and could not find you."

"Well, I am glad that you, and she are safe and neither angry with me," he replied. "I take it Tahto is not so critical that they kept you near him. Therefore, with such doctors as Esther and your mother, I am sure he'll soon be well."

Natan had not been following their words, as he often did by staring at their lips. But now he pulled their arms and pointed with excitement. A crowd was forming by a booth set up on risers in the square. On it the poet boy appeared and, dressed in royal togs, was dancing. They hurried there to find a place and watched as he, ignoring vicious taunts and teasing from the crowd, began to sing.

"I tell a tale of wealthy folk," he sang, "who lived across the seas. Great founder of old Rome was he, a fellow named Aeneas. If you wish to hear my tale, you must well listen. For a tiny man am I and my voice is rather thin."

Despite this disclaimer, the timber of his voice was hearty and, furthermore, had such a curious tone that all the crowd at once hushed to hear him. Then he pulled the harp from his shoulder and struck a chord. An arpeggio of notes soon followed, and to this, he danced, balancing on one toe and while pointing his other in the air. Then he leapt and came down in a curtsy. All the while his harp accompanied him.

"I thought he said he did not play it well," Achtriel remarked.

"You know him?" Naadasya asked.

"Yes, I met him several days ago. He performed for the castell feast and was asked to stay in their employ. He asked me who could help him play that harp the castell bard gave him. I told him to find you."

"I thank you for promoting me," Naadasya said. "But I doubt I've much to teach him. In fact, this instrument is one I traveled here to learn. But hush, we'll miss the tale."

The boy strummed on his harp and, jigging, sang the following verse:

"Aeneas was the son of Venus and a lusty sort. In mighty Troy, he lived and grew, a favorite at court. When Minerva with the Greeks her ten-year war began, Aeneas, save for Hector, was the fiercest fighting man." The boy bowed after his verse and chanted this cho-

150

rus: "Aeneas was a hero; from the goddess he did come. He sailed the sea destined to be the founder of old Rome." Then he made a circle on his toes and leapt and strummed a long chord on his harp and began again.

"Alas, the Greeks brought down that town, finest in history. But, through Aenaes, Troy lived on to found a great city. Mighty Troy in ruins lay, all but a score were slain. Of all the proudest warriors but Aeneas did remain." This time, the crowd joined in on the chorus, imitating his dance routine and clapping loudly till his verse continued. "When at last to aid him at his side, there came no one, he left the battle to the Greeks to find his wife and son. Venus, lady of the skies, had mated with his sire; she followed by invisibly and kept him from the fire. With wife and son in hand, his aged father on his back, Aeneus left his city, which the Hellens then did sack. But alas his wife and son were lost, burnt up in bloody flames, weeping Aeneas fled the gates and called to his boatswain. Make fast my ship, and we will sail away from our lost home, for we are destined to live on to found great glorious Rome." At this, the boy made a sumptuous bow, and the crowd burst into cheers.

"Another, another!" they cried to him. But he called, his voice large now and easily penetrating their din. "I will soon return my friends. But first I must seek refreshment. When I come back, I will tell you how Aeneas seduced Dido, the most beautiful and haughty queen and founder of Carthage!" He climbed down from the platform then, and Achtriel did not see him until he emerged through the crowd and spotted her.

"Hello!" he called. "You came. I'm glad. I hope your grandfather is improved."

"He is not well, but he is better," she replied. "They made me leave him for they said my fear upset him."

"A wise instruction. Such illnesses are best managed cheerfully."

"This is Natan," she said, noticing how eagerly Natan regarded the young man.

"Charmed to make your acquaintance," the boy said with a flourish. Natan, thinking he was jesting, returned a faux aristocratic bow.

"I like your face, my friend." The boy laughed. "You must be oft at court to imitate the men so well." Natan shook his head and pointed to his eyes.

"It's just as well," the boy said smiling. "It can be unsettling to observe them much in their own habitat."

"And this is Naadasya, the musician."

"Achtriel tells me you are interested in improving your harp work," Naadasya said. "I would love to help you, but I, too, am but a student of that instrument."

"Not so a score of others though," Achtriel insisted.

"How fortunate. What instruments have you?" the poet boy asked.

"Come by my tent tomorrow. We'll have a chat."

"A most welcome one!" the boy asserted. "Well, I must return to my profession now. The audience grows restless." Indeed, the crowd had begun stamping rhythmically while shouting, "Anus! Anus!"

When the boy resumed the stage, the crowd behaved quite differently than they had when they had first seen him. Now they produced an excited buzz and admonishments to friends and neighbors to be still. Soon, everyone stood rapt awaiting his performance. Achtriel had never seen the townsfolk so attentive.

Fingering his harp strings, the boy now strolled along the platform's edge as if it were a riverbank, and he a meditative wanderer. He began to sing a plaintive melody; his resonant voice shaded with sadness. The song was from a woman's point of view and told how fickle love is, how it alights, delights us, then takes flight like an elusive bird. The refrain repeated, "Ah, how sad is love, she brings to mortals fierce and sweet desire, she fills our thoughts with happiness, our bodies with her golden fire, she pricks us gaily with her plumaged darts, only to fly away and with her take our hearts." When he stopped singing, not a few of the audience members were seen to be weeping.

But then he began a bawdy strum on his harp, and stamping his foot in time, he roused them and resumed his stirring ballad.

"The rivalry of womenfolk! What man has never felt
that sting?
My tale concerns a greater feud, it is of goddesses I sing.
Hear now of Aeneas, our fearsome hero brave.
See how in innocence of women's wiles, this king was
nearly made a slave.

On Mount Olympus lived two beauties who since
time began had vied for power,
Venus and that queen whose mighty throne was
Jupiter's dower.
Glorious Juno, heaven's sovereign,
She who rules the womb and through that channel
every being.

From the very first beginnings of the Trojan
conflagration,
Juno for reasons you shall learn was angered toward
that nation.
So as the Trojan warriors fought, wresting in the breech,
And the Greeks, whom Juno championed, were
beaten to the beach,

Went she to Jupiter with kisses and sweet wiles,
Dressed in Venus' girdle, her own husband to beguile.
With ivory skin and scented breast she so enticed her king,
Who with a drought was then knocked out, the
Trojans forgetting.

Yet, after Troy had fallen her rancor not assuaged,
She cursed Aeneas and his men who from Troy he did
save.
For as his sailors plied their way upon the sea,
She avenged herself on that Trojan who had slighted
her beauty.

Those who know this tale remember well how all
began,
Goddesses three, in jealousy, sought Paris, though a
mortal man.
When the three celestial queens forced him to choose
the loveliest,
He slighted Minerva, and Juno, saying Venus was the
best.

So unto Paris' kinsman, Juno was thenceforth
foresworn,
Thus from her kin, the foul North Wind, she bade
bring forth a storm.
But her brother, Neptune, mighty ruler of the waves,
Calmed the sea and stilled the winds, the Trojan men
to save.
Their ships, storm tossed and broken to the shores of
Carthage made,
But this was Juno's city—rich and well in its heyday.
Bright Juno saw, being a god, what Fates decreed for
men,
She knew Aeneas could found Rome and bring
Carthage to ruin.

Now at that time, my goodly friends, Carthage was
glorious strong,
Lovely Dido founded it and ruled it all alone.
Gentle, sweet and kind was she, a widow, and wealthy.
Aeneas too had lost his mate, in fire, all Troia's destiny.

Scheming Juno now laid out another plan,
Aeneas, though a warrior, was also just a man,
And therefore, like all men in history,
Might yield to women's treasure trove and forget Italy.

And here he had them all sing together a new chorus of his tale:

Oh, Lady of the amber dawn,
She who brings forth rain and sun,
Look well upon your mortal children,
And bring them to lie in your Heaven.

Now, my good friends did not I tell to you,
That in this tale there was not one goddess but two?
Indeed, that loveliest of every female formed,
She whose match in beauty never shall be born.
Lovely Venus I intend to praise,
At one sight of whose sweet face all men become
enslaved.

Now Venus, being Love's champion, was not opposed
to all.
She thought it fine that Dido for her son's beauty
should fall.
For Dido was so virtuous and free of love's allure,
That Venus slighted felt and sought some vengeance
against her.

For of all the insults which men to her may give,
The ignorance of Love is worst, for without it none
would live.
Now, the lovely Venus has another precious child,
By whose arrows Gods and even Holy men may be
defiled.

To impish Cupid I refer,
Whose darts love's longings will ensure.
Woe to the man or woman
Who doth choose to slight him,
Be they shy or ugly, bold or prim.
For he will with his missiles pierce their hearts,

And cause such throbbing in their nether parts,
That soon whatever comforts they felt certain of,
Are become but useless profferings to love.

Now as Aeneas and his men lay shipwrecked on the
strand,
Wary were they of the dangers in this foreign land.
So Aeneas with his comrade Achates
Left the crew and went to scout about the strange
country
When, lo, a huntress came to them, appearing on the
rise
The two did not suspect that she was Venus in disguise.
She told them to go forth and find Carathage's dusky
queen,
And cloaked them in a secret mist so they might walk
unseen.

Thus through the streets they went, although they
were but lone strangers,
The mist hid them from view and thereby kept them
out of danger.
There they passed a great temple and nearly wept
with joy,
The walls were carven with the scenes and fighting
men of Troy

Just then the royal procession did go by
Whilst, amidst them, Dido cast her weary eye.
But just as she her courtiers was about to follow,
Venus' mist dissolved and there stood Aeneas—lovely
as Apollo.

He bowed sweetly and told her of his plight.
She bade him bring his men and at her palace pass
the night.

For as we might suspect,
When she Aeneas met,
An arrow flew, and Dido too,
Became as all must be,
The slave of She who rules the very skies with her
beauty."

This time as the audience sang the chorus some rowdies swung each other about with merriment. When he began his next verse, however, they stopped at once to listen.

"Poor Dido, all her power now was forfeit to a man,
Her city and her riches she gave up to his command.
To please the Trojans she put on such feasts and pageantry,
That all were happily content to stay in her city.

Aeneas was then pleasantly diverted from his sacred mission,
But Jupiter was not amused, for Rome was his most cherished vision.
He sent that dangerous sly God whose winged feet all warnings bring,
Mercury to Dido's garden flew as in it Aeneas was strolling."

"Oh, blind and simple man thou art who lingers here in ease,
My father tells you to resume that task which is your destiny.
Seek that mighty kingdom the gods spared your life to found,
Leave this life of luxury although it will your fair queen wound.

For no man can long avoid his chosen path,
And the tears of women are no match for heaven's wrath.
Then like a falcon swiftly rose and vanished he,
That fleetest winged God, mischievous Mercury.

What could our hero choose to do but act as he was told,
Besides, in truth, Dido on him had not so strong a
hold.
So he summoned forth his loyal men,
And told them to in secrecy prepare the ships again.

But he warned them to do all unseen,
To thus postpone the sorrow of his loving queen.
Yet their actions soon gave them away,
And Dido, unbelieving, begged Aeneas now to stay.

Have not I given to you all things which you desired,
Been at your side by day and at night to your bed retired?
Did not I my worldly riches well forfeit,
So that you and yours might live in comfort and
surfeit?

Why then do you quit of my most wonderful embrace,
And with your men, to treacherous seas prepare in
secret haste?
Aeneas, ashamed and angered, however was not loathe,
To remind her that they had not ever truly been
betrothed.

The Gods, he said, command me, lady, to be off and free,
To set sail through storm and gale and find my destiny.
As all her tears and all her pleadings could not him
dissuade,
So from his side she stumbled weeping, and to her
bedchamber she made.

And as the Trojan boatmen to the open seas did turn,
They saw fires on Carthage shores and heard that city
wail and mourn.
And yet Aeneas never knew that she who loved him
like a wife,
Had watched him sail and then had jumped and
taken her own life.

So my friends to Love pay all your due.
Lest She wreak Her fortune and Her powers against you.
And do not set forth proudly, you who travel on the seas,
Without remembering my tale, the voyage of Aeneas."

The boy bowed then and set forth a last long strum on his harp. The crowd exploded in a chorus of approval and beseechments for him to continue. "Alas, my friends, my turn is over. Another bard will entertain you now, and I shall see you here tomorrow night."

The crowd protested at the thought of losing him, but let him pass with a much different attitude than it had treated him at first. Now they doffed their hats and pressed his hand with thanks. He smiled and bowed politely and took the coins they pressed on him. But all the while, his eyes were scanning past them.

At last, the second bard began his act. He was an older man, whose gray head wobbled when he spoke. But nonetheless, his voice was strong and while not as lively as the boy's, it told a steady tale. The boy emerged from the crowd of onlookers and spotted Achtriel. With a satisfied expression, he joined her and her friends.

"I have not heard such a tale outside Ravenna," Naadasya exclaimed.

"Yes, they keep the old stories up in those parts," the boy agreed. "Along with those of the Goths and Celti. I spend some years there as a boy and trained with several teachers there." Natan laughed and pulled on an imaginary beard then bent his back as if with rheumatism.

"True, I am not an old man yet," the boy conceded. "Although I sometimes feel like one."

"Notwithstanding, it seems you have studied for many years and in many places," Naadasya said admiringly.

"A bard who wants to earn the title must begin at an early age and study diligently to an old one. It is a competitive profession and one not readily to tolerate a stranger. I had thus to be more diligent than those who are by family or recognition picked for the profession."

"Why were you a stranger?" Achtriel inquired. "Did not you have family of your own?"

"I may have once upon a time, I do not know," he answered. "I was adopted by a courtier when I was small, and he raised me with indulgence. Yet even he did not know my true parentage. He bought me from a slaver when I was but two or three."

"So you were raised among the courtiers?" Naadasya said, "That explains your careful tongue and stylish manner."

"One's tongue and manners are the mark of entry in that society," said the boy. "That is as far, alas, as its civility extends. But now I wish to learn from you, my friends. I fear you must be my refuge in the days ahead. I've been employed to stay here for a while by your new duke."

"How wonderful," cried Achtriel and meant it, though the boy glanced at her sharply as if to question her sincerity.

"Yes, it may well be," he then agreed and smiled.

A girl with auburn hair walked by and let her large eyes linger on Natan's. He patted Achtriel's arm with fervor and pointed to Naadasya and the boy. She knew he meant for her to stay with them. Then she nodded, and Natan went after the girl like a long-legged pup.

"That must be Violette," Achtriel guessed.

"She seems to like him," Naadasya observed as Natan caught up with her. The girl, with a coquettish glance, took his hand and led him toward the fields. Musicians there were tuning up their instruments.

"Let us go and dance as well!" Naadasya suggested and taking Achtriel's hand followed Natan toward the gathering crowd.

On this second evening of festivities, the mood was different. There were more families about and older couples. The men stood rather stolidly and looked about, as if to broadcast their proprietary rights. The women, though, were gay. They had cleaned themselves up and brushed their hair. Many were wearing new dresses much like those of the Hildebards, which she had helped design. There was a general air of pride and fastidiousness to folk that had not been evident before. Even the children inspected their peers with evaluating glances.

Achtriel, of course, was not included in these appraisals. The moment an adult's gaze took her in it seemed to bounce and come to rest elsewhere. Some children though, looked long at her and at the poet boy beside her. Although Naadasya was a foreigner with dark brown skin and strange clothing, their glances took him in with equanimity. It was just the sight of Achtriel and the bard that aroused their keen attention. Achtriel could have wished she was naive enough to wonder why, but she had long ago discerned this fact. To be unusual in human form marked one as more outworldly than an elephant.

Even so, her habitual sense of her own strangeness had been somewhat mitigated. The pageant atmosphere, aided perhaps by the consumption of much beer, had heightened the conviviality of the crowds. Now the sunset lent an air of quaintness to the scene. Achtriel found herself, in spite of her difference, feeling a kinship with the townsfolk, a sense that these people belonged to her in some unspoken way.

Chapter 17

Now amidst the crowd, a singer stepped forth and clapped her hands abruptly. She began a song in Frankish which she accompanied with courtly dance steps. The song concerned two lovers who had met in a palace, but one, the girl, was married to the king. The boy was the king's comrade and had sworn him fealty but could not help loving the girl.

The verses told of their embraces and their trysts, their stolen kisses underneath the forest moon. But as in such songs, things quickly made their way toward tragedy. The couple was disgraced, and she was forced to go back to the king. Achtriel remembered Bonda then and wondered where she was. It was sad that such a gift of beauty should bring its owner only doom.

Another singer strolled about the crowd, banging on his hands a kind of round tambour with little cymbals. The tambour made a lively beat to which his song added inflection. The song told of two slaves who looked alike, so much so that each one's master could not tell him from the other. Their masters looked alike as well.

Neither the two masters, nor the two slaves knew their counterparts existed, for they were both sets of twins who had been separated in infancy. So each slave kept thinking that his master's mind was addled. And each master raged and more comically berated his slave. There was a mix up about a necklace one slave was to have sold but gave to a woman instead and then was beaten for it. The slave sang a funny song, and soon, people were repeating the refrain.

"Do not call me fool for you are far more fool than I,
Great Lord who was decreed to rule me, though I cannot tell you why.
For he who rules should be one who stands high above disgrace,
And clearly you're too drunk to see what stands before your face."

The crowds began to sway and step in time to the tune. Soon, there was a circle of townsfolk, mostly couples but some families and elders, who were dancing to it.

"Would you do me the honor?" a voice addressed her, and she looked to see the poet boy extend his hands.

"I cannot dance..." she mumbled, turning red, and looked down at her twisted foot.

"Of course you can!" He laughed.

"Oh no, I would only look ridiculous."

"To most folk, we are ridiculous if we but stand here," he replied. "Why should we care what they will think if we now move about?"

"I doubt you are as unschooled a dancer as you claim," Naadasya added. "For I saw you in our performance, capering quite deftly."

"Oh, I was only being silly then," she protested.

"Oh, well, by all means, we must be very solemn now," the boy said. He stood in such a pose of miserable contemplation, looking at her every now and then with a lordly scowl, that at last she had to laugh. Then he took her hands and led her toward the circle.

To her surprise, people gave way for them and even smiled approvingly. Her first wobbly attempts at dancing almost made her fall, but the boy put his hand on her waist to steady her. Soon, the music caught her feet up like the ocean, and she let them hop. The boy guided her hoppings.

"You are not silly now," he smiled. "You dance quite well."

"It is only because you are pulling me," she told him, but in spite of this enjoyed the motion. It was like bouncing on music, the notes lifting even her lame foot to free it.

"Have you never danced before?" the boy was asking.

"No," she told him, watching her feet move over the grass.

"Well, I'd never guess it. But for one thing."

"What is that?"

"You are supposed to look up at your partner. You will find your feet can manage on their own."

"Oh," she said and looked at him.

"Very good. Now don't-ah-don't look down. That is better. Very good."

"What if I fall?"

"I wouldn't let you."

"But…"

"You are not a trusting soul."

"Perhaps you are right," she said, stealing a quick downward glance.

"Tell me then, how came you here. It is a highly interesting town in spite of its provincial placement."

"It has not been interesting till now," she said, trying to ignore her feet.

"You mean because the castellan arrives?"

"Yes. Before that it was dull and mean."

"But I have met so many interesting people! There is Naadasya and Natan and you…"

"Naadasya only came a week ago. Natan is interesting because his mother and her sister are so. They came here from Austrasia. Tahto is interesting," she added after a pause.

"That is your grandfather?"

"Yes. Well, he is not really. He found me when I was an infant and adopted me."

"I see. And why is he so interesting?"

"Oh, he is very wise and learned. He studied in the East when he was small and collects and copies manuscripts and teaches students."

"Indeed! I will have to meet this man."

"I hope you will be able to," she said and became quiet. "He has been ill."

"But is it really serious?"

"I think so. Esther says he has some fluid in his lungs."

"Ah, yes. A common ailment among older folk. But Esther tends him well?"

"Oh, yes. She and Natan's mother, Fagim, are the best doctors in the nearby villages. People come to them from all about when their kin are ill."

"Well, then, I'm sure he will be better soon."

"I hope so."

The song concluded, but another singer started on a tune. It was gayer and more ribald than the one before, and he looked at her briefly to assess her reaction.

"Would you like to dance some more?" he asked.

"Yes, please," she told him. "It is wonderful." So they danced and talked and laughed through several songs until Naadasya came to them and shared his mug of cider.

"How is Tahto today?" he inquired, and Achtriel grew suddenly quite grave.

"I don't know. I should go and see to him. Where is Natan?"

"Oh, I've spotted him," the boy said. "He is with a group of friends. If you like, I can walk you home."

"All right," she agreed.

"When you get there, Achtriel," Naadasya said. "See if you can persuade that pretty nurse to come and dance with me."

"I will," she promised and set off toward home beside the boy.

"Your name is most unusual," he commented as they walked.

"It is an angel's name from a text Tahto read when he was growing up."

"And very apt," he complimented. "But you do not know my name."

"Oh. I never even asked. I'm sorry. What is it?"

"It is Frans. I had another name once. A court name. It was a silly title that they employed only to make sport of me. I prefer Frans for I chose it myself."

"You named yourself?"

"Indeed I did. When I left court and went to seek my bardship."

"I had another name as well. But Tahto did not like it."

165

"And so we both are twice born, as it were. Improved upon reflection."

"I suppose," she answered. "I do not remember being Agoberthe."

"I do, alas, remember being Ambsace."

"That was your court name?"

"It was. It means the lowest throw upon the dice. A symbol of my popularity."

"What was court like?"

"A horrid bore. Stuffy conversations in stuffier rooms. The smell of foul bodies and hair grease in every garment. Cold stone hallways also odiferous. People who wait until they think they are in private, a dwarf doesn't count as human company you see, and proceed to evidence how treacherous and insipid one may become. And endless gatherings. My master was only a minor lord, but still he was required to attend such lengthy ones that I soon learned to read to occupy myself. That is, when I was not required to entertain."

"What were the gatherings about?"

"Constant machinations, gossip, intrigue, evil plots. I heard enough to know only that I wished to leave that world as soon as possible. So when I was eight…"

"That is my age now…"

"Is it? Mine is sixteen."

"So for eight years, you have been traveling?"

"That's right. But now, perhaps, my fortunes will allow me to stop for a while."

"Well, that is wonderful that you will be the court's poet."

"It is not wonderful, but it is good. A bard must find such kinds of employment. It is considered very mete."

"But you will have to live among the lords again."

"Indeed. But now I have found you and all your friends. And that will sustain me. Besides, I am older now and can stand it better."

They had reached the footbridge. The light in the woods was fading quickly. They picked up their pace.

Suddenly from between some trees, a crowd of boys and men emerged. They were holding cups of beer and laughing loudly. One of them spied Achtriel and Frans and motioned to the others. The group, to Achtriel's dismay, came hurrying to stare at them.

"He's a mite! And she's unshapen!" crowed a boy, the fattest of them, and laughed so loudly that the others were inspired.

"No. She's a gargoyle, look at her claws!" another cried.

"They're uglier than Pan and not amusing!"

"Indeed?" Frans interjected quietly. "I'd say we were amusing and as talented as Pan. I will prove it." He took a flute from his pocket and began to blow on it. At first, the men and boys were taken aback, but then they only laughed and danced about with monstrous grimaces.

"Let's toss them about. They look like puppets!" the fat boy cried and stepped closer to Achtriel. She picked up a rock and readied herself to throw it at him.

"But listen briefly to my tale, good fellows," Frans implored them. "Truly it will make you laugh. And if it doesn't, you may throw us about as you please."

"Well, tell it then," sneered the fat boy.

Frans said some words in a dialect she had never heard, and suddenly, the men were sneezing, coughing, and scratching themselves. The itch seemed to grow on them until they could do nothing but scratch as if their clothing were on fire. Frans put his flute back in his pocket and took Achtriel's hand. "Good day, gentlemen," he said and led her away. She looked back to see them rolling on the ground with cries of great discomfort.

"How did that happen?" she asked astonished.

"An art I learned from the Celtic bards," he told her. "They have many interesting tricks."

"But how did you…"

"Ah. I cannot tell you. It is a piece of bardic wisdom reserved for only those who have learned many, many poems."

"How many?"

"Oh, thousands at least."

"You have learned thousands?"

"And more. The bardic tradition is very old and quite complex. I was most fortunate to be admitted to its ranks. But then good fortune seems to follow me." He smiled at her.

"Can you make Tahto well?" she asked as they neared her part of town.

"Alas, I know no spells for that. But it may be the women need none. They have experience and skill which is always better." They now approached her house, and she stood at the door. She could not open it at first for fear of what she might encounter on its other side. Then she heard Fagim chuckling and felt it could not be so dire. They opened the door and came into the foyer.

"His fever has broken!" Esther cried when she saw her. "He will be alright."

Tears began to make their way down Achtriel's cheeks and Esther came and held her. The relief that encompassed them was like a lovely bath. Her heart, which she now realized, had been beating rapidly since Tahto first got ill, sank happily into it. "Thank you," she said to Esther and Fagim.

"He will need a lot of care, my dear," Fagim said, looking closely at Achtriel. "It will be many months before he can resume his teaching."

"I will do it for him," she announced. "And I will draw each day, on leather if I must, till the festivities end."

"Well, he is lucky he has you now," Fagim said nodding.

"And who is this?" Esther asked then, smiling at Frans.

"Oh, I am sorry." Achtriel dried her tears on the back of her hand. "This is the poet I told you about. He is a bard really and knows over a thousand tales."

"Welcome, bard, to our community. But we cannot call you bard forever," said Fagim.

"Oh! His name is Frans. He is a wonderful singer and storyteller. Everyone in town was entranced."

"Except those fellows we met on the road," he muttered.

"Yes, he made them…"

"I am happy to be here," Frans interrupted her. "I have met Naadasya and your son, Natan, a lively fellow. Achtriel informed me that you were both medically skilled, but she did not prepare me for two such beauteous practitioners."

Fagim introduced herself and to Achtriel's surprise allowed a feminine smile to lighten her features.

"And I am her sister, Esther."

"I am delighted to meet you both. I shall most likely be in this town for a while and am most desirous of good company. Soon I hope Tahto will be able to converse with me as well. I am also learned and have traveled much. I welcome the chance to share my views with him."

"He will enjoy that too," Fagim assured him.

"Well, I should go," Frans told them, although it did not seem that he wished to.

"Oh, and Esther must go out and dance. Naadasya waits for her," Achtriel remembered.

"I cannot leave…" Esther began, but Fagim said, "Of course you can. There is nothing more for you to do, he is asleep. The child and I will manage."

"So then you approve of him?" Esther queried her sister.

"So far," she answered, "now be off."

"I will walk back with you," Frans offered and held his elbow out.

"Thank you, kind sir," Esther said smiling and linked her hand through it.

"Thank you also for your help. I did enjoy your tales," Achtriel told Frans who smiled at her as they departed.

"He seems a bright young man, how old is he?" Fagim asked when they were gone.

"Sixteen."

"Only a bit older than Natan."

"Natan was dancing with a girl."

"Violette," Fagim did not look pleased.

"You do not like her?"

"I do not trust her, no. I think she means to break his heart."

"What can you do?"

"Nothing," Fagim said. "Now let's go to bed."

Chapter 18

In the morning, Achtriel awoke feeling inspired. The air was warm and augured a sunny day. She would meet the man from the castell and see if he would sell her another roll of vellum. It was a bold request, but Tahto's health depended on it. Ordinarily, the thought of asking such a thing of some great lord would have been terrifying. But in this bright morning, she was hopeful, as if anything wonderful could easily happen.

She dressed and washed with more than ordinary care. She did not want the lord to change his mind. She even took a scarf that Esther had forgotten and wound it prettily about her head. It would also serve to keep the sun's heat from her eyes when noon arose. Fagim was asleep by Tahto, and the fire embers smoked beside them. She must have let the fire die, a sign that she considered Tahto's illness better. There were several cakes and some bread from yesterday for them to eat. Today, she would try to earn enough to buy some eggs, pulse and lentils. She would have to think carefully about money for the next few months. She must earn as much as she could now and then plan how to make it last.

Tahto's students would not mind if she took over for him for they liked her and would feel they were helping him too. Besides, she could correct their Latin and Greek grammar. They somehow could forget their lessons overnight or after time, which she found astonishing. Did not older people learn things better than children, and if not, why did they pretend such vast superiority? Perhaps these students were not very smart, but then why did they wish to study? She herself could not forget a thing once learned. She would have liked to ask them how they did it. It might help her to forget the things she wished had never happened.

She took a pulse cake and a drink of water. The thing now would be to get money, for this food would only last so many days. She needed coins to save for future necessities. The courtier would not be there till noon. She must find another way to earn before that.

She left the house, closing the door as softly as she could. Fagim had been awake for days and sleep was precious both to her and Tahto. Once outside the door, however, Achtriel began to hum. It was a lovely morning, birds trilled, and everything smelled clean. She hurried in her uneven gait, wishing her weak leg were stronger so that she might run. The pie sellers would be readying their wares, perhaps they could suggest a way for her to earn some extra coins that morning.

On the town road, she passed the spot where the men and boys had fallen down. There was no one there now—they were not dead at least. She had pitied them, itching and groaning in the dirt.

How capricious human feelings were. Why should hearty folk want to hurt smaller and less perfect ones? What impetus brought forth that cruelty? She and Frans were certainly no threat, so it could not be fear that drove them. If she were strong and finely made she would be thankful and thus kind to everyone. But perhaps she did not know how she would be. Perhaps to be so hale in circumstance made one less cautious of God's grace.

Near the place where the musicians had been stationed, scattered groups of people lay sleeping. Their faces, even slack in sleep, seemed happier than usual. Music and celebration seemed to fill a longing people had, one that could be sated in no other way. But if such joy were salutary, which it clearly was, why did men not practice it more often?

Why have pageants only once in many years and spend the other time enmired in work? Why not have a pageant every Fall and let merchants come from outlying villages to sell? They would find eager new markets for their wares and musicians and bakers and other tradesmen too would prosper. She decided she must share this thought with Tahto. He would know how to propose such measures to people who had influence.

When she neared the town, she saw familiar faces. Naadasya and Esther were walking together, looking unkempt but extremely happy. When they saw her, they appeared distraught and smoothed their hair and clothes and put on different expressions.

"Good morning! You're up early!" Naadasya said a bit too gaily.

"Yes. I need to find a way to earn money. I thought I'd ask the pie sellers if they'd hire me."

"Why should someone of your talents now sink to selling pie?" he asked.

"I have no more vellum. A castellan said he might bring me some at noon. Till then, I must make use of the time."

"I speak not of your drawing skills, but of your musical ones. You shall accompany me on the drums, and we will play for folk as they breakfast."

"That would be wonderful!" she said.

"I must go back and see to Tahto," Esther said and eyed Achtriel uncomfortably. "Please do not tell Fagim that you found me so…this morning."

"What do you mean?" Achtriel asked.

"Just do not mention that you saw me. I plan to tell her that I slept at home."

"But I thought she liked him…"

"Hush, child," Esther said, and Naadasya broke into loud laughter.

"Do not think yourself so highly placed, my man," Esther scolded. "For I have yet to give my own approval."

"Madam, I know full well my future, and that also of my heart, waits on your mercy."

"Indeed," she said and kissed him lightly on his cheek. Then she lifted her skirts to her knees and ran across the field. He watched her disappear over the ridge and stood there for a while as if he had forgotten Achtriel.

"Shall we go to get your instruments?" she prompted.

"Oh, yes. We shall most certainly do that. Come follow me, my angel." Then he smiled so gaily that his face shone like the rising day.

When they returned with drums and reeds, the square was bustling with people. Merchants who had recently arrived were arguing with those who had established posts from which to sell their wares.

"We've spent weeks upon the roads, and you show us no mercy!" one complained.

"Why should I lower my profits for you? I owe you naught," another answered.

"Where is good Christian kindness in this evil place?" A woman with a scarf hiding her hair bemoaned.

"Here, madam, you may work by me," Margit told her.

"And if your merchandise outsells our own, don't you forget the kindness," Duggan warned the woman.

"My tarts were baked this morning with fresh fruit and butter," Margit advertised. "I've naught to fear from ary competitor."

"My dear, I would not steal your business," the newcomer said. "I am selling cheeses which will go well with your pastry."

"We can offer them together for a higher price!" Margit smiled and cleared a space beside her for the woman.

"Ah, here's the little Jewish girl," Duggan said, spotting Achtriel. "You must set up here for us and bring the crowds by."

"Alas, I have nothing to draw on," Achtriel told her. "But my friend and I will make such lovely music that the crowds will quickly come."

"A court man was here earlier, talking about fees and such rot." Duggan frowned, scanning the early morning marketers. "Leave it to them to try to find a way to line their pockets with the comforts of the poor."

"Well, if they bid us pay a fair tax, we shall do so," Naadasya said, taking up his flute.

"Fairness and fineness ain't fast friends," Margit said, surveying Naadasya with her large green eyes.

"Ah, not so. My music is both fair and fine, and I share it for whatsoever rewards may come my way." He laughed.

"Perhaps they maunt all be coins and such," Margit said, flirtatiously.

They played all morning, and several people did give them coins. But it was clear to Achtriel that her drawing had brought a much greater profit. She looked impatiently toward the castell hill, as if her gaze could call from it the wealthy man and his supply of vellum. But at noon, a different castellan approached, one with a pinched face and pale thin lips.

"Where is your permit, sir?" he addressed Naadasya.

"I have none." Naadasya smiled. "But I will gladly purchase one. How much are they?"

The man looked down at the small pile of coins at Achtriel's feet and rubbed his chin. "Those will do," he said.

"But, sir, that is all we have!" she protested.

"And better you should pay it me than twice its number for a fine," he said, looking about. "The mayor bid me see to this, else he will come after me and throw you both into a cell."

"Here," Nadaasya said, bending and scooping the pile of coins into his hand, "Take this and be gone. But how are we to know that this now covers our permit?"

"You have my word," said the lord contemptuously and walked on.

"If the word is as good as the man," Margit said, "you will make no coin today."

"What will we do?" Achtriel worried. "I must get money for Tahto. The pageant will be only one day more. I could buy some leather but my pen would soon dull and I have no other. Besides, it is very hard to cut."

"And rare to find," Margit added.

"They wealthy have those wax tally sheets," Duggen suggested.

"She can't use those, aunt," Margit said, "They'd melt."

"They don't afford an easy way to copy the drawings, anyway," Achtriel sighed. "I will just have to hope the gentleman will sell me some vellum." She looked forlornly toward the castell hill, but only its trees were moving.

"Well, let us continue," Naadasya said. "Perhaps if we make money, we can sneak away before the lord returns."

But after they had played all morning, just as the amount of coins looked promising and Achtriel was calculating how to spend her share, the pale man returned. Naadasya saw him coming and scooped up the coins and put them in his pocket. He had taken Achtriel's hand and begun to hurry off when the castellan barked, "You. Black creature, do you thwart the mandate of your nobility?" He pulled his dagger from its sheath. Naadasya stopped and turned around. "Why no, sir, I was but packing up and heading home."

"And what of the taxes?" the man bellowed.

"Taxes, I was never told of..."

"I know not what benighted lands you hail from, but here in civilization, every profit must be taxed. The only reason that your fellow merchants do not know this is because they have lived so long in barbary, without the benefit of a presiding noble. Now, praise God, your little town has returned to the bosom of society."

"There are other bosoms I would more happily lie upon." A nearby fig seller sighed.

"Quiet, lout," the pale lord barked, "I have not yet assessed your due."

"Till now, we folk have used our local taxes to support the poor," Margit stated. "Like as the Jews do. It works well for..."

"Shut your mouth, woman!" the castellan snarled and turned the point of his dagger toward her. "I have no patience today with your whoring sex. The Jews..." he said this word as if describing excrement, "because they are not fit to live in the same good Christian world as we, must suffer for their ignorance. Their just reward awaits them in the fires of hell. Besides, we will not spend their sin-got wages. Child eaters and witches all, if I know aught. But our church and royal custom is to let the long nosed dig their graves. There are none here among you I should hope."

"Of course not, sir," Duggan insisted. "Now take this coin for all of us and be about your business."

He took the coin and turned it over in his hand. "It bears the face of Clothair. Hah! Look at his fat chin. I thank you dame, for

175

your cooperation. Your fellows must thank you. But they shall not get by so easily. All must give me one good tenth of his earnings from now on. And you," he turned again to Naadasya, "foreign monkey, I will take your purse."

"That is not right!" Margit cried and the others echoed her dismay.

"Shut your mouth, or I shall fill it for you," he said, advancing toward her menacingly.

"Here, have all of it. I gladly pay," Naadasya said and gave over the money they had earned that day. Achtriel started to protest, but Duggan silenced her with a warning look.

"Well done. Well done," the pale man murmured, distracted from Margit by the sight of money. Then as if he had remembered suddenly an important engagement, he looked across the square to where the beer stands stood. "Thank you, good folk all," he said and pocketed the coins.

"But, sir, my grandfather is ill, and we must..." Achtriel began.

"Shut your beak, misshapen crow." The man stepped around her as if she were diseased. "Or you shall wither in a cage."

Naadasya held her head against his side until the man had walked away.

"Did you save anything?" she asked him when the man had gone.

"Only this, I am afraid." He handed her a pentanummum.

"But what will you have earned?" she protested.

"I am a man so glad today," he smiled, "That I can live on air. Besides, Tahto needs food, and that is my concern as well."

"Thank you, Naadasya," she said.

"Let's hope that weasel is the worst of his lot and not the best," Duggan remarked.

"Let us hope he chokes upon his spittle," the fig vender amended.

"I'd be happy to assist in that," another merchant muttered.

"Now, let us not think on violence." Naadasya shook his head. "For, once it has opened its maw; there is no telling who will fall between its teeth."

"You come and sleep at my house, child," Duggan insisted to Margit. "A maiden's not safe on her own with such polecats about."

"Same's true, Aunt, for all the daughters of this place," Margit said, pulling her shawl tighter.

"Well, you and they are all welcome with me. We will build a fire and heat some oil, and if any dare break o'er our threshold, we shall singe them to a pretty turn." The others laughed at this and seemed to relax slightly.

But Achtriel looked at the penta Naadasya had saved for her and felt like crying. She had counted on her drawing to see them through the rest of Tahto's illness. The Hildebard's tutor would not leave for months. Tomorrow, the pageant-goers would pack up and leave. Even tailoring work would be impossible to find now, for the local moneyed class had spent their savings.

Just then, the red-dressed woman who had accompanied the castellan the night before appeared on the edges of the crowd. She looked about, then signaled with her eyes for Achtriel to come to her. When Achtriel approached the woman, who smelled of wine and sweat and fire ashes, whispered, "I have for you." She pulled a roll of parchment from her bodice and gave it to Achtriel.

"Oh! I thank you," she stammered, "and please do thank the gentleman! Now I can..."

"Gentleman knows aught." The woman sneered as she fixed her dress. "He and friends lie down with drink since dawn."

"Then how did you..."

"I in every room," she gave a bitter laugh, "and work no turn my eye from what not be missed. This, for you, for my little sister do you ill."

"She did not hurt me, but for this, I thank you..." Achtriel said gratefully.

"You never seen me!" warned the woman and wrapped herself in her cloak and hurried away.

With the gift of parchment, Achtriel was able to earn more than she had in the previous two days. Word of her drawings had spread, and everyone, it seemed, desired to have a portrait or memento of the pageant. Naadasya played his drum and entertained those who waited for their turn. The food sellers did brisk business with the bystanders, and soon, other performers came and added to the festivity.

The merchants pooled some coins and hired a boy to follow the pale man and tell them of his whereabouts. The child's job was easy, for it seemed the man had no intent to quit the hut that sold mead, beer and other liquor. At dusk, the child returned and told them that the man was lying in a stupor. He also said that several boys had searched the royal's pockets for remaining coin but had found none. They would have beaten him but feared his wrath and that of his powerful friends. So they contented themselves with taking off his pants and hiding them.

"I should take you home now," Naadasya told Achtriel. "You have earned a wealth of coin here, and there will be those who'll try to take it from you." Achtriel agreed and rolled up the last of her parchment.

"I like this work so much I could do it every day," she told him. "But now things will return to the dull way they were before. The only pictures will be on the church wall, of tortured sinners. I would do that as well, but the priest said he would never hire me."

"But look what you have done!" Naadasya crowed. "Not only will those earnings buy food and medicine for months but you have made a marvel."

"What is that?"

"You have created a new form of art for your countrymen."

"Don't be silly, Naadasya." She laughed as she secured her coin purse in her shirt. "I've only drawn pictures of them."

Chapter 19

By October, Tahto's healing had progressed quite well. Remarkably for a man his age, Fagim declared. Tahto insisted that it was his meatless diet, but she dismissed the idea.

"If I told my patients to forebear what little nourishment they find, they all would starve," she told him. "Without the occasional fresh meat, they would begin to suffer from bow leggedness and sores. They cannot afford milk, eggs, and whey as you do."

"And I," Tahto smiled patting Achtriel, "can but afford it due to my sweet benefactor. She works for a wealthy family now, tutoring their sons. I think I shall retire from teaching and leave our livelihood to her."

"If I added three more classes..." Achtriel began.

"No, no, my child," Tahto protested, "I was only joking. Besides what would I do with myself if I did not teach? I would grow old simply from boredom."

"I don't want you ever to grow old," Achtriel said and hugged him.

"Too late for that." He chuckled. "But I shall do my best to never age a moment more."

"The way to do that is to rest yourself when I tell you," Fagim admonished. "Something you were never wont to do before the illness."

"I do it poorly even now," he said, eying the pile of texts that she had piled up and taken from him.

"It is time for your nap," she announced and stood glaring at him until he sighed and, giving Achtriel a martyred look, went off to his bedroom.

"How do you like working for the Hildebards?" Fagim asked when he had gone.

"I like it very much," she said. "The boys are reluctant students, but they are amusing. I think I shall be a teacher always since I cannot draw for living."

"Mayhap someday you will be able to," Fagim remarked with a faraway look. "Sometimes, the things we least hope for can come to our lives."

Two days later at the Sabbath meal, the reason for Fagim's optimism revealed itself. At her announcement, the chevara sat stupefied, Macha's turnip porridge cooling in their bowls. Achtriel was the least surprised. For once, she was the one to experience a superior sense of foreknowledge. Since the pageant, she had been less reclusive and gone much about the town. She found herself in places now where gossip was relished. She had to admit that she enjoyed it. She had heard hints before today that her chevara must soon plan for a wedding.

When all those at Tahto's table overcame their shock, they began to discuss the matter with much excitement.

"Well, we will not have to search far for musicians," Tahto said.

"And Frans will perform for us I'm sure." Naadasya nodded.

"I have made good friends with the pie and tart sellers, and they will gladly sell their wares to us cheaply," Achtriel added.

"We shall have more amusement than we did at the pageant!" Mosse declared.

"And how did all this come about pray tell us…" they all asked.

So they were informed of the clandestine love affair that had flourished unknown to almost everyone in town. They were brought up to date on the secret plans, careerings from elation to hopelessness, fears, and missives.

"I must learn to lift my nose out of my needlework." Profait shook his head. "I was once astute about such things, but I had no idea…"

"Nor I," said Samiel, "But I must admit I am so happy for you both it warms my wicked heart."

"Esther, why did you never drop a hint to anyone?" Tahto teased playfully.

"It was not my place to say." She laughed.

"Well, congratulations both, and all the best, Fagim." They raised their glasses to her. "And to you, you old satyr." Samiel patted Mosse on the back.

Of course, they had not dared to dream, they told their friends, that they could ever wed. But some months ago, Fagim had met an old friend from the village in Austrasia where she had once lived with her husband. The friend said that Fagim's husband had remarried only months after Fagim and Natan ran away. This news in itself would not have made a difference, for without an official divorce decree, Fagim would still not be free.

But the friend revealed also that the husband had gone missing, and that his present wife now planned herself to be rewed. She was much younger than Fagim's husband, and when he left on a five-year-trading voyage, she had fallen in love. Her new suitor was wealthy and after several years had passed, he had the means to finance letters to Babylon to enquire of the rabbis there. The rabbis said that since the merchant had not been gone the requisite amount of time to be claimed dead, the only way to prove him so was by a witness. This was usually quite difficult to do.

If a ship or other merchant venture was waylaid, the captured Jews were often ransomed at the nearest Jewish settlement. Word of their survival would be forwarded from there or they themselves would send word home to family or friends. Because most Jews were faithful husbands and would miss their families, if means existed, they usually came home. But as no one had returned from the voyage which Fagim's husband had led, the likelihood was that all, including any potential witnesses, were dead.

No news of the Fagim's husband's death or survival had come to this present wife for many years, during which time she could not wed. But when she bore a son, her suitor was determined to legit-imize their marriage. He had offered a sizeable reward to any who could prove the merchant dead. Within several months, a man, who had been among those on that waylaid ship, came forward. It seems he had stayed "missing" for he loathed his wife. However, with the reward, he could petition the Tennaium for divorce. So he braved the censure of the Jewish world and contacted his home village. He claimed he could not return to his first wife for he had wed a widow and had several sons. He also declared that he had watched Fagim's husband drown after the wreck of their ship.

He himself had been spared, he said, because he had caught hold of a timber and had drifted to the shores of Sicily. It was a very high civilization there and having been restored to health and a comfortable financial provision by his current wife, he saw no reason to leave it. Until the reward. Evidently, the rabbis found his story verifiable, for they granted Fagim's husband's second wife the right to rewed. With her husband proven dead, Fagim was also free to remarry.

Tahto had not known of his friend Mosses' love affair. Neither, it seems, had any but Natan who had no wish to broadcast information which could taint his mother's reputation. But word of the affair had leaked out to the Hildebards when they were in Rodom. They had a Jewish seamstress there who hailed from Fagim's original Austrasian town. It seems that seamstress knew the woman to whom Fagim confided, in her joy, when word of the second wife's marriage was confirmed.

Ordinarily, Fagim would have been beneath the notice of the Hildebards. She was not beautiful, went dutifully about her business, and offended no one. Even word of Fagim and Mosses' indiscretion would not have caused much stir. But with this delicious story and its happy ending, the affair had become the talk of those who loved to talk, and those, of course, included the Hildebards.

"Everyone will want to come, you know," Esther chided her sister. "It will be a grand event."

"Oh no, I cannot have anything like that..." Fagim fussed and looked at Mosse.

"We will do what we can and let whoever wishes attend," he said. "But we cannot afford a lavish..."

"What will you wear?" Esther ignored him. "I know! I have a fabric left over from Bonda's wedding dress..."

"Oh no! I could absolutely not..."

"Psch. Hush!" Esther commanded, "You will not dissuade me. I can see the garment in my mind; Achtriel will draw it. You shall look a vision."

"I am not a vision," Fagim protested. "I am an old spinster, and if I try to look otherwise, I will be laughed at."

"Nonsense," Ester said. "You are only twenty-nine and with a little artfulness and some wonderful design, we shall surprise the whole town with your beauty."

"Don't be ridiculous..."

I find you beautiful," Mosse declared. "If others see you so, they will simply see you as I do, and that makes them highly privileged.

"With your hair so..." Esther lifted her sister's dark locks and twisted them into a pile. "Oh yes!"

"Oh no," Fagim groaned, and everyone laughed.

For Achtriel, the most exciting event related to the impending wedding came two days after that Sabbath dinner. Fagim announced that she and Mosse would be taking her with them to Rodom to purchase cloth. Natan was to come also. He and Achtriel could explore the market streets while the adults managed their business. Rodom was the oldest and most extensive Jewish market outside Paris. Goods from all corners of the earth would be on view there from Oriental silks to Arabian lyres. Achtriel bounced about the house in such a fever of anticipation that neither Tahto nor Macha could long restrain her.

Macha had never been out of town and so could not answer the incessant questions with which the child assaulted her. She was, however, a great source of rumors and cautionary tales about river demons and all manner of foul spirits who were sure to abound on the roads and waterways. Tahto privately advised Achtriel not to set great store by this information, and she did not, except at night. Then sometimes she found herself unable to sleep imagining a variety of horrors. But by the morning, these thoughts would have lifted, and she would spring out of bed to excite herself once more with incessant chattering about the upcoming excursion.

For the first time in her life, she was interested in her dress and spent many hours sorting and matching the clothing that lined her room. Macha was very helpful in this regard especially in the determination of which items were suitable due to their poor upkeep, only for scrap. She did undertake to patch and refashion some of the more acceptable pieces and even made Achtriel a lovely two-piece kirtle with a ribbon trim.

"You shall represent us well," she declared, fitting Achtriel for the final hemming. "Let no one say I've let you go to the city like an urchin."

"Who would say that?" Achtriel asked, fingering the ribbon on her sleeves."

"Those who like to wag tongues. Which is everyone in this town."

"Everyone says you have improved me admirably. Especially since the pageant."

"Pshh. I had nothing to do with that. It was your friends and your new interests. And coming out of the woods."

"But without you, I would never even have walked, Macha."

"Nonsense. You were determined to do so. Never gave me a moment's peace as a babe unless I played with you and taught you. I had no choice."

"Nonetheless, you have made me as close to a lady as I shall ever hope to be in this life." Achtriel gave her a kiss.

"Ladies, pooh! What is highborn in you comes from your own spirit."

"Still I shall never forget what I owe. What shall I bring you from Rodom?"

"A husband."

"What sort of husband?"

"A rich one of course. And, please, one not overly dull."

"Perhaps those two qualities are rare in one individual."

"You sound more and more like your grandfather every day," she said, shaking her head.

Chapter 20

Throughout the month with travel preparations, her teaching schedule and Tahto's care, Achtriel was so busy that she forgot about the other much anticipated date. So she was startled when Tahto announced that his brother would be there in time to see the wedding.

"Are you quite sure, Tahto? How do you know?" she asked. She was fitting him for a new overshirt.

"His letter was posted six months ago, and in it, he said he would be here several months after Adar. As Fagim and Mosses' wedding will be held before Purim, he should be here to attend it. Perhaps we can sing the Xenophorion together as we once did. I must be able to sing without coughing by then."

"Yes, you must!" she agreed. "Else your brother will blame me for overtaxing you."

And as if her demand carried a potent spell, he did recuperate. By November, he was able to walk around the town and visit members of the synagogue. It was astonishing to Achtriel how these people, who for years had regarded Tahto as dangerous, now stopped to smile and wish him good health. He would come home from a walk humming tunes he had not sung since her infancy. Was it their solicitude that cheered him? Odd, because he had not before seemed to note its absence.

The doings of the synagogue community had concerned him as little as the squawking of chickens. Yet now he would comment at dinner about Michal's progress in the Torah or Yonaton's polite children. Perhaps such social acceptance was a universal balm, as indiscriminately necessary as water. Yet she wondered uneasily if his illness had somehow changed him, making him more ordinary.

When another letter from his brother, appended to a neighbor's enquiry about a shipment of furs, said that he and his wife were well and would be here soon, she did not begrudge his open joy. He seemed buoyed with it and danced her around the kitchen like a boy.

"You will be so happy to see your brother," she smiled when he let her go.

"Oh, I should think so!" he said and went humming off to his study.

That night, she awoke in the darkness. An owl spoke in a nearby tree, and she shivered under her blanket. Now that Tahto had real family, she wondered, would he need her less? Perhaps the new relatives would find her cumbersome and convince him to send her away. She remembered the twisted beings she and Frans had seen at the fair. Would that become her fate at last when she had lost the strength to work in fields or scrub a lady's floor? She told herself such thoughts were drastic, but all that night, they kept her from sleep.

"Tahto?" she questioned him at breakfast. "Will I be in the way when your brother comes?"

"In the way of what?" he asked, munching his rye bread.

"Well, you will have your family then and..."

"And as you are my family so shall you," he replied. "And besides, we shall need your assistance with the other girl."

Her hand, lifting a spoon toward her mouth, stayed suspended in midair. "Other girl?"

"Yes. Apparently the serving woman they bring with them is in fact not much older than you. She speaks Greek, but knows no Latin, and cannot read or write in the common tongue. She will require instruction."

Achtriel was speechless. When she could make utterance, she scolded him loudly. "Why did you not tell me of this?"

"Oh, didn't I?" he said and looked at her with a sly sideward's glance. "Well, perhaps I had forgotten."

"A girl? What is she like? How old is she? Was she slave or free? How did she come to be their servant? Is she from their city? Is she a Jew?" She jumped from her chair upsetting his crockery.

"I see now why I may have forgotten to mention it, "he said, steadying his cup. "Of this girl, I know little else than that she came to them for sanctuary."

"Sanctuary?" Achtriel's amazement rendered her speechless.

"We shall hear the full story soon enough. What is important is that you make her welcome for she will be unused to our dusty ways."

"Of course…" she answered. But in her mind, the questions persisted. Was the girl an orphan too, and so likely to feel friendly to her? Might she be mean spirited like Sorgen or simply have no use for a crippled girl? Would she be even interested in learning or find it a chore as most people did and thus make problems for Achtriel? What if she were stupid? If her tutelage was to be Achtriel's anchor to this family, could she in fact accomplish it?

"For once you are quiet," Tahto said. But rather than return his bantering tone, she smiled sweetly and began to clear her breakfast dishes.

The subject of the new girl was too sensitive to broach with anyone. They would cajole her, as adults were wont to do, with their deliberate or unwitting ignorance of childhood truths. If a girl, especially if close in age, were not one's friend, then the chances of her becoming one's enemy were very high. If the girl loathed Achtriel, it would not be obvious to Tahto. He would simply counsel her to be more civil. She herself would have to bear whatever slights and machinations this rival devised. As time and maturity forced on them its necessary jurisdictions in the marriage world, would their discrepancies render one mistress and the other slave?

The life of a lady's servant was not strenuous. In fact, for one with her defects, it would be considered a godsend. She might perhaps continue studying, if only to provide tutelage to the inevitable offspring. But things could always go unexpectedly for good or ill. Life was ever uncertain. She sighed, but beneath her troubled thoughts, there could not be extinguished a sincere curiosity.

By the time the day arrived for her departure to Rodom, she had developed a veneer regarding the subject of the girl. When questioned, she pretended only eagerness and acquiescence. No one guessed at her darker fears. None, in fact, had time to give thought to any worries for the details of the trip were endless.

Many folk in town had employed Fagim to purchase for them in the city. In itself, this was a pleasant prospect. But the need for scrupulous accounting and legal preparations, the details of the lading and the wrangling, between buying parties, for the use of cartage space kept Fagim and Mosse in long discussions with innumerable townsfolk.

And there were precautions to be taken. The money, and later the returning goods, must be well hidden for the possibility of thievery was never far. Mosse had a covered wagon with a false floor which was kept completely hidden under grain-filled sacks. Below the floorboards were secret compartments that even the cleverest of thieves, and they did not tend to be clever, would overlook. The travelers must take care to seem impecunious, concealing their money and better garments in the compartments. The travel food must be planned and purchased to provide the most nutrition in the smallest space. They must practice their Frankish and all the other dialects one might encounter on the road or in the market stalls.

They studied maps and planned alternatives and stratagems in case of some emergency. Natan was quick and sly and good at fighting. In addition, Mosses' cloak harbored a large cudgel. Jews were not known to be fearsome. Most abhorred violence because of their teachings and had never been schooled in the use of it. But Mosse had traveled much in his early years and had learned the effectiveness of a good weapon. He hoped he would not have recourse to need it, but nonetheless, it was there.

When the day arrived for their departure, Fagim and Mosse were both weary. Natan had been up all night with them, loading and arranging the provisions and checking accounts, for he was skilled at

numbers and the documents of trade. As soon as they bade farewell
to the small party who had come in the predawn light to see them
off, Natan fell asleep. Achtriel could not ask the questions which her
eager curiosity set forth, like morsels from the never empty braziers
of legend.

She watched in silence the city walls grow shorter, then shrink
below the hills and disappear. How quickly and completely they were
gone, and nothing but wildness seemed ever to have been there. It
was frightening at first to realize that they were so alone. Beyond the
reach of voice, camaraderie or succor, which a village provided, even
to ones not always welcome there.

They juddered a while on rough cart tracks but came eventually to wider roads. These sturdy remnants of the Roman occupation would make travel a much safer proposition. Better than the
canals. These waterways were frequented by keen unsavory fellows.
Jews in particular, it was said, were targeted by ferrymen for robbery
or mayhem.

But the Northbound roads were visible from far away and
guarded by the merchants who paid for outposts, staffed with fighting men, to tend them. The land around the roadways had been
burned free of trees and underbrush to hinder ambush. Thieves
would have had to risk attack by archers to waylay them. Because
the services of merchants were necessary to the gentry, they also paid
equestrian patrols to scout the roads. So, despite potential dangers,
it was with relative security that the party made its way. Mosse had
rented two strong mules, Valeria and Plautus, whose burnished backs
swayed them genially forward.

The journey to Rodom took nine days. At night, if they found
suitable cover, they tethered the mules and slept in shifts. Achtriel
took longer turns at night watch than Mosse and Fagim who did not
sleep well in daytime and were grateful for the rest. They complained
of the difficulties of sleeping while traveling, a problem unknown to
Achtriel who could happily avoid a boring, rainy travel day with the
rare privilege of a daytime nap.

Natan, under Naadasya tutelage, had built a small Chaturanga
board and little wooden figures to go with it. He and Achtriel spent

much of their time in the back of the cart playing the game or retrieving the pieces that tumbled to the floor and lodged themselves in intractible spots. After several hours of play, Achtriel would grow weary of the game.

Natan, however, could spend days arranging and rearranging the figurines in ever more complicated relationships. She preferred to lie in a corner and daydream. Her thoughts would be interrupted from time to time by his intrigued or satisfied utterances.

The morning of the day that would bring them into Rodom began cold and damp. Achtriel peeked from the cart to discover a surrounding fog, so thick that the world was all but invisible. No one else had awoken. She was alone in the whiteness. A mist such as this would be the ideal setting for an enchantment.

She slipped quietly from the cart and went to pass water. Her urine as it hit the ground made mists of its own. The breaths from her mouth did also. What made such phenomena? She pulled up her undergarments and stood up. Silence encircled her like a spell.

It seemed that mist muffled sound as it did sight. What was it in the changed air that could account for this? She walked about, breathing the smells of trees and moistened earth. Truly, the world was already magic. Too many people had forgotten this. Animals, as babies did, knew each thing that God had fashioned was a wonder.

"Raugh!" It was Natan, emerging from invisibility, to startle her and grab her shoulders. She laughed and tried to run from him, but he was faster and caught up to her. He lifted her and swung her around, and the silence was destroyed by their playful laughter.

Later, on the road, when they had eaten their midday bread, Natan crawled to the wagon front and stuck his head between his mother's and Mosses'. He turned back to her and gestured frantically. She came behind him and looked out. The cart was in the highlands. Below them the roofs of Roman buildings could be seen above the trees. As they neared, smaller wooden structures appeared, oddly insubstantial beside the remnants of that vanished kingdom.

There was something about a city, even a second-class one like Rodom, that bespoke excitement. To Achtriel, it seemed almost as otherworldly as the mist. Entirely different lives were led by those residing here, even the Jews, whose community was said to have been established hundreds of years ago by the wealthy Jewish families of Rome. They were rumored to have large houses and estates rivaling those of the gentry.

Their schuls were often visited by traveling scholars. She wondered what it would be like to study in them. But Tahto, Esther, and Fagim remarked disdainfully about the caliber of education they provided. Esther said she had attended, out of curiosity, some programs offered there. They were mostly full of men who argued about the Talmud. More imaginative subjects, speculations on the nature of existence or on Greek and Persian texts, were unheard of.

Still to live in such immense communities, where Jews had influence among the merchant classes, seemed enviable. Not to live in fear of the whims of local government or the perennial uprisings of disgruntled neighbors would make for a privileged life. Still, as it was, these wealthy Jews provided a steady market for the luxury fabrics which Esther and Fagim imported, and the rare books, which Tahto copied and sold to augment his income.

"Now do not look about you so excitedly," Mosse admonished them over his shoulder. "Or the townsfolk will think we have arrived solely to be robbed."

"Oh, let them look, Mosse," Fagim said. "They are children after all." Natan pushed his mother's arm and frowned. "To me, you will be a child," she responded, patting his arm. "Always." He made a sour face at her, and they all laughed. Thus, their entrance to the city was not as dignified, perhaps, as Mosse might have wished.

Chapter 21

The outskirts of Rodom were, in fact, a humble affair. One-story wooden dwellings, no more elegant than those of Briga, shared the streets with taller apartment houses. These were several stories high and leaned close upon each other as if to keep themselves from collapsing. Toothless crones and barely clad infants wandered among them. The front doorways were attended by seated men who looked up suspiciously at passersby.

They went through many of these apartment neighborhoods, each of them attended by energetic vendors. Food sellers, soothsayers, herbalists, and beggars plied trades beside scurrying slaves and house-holders. Their singsong advertisements and aggressive harangues and the no less vociferous responses from pedestrians created a brash cacophony. Carts and wagons pulled by animals or people hustled by, oblivious to the commotion. Everyone seemed in a rush as if late for some critical event.

In the center of the town, they came to a long straight street. It was flanked by Romanesque governmental buildings, unchanged, but for some wear, since ancient times. One declared itself, in ancient Latin carved above its gallery, to be a synagogue. Beyond it sat a giant archway, decorated with reliefs and identified as The Street of Jews. Much like its namesake in Briga, this thoroughfare was occupied by venders of many nationalities.

The street, which seemed immeasurably long, was crowded even at this early hour. They could see brightly colored storefronts and street stalls boasting every kind of rarity: weaponry, metalware, artifacts, jewelry, embroidered cloth, and silk. Street venders touted hot porridge, pickles, wine, sweetbreads, cheeses, dates, and olives. Unfortunate pigs and goats stood in cages awaiting their demise.

The second hand finery of Byzantines, Moors and Armenians rubbed shoulders with the hand-wrought woolens of Visigoths and Burgundians. Representatives of far-flung clans set up their stalls beside Persians, Africans, and venders from the British Isles. None, even the Franks and Lombards, habitually at odds, seemed bent on warfare. All, in fact, were so intent upon their business; they hardly glanced at one another.

Only the armed guards, employed by wealthy merchants, bothered to look menacing. Even so, the shoppers stepped around them with little fear, their faces bearing an odd admixture of apathy and vigilance. Although most people appeared well-fed, not so the animals among them. No herdsman would have dared to own such bony beasts. Even the ubiquitous street fowl were little more than feathers. Now and then, a pack of dogs would appear beside Mosse's cart and look at them with sad and hungry eyes.

To her surprise, Mosse did not stop on the merchant street but traversed it. Its adjacent roads gave way to smaller, less populated ones where commerce became gradually less active. They led at last to a region of relative quiet. Here, the streets were bordered by great overhanging trees. The sizeable houses behind them were obscured by stone walls or sharpened pallisades. Mosse stopped the cart and looked about as if to reacquaint himself with the area.

"Where are we?" Achtriel asked him.

"I have a relative who lives in one of these estates," he told her. "She has agreed to put us up while we do business in Rodom. That is, if we want to stay with her." He eyed Fagim, somewhat uncomfortably.

Fagim nodded, the thought of such accommodations overcoming, perhaps, whatever disapproval he had anticipated. He got down from the front of the cart and stood a moment stretching his long limbs. Natan jumped down too and went to stand beside the older man.

"You shall accompany me, eh?" Mosse acknowledged.

"He oversees my interests," Fagim said slyly.

"She is my sister-in-law!" Mosse protested to him with somewhat ineffectual gestures, but Natan merely slipped an arm through his and led him onward. Mosse looked back helplessly, but Fagim only laughed.

"He was expected to marry her when his brother died last year," Fagim explained to Achtriel. "I hope she does not bear me malice."

"Natan will stare her into compliance," Achtriel assured her.

"Who would have thought that I, old crow that I am, would play the part of temptress? Just remember, Achtriel, the roads of love are unpredictable." Achtriel said nothing but thought that, for herself, those roads would remain predictably closed.

When Mosse returned, he brought with him a round-faced woman, so short of build that she reached only to his chest. Natan had neglected to return with them. Achtriel spied him farther down the street standing before a walled courtyard, attempting to seem interested in some flowers being tended by a young housegirl.

"Welcome, welcome," the woman exclaimed, stretching her arms to include Fagim, Achtriel, the mules, perhaps the wagon itself. "I am Mayim, and you shall all be my guests! Mosh, now you must bring your wagon around back to my stables. These poor creatures (it was unclear if she was referring to the mules or their human cargo) look much the worse for road dust. Well, a good wash and a luncheon await you all."

"Thank you for your hospitality." Fagim smiled down at her, extending her hand. "We are most fortunate."

"Oh, but what foolishness!" the woman said, taking Fagim's hand. "I could have hoped for no better fortune myself than a house full of interesting friends. The last months have been so dull. There has been little company, and none of it interesting in the year since Dovid died. I was nearly hopping about like a sparrow in anticipation. Leyal!" She turned her head and shouted to the housegirl, "Call the stable boy."

"Oh, we can see to our animals," Mosse offered.

"What nonsense! You must not let your lovely bride be seen clucking at mules like a farm hand. Get up there beside her and escort your party forth like propertied folk."

"I shall do as you request," he acquiesced as he mounted the wagon. "Although we shall be thus imposters."

"But Fagim has a house!" Achtriel pointed out. "And built it with her own hands."

"Then she, at least, shall be conveyed as befits her," he said to his betrothed.

"And when you are married, you shall live there, and so you shall be propertied as well," Achtriel said.

"My small shack is hardly in the category of your sister's elegant home," Fagim remarked.

"Built it yourself!" Mayim exclaimed. "Well, indeed mine was not got by my own handiwork. I cannot claim it with the pride you do yours." She continued to eye Fagim, her face displaying an obscure emotion. Then she turned and trotted ahead of them, her head lifted like a little dog's, and went to unbar the double gate in the courtyard's wall.

As they came through the gate, a boy came forward to take the mules. He was about Achtriel's age and upon catching sight of her stuck out his tongue. He was gone by the time she had gotten down from the wagon. There was no time to look about for him because they were greeted loudly by Mayim, standing before her columned veranda and waving her arms. "This way, this way," she called.

They brushed as much dust from their clothing as they could and approached the house. It was, by Briga standards, immense. Its front door was made up of two huge and intricately carved panels. Mayim hustled them through it and into her foyer. This entry room was bigger than either Tahto's or Fagim's entire house. Its high ceilings were decorated with architectural flourishes and artful frescoes. The walls were painted with Hebrew themes, the tree of life, the flight out of Egypt and Moses on the mountain. The room was delightfully cool, and Achtriel would have liked to remain in it, but Mayim led them through it into an even larger space.

It would not have been accurate to call this a room exactly, for it seemed to be a central area contiguous to numerous hallways. In the center of it, there was a large stairway resembling the Hildebard's. But unlike theirs, this one shone with polished wood and had been scrupulously cleaned and swept. To the right of it lay a sumptuous room, in the middle of which stood a long and elegantly appointed table.

"We shall have lunch as soon as you all have had a moment to refresh yourselves. You shall share my bedroom, Fagim and Mosh and Natan shall be in the guest quarters. Layel will show your…?"

"Achtriel," Fagim supplied.

"Yes. Layel will show you to your room. Do not tarry, for a spectacular lunch awaits you all. Oh! Can she manage the stairs?" she whispered, not very quietly, to Fagim.

"Yes," Fagim assured her and looked over at Achtriel apologetically.

"Good. Then follow Leyel, and she shall show you up." The girl who had been taking care of the flowers was now beside her and took her hand in a proprietary fashion. She led her rather brusquely up the stairway, through a long hall, and then up a second, less presentable set of stairs.

"These are the rooms," Leyel said, eying her. "Whose servant are you? His or hers?"

Achtriel colored slightly and replied, "Neither. I am a friend."

"Indeed," Leyel said, doubtfully. "Well, you shall sleep with us no matter, "friend." This is my bed, and that's yours. And never doubt we will be watching you. Don't try to take anything."

"I am not a thief!" Achtriel protested loudly.

"So say they all," Leyel said and promptly left.

It took some minutes for Achtriel to calm herself. She had never been accused of thievery, although she was accustomed to being taken for a servant. She thought maliciously of wiping her now filthy boots across the servant's pillow, but she did not. Instead, she sighed and looked around.

Room was perhaps an exaggeration for there was little of it. The space was built below slanting cantilevered roof, which took up most of the headroom. Under it stood four small beds, all close together and smelling none too clean. She tested the one which had been designated hers. Although it smelled of sweat and dirty feet, it felt luxurious compared to the cart floor. She did not have time to rest, however, for Fagim called up the stairs and told her to wash and come down to lunch.

The meal was indeed elegant. There were breads and cheeses, spinach soufflé, pickled onion and olives, apple butter and salad. In the middle of the table, there was a bowl of pears. Achtriel ate quickly and then noticed that the other three—Natan was taking his meal outside with the stable boy—were lingering over their food. She knew they must be as hungry as she was but seemed to be pretending otherwise. Instead, they were talking.

"And he has not seen this brother since they were children?" Mayim was saying. "How astonishing!"

"Yes. We are all waiting anxiously for their arrival," Fagim said, reaching daintily for the bread basket.

"Perhaps he brings riches from the east?"

"No," Mosse said. "They had to leave suddenly. We do not know the full story as yet."

"Well, if he were a wealthy man, even under such circumstances, he would have jewels."

"Perhaps. We do not know." Mosse looked uncomfortable and glanced at Fagim, but she was studiously buttering her piece of bread. "We do not know much of the ways of the wealthy, I'm afraid."

"Now don't pretend to be a pauper, Mosh. You know we come originally from a well-off family. If you had not quarreled with your father and had taken up his business…"

"I made my choice then, and I am not ashamed of it," Mosse said, frowning. This seemed to end the conversation and allow them all to eat.

Achtriel was anxious to leave for the market, but she had to remind herself that she was a guest, and so must not badger, as Tahto put it, with veiled suggestions to eat more swiftly. Nonetheless, her impatience must have been noticeable for Mosse shot her looks under his eyebrows warning her not to fidget.

Lucky Natan did not have to be glowered at, for he was not trapped in this stifling room. The sound of his raucous laughter could be heard from time to time. Once Natan peeked in the door at them, his face happily besmeared with dust. He was undoubtedly playing chase and wrestling with the stable boy, stretching his limbs after the long journey.

She, however, was condemned to sit quietly while the grown folk talked. They could be so tiresome. Why must they say only the things one could predict. It seemed as if someone had written the words for them, and they bespoke their lines like playactors. She would much rather have gone with Natan.

"I can help clean up," she offered brightly. "Shall I clear the table?"

"I shall not let a guest of mine be put to work!" Mayim exclaimed.

"I do not mind, madam…" Achtriel began, but Mayim shushed her.

"No, no, no! Mosh has told me that you are a scholar," she said, spooning a prodigious helping of salad onto her own already crowded plate. "I would not demean you by letting you near my kitchen."

"But…" Achtriel caught another of Mosses' looks and managed to silence herself.

"The two of you will live in the shop then, after the wedding?"

"My son will have my house," Fagim said. "He is a man now."

"But he is… does he not need a warden to look out for him?"

"Natan cannot hear well. That is the full extent of his deficiencies. In all other matters, he is more competent than most." Fagim's lips drew into a tight little twist that was the only sign of what Achtriel knew was considerable anger.

"I see…" Mayim said, looking confused. Glancing at Achtriel, she remarked, "We must all be forebearant with the afflicted. You are to be commended both of you." Achtriel could feel her face becoming red. She wished that decorum permitted her to lose the impolite words that filled her mind. But Mosses' eyes narrowed at her under his considerable eyebrows, and she said nothing.

Finally, the conversation faltered as even Mayim became aware that they had exhausted their repertoire of mundane topics. "Well,

I suppose you will be wanting to go on now," she said with a hint of irritation. "Take my mules but keep an eye on them at market and do not leave them unattended. And watch your purses the place is full of thievery."

"Fagim has been merchanting in Rodom for many years now," Mosse said. "I am sure she knows how to conduct us in the city."

"Indeed? How unusual a thing! But just one more absorbing fact about your bride, Mosh. You do have such…interesting friends in Briga."

"My sister and I began the trade for want of a better one," Fagim explained. "And finding it an easy one we stayed with it. We had my son to feed, and neither of us any marriage prospects."

"Well, that has changed indeed," Mayim said, a bit too briskly. "Ah, well now, you must be off. I will call the boys to bring the cart around."

"I can go and tell them," Achtriel offered.

"A young lady does not consort with stable boys," Mayim admonished.

"But Natan is not a stable boy and…"

"Finish your tea now," Fagim advised her.

"You only need to sit there and look pretty," Mayim said. But it was clear she did not believe that Achtriel, with her crooked arm and limp, could ever achieve that.

Chapter 22

At last the interminable lunch was cleared away, and the preparations made for their excursion. The trade goods had been sorted into saleable packets and bundled beneath the wagon's floor. A hidden coin box was secured beneath the seat, and a leather purse strapped on Mosse's belt. As they retraced their route down Mayim's street, they were scrutinized by her neighbors who, it seemed, had discovered a sudden need to water their flowers. They appeared just as eager to ogle country folk as Achtriel was to stare at them.

The two did indeed seem to be of different breeds. The city people were cleaner and more brightly clad. And yet their faces, although their work was far less strenuous, bore the pale hues of exhaustion. The children stood, hemmed in about the grounds, like house slaves. They whispered haughtily among themselves and pointed at Achtriel with derision. When the cart left them behind, she was relieved.

Natan, now that the stable boy was not there, soon became friendlier, leaning beside Achtriel and gesturing at all the passing sights.

"Is that a riverway?" Achtriel asked Fagim, as she noticed a small stream beside one street.

"Yes. It serves as that and also as an outlet for the city waste." The children made faces at each other and laughed.

"I hope they don't bathe or wash their clothes in it!" said Achtriel. Natan mimicked a proud city man suddenly sniffing at his shirt.

"Where do all these people live?" Achtriel asked.

"They live where they may or where they can," answered Fagim. "These apartment blocks are overcrowded and new ones are continually being built."

"They are so squalid that they inspire their residents to industry, so they may live in better circumstances," Mosse joked.

"How do they eat? There are so many people here and no fields about."

"The farmers bring in food from the country and sell it at market."

"Can that feed so many people?"

"That depends on the crops. But those who have money will always be the last to starve." Mosse looked over at Fagim. "And I do not intend for that to happen to the ones I love."

"Very clever." Fagim narrowed her eyes. "He wants me to raise my prices," she explained, "even for the customers I have long done business with."

"She fears losing their custom. But in truth, her prices are already lower than the markets'. I am simply trying to improve her negotiation skills."

"I have been in business for almost ten years," Fagim told him. "I can judge my customer's temperaments well enough." There was silence in the front of the wagon then, and Achtriel looked nervously at Natan. He rolled his eyes, as if to say, "They do this all the time." They spent the rest of the ride in an uncomfortable silence.

As they neared the Street of Jews, they could hear the tumult long before they saw it.

"This is close enough, I think," Mosse said, pulling the cart into an alley some streets away from the main market. "Do you agree?" he asked Fagim sheepishly.

"It looks fine, providing you give that lad over there a coin. Otherwise, the cart will not be here when we return."

"How much does he require then?" Mosse asked.

"Here, Natan. Give him this nummus," Fagim said, taking a small purse from under her tunic.

"Can I go too?" Achtriel cried.

"Yes, but you must stay beside Natan."

The two young people bounded from the cart and gaped about in the sooty air. Even on this side street, there were crowds speaking so many differing dialects that the amalgam of their voices became a singsong hum. They hurried by in small and large groups, singly and in pairs. But all, without exception, trained a wary eye on everything and everyone about. It appeared that the powers of vision, which in the country might rest and muse, here must be quite circumspect to ensure survival. Achtriel glanced about to see what required such attention.

Mostly, there were only people, talking loudly at each other. One group nearby, a seller of roots and his would-be buyers, spoke divergent tongues and so raised their voices to a crescendo in lieu of communication. Another group, consisting of a woman with five ragged and fly-plagued boys, shouted at every passerby while dangling a slimy fish. Behind her, a motley throng stood about a wagon examining its wares.

Between their backs, Achtriel could see clay jars and boots, crockery, tools, rope, and hides. On a nearby table, about which a more pecunious class was gathered, lay horse gear, furs, and glassware. Natan pushed her shoulder and pointed at some fur clad men who were selling golden belt buckles and fine grooming tools, carved ivory boxes, and silver pins.

Mosse and Fagim stepped down from the cart, and the street boy nodded at them, acknowledging his receipt of payment. "There will be the same and a half for you when we return and find all well." Mosse told him, handing him the reins and patting the mules' brown heads. Fagim gave the boy a parcel filled with dried meats and fruits. "You shall have a full meal when we return." She smiled at the boy who broke into a gap-toothed grin.

"We are going to set up a stall in the main street," Fagim told Achtriel and Natan. "It is that way. If you need us, you cannot miss it. The two of you may look about but only with each other." Fagim told them. Natan, who had been to the city before, made a disappointed face.

"You must watch Achtriel closely," Mosse told him. "She is small and can easily be trampled."

Natan gave a wounded sigh but took her hand.

"I am sorry you have to watch me," she told him when the adults were gone. He shrugged but continued to look discouraged.

"I will be alright by myself," she insisted. "I have been to cities before." He looked down at her, skeptically. "With Tahto! When we went to the coast. To get his brother's letter." Natan nodded, remembering. He looked at her again and then about him greedily. Then he made a stern face at her and pushed her to the side of the crowds, near a crumbled wall.

"I will stay right here. I promise," she told him. "Now run before they see you." He gave her one last warning look and sped away, soon disappearing into the mill of bodies.

Achtriel stood against the wall and looked around. The city did not seem so very frightening. In fact, there was an excitement to it. People's faces, enlivened and cunning, looked sharply about. Not so the nomadic tribesmen with their wives and flocks. Such dissemblance was beyond them. They gaped like children. Especially at some people walking by on stilts, dressed up like Catholic saints. Suddenly, she felt a pincer seize her arm.

"So. You have betrayed me," a voice hissed in her ear. She turned to see a girl, a few years older than herself, dressed in expensive clothing, although dusty and torn. Her face was very pretty and somehow familiar.

"Don't pretend you don't know me, crippled girl. I knew sooner or later, you'd be starving and eager to be of use to them."

"Who are you?" Achtriel stammered, feeling the bite of the girl's ragged fingernails on her skin. The girl's face dropped its venomous look in a moment of surprise. "Am I that changed really?" But then she laughed ruefully. "Well, I am glad of it." It was the bitter downturn at the corners of her mouth that sparked recognition.

"Bonda?" Achtriel gasped. "What are you doing here?"

"Then you had not heard."

"I have heard nothing concerning you."

The girl loosened her grip slightly on Achtriel's arm. "You have not come for me? They did not send you? They are not here?"

"I came with Fagim to help her. She is getting married." At that word, the bitterness in Bonda's lips twisted her mouth into an awful smile. "Is she now? That aged crow. How life mocks us."

"What happened to your..."

"My marriage. To that ass. I ran away." She looked about, her face scanning the crowds.

"Who is looking for you?"

"Who are you to know my doings?" she spat. "You are nothing but a slave."

"I am not," Achtriel insisted. "I have a grandfather who has given me more than you will ever have."

Bonda's eyes stopped their ceaseless scanning and focused on Achtriel's face. "Yes, you are fortunate. Mayhap the gods favor you. You might bring me luck. Swear you will not tell them."

"Tell who?"

Bonda narrowed her eyes like a striking snake. "My father searches for me. He is my blood unlike your grandpa, yet he would bring my corpse back to retrieve its dower. But he cannot harm me now. He would be foolhardy to pursue me."

"But your mother...don't you think she would want to help you?"

"She is a mouse who would soon betray me. No. My freedom's won at a dear price, her mourning is a small expense. Step back into the shadows, girl. I cannot be here." Bonda pulled Achtriel with her toward the wall and into an alley that smelled of human waste. Here she crouched, looked about, and pulled a wineskin from her skirt folds. "Care for some?" she offered and then shook her head. "That's right—a Jew girl. Keep your innocence, my friend. Mine has been mongered." She took a long drink of her wine.

"What happened to you?" Achtriel asked, bending somewhat clumsily to crouch beside her.

"A long tale. Not a pleasant one." She tipped the flask again to her lips. "The old man..." her face paled momentarily until she let out a resounding belch. Then she wiped a lock of greasy hair from off her forehead. "He had a son who wanted me. They fell to fighting, and the son was killed. From then on, the old man kept me inside a chamber with a watch set on me night and day. But there was a young guard, he wanted me. We escaped and came here."

"Is he with you still?"

"They killed him."

"Who?"

"The ones who have me now. But it is better. I am free."

Achtriel was aghast. This girl, only a few years older than her-self, had met such a cruel destiny. In unguarded instants, one could still see the childishness in her face. "Where will you go?" she asked at last.

"Go? Where should I go? I am here."

"But where do you sleep? Who feeds you?"

"I feed myself!" she said indignantly. "And far better than many in this hell. And I sleep where there is none to poke me unless it be for money and at my will."

"But..."

"Don't fret for me, you withered goat, and do not ask who keeps me, or I shall have to kill you. Know this, though. If you tell anyone in Briga you have seen me, I shall send my owners there to slay you. They are skilled in it."

"I would not tell leastways if it might bring you harm."

Bonda stared at Achtriel, sighed and shook her head. "Well, you Jews must be kind I suppose," she said, appearing almost grateful. "Fortune has been good to you that you are not as mercenary as the rest. May your luck come to me. Now go away before I change my mind, and my knife shall end your luck for good. Begone!"

She pushed Achtriel who lost her balance and toppled into the dirt. "Go, you puny cripple," Bonda said, rising. "I pray you are the last thing from my past I shall ever see." Then she ran further into the darkness of the alleyway and was gone.

When Achtriel reemerged into the sunlit street, her eyesight was briefly blurred. It was in that instant that a well-aimed blow struck her on the side of her arm. She turned to see the rubicund and fuming face of her assailant. It was Natan, and he was screaming at her. His vociferations, untutored by the world's, expressed this as a course of violent and grating yelps, rendered further inarticulate by his attempts to mold them to speech. She knew he must be vastly out of sorts for he had, since childhood, never let such sounds escape him. But the worst of it was that he looked absurdly funny.

She tried for some moments to appear contrite, for she knew he must have been afraid. But his wild gesticulations, his moos and barks, were so incongruous to the dignity that was his wont, that she could not help herself. A smile began to seep from the corners of her mouth. Seeing it, he fumed anew and magnified his loud vituperations until she could not stop her own helpless collapse into laughter. She felt another blow upon her arm and then another lighter one, and finally, the sound of his rueful chuckle, which was curiously identical to a hearing person's.

"I'm sorry," she managed to say when she had gained control of her mirth. "I didn't mean to laugh at you." He gave her a murderous look but breathed with relief. Then he made a questioning face and gestured about.

"I didn't go far, I...I saw something, and I got somehow lost." He looked skeptically at her but finally shrugged and accepted her explanation. His composure having returned he looked back toward the main street. Fagim was nowhere visible, and a sigh of profound gratitude escaped him. Then he turned to her and ringed her forearm in a viselike grip.

"Since they aren't here, we could explore a bit," she offered. "They wouldn't mind as long as you are with me." He looked doubtful but severely tempted. Then with a furtive scan of the environment, he pulled her forth.

They examined many booths of which her favorite was the one with little figurines, carved in marble, wood or metal, charms of gods and demigods. Natan did not want to leave the booth that bartered Roman war goods. The bright shields, armor, javelins, and swords seemed only slightly tarnished by the past one hundred and fifty years.

There were craftsmen selling furniture, wooden beds, chairs, and cupboards. Roman brickwork could be had as well as mummified birds and bats from Egypt. Closely guarded were the stalls that dealt in jewelry: golden ornaments and toques, cloak pins, and dangling earrings set with gems. She had been pushed aside while ogling some of these when she looked up to see a person unlike any she had seen before, even in this metropolis.

She was a tall woman of middle years, her head and body cloaked in brown robes that descended to her feet. Her hands were tucked up in it too so that she seemed otherwordly. Her sandled feet were black with dirt, as if she had walked a long way. Her face was rough but steeped in kindness and a sense of profound peace. Indeed, she was radiant, here among the tumult. The woman caught sight of Achtriel and smiling, came to her.

"Are you a holy woman?" Achtriel asked.

"None is holy but Our Lord." She laughed gently. "But I serve Him as I can." She gestured toward her nearby table, which was covered with codices, scrolls, and even some elaborate and intricately designed books.

"Where did you get those?" Achtriel asked.

"From monasteries on the Western isles. Some are very old or copies of much older ones. Come and look." She led Achtriel to her stall where another figure, also robed, sat on a wooden crate.

The manuscripts were unusual, unlike those which Tahto often found. The recently copied texts were neatly scrolled, but the older ones lay open. Some were so ancient that their edges were brown, curled, and worm eaten. She recognized the Latin and Greek lettering, but there were others whose letters seemed merely clever squiggles.

Natan had come to stand beside her and made a face which pronounced the oddity of the curlicue words. He looked questioningly at the woman, and Achtriel translated. "What are these?" she asked.

"I do not know. I was given them by a monk who had traveled to Byzantium. He says they are Persian or Arabic."

"My grandfather would love to see these," she said, tracing the lovely swirls with her fingertip. He finds old books and copies and sells them too. But they are not as nice as these," she said. "Are they very costly?"

"I am afraid so," the woman said. "We do not come across the sea, but several times a decade. We wait here for a group of buyers for a prenegotiated sale. Elsewise, I would have sold you one less dear.

I can give you something, though!" Achtriel watched as the woman went into a tent set up behind their stall and re-emerged. She was carrying two small animals, which Achtriel belatedly identified as a miniature form of bobcat.

"These are for you and your friend," the woman said. "They will bring you custom. They are excellent ratters and, being rare hereabouts, will be much in demand. Give them milk and water and whatever else they like. When they become large and clever, let them roam about. The mice and other vermin are their provender. Right now, they are just children. One is male, one female. Breed them when they are grown, and you will have a business." The woman lifted the cats, and Achtriel and Natan each took one. The creatures made high-pitched mewling sounds and looked up at them beseechingly.

"Oh, they are wonderful!" Achtriel exclaimed.

"Oh yes, you will come to love them. And they will deeply befriend you," the woman said. "Better companions one could not wish for."

"Oh, how can I thank you?" Achtriel cried.

"Your tender faces have done so already," the woman told Achtriel. And indeed, she and Natan were entranced. The wonders of the market dimmed beside these appealing creatures.

They spent the next few hours, huddled by the wall where they were to meet Fagim and Mosse, utterly enraptured with the kittens. A kindly farmer gave them milk and a concave wooden cap from his pail for a feeding dish. Natan used the money he had saved for weeks to buy dried meat, which the little cats ferociously consumed.

"I hope Tahto does not mind that they are meat eaters," Achtriel worried. "For I shall have to feed them for a while until they're grown." Natan looked down at the kitten asleep in his lap. He shook his head as if to say, "Who could dislike these?"

When Fagim and Mosse returned, it was growing dark. Their quarrel seemed to have been forgotten for their faces were flushed with happiness.

"What have we here?" Mosse exclaimed.

"They are baby cats," Achtriel told him.

"I can see that," he said. "But what are they…"

"We are going to take them home with us and raise them to eat vermin!" she explained happily.

"But how are we to get them home with us?"

Natan quickly began a pantomime showing how they would protect the cats on the journey home and how, if the need arose, they would take them outside for their excretions.

"I think they are brilliant," Fagim said. "We had many of these creatures in Austrasia, and our grain bins were free of mice and snakes even in summer."

"But who will feed them till they are grown?" Mosse asked doubtfully.

Natan gestured to explain that Achtriel would take the female cat and he the male, provided they could decide which was which.

"And when they are grown, we'll sell their children and get rich!" she added.

"I see," said Mosse.

"What a generous contribution to the town," Fagim said, giving Mosse a disapproving look and bending to examine the cats. "They certainly are dear. Can I hold one?" Natan proffered his kitten who mewed plaintively or perhaps with some annoyance at having been awoken.

"I can see my family will not be persuaded to forego this new husbandry." Mosse sighed. "I will explain to Tahto that I had nothing to do with the idea."

"Tahto will love them," Achtriel insisted. "For all living things are the face of God."

"Very well," Mosse said. "But please have these visages of God attend to their eliminations before we return to Mayim's."

The little animals proved easy to care for. Once settled in the wagon, they commenced an inspection of it, sniffing at every object as if committing it to memory. After a second meal of Natan's dried meat, they became antic and jumped on each other in the most comical way.

Mayim proclaimed them charming but insisted that they lodge with the stable boy until the morrow. Still, Achtriel could hardly sleep, worrying for her charges. In the morning, she hurried to the stables and found Natan asleep on a hay mound. The little cats had curled themselves under his chin.

With the kittens to amuse them, the trip home was much more interesting. Achtriel hoped that such lovely gifts might signal a thorough change in her fortunes. The townsfolk and even their children had seemed kinder since Tahto's illness, she had Frans and Naadasya and now the little cat. If Tahto continued healthy, all would be very well.

Chapter 23

When they reached the village, Mosse drew the wagon close to Tahto's house so that she did not have far to walk. Holding the cat, she got down from the wagon and hurried into the house. She was about to proclaim her excitement to Tahto, but then she froze, openmouthed. The man she was about to speak to was not Tahto, or he was, but a taller Tahto with less gray in his head and beard. Behind him at the table, with the real Tahto, sat a well-dressed woman and, standing beside her, regarding Achtriel with an unreadable expression, was the most beautiful girl she had ever seen.

She was perhaps thirteen and seemed to inhabit that spectral realm twixt child and maiden. Yet one could tell that at any age she would astound. The fact of her existence, a masterwork of line and form, was itself astonishing. Her skin had the hue and radiance of polished sard and her face was an almost perfect triangle, like a cat's. Like that animal, her eyes were large, arresting and slightly tilted.

She had a straight nose and widely angled cheekbones whose shadows drew the eye to her mouth and tapered chin. Her lips were both generous and marvelously contoured like the finely wrought outlines of a petal. Even the sable hair which wreathed her head and shoulders seemed shaped by Theano of the golden mean. It seemed one could, like Tiresius, in gazing too long at her perfection, be stricken blind.

Indeed, there was about her some mythical dread too near divine for ordinary life. Perhaps the Creator meant such beauty to disquiet, to remind man of His prime antilogy. For she was a vessel of both innocence and provocation, sensuality and holy grace. Compared to her, Bonda would have seemed a halfplucked pullet beside a swan.

"Ah, you are home!" Tahto called from the table. "Come and meet our new family. This is my brother, Nimrode, and his wife, Berthe. This is Achtriel, my ward."

"We may greet you at last." The brother smiled. "But we feel we know you already so much has Tahto talked of you. I think he has missed you these past weeks."

"And this is Tirzah," Berthe said, gesturing at the girl. Tirzah bent her head by way of formal greeting. "She grew up speaking Greek and she has learned your Frankish Latin from the crewmen of our vessel."

The two girls eyed each other in a somewhat awkward silence. Then Achtriel lifted her cat and said, "Look what I was given by a woman in the market street!" The girl surveyed the cat with a wariness equal to that with which she regarded Achtriel. "I was given her by a bookseller!" Achtriel repeated in Greek. She had been sure that no one in the world could not have loved this little cat. It widened its eyes and mewed endearingly. But Tirzah did not come forth to see it, nor did she smile.

"We are having dinner soon," Berthe announced. "You girls come in and help me serve."

Achtriel turned to look at Berthe. It was clear that in the weeks that Achtriel had been gone, this woman had assumed completely the authority to run the household. Swallowing her discomfiture, Achtriel put down the cat and followed the woman to the kitchen. Tirzah came also, obedient but somewhat distracted.

In the kitchen, she watched as Achtriel collected wooden dishes. "The larger serving boards are over there," Achtriel told her, again in Greek. Tirzah looked in the direction she had indicated but made no further movement. Did the girl not understand the simple task of table setting? Achtriel looked more closely at her face to spot signs of idiocy. She saw only a profound apathy overlaid with the knowledge of her obligation to appear cooperative.

"Tirzah," the brother's wife said, "here are the bread loaves we made. Can you put them on the table?" The girl, clearly understanding, took the loaves and left the room, looking indifferently at Achtriel as she brushed past.

"What will you call your little cat?" Berthe inquired.

Achtriel realized she had forgotten the cat and looked anxiously about. But there was no need to fear. The cat, as if it had been born to live in a house, had appropriated some cloaks which had come with the guests and lay atop them, licking its fur. It looked up at Achtriel briefly then resumed its ablutions. Achtriel decided that, despite its demarcation as a different species, this animal was a great deal more personable than Tirzah.

At dinner, Tahto and his brother talked excitedly, laughing, although often with tearful eyes. Achtriel had never seen Tahto so animated. They were speaking Aramaic, so she caught only words and phrases, all about a time long past. It seemed they were not even in this room but in an altogether different life. Achtriel turned her attention to Berthe. She was much younger than her husband, a kind person clearly, and one who did not need others to notice it. She sat listening to her husband and new brother-in-law with a quiet smile. Tirzah looked only at her food and ate it uncomfortably.

"But I have forgotten you," Tahto said, turning to Achtriel. "How was your expedition? Did Fagim sell very much?"

"I think so," Achtriel replied. "She seemed pleased."

At the mention of the journey, Tirzah looked up to reassess her. It seemed that for her, a certain prestige attended travel. Brief interest kindled in her eyes.

"Who did you say gave you the kitten?" Tahto asked, "It is a lovely prize. Most rare around these inland parts."

"A bookseller. She had the most amazing manuscripts, even Arabic ones. She could not sell us one because they were too expensive. She had come to sell all of them to someone prearranged. But she gave us the cats. Natan has one too, the boy, we think. We were going to have babies and sell them, but Mosse says that after their first litter, we would have to eliminate all the other female kittens; otherwise, they would populate quite thoroughly by themselves. So, after we sell the first litter, we are just going to let them."

"Ah. Yes." Tahto nodded. "Where we grew up, on an island, the cats had populated so thoroughly that every household had several, and more survived unaided on forage. It became a problem for they hunted the local fauna."

"What did you do?" Achtriel asked, not sure that she wanted to know.

"We gave many to the merchants. Cats live happily the shipboard life and keep the vessels free of rats."

"Yes. I remember now." Nimrode nodded. "There were a great many of them, were there not before the..."

"Yes, yes," Tahto cut his brother short.

"Before what?" Achtriel asked. The men exchanged looks.

"There was a famine when we were besieged by the Byzantines," Nimrode said.

"Oh. Yes, I remember," Achtriel said and frowned. "Then I suppose people ate them. How awful."

"I'm afraid so," Nimrode admitted, "although Tahto and I refused."

"Why?" Achtriel asked.

"Well, we do not eat flesh, as our scriptures tell us, but had I not took ship I might have come to that." Nimrode looked unhappy.

"I wondered if you would succumb to that after I left."

"At first, I was able to earn a small living at the synagogue. Enough to feed the rabbis and myself. But as time went on, there simply was no food to be had. Had not the pirates offered me a berth, I might have starved. But they seldom lacked for food."

"Pirates?"

"Oh yes, that they were. And a clever lot. They knew the seas and coasts like none else and used this knowledge as a form of barter. Even though the siege had cut us off, the pirates slipped round to the island's back to sell food to the wealthy. I happened to be walking there one day and spotted them. I begged them to employ me, and they very kindly did.

"What was it like?" Achtriel asked, her eyes widening.

"Oh, be careful brother." Tahto chuckled. "This child, once she has sniffed a single grain of information in your keeping, will not let you rest until you have spilled the whole barrel."

"I will tell you all about my nefarious past." He winked at her. "But later. Now I wish to…"

"But what happened to the others? The ones left behind."

"Well, the siege as always proved successful. The isle surrendered. But even then, the Byzantines choked off our business, and our people were forced to work for them or starve. In the end, food is the victor. I imagine the cats knew that already."

"How many creatures live for sustenance alone? It is a jealous lord," Tahto observed.

"There are people in the Far East," Nimrode said brightly, "who go without food for many months. Sometimes years!"

"No, they cannot do that." Achtriel shook her head. "You think that I am gullible."

"But in fact they do or claim to do so," he insisted, "Indeed, they look like bones encased in meager flesh, so if they do not live on nothing, it is near to that."

"But why?" Achtriel asked, puzzled. She took a bite of bread and held it in her mouth before she chewed it. What would it feel like never to eat? She swallowed the bread, grateful for its savory warmth. "Do not their insides shrivel?"

"These people say that they live on contemplation of the Divine."

"I don't believe they can live on nothing. Perhaps they die, just after you have seen them," she reasoned, chewing her bread.

"You may be right," Nimrode admitted, amused.

"Or perhaps they are like some frogs and bugs who curl into seeds until a rainy year. But if they are awake and walk about…"

"Oh, they are as spry as sparrows," he assured her. "They heal the sick and counsel magistrates to circumvent their wars."

"Then why could not the islanders have stood the siege and let the cats alone?"

Nimrode looked startled then sat back in his seat and laughed. "I see she is as quick as you say," he said to Tahto.

"Oh, but ever more so." Tahto wiped his beard to clean it. "She taught my Greek and Latin scholars when I was taken ill." Nimrode and Berthe regarded Achtriel with new respect. Even Tirzah ceased her observations of the wall to glance at her. Those unearthly features formed into a new expression. One of suspicion.

After dinner had been cleared and the dishes cleaned, Tahto and Nimrode went to his study.

"Tirzah will be sleeping with you," Berthe told Achtriel. "I have added wool to enlarge your bed."

"Of course," she said politely but wondered if she could feel safe enough to fall asleep. There was something of the animal about that girl, a Cerberean quality. She would not make a pleasant bed-mate.

When the kitchen was cleaned, Achtriel began to feel very tired. She glanced at Tirzah uncertainly. The girl seemed to have no interest in sleep or as little as her interest for all things. She was sitting idly at the table beside Berth who sewed by candlelight. Achtriel thus went alone to her room, thankful to be by herself. She put on her night clothes and located her doll, whom Macha had thoughtfully stationed on the wooden chest. Rael looked really much bedraggled, and she wondered if Tirzah had interfered with her.

Remembering that Tahto valued generosity, she stifled her annoyance at the thought and, holding Rael in a firm embrace curled up on the bed. Although she was exhausted from her journey, it became impossible to sleep. After some discomfited hours, Tirzah came into the room and stretched out flat beside her. It was like sharing the bed with an icicle.

Nonetheless, she must have slept for she woke at daybreak to the choir of birds. She turned to look at Tirzah who lay unbent as if in a tomb. In sleep, the girl's face was not quite so frightening. A dream of some emotive content must have broken through her masque. Her forehead was pursed in fear or confusion. A tiny cry escaped her lips.

Achtriel slipped from behind her and out of bed, relieved to see the girl had not awoken. Now she could have her world to herself, if only temporarily. She scanned her room. Berthe and Macha had been thorough, and things were not as she had left them, scattered and familiar. She could not get Macha to understand that when things were put away, she never could find anything. And now Berthe would doubtless impose unending order.

And indeed the woman now peered into the room. "Good morning, girls!" she said and woke the sleeping dragon. Tirzah's features lost whatever pliancy they'd held in sleep and hardened to their usual frostiness. She looked up at Berthe and then with some alarm at Achtriel. "Good morning, dear," Berthe said, gently for Tirzah seemed confused, momentarily, and anxious.

"Good morning," she replied dully and looked around the room as if to get her bearings.

"Come and help me make some bread," Berthe said, smiling. "In three days is the Sabbath, and we must be prepared." Tirzah glanced at Achtriel, a fellow servant's scrutiny perhaps.

"We can make food on the Sabbath," Achtriel offered. "We do not follow every law."

"Oh yes, I know this." Berthe laughed. "I meant only that we must prepare well for that dinner. There will be a large gathering in honor of Fagim and Mosse and to herald our arrival. We have much to do."

"We will wash and dress ourselves and come there shortly," Achtriel agreed and looked to Tirzah for confirmation. The girl's face showed only resentment, and something Achtriel could not define. The wish to stay asleep forever was what it seemed. Nevertheless, the girl rose and dressed herself in the worn but expensive garments she had worn the day before.

"I have many clothes there in the trunk," Achtriel said pleasantly. "People give them to me for…"

"No, thank you," Tirzah said.

Achtriel opened her trunk and found some work clothes for herself. The girl did not even glance in her direction. Her face was as inert as a stone. Nonetheless, she followed Achtriel out to the kitchen.

The cat awoke as they passed and jumped from its perch to prance beside them. Achtriel went through the kitchen to the back door and opened it to look out at the day. It was cold, and would likely rain. This would be an early winter. The garden vines were spent and shriveled. Only some root vegetables had survived.

The cat bounded eagerly out the door and then stopped, astonished, it seemed, by the coldness on its feet. Nonetheless, it began to explore, sniffing daintily at the weeds.

Achtriel, picking up the little cat, went toward the washhouse. Tirzah followed her, looking disgusted, but seeming to have resigned herself to such indignities. Achtriel could not tell which was more comical, the cats discomfiture at icy ground or Tirzah's shock at the coldness of the wash-bowl water. Neither, perhaps, was finding this home as they expected, although the cat was clearly the more eager to acquaint itself.

"It will be warm later, when the sun is high," Achtriel offered.

"But it will still be filthy," Tirzah muttered, looking at the water.

Achtriel was shocked. This water was much cleaner than that in Rodom. She herself refilled the basin many times a day. There were no traces of bracken or foul odor in their well. Even at the Hildebard's, the water had had a sulpherous smell. What had this girl been used to?

She found cause to wonder this on more occasions throughout the morning. Tirzah did not know how to prepare dough and had to be instructed at each step. She did not appear to recognize simple cooking utensils, did not know the difference between bread or butter knives, or between brooms and mops, bowls and cups, ladles and soup spoons. Neither could she distinguish between dulce and grain, wheat and rye.

At first, Achtriel assumed the words were unfamiliar. But she realized that Berthe was speaking them in Greek, the language in which this girl had ostensibly been raised. At one point, when Berthe had left the kitchen, it was necessary to remind Tirzah to cleanse her hands before kneading the loaves. "I know! I am not stupid!" she hissed. It was but another curiosity of the girl's odd background. She had found clean country water filthy yet did not know simple rules of health.

When morning preparations were completed and the bread was in the hearth, Berthe suggested that the girls go for a walk. At the mention of this, Tirzah paled; but seeing Achtriel had noticed this, she shrugged her acquiescence. Their clothes were covered now with flour, so she led Tirzah back to the bedroom.

"Take whatever clothes you like," she offered. The girl approached the trunk with some minor interest, the first thing to elicit some response.

Not wishing to embarrass Tirzah with her own habitual disregard for fashion, Achtriel chose a matching kirtle and smock. Tirzah, however, chose a filmy festive gown, worn at someone's wedding or bar mitzvah feast. She did not seem to find it inappropriate for potentially rainy day, so Achtriel said nothing.

Heading toward town, however, it seemed the girl must reckon her mistake. Everyone they passed was wearing working clothes or simple tunics. People stopped and stared at her and watched them pass. Children laughed at them, and one group of urchins ran to block their passage.

"Look, the princess and her dwarf have come to town," a boy said loudly.

"Go away, you smell like rotten eggs," Achtriel retorted. His companions made as if to throw dirt at them, but she hurried Tirzah past.

"Who are they?" Tirzah asked when they were safely away.

"The children of the town."

"Why do they speak so to you?"

Achtriel found it curious that Tirzah had not included herself as an object of ridicule. "They have always done so and will do so, I'm afraid, until I die."

"For what reason?" she inquired.

"I am deformed," Achtriel said quietly, amazed that it should need to be explained.

"But is not this common?"

"Not here. Was it common in the city you come from?"

"I would not know such things," Tirzah replied.

Achtriel longed to question her more. How could she be so ignorant? Did she not go out into the world? Was she of a rich family? But even such girls went about in litters and observed the city. What kind of person lived for years in a metropolis and would not know such things? Something told her not to ask, however. Perhaps it was the distant look that fell on Tirzah's features after she had spoken.

"I am cold," she then announced and turned back toward the house. Achtriel followed her reluctantly. Didn't she know that if they went back home, they would have to work all day? But it was clear that if this girl wished not to speak, there would be no point in asking.

Later that morning, however, curiosity inspired her to try. They had finished chopping vegetables, and the beans were in to soak. Berthe asked if they could go out again for milk.

"We would have to go into town," Achtriel said, looking sideways at Tirzah. The girl glanced up, uncomfortable. Berthe seemed to understand her reluctance and offered to fetch the milk herself. She instructed Achtriel and Tirzah to clean and wash down the kitchen in her absence. This became a tiresome task because it required explanation at every step. Tirzah did not know that fire boiled water, that lye was dangerous, that a mop must be wrung out.

"Did you have a mother?" Achtriel asked delicately. Tirzah was kneeling, ineffectually dragging a rag, long overdue for rinsing, over the floor. At first, she made no move to answer. Then she said, "I am told that I did."

"Do you remember her?"

"No."

"I had one for a day or two, but I know nothing of her," Achtriel said.

"Why?" Tirzah regarded her with a kind of distant curiosity.

"She left me in Tahto's alley when I was a few days old."

Tirzah returned to her scrubbing. "Mine gave me over to the care of her friend."

"Why?"

"She died."

Achtriel opened her mouth but saw from Tirzah's fierce expression that their talk had reached its end. When they were done with the kitchen, Tirzah went into the bedroom and lay down.

"Are you unwell?" Achtriel inquired, hurrying after her.

"No," she said and turned her face toward the wall.

When Berthe came back, Achtriel ran to tell her that Tirzah was in bed. Berthe only nodded and did not seem concerned. Achtriel was stunned. Was lying down in the day a custom where they came from? She had only known it to be done when one was ill or giving birth. She was trying to think how best to broach this, and many other topics, when Berthe spoke loudly.

"I have ordered some cloth from Profait, can you fetch it for me?" she asked. Although framed as a request it clearly wasn't. "I have had him put it in two sacks so you and Natan can carry them back. Here is payment." She reached into her bodice and pulled out a leathern pouch. When she counted out the purchase price, Achtriel was startled to see gold and silver coins, inlaid ivory, and several exotic jewels. Seeing her surprise, Berthe explained, "We were wealthy you see in Constantinople. I came from a rich family, and when I married your uncle, we lived very well."

"Why did you leave then?" Achtriel asked, but Berthe was musing.

"We had a Roman villa, baths and gardens, many servants. They were slaves originally of course, but your uncle taught me this was sinful, and we gave them all their freedom. Many Jews in Byzantium do this you see, but usually, the family requires that the slaves become Jews also. We did not care what worship they professed. Our servants practiced Gnostic meditations, rites for Ahura Mazda, Christ, and all the gods from Africa and many other lands… It was fascinating. I have thought myself to write about the different practices, now that I have the time."

"Why did you not have time then, if you were rich?"

Berthe smiled. "Even wealth does not bequeath a leisure life for women, child. We are responsible for everything and everyone within our households. There is the cultivation of the crops to oversee, the market fluctuations governing their sale, the upbringing and education of the staff and their children, the entertainments, the husbanding of all resources.

There are marriages and births and illnesses and deaths that all must be attended to. I had a staff of doctors, much the best in the city, I'm told, and studying with them, scholars, philosophers, medical students. It was a very lively place!"

"But lots of work for you."

"Oh yes. But work I loved."

"Then why did you…"

"Such things are over, and we will not dwell on them today," Berthe said, cinching the coin purse. "Here is the payment; I would have given more for they are expecting a child, but we must use caution now, our funds are limited." Berthe handed Achtriel a tsimissis and watched as she secured it in her money belt. "Natan is waiting for you. Hurry now for he has other work to do for Mosse."

Achtriel did hurry to the best of her ability but could not shake the suspicion that Berthe had wanted to be rid of her. After all, Natan was almost fifteen and was tall and strong. He certainly did not need her help to carry a few parcels. It must have something to do with Tirzah, but what? These people from the east were very odd, she concluded. It was both intriguing and a bit disturbing to have them under her roof.

Natan was also curious about her houseguests. On their walk back to her house, Achtriel told him what she could. "There is much I do not know, and no one seems inclined to tell me. Most mysterious is that girl, Tirzah. A denizen of some strange other world it seems."

Natan stopped walking and stood before her, all insistent inquiry. "All I know is what I've told you. If she were a *naiad* or a *chayot*, it would not surprise me." Natan gestured insistently at his face and body. "I have told you several times, Natan, she is more beautiful than anyone you can imagine," Achtriel sighed impatiently. "She makes your Violette look like a boar."

Natan grew angry at this, as Achtriel had hoped he would, and asked no further questions. When they reached the house, however, he came in, set down the parcels, and began to peer about as if for treasure.

"Tirzah is resting now," said Berthe, guessing his motivation. "When you come for Sabbath, she will welcome you." Natan's face blanched, and he nodded with embarrassment. Then shooting Achtriel an angry look, he left the house.

"Is this material for Fagim's wedding clothes?" Achtriel asked, "I can help you with them."

"Yes. We shall all need some finery for that, and we have not much time to make it. I will need your help with it all I'm sure," Berthe told her.

"Does Tirzah know how to make clothing?" she asked slyly, already knowing the answer.

"No," Berthe answered. "But she is interested to learn, and you and I shall help her with that." Achtriel could have expressed some doubt about Tirzah's willingness, but she did not.

"For now, however, you may go and play. Where is your kitten? I think she needs some company. By the way I do not think you will need to fear the predators. The trees are thick and the crows set up such a racket, just now, when they spotted one that your clever cat ran into the house. By the time the leaves have thinned she will have grown large."

"Thank you. But what about my students and my classes? They will be here this afternoon."

"We decided to cancel them for a while until things get organized."

"But what about the money?"

"Don't worry. Nimrode and I can help out for a few months. Then you can resume classes."

"Oh," Achtriel was not sure whether to be angry or thrilled. But she liked the idea of a free afternoon and went to find her kitten. She discovered it chasing moths in the garden. At least this creature had no secrets but seemed delighted to be noticed and ran eagerly to her. She decided to name the kitten *Sachela* from the Hebrew for native sense. It was clear that this cat was the female. She had made herself immediately useful, as women did. It was as if she knew already that this was her home.

Sachela followed her back to the house. As Achtriel crept warily into her room to find her doll, the kitten followed, much intrigued by the stealth required. Tirzah lay on the bed, as if she had not moved since this morning. Achtriel found Rael and quickly left. Then she and Sachela spent the rest of the morning companionably in the garden.

When it came time to make the midday meal, Achtriel washed up and came inside. There she found Berthe and Tirzah in the kitchen. They were discussing something in furtive tones and stopped as soon as Achtriel came toward them. "I am teaching Tirzah to inspect the greens for insects, would you like to show her how you do it?" Berthe asked brightly.

"I am not as thorough as some people," Achtriel admitted. "If the bugs are too small to be seen easily, I just forget about them."

Tirzah looked horrified and took the greens from Berthe's hands. "I can do it," she said with a haughty glance. It dawned on Achtriel that this could be a helpful tactic in enlisting Tirzah's interest. If she herself appeared incompetent, the girl would be inspired to learn, if only to best her.

Obviously, she saw things as a competition. But why on earth? How little she must be aware of the worth of her unworldly beauty. And what was there worth fighting for in this house? After the meal as they sat around the table, Berthe suggested that the two girls take a little walk.

"Are there wild beasts?" Tirzah asked her quietly.

"They don't come into town," Achtriel explained.

"Why not?"

"The dogs would set on them, or townsfolk fire arrows at them. Besides the woodlands are their home, and they do not like to leave there. Only sick and injured wild things come into the town. Bears and wolves and foxes wait about the farms to steal the livestock, but they are too smart to show their faces here. The only wild animals in town are birds and smaller rodents, and they cannot hurt us." Tahto was looking at her with approval, so she stood and looked at Tirzah with an inviting smile. Tirzah looked at Berthe and rose out of her chair, whether from boredom or embarrassment it was hard to tell. Nonetheless, she followed Achtriel outside.

"Where shall we go?" Achtriel offered. "There are markets set up in town. They sell all kinds of useful things and sometimes pretty ones."

"What kinds of pretty ones?" Tirzah asked, looking askance as if for predators.

"Ribbon, dyed cloth, embroidery." Tirzah did not reply so Achtriel took this for acquiescence. As they walked over the foot-bridge, Tirzah slowed for Achtriel to stay beside her. Was this an indication of a nascent friendliness? "Do you like it here?" Achtriel asked.

Tirzah looked annoyed. Then she answered, "It is fine."

"Is it like your home, the land you come from?"

"Not at all," she frowned and said no more.

In town, the merchant's booths were up, circled by afternoon shoppers, wives who would prolong their absences from home as long as possible. Tirzah looked about with mild curiosity but made no move to venture closer.

"Come, I know some of the merchants; I will introduce you," Achtriel told her.

"No, no," Tirzah objected. "I do not want to know them. Or others."

"But if you are to live here for a while, it will be lonely not to know anyone."

"What have I to say to them?"

"It doesn't matter what you say. The point is simply to be friendly."

"I am not friendly," she stated flatly.

"Watch me," Achtriel said and walked up to her friends the baker and the tart girl.

"It's the child, the drawing girl!" Duggan exclaimed. "Where have ye been, miss?"

"My grandpa was ill, and then I went to Rouen with Fagim and Mosse."

"Oo, a grand traveler she is. What is in Rouen, I have never been there."

"A lot of merchants and a lot of people," Achtriel replied. "This is Tirzah; she has come to stay with us."

"Holy Bridhe, child, aren't you the pretty one?" Duggan said admiringly. "Like a nymph, she is, or a fairy." Other shoppers had noticed Tirzah as well and stood agape until their manners bade them look away.

"Tirzah is from the east. She traveled here by boat," Achtriel said and turned to see that Tirzah's face had turned a redder shade of amber.

"Oh, you must come sit with us tomorrow day!" Margit insisted. "We want to know about your voyage. That is the closest us will ever get to a sea or a ride upon it."

"Perhaps one day if I am wealthy, I will buy a boat and take you there," Achtriel said.

"Then be about it!" laughed Duggan. "Why do you not bring your drawing cloth and draw here as you did at the fair?"

"That was parchment. It was a gift, and I have used it up. I do not know where to get more."

"I imagine such things are all easy to be had in Eastern cities?" Duggan said to Tirzah.

"Riches we could never dream of," speculated Margit.

There was a silence. "Riches are there," Tirzah spoke at last. "And are much valued. More than the people who would own them."

The bakers nodded. "True as not I would imagine," Duggan agreed. "More than us like to be sure."

"Come out tomorrow day. Sit by with us," the younger girl repeated. She was not much older than Tirzah.

"Thank you. We will try to do it," Achtriel replied for her and waved to them as she and Tirzah walked away. The townsfolk turned self-consciously back to conversations that had faltered as they stared at Tirzah. All the men and many women kept watching her over the shoulders of their cronies. It was as if a queen walked by. But Tirzah was intent upon her inner thoughts and did not seem to notice. Nonetheless, she seemed slightly less miserable.

The next morning dawned warm and sunny. Such a day had not been seen since midsummer and seemed like a gift. Achtriel sat up and smelled the air. Sachela, who had slept on top of her, sprang deftly off the bed. This woke Tirzah who, in spite of her usual sour temperament, sat up and looked about.

"It is beautiful," Achtriel told her excitedly. "And the bread and stew are made for Sabbath meal tomorrow, and nothing is left for us to do!" Tirzah did not reply, but neither did she lie back down and sleep.

"What is that noise?" she frowned.

"The birds. They wake each other up like this at dawn. Let's go out to see them!"

"The beasts…" she said uncertainly.

"They are all in the woods. Let's go!" Achtriel's excitement seemed to have some pull on Tirzah, for she did rise and sit up. Achtriel lifted the trunk lid to remove some clothes and stifled a laugh as Sachela raised her paws to the side of the trunk and tried to jump inside it. She picked up the kitten and closed the lid as silently as possible.

The common room was quiet as they crept through it. They could hear Tahto snoring in his den, and his brother doing likewise in the other bedroom. The kitchen, still spotless from their earlier work, sparkled; and the stew pot simmering on the hearth spit smelled wonderful.

Outside the ground was warmer. On the way to the washhouse, Sachela scampered off to chase a dragonfly.

"We can go and look about and visit with the bakers," Achtriel whispered as they hurried to the washhouse. "They will give us breakfast!" she explained excitedly and splashed wash water on her face.

"I do not want to go there," Tirzah said.

"Why? Do you not like them? They are very friendly."

"No. I like them. It is the others."

"Oh, the townsfolk are just rude," she said, drying her face on her nightshirt. But once they get to know you, they will be better."

"Like those awful children?"

"Pay no mind to them. On days like this, their venom cannot harm me. Besides we are together. We can laugh at them."

"I do not find them amusing."

"Nor do I. But they use derision as a weapon and so can we. I cannot do that when I'm by myself."

"Are you sure it's safe?"

"Of course. No one will harm us. It's the law." Tirzah considered this information and at last washed and dried her face. "I brought clean clothes for us." Achtriel proffered a dress she'd hoped the girl would not object to. It was the most ornate one she could find. She donned her own rough garment eagerly and rushed out to the yard. The air was like some kind of music; a kind you could smell. "Let's go!" she cried. Tirzah emerged from the washhouse, looking celestial. "I have no shoes," she said.

"We don't need them today, the earth is warm." Tirzah looked at the dirt and stepped uncertainly onto it. The ground was wet, and her feet sank in the mud. She looked horrified, but Achtriel laughed and began to walk and soon, from pride or defiance, Tirzah followed. Her every step seemed to be a further resignation to fate. But by the time they reached the river bridge, they had become brisker and more careless. She turned and waited for Achtriel's slower pace.

"This is where they grow the food?" she asked when Achtriel caught up to her.

"Yes."

"Why are so many fields overgrown?"

"It is because they leave some plots to fallow every year, so the land will thrive."

"It is stronger if it is left alone?"

"Yes," Achtriel said. "It must rest, like us."

"It must have its Sabbath."

"Yes!" she replied delighted with the analogy. "And the field hands feed it a rich supper of manure and rotting waste." Tirzah looked so sickened that Achtriel had to laugh.

"You are trying to fool me," Tirzah stated suddenly and stopped walking. Then she turned back toward home.

"No! No, it is true!" Achtriel cried, hurrying to overtake her. "The land is strengthened by these things and can grow richer food. And nothing is useless to it, all that dies or rots, especially from animals, it uses to bring new strength, new life." Tirzah turned back toward the road and scanned the fields uncertainly. "Is that why they bury the dead in it?"

"Yes, I suppose it is. So their bodies, which they do not need, can bring health to the plant life."

"It is so..." Tirzah faltered.

"What?" Achtriel asked as they resumed walking.

"It is so much different than I thought. They must have thought us idiots to frighten with fairy tales. None of it true."

"Who told you fairy tales?" she asked but knew even as she did that she would get no answer.

When they reached the town, the market stalls were up and doing business. The bakers smiled delightedly at them behind their customers, and Margit waved them forward.

"You've come!" she cried when some shoppers left, laden with fragrant rolls and loaves of bread. "Now we can keep company and make the long day shorter."

"And your beauty," exclaimed Duggan, shaking her head with disbelief, "such loveliness will bring us custom all the day."

Seeing the darkening expression on Tirzah's face, Margit insisted, "But that's not why we asked you!"

"Oh no, love. We don't care if you are a queen or a crone, for our part, if you are pleasant company. But first things first. My name is Duggen, and this, my niece, is Margit. I've brought her up since she was wee, her folks was killed by brigands."

"This is Tirzah. And we are orphans all!" Achtriel exclaimed.

"Ah, do I wish it." Duggen sighed. "My old ones live with me and run me round like a drudge. These hours at my stall are the finest of my day."

"But I help you, Aunt," Margit said.

"Yes, my child, without you, I'd have fed them poisoned mushrooms long ago. No matter that the preacher tells us to honor our parents."

"How can we help you?" Achtriel asked, knowing she did not have beauty, but only its opposite, to offer them.

"My dough has risen, girls, and needs a pounding. Who wants to give it blows?" Duggen asked them.

"We will do it!" Achtriel offered and led Tirzah to the floured board behind them.

"Why does it need to be beaten?" Tirzah asked her in a whisper. But Duggen heard her and called out.

"It is like the kind of man who thinks too high of himself," she said.

"If we did not chasten him, he would grow till he bursts!" Margit added, and they all laughed at this. By the time the dough had risen twice, the morning sun was high, and they were in similarly healthy spirits.

They spent a lovely morning baking bread on their outdoor oven and selling it. The bakers taught them ways to spice the dough with herbs and buttermilk to flavor it. When noontime came, they sat beneath a tree and sampled their work.

"How do you like the anise?" Duggen asked. "It is my invention and seems to now be popular."

"It's…interesting," Achtriel offered, and Tirzah said, "It tastes like something which the Hindu women bake."

"I think it's horrid," Margit said. "What d'you think of my creation here!" she handed them some convoluted rolls of puffy dough as soft as cake but with more bite to it.

"Delicious!" both the girls agreed.

"I'll show you how to make them later. You roll the dough out thin, see, and lay it with butter. And the rolls stay fresh for days, if ever they do last that long!"

"These I'm sure will not," said Achtriel eating hers.

"I don't suppose you've heard the news since you've been long away," said Duggen slyly.

"About your friend, the red lady," Margit raised her eyebrows.

"The woman who gave me parchment? What has happened?"

"Well," Duggan began, obviously warming to her story, "the Lords and all their drunken lot made use of her. And then she came up with child. Now this is not so strange and all but what happened later is."

"Naturally she went back into the woods, they say, back with all her sorcerors and thieves," Margit added, not without a hint of disdain.

"And then the truly interesting thing. One lord went off to find her. Rode out one day and has not since returned!" She looked from one to the other as if even now she could not believe it.

"What royal man would leave his beds and mead, and all his comfort to go to find a whore?" Margit scoffed.

"Perhaps he loved her," Achtriel surmised.

"If so, he would have set her up and kept her."

"Perhaps she refused," Tirzah said.

"Well, he must have been a horrid lout for her to turn down riches!" Duggen laughed.

"If it were me, I would have taken all his gold before I run away, but they say she had none," Margit said. "First, his men thought she robbed him and that he went to get his goods. But they found she never taken anything, but he had neither. He went off with but the clothes on his back."

"What a mystery," Achtriel said, "I hope they come back soon so we will know what happened."

"Them she lives with rarely come to town. They live in some strange forest place," Margit said, "They like to keep their secrets."

"Perhaps he did try to leave her tribe and return, but they have killed him!" Achtriel said with widening eyes.

"He would've taken his weapons. That I know!" Duggen said,

"Yes, but witches have no fear of blades and arrows, do they, when they have their conjury," Margit said, catching Achtriel's excitement.

"Well, let us hope he does survive or his cronies will punish us." Duggen sighed. "Even now they want to raise the tax beyond the means of any poor man."

"There are not many of them surely," Achtriel said mysteriously.

"What d'you mean?" Margit gasped.

"Our folk could take them in the night, and none would be the wiser."

"Ooh, you are a wicked child," Duggen cackled.

"I would fight them," Margit declared.

"Girls, I say we talk no more of this," Duggen told them quietly. "If the wealthies heard us, they would have our heads."

"How would they hear us?" Achtriel asked. "Do they often come to town?"

"No. But they send their slaves to shop, and that is not the only danger."

"What is it then?" Tirzah asked fearfully.

Duggen looked around then crouched to shield her next words. "They've got spies about," she whispered. "That old priest is one and so's the jongleur."

"Which one, it would not be Frans!" Achtriel protested.

"Ah no. The dwarf's as good a one as any in this town, and much the better."

"Not Naadasya either."

"Of course not. All he does is hearten us with music. It's the other one."

"I do not know who that would be."

"He's over there." Margit indicated with her head a grinning fellow, accosting passersby with juggling tricks and somersaults.

"I've never seen him here before," Achtriel said.

"He came in with the fair and never left us," Margit said. "He plies our customers with jokes and dirty tales for which he then demands coin. When they get to us, they can't afford no more than crust."

"He bothers your friends too, I hear, and steals their business."

"Frans and Naadasya?"

"Them and that fine pretty girl of his."

"Do you mean Esther?" Achtriel asked, shocked.

"Why yes. Where have ye been? Oh, right, you was busy with your grandpa and then out of town," Margit remembered. "They say those two would wed except the priest won't let them."

"Say's they're heathens," Duggen said sarcastically.

"That priest," said Achtriel, "I saw him drunk carousing with the whores the night of festival."

"Hush now," Duggen told her. "I would not want your grandfather to see you know such words. He'd say we taught you."

"No, he wouldn't," she protested but rephrased her words. "I saw him doing most unchurchly things with those women from the woods."

"Are they common prostitutes?" asked Tirzah who till now had mostly listened, but attentively.

"They have different ways from us and from the rent girls of our town too," Duggen said. "They live free, have since ancient time. Speak a language older than Rome's, some say, and do spells unknown even to the local witches. But to be fair, they're decent folk as well. Have brought us food in times of famine and have doctoring skills."

"I know Fagim consulted with them when there was that plague some years ago," Achtriel agreed. "And that red-dressed one was keen to make amends for Sorgen. On the pageant's first night, the slave girl waylayed me, thinking I sought to take her place at the Hildebards."

"At least those doxies don't fancy themselves the gatekeeps of God, like the priest." Margit said. "He talks of fornication and yet..."

"Well, that's entirely too much talk of this for young ones," Duggan interrupted her. "We'll speak of better things now. That jongleur's not the only one who can caper. I say we put on some entertainment of our own. What say you pretty girls go about him and dance."

"No," said Tirzah, suddenly pale. After a short silence she said quietly, "I will never dance again." They all looked at her but no one could think of anything to say.

By the end of the day, it could have been supposed that a miracle had occurred. Tirzah, while not precisely friendly, was entering in conversations and adding her opinions. At one point, she even smiled at something Margit whispered in her ear. Achtriel was surprised to find herself jealous of this intimacy. Perhaps Tirzah had been so cold because she knew a crippled girl was not worth noticing.

But something told her it was simply that Margit was closer in age to her, and that Tirzah had begun to feel more comfortable. When the sun descended in the sky, they bade the bakers a warm farewell and promised to come back after the Sabbath.

The next morning, everyone in Tahto's home was cheerful. Tahto, himself, seemed another man, now that their house was full of lively people. He had always enjoyed witty conversation, and Berthe and Nimrode both excelled at this. The atmosphere affected Achtriel and Tirzah too. They spent the day, if not amicably, at least in a companionable comfort. They spoke little, but it did not seem to matter.

Something had changed in Tirzah's outlook. That her coldness had begun to thaw was evident in subtle ways. She no longer looked discomfited when Achtriel approached or came into a room. Even her dour reveries had lessened in intensity. Once when Achtriel was playing with the kitten, Tirzah actually joined her and smiled, in spite of herself, at the creature's antics.

When dinnertime approached, Berthe instructed them to wash and change their clothes. "And Achtriel, put on something pretty for the Sabbath," she called after them. "Tirzah kindly see to that."

A further consequence of Tirzah's improved mood was her interest in the clothing trunk. Now she carefully removed each folded garment and inspected it. Then she refolded it, patting it onto its pile with a proprietary air." These garments are so simple," she remarked at last. "But some look well made."

"People give me all their outgrown things," Achtriel said, sitting on her bed. "Not wishing to embarrass themselves by revealing any shabbiness, they give me only what is fresh."

"And odd," Tirzah added, examining a dress made with lush materials but ineptly cut.

"I never notice what I wear." Achtriel shrugged.

"I see," Tirzah said, turning to look at her. "Well, today, you shall notice, and we will comb your hair besides."

"But I don't…" Achtriel began, but she was shushed. "Come," Tirzah said in a commanding tone.

"I can dress myself."

"Clearly. That has been the problem. Now come here" Chagrined, but amused by this sign of interest in her shy companion, Achtriel approached." Now. You have a pretty face."

"I do?"

"For a barbarian. Your eyes are very charming too." She held a dress to Achtriel's face and squinted at her. "Yes. Blue, I think, will suit you well. Here, put this on." She handed Achtriel a festive garment, something that a wealthy merchant's girl had worn to some lush occasion.

"I can't wear that!" Achtriel scoffed.

"Of course you can. Now put it on."

"But it's…"

"Does the helot contradict?"

"You are not my master!"

"In this case, I am." She gave Achtriel a gentle shove and motioned for her to obey. Groaning, Achtriel put on the dress and turned around to be inspected.

"Very nice," Tirzah proclaimed officiously. "Now where is your comb?"

"I do not know."

"Well, find it then. And hurry up about it."

Feeling like a costumed dramatist, Achtriel poked about her room. The comb, unfortunately, was atop the dresser, placed there prominently by Macha.

"Come then," Tirzah beckoned, as if there were no other option. Achtriel gave her the comb and stood to have her hair attended to.

"That hurts," she objected as Tirzah pulled painfully at tangles.

"Next time, it will hurt much less."

"Next time? Ouch!"

"Yes."

Achtriel winced as her head was tormented. Having a sister, one who styled herself a slave owner no less, was beginning to seem a bad idea. A plan began to form in her mind. She would wake tomorrow and every other day before this slavedriver arose. She would take food for the day and return to the woods. She would stay in her private lair until it was time to resume teaching. At last her hair ministrations neared an end.

"There," said Tirzah turning Achtriel's combed and braided head to and fro as if she were contriving a painting. "Now I'll show you how to walk."

"I walk the only way I can!" she protested.

"Precisely. And you can do it better." She made Achtriel walk across the room and studied every step. "You sway too much," she commented. "Now. Let me see your hip."

"No!" Achtriel backed away.

235

"Come here. I have seen worse sights."

Like a calf presented for branding, Achtriel approached and lifted up her skirt.

"Step on your foot and let me see." Tirzah commanded.

"Why?" If she went to bed earlier each night, it would be easy to wake before dawn and stay away until nighttime.

"Now, watch how I put down my foot," Tirzah instructed. Despite herself, Achtriel observed the girl's technique. By slightly shifting her weight to the other leg, it seemed she might achieve a smoother gait. "Now you shall practice every eve and morn, and by the end of a month, you will sway much less." By month's end, Achtriel planned to have completed a hut for herself so she could sleep in the forest.

"Let me see you, girls," Berthe came in to the room and stopped short. "Why Achtriel! You seem a different person!"

"I'm not," she said gloomily.

"Tirzah, you have made a miracle. Tahto, come here!" Berthe hurried to the common room. Soon, Tahto and Nimrode too were standing in her doorway.

"Achtriel!" Tahto exclaimed warmly.

"My gracious, you have made a princess of her," Nimrode said approvingly to Tirzah.

"Tirzah's gifts are many. We know so little of them yet." Berthe smiled and went to finish dinner preparations.

"Well, clearly she can spin gold thread from chaff," Nimrode remarked.

"You have accomplished what few have dared attempt," Tahto agreed. Tirzah bowed humbly but clearly, self-congratulation was uppermost in her thoughts. It was infuriating. When Tahto and his brother left to wash themselves for Sabbath, Achtriel could bear no more. She flung herself facedown onto the bed.

"You will learn to like it," Tirzah said and left the room.

A maelstrom of emotions, tears of rage and protest, overcame her. They had all conspired in her humiliation. She knew well she would never be like other girls. And so did they. They only praised her out of pity.

And more alarming was the sense that this new state of things, with Tirzah in command, was destined to continue. Now there would be someone to instruct her, insisting on obedience. Worse than Macha. Now her time would be constrained in countless ways that she did not desire.

And Tahto, even Tahto, would not rescue her. Their time of freedom as a happy pair, sufficient to themselves was gone forever. And more trying than that, if such a thing were possible, was the immediate necessity of being displayed. Before Natan and Mosse, Fagim, Naadasya, Esther, Frans, Profait, everyone. How would she endure it? By the time Berthe called her in for the Sabbath meal, her plan for moving to the woods was nearing completion.

She came into the common room furtively, hoping to find an unlit corner. Nadaasya and Esther were there, greeting Nimrode and Berthe and inquiring about their voyage. Then Naadasya turned around and saw her. His eyes went wide and became merry. But then he looked more closely at her face. He turned back to the conversation considerately, allowing her to find a shadow. The day was waning and without the candlelight, one corner was invisible. A haven at least for now.

Then Esther turned around. "Oh my goodness! Achtriel," she cried. They all turned to look at her as she sought the further reaches of the corner.

"Come here, child," Berthe said. "I want them to see what Tirzah has accomplished." Unwillingly, she stepped into the light.

"Why you look like a different girl," Esther said coming to Achtriel and turning her around. "And your braids are perfect! What was her secret?" Torture, Achtriel said, but to herself. "And look how lovely her hair is, golden in the light. Come closer."

"She looks as she has always done," Naadasya said. "She has always been beautiful."

"But now she is appropriately adorned," Esther said, smiling.

"How do you like it?" Nadaasya asked her.

"It's fine," she mumbled. Thankfully, the door now opened, and Mosse and Fagim came in. Natan was not with them. God was kind in this at least.

"Hello, hello," Mosse greeted everyone. He did not notice Achtriel and engaged the others in some cheerful conversation. Fagim, however, turned around and said, "Brilliant. And who has brought this butterfly out of its casing?"

"It was our ward, Tirzah. Tirzah, come out of the kitchen and meet our guests." Tirzah came into the room and bowed politely. There was stunned silence for a moment.

"Aphrodite," Naadasya said.

"She is not only beautiful but wise as well," Berthe said, beckoning the girl to join the circle.

"Where are you from, child?" Esther asked.

"Constantinople," she replied.

"She came to us last year at December," Nimrode explained, "and has been with us since. When we left our home..." his face darkened briefly, "she came with us. Here to this great city."

Everyone chuckled at his sarcasm.

"It is indeed the greater for your advent," Mosse told him. "Now we shall have two great scholars."

"I'm afraid I am no Tahto," Nimrode said. "He was always the shining star."

"Well, thank God you are here to help him," Fagim said. "He needs someone who does not live up in the clouds to help him manage the quotidian." Achtriel felt her stomach seize at Fagim's statement. Would Nimrode soon replace her as Tahto's aide? And now they had Tirzah, a beauty and an artist. What use could such a household have for a cripple?

Just then, the door opened, and Natan walked in. His face was tanned from the past bright days. He looked older somehow. Even his style of dress was neater. He looked at Tirzah for a moment, like a mariner shading his eyes at daybreak. Then he glanced away quickly.

"This is my son, Natan," Fagim said to the new arrivals. "He is apprenticed to an artisan who tells me he will go far."

"Where are Samiel and Profait?" Mosse said. "Are they in Tahto's study and both their noses in a book?"

"Profait cannot come because his wife is having pains," Esther said.

"Already?" Fagim looked worried.

"She is only ending her seventh month," Esther said. "Most likely, these pains will subside. But Profait felt he must stay with her."

When Tahto and Samiel emerged from his study, they seemed surprised but very pleased to see visitors." Ah, you have come already," Tahto said delightedly.

"It is sundown," Nimrode told him.

"Yes, but the travels of these earthly orbs have little meaning for him," Esther teased.

"Untrue. I simply was involved in reading and forgot the time," Tahto said. "A most interesting manuscript I received last year. I had not looked at it till now, but it is fascinating. A lost text by Lucretius. One of the great humanists of the ancient world."

"Well, now, we shall be fascinated by my cooking," Berthe said. "Although I did have assistance. From Tirzah and Achtriel, of course." From the corner to which she had retreated, Achtriel detected a tone of dismissal in Berthe's words. "Why 'Achtriel, of course'? Had they already begun to see her as a lesser being? Soon, Tahto would forget all about her. Now he had Nimrode to share ideas with.

Natan had been nonchalantly circling the room, as if in search of a lost button, but glancing up whenever he thought no one would notice to stare at Tirzah. Now he reached the corner where Achtriel was hiding and gave a squawk. Of course, he would be furious with her now. He would not have wanted Tirzah to know that he was deaf.

These noises were familiar to the town and to the folk who knew him, but she knew they embarrassed him nonetheless. Gaining his composure, Natan smiled. A mean smile, then he began to laugh at her.

No one noticed this. They were preparing to sit down at the table. But to Achtriel, his derision was a wounding blow. She felt the tears returning and struggled mightily to stop them. Now Natan was gesturing to say that she looked very nice. But she knew he only did it to so he would not be scolded. When next they met, he would tease her unmercifully.

She looked behind her at the door. Could she make it out in such a way that no one noticed? She would hurry at her fastest pace and leave this room, this town, behind. Berthe called, "Achtriel, come, sit at table." She was doomed. She dried her tears as thoroughly as possible and prepared for further degradation.

Tirzah lowered herself into a seat across the table. In the candle's glow, she truly seemed unearthly. Her cheekbones cast piquant shadows that etched her face and perfect mouth as if they were carved in marble. Although Achtriel felt a pang of envy, she was glad the girl was present. In her shadow, no one would notice the costumed gargoyle that sat across from her.

Berthe began the Sabbath ceremony, one more formal than any that had taken place in Tahto's house before. The lilt of the familiar Hebrew words brought Achtriel some comfort. Maybe YWHW could help her find a way to get out of this room.

Everyone at the table looked supremely happy. Tahto's face beamed in the candlelight, and the whole chevara was excited to welcome the newcomers. Natan seemed more jovial than usual and exaggerated all his pantomimes till they seemed theatrical and very funny. Fagim had softened since her engagement to Mosse and did not engage in her usual sarcasm.

The men seemed energized by their new companions and intermittently stole glances at Tirzah. Although they pretended not to notice her, they joked and gestured with greater animation. Nevertheless their wit and merriment were infectious and the conversation interesting. Ordinarily, it would have been, for Achtriel, a delight. But tonight, her thoughts drifted away into worrisome questions about her future.

What if they tired of her? Where would she go? She was only passably competent at things that even average slaves could do. Other than her learning, she had little to offer. She could work for Profait designing clothing. That did not earn much, but if they let her sleep in the shop room, she might manage. But such a prospect, although somewhat reassuring, was hardly cheerful. How would she occupy her mind for all those tedious hours? Perhaps Tahto would still let her attend his classes, and she could think about the things she learned to make the time more pleasant.

"Achtriel, you seem lost in contemplation." Esther leaned close to her.

"Yes. You are not adding your usual commentary," Mosse added.

"You haven't touched my souffle," Berthe cajoled.

"And here you are looking so impressive tonight; you should be full of vinegar." Fagim laughed. Only Naadasya discerned that something troubled her. And he remained discreet. The door opened then, and Frans came in. "I stole away and came to join you," he said merrily. "They will not send for me tonight. There was some happening afoot. And thus they did not notice this!" He held a bag up for them to see.

"What is it?" they all clamored. Berthe went to fetch another seat for Frans, thoughtfully folding a cloak on it to make it higher. After he was seated, he spread the contents of the bag onto the table. Sweetmeats, fruit, and dates abounded. The exclamation at these riches went on for several minutes with Frans explaining how he'd stored the things behind a cupboard in the larder and waited for the lords to drink their mead, quarrel, fall asleep, or otherwise achieve unconsciousness.

"We are fortunate that they are so occupied," Fagim said. "The townsfolk fear that they would otherwise turn on them and raise taxes or simply resort to plunder."

"It is a delicate thing, living near royals." Naadasya nodded. "In India, they routinely treat the villagers as chattel. Royal wives of course are below even this; they are killed by the hundreds when their husbands die, to go with him to the afterlife. Thoroughly savage."

"Perhaps in wild Ebon lands, the people live more peaceably than in our so-called civilization," Esther mused.

"Many do. Some are worse," he said. "I have heard of a tribe that routinely beheads large groups of citizens simply as a celebratory rite." No one noticed that Tirzah had turned pale. But Achtriel could see that this discussion was a trial for her.

"Can we not talk of something else?" Achtriel proposed. As everyone turned to look at her, she realized too late that she would now become the focus of attention.

"Why I did not recognize you!" Frans exclaimed. "Where did this lovely girl come from?"

"Tirzah has accomplished the impossible," Fagim said. "Our wild boar is not only in clean clothing, but her hair is neat."

"I think I can still recognize her." Frans squinted at her playfully. "Such a person one does not forget, even in rags."

"Let us drink to Tirzah," Berthe suggested. They all raised their wine cups and shouted. "Chaim."

"And to our new arrivals," Tahto added.

"Why did you leave the East?" Esther inquired politely. Tirzah now turned almost white.

"I smell something burning," Achtriel said, rising from her seat. "Tirzah and I have made some special rolls we copied from the bakers. I think we need to see if they are ready." Tirzah looked across at her.

"Yes. We must look to them," she mumbled and left the room. Achtriel followed her.

Beside the oven, Tirzah was standing unsteadily. "That was kind," she said to Achtriel.

"I wanted to get away too," she said, opening the oven to see to the rolls.

"I think they're done," Tirzah said. "Move away so I can remove them."

"I can do it," Achtriel protested, but Tirzah elbowed her aside and taking the dishcloth, lifted out the pan.

"You can make sure that the fire is dampened," she said in a commanding tone. This assumption of superiority seemed to bring her color back. Her face looked settled now, calmer and determined. "Make sure the embers are completely separated," she called to Achtriel as she carried the rolls in to the common room.

Achtriel stood still looking at the stove. So it was true. This girl meant to usurp her every function and get rid of her. Or at least solidify her own authority as taskmaster. Exclamations of appreciation resounded from the other room. The lively conversation now resumed, albeit in a less gruesome tone. From Tirzah's polite but charming disavowals of praise, one thing was clear. She could control whatever turbulent emotions boiled beneath her skin.

If she had mastered the adult art of dissimulation, what other devious skills might she attain? Achtriel would by degrees be relegated to the tasks that were demanded of her. Everything she had once overseen—the cooking, shopping, cleaning—would be subject to the older girl's direction. Soon, her obsolescence would be complete.

She realized then that her opportunity to escape was in front of her. Opening the kitchen door, she slipped outside. No one would miss her. They would assume she had gone to the wash-house and would not note her absence for a while.

The evening had cooled the air, and all resemblance to spring-time was now gone. She rubbed her arms and cursed the uselessness of this ungainly clothing. It protected neither legs nor arms from the chill. And it was difficult to walk in, she learned as she made her way through the yard. A garment not for cripples or for slaves, it hung about her frame and made her stumble. She looked back at the house, her home since infancy. Tomorrow, she would leave it.

At the thought of this, her tears began. This had all happened so quickly, and yet she was foolish not to have expected it. She had been so fortunate, it had almost seemed that heaven's hand had saved her from her fate. But that was but false pride, and now she would be punished for it. Foundling that she was, she surely had extracted all the luck that life would give her. Now she would see the real world, as Bonda said. And for her, even resorting to Bonda's way of life was not a possibility. No one found cripples enticing. They wished rather to think they did not exist.

She looked down at her withered hand. It looked like something twisted, something dead. Her bad foot, exposed so cruelly by this useless garment, was like the claw of murdered chicken. Hideous. Deformed. She herself was nothing but an eyesore. And as such the road ahead for her did not look promising. Her weeping became louder, though she struggled to contain it.

Moments later, she felt a soft warmth against her leg. She glanced up and saw her cat, looking at her, for all the world like a worried friend. Wordlessly, she opened her arms and pulled the kitten to her. It sniffed her curiously then licked her chin. A soothing whirr was emanating from it. The sound was comforting.

"Hello?" a voice startled her. Naadasya was there, kneeling by her. "I knew something had bothered you. Don't worry, I have not told the others. They think I am in the wash house." He sat down next to her and straightened his long legs. "Can I be of any help?" He put his warm hand on her shoulder. The little cat's body radiated comfort. From the nearby river came the trill of frogs. She rubbed her face quickly to hide the traces of crying.

"Can you tell me?" Naadasya asked. His concern was genuine and his voice inviting.

She looked down at Sachela. "It's just that…now I have to go." A fresh wave of tears overtook her.

"I don't understand."

"Now Tahto has his brother and two women looking out for him. What does he want with me? I shall have to find some meager dull employment now to earn my keep."

"Ahhh. I see, "Naadasya said. Then he looked at her gravely. "Listen to me, young one," he told her. "There is something you are not apprised of, something that you need to know. I have traveled long in many lands. I have been at the courts of emperors and kings. I have been hired to teach in the most learned places in the world. Academies in Babylon and palaces in Ravenna.

I have taught the sons of wealthy, brilliant Jews who could remember whole verses from the Talmud after a single reading. I have seen many a bright pupil. But rarely, perhaps never, not among the sons of kings or the synagogue devotees have I met a child with your capacities."

She started to protest, but he put his finger upon her lips. "Listen to me. Every child comes with certain things. Qualities, abilities, propensities, skills. Some are dazzling, some horrific. Sons of kings for instance can be so savage in their nature that murder and betrayal seem their due inheritance. Some are gifted musically, some in battle prowess. Some are born with a mind so rich and capable, so complex and apperceptive that we must stand in awe of them. You are one of those."

"But I am only…"

"Hush," he said, "this is not flattery or sympathy. I can see you do not know this. Yet it is true. Someday, you will surely contribute great things to history. You are not like other children.

Perhaps you have known this a while. And here in Briga, you are not likely to encounter souls with wide enough experience to fairly judge you. Because I have been a prodigious child myself, in a country of accomplished people, I can see your value. Tahto also understands this. He sees in you the brilliant child he once was. He does not keep you here because he needs someone to tend to him. He keeps you because he knows that you are something rare, a treasure. And because he loves you."

"But…" she stammered, "how can you tell these things about me?"

"Do you see that tree there? It's an apricot tree. I know that from its bark and its shape and the way it smells. When it puts forth new leaves, they will be apricot leaves, and the fruit it bears will be the only kind it can produce. It is not possible for it to do otherwise. So do I know what you are. You must have time and sanctuary to put out your foliage. But when you are ready, you will reach to the sun."

"No. But I mean Tahto. How can you know he loves me?"

Naadasya laughed. "Who could not?"

"Tirzah."

"Ah yes." He smiled wryly. "She is formidable it is true. But she has survived by that ability. Perhaps when she settles in, she will be easier."

"I don't think so."

"Well then, you must find a way to bear it. All you need do is remind yourself that she has been frightened too. Probably a great deal. Her actions are those of a desperate soul. You can see that. Now you need a strategy to use with her. I'm sure you will come up with something. You are a clever child." Achtriel sat beside him thinking. He was right. She could find ways around that authoritarian. It would be simpler than many things she had already accomplished.

"Thank you, Naadasya," she said. "I see now. I will find a way."

"Of course you will." He smiled. "I have no doubt. Now it is getting cold here. Let's go back in and join the others."

"Where have you two been?" Esther inquired discretely as they came back to the table.

"I was teaching Achtriel about trees," he said, sitting beside her. "There is an apricot tree out there. Unusual for this climate. How did it get here?"

"That tree was here when I constructed this house," Tahto said. "I purposefully built beside it."

"Some travelers from Armenia must have passed through here. That is where the tree originated. Although the Romans cultivated them too," Nimrode said.

"We are on an ancient trade route which the Greeks and Romans used. Certainly, it predated them. One can only speculate on its origins," Tahto said.

"What were they trading, Tahto?" Achtriel asked, feeling a rush of gratitude for his familiar face. The one she loved above all others.

"Goods from across the Eastern sea, from Persia, Arabia, even the Orient. If it were not for trade, the winds of change would never reach the wider world. But they do. Along with their exotic toys."

"They say the figurines of Buddha can now be found in Africa," Nimrode said. "And the gold work of the Celts in Sicily."

"It is not a settled world indeed. I did not know it so well where I lived before," Berthe said. "It was mostly through our servants that we learned of other lands."

"You were fortunate, my love, to have been born into a great estate," Nimrode said. "In such places, change comes politely in measured step. It is as if all the world must stand in awe of such prosperity."

"Yes. It can almost seem, there, as if the Roman world were still as it was, if one does not venture into certain parts of the city."

"What is there?" Achtriel asked.

"Wherever there is regal power to be won, no one is sure of safety," Berthe said quietly. Something in her tone left a hollowness behind it, which turned the conversation to lighter subjects.

Chapter 24

After dinner, Achtriel preempted Tirzah by rising before her to clear the table. In the kitchen, she took advantage of Tirzah's relative inexperience to tell her pleasantly how to soak the bowls in heated water to clean them. She could see that Tirzah was discomfited by this lack of acquiescence to her authority. Achtriel felt glad of that, but then remembered that she, herself, had been the first to take a pedagogic tone with Tirzah. Now she realized how rude that was.

"Do you think we should leave this dough out as Margit suggested?" she asked by way of conciliation. "She said it would keep well overnight, but I don't know..." Tirzah frowned, but then she took a long breath and replied, "It will be fine." Achtriel noticed out of the corner of her eye, as she bent to scrape the bowl clean, that Tirzah seemed resigned, at least for the moment, to this balance of power.

That night, Tirzah awoke screaming, and her cries woke Achtriel too.

"Are you all right?" she asked uncertainly. Tirzah did not answer but did seem to have been startled from her paralysis by the question. She looked over at Achtriel as if unsure who she was. For a moment, neither of the girls said anything.

"Are you...?" Achtriel began.

"No," Tirzah said hoarsely, "I am not. Do not talk please."

Achtriel waited while the girl managed to calm herself gradually and begin breathing normally.

"Can I help you?" she asked, feeling genuinely concerned now.

Tirzah looked at Achtriel, her pupils widening as if to take her in. "I am fine," she said unconvincingly, "I had a bad dream."

"I have had bad dreams," Achtriel said, lying down with her head next to Tirzah's in what she hoped was a companionable way. "Sometimes, I dream I am drying up, like a drop of water in summer. I feel so hungry and thirsty that I cannot stand it. Usually, that's what wakes me up." She waited hopefully. Perhaps Tirzah would respond. "Sometimes, I dream I am running from a crowd of horrible people. They are chasing me and trying to burn me up with fire. The more I try to run away, the less I am able to. It is as if my whole body were— like my arm and leg—lame."

Tirzah was silent. Nevertheless, it seemed to Achtriel that a certain change had taken place between them. As they drifted back to sleep, it felt, unlike before, as if they slept beside each other. In the morning, Achtriel woke with the breaking day. Tirzah looked relaxed now in her sleep. There were few traces of the terror of the previous night. Only a slight furrow between her brows gave evidence of perturbation.

As they were sitting down for breakfast, they heard a loud knocking at the door. Achtriel went to open it and was stunned to see Margit standing there.

"Forgive me," she said. "Just give me a moment to catch my breath. I've run here as fast as I could."

"Come in," Achtriel offered. "We are eating the rolls you showed us…"

"No, I've come for her." She pointed at Berthe. "The tailor's wife is having her child. It is past a month early, and she fears mighty for its life."

"I will come at once," Berthe said, rising quickly from her seat. "Achtriel, go and fetch Fagim and Esther," she said. "Tirzah, come with me." Before Achtriel could protest, Berthe had shuttled Tirzah out the door. "And bring some firewood!" she called back.

Achtriel looked around for Tahto, but he was in his study. She dressed herself and went out into the sunshine, but her thoughts were dour. Why should she be the one sent to fetch Fagim? Tirzah had two strong legs and could undoubtedly run faster. The only explanation could be that Berthe wanted Tirzah more, who surely, in her odd, but obviously sheltered life, had never helped in a delivery. Yet clearly, Berthe preferred her assistance to Achtriel's.

As she climbed the hill to Fagim's house, she struggled with her anger. Who was she to question Berthe who had spent years attending the women in her household? Perhaps, in the instant that it took to make her choice, Berthe discerned an inner character of Tirzah that was not clear upon the surface. Until now, Achtriel would have supposed herself the more intelligent, the more responsible and sober in the face of crisis.

Of course, it was a vain and evil thing to be so thoughtful of her own concerns when someone's baby might be dying. As she proceeded up the dusty path that led to Fagim's house, she felt herself to be disgraceful. When she reached the front door, Fagim came to meet her.

"Profait's baby is coming early," she explained to Fagim and Natan.

"Go fetch Esther, "Fagim told her son. "And bring some firewood to Profait's shop. Achtriel, come with me."

In spite of her own self-recriminations on selfishness, Achtriel felt her spirits lift. At least someone could judge her strengths appropriately.

"Is there anything that I need to know?" she asked as they descended hurriedly to town.

"Early births are often fatal, it is true." Fagim frowned. "But sometimes, fortune favors them. Mayhap the child is not as young as they have calculated and will be in no more danger than others."

"I think Profait is known to be precise."

"You are right as usual," Fagim said, her frown lines deepening. "But there is hope yet. We will do the best we can." She took Achtriel's hand and briefly squeezed it.

At the tailor's house, the pandemonium that Achtriel expected was absent. In fact, the place was deadly silent. "Hello?" Fagim called.

"We are here," Berthe's voice came from the antechamber.

"Natan is fetching firewood and my sister," Fagim said cheerfully as they joined the others at the young wife's bedside.

"Ardith is quite the soldier," Berthe said, smiling at the pregnant woman. "She has not cried out once, or so her husband said e'er he left us."

"I have," Ardith said, grimacing, and let out a little groan of pain.

"No need to stifle yourself now," Fagim said, wiping Ardith's brow. "Your husband's gone. We all know how weak the poor things are on such occasions."

Ardith smiled and looked at Fagim gratefully. "Thank you both for coming," she said to Berthe and Fagim. "And you girls also." She nodded at Achtriel and Tirzah. Her face began to show the signs of pain again, and Berthe glanced at Fagim with a worried look.

This time, Ardith did not close her mouth, and her groans escaped it. Tirzah, who had retreated to the farthest corner of the room, seemed increasingly ill at ease. No one but Achtriel seemed to notice this. Remembering the girl's cries of terror in the night, she went to stand beside her.

"It will be all right," Achtriel whispered uncertainly. Tirzah did not answer but looked at Achtriel with such profound antipathy that she did not know how to respond.

"The child will be here very soon," Berthe announced, feeling underneath Ardith's bedclothes. "We must prepare."

"Where is Natan with that firewood?" Fagim said angrily.

"I will go and fetch him," Tirzah said quickly and bounded out the front door.

"We must have warmth of any kind," Berthe scanned the room. "Child, go and see what you can find out there," she indicated with her head the tailor's shop.

"Yes, Berthe," Achtriel said and went into the other room. There were linen dresses, dyed woolen cloth, and piles of filigree. None of these would do. She spotted a trunk under some woolen capes and opened it to look inside. To her delight, there was a calfskin shawl lined with fur. Hurrying back to the anteroom, she asked, "Will this be good?"

"Wonderful!" Berthe said with some astonishment.

"It was…my dowry…was my grandmother's," Ardith explained. "I did not sell it, kept it for emergencies."

"Well, this is surely one," Fagim said taking the fur shawl from Achtriel.

"We have some kindling in the back," Ardith said, her words devolving into groans of agony.

"Achtriel…" Berthe said.

"Yes," she answered, already headed to the door.

In the back, a large pile of twigs lay strewn about the chopping block. Achtriel grabbed the kindling and smaller pieces which would quickly burn. Using her skirt as a basket, she hurried to the shop and put them in the oven. Above the oven stood a fire flint which she used to light a twig and with that the kindling. When the fire had caught she went outside to get more wood.

Soon the room was comfortably warm, and Fagim came out from behind the cloth that separated the two rooms. "Good work!" she said approvingly. Now can you find a stew pot?"

"She says there is one in the corner," Berthe called. Behind her, Ardith's screams heightened in intensity and volume.

"I must get back to her," Fagim said quickly. "Warm some water in the pot and keep the fire going."

Just then, Natan came in with more wood. Tirzah was not with him. "Where have you been?" his mother scolded as he dropped the wood beside the oven. He gestured apologetically, pointing back toward the street, and quickly left.

"We will need more tomorrow," she muttered gazing at the firewood, "or need none at all."

As Fagim returned to the birthing room, Achtriel caught a glimpse of Ardith. Her head was thrown back in an expression of unspeakable pain that told of her distress far louder than her cries. Suddenly, there was another sound. Something creaky like a chipmunk. "He is alive!" Fagim announced.

"Wrap him immediately." She heard Berthe instruct. Rushing to peek through the curtains, Achtriel glimpsed a tiny body being handed from one woman to the other. Fagim said, "He is small but hardy." And looked encouragingly at Ardith.

"The Lord preserves…" Ardith said and fell back heavily onto the pillows.

"Let us hope so," Fagim muttered. She was cleaning the child as Berthe tended to Ardith. She pinched the child's cord and cut it with a tailoring scissors. Then she wrapped the baby tightly in the furry shawl. "Is the water warm?" she called to Achtriel.

"A little," she replied.

"A little is exactly what we want," she said, rising and carrying the child to the stove. "We do not want to boil him." She removed the infant from the shawl and placed him gently in the water. "Hold his head so he may breathe," Fagim instructed her. "And make sure the water temperature stays as it is now. If it gets too warm, push the basin from the flame and let it cool. I will be back as soon as I can."

"Yes, Fagim," she said and took the tiny head into her palm. The small face was peaceful, somewhat concerned but not afraid. His eyes, surprisingly alert, looked up and seemed to focus on her face. In them, she recognized the unpropitious infant she had been. Uncertain of continued life but willing to attempt it.

"You are going to live," she told the little boy. "Next spring, we will pick flowers in the woods."

How small he was. But in spite of that, he did not appear frail. His body was well formed, and his little fists were clenched as if to ward off adversity. He began to make small utterances, for all the world as if he were trying to tell her something. At that moment, her self-concern retreated. The shame of her infirmity, her jealousy of Tirzah…it all seemed trivial and distant. She reached into the water to check the temperature and let her fingers touch the little boy's hand. He held it and began to wave it in the water.

"You are going to live," she said again.

Fagim pushed aside the curtain and hurried to the stove. She looked down at the boy and carefully felt his arms and legs. Then she gave a resolute nod. "We will let him warm a minute more. Then we will keep him wrapped in the shawl. It shall be his ark of bulrushes. We will see him safely afloat."

"Yes, Fagim," Achtriel said. When the child was wrapped in his fur, she carried him to the window. There she spotted Tirzah hurrying between adjacent houses like a frightened animal. She remembered what Naadasya had said, that fear and trouble surely had long been companions of that girl.

How lucky I am, she realized. I have been loved and protected, encouraged and educated. Because of Tahto, I have never been enslaved or, worse, exposed to die. And although I came into the world as ill equipped as Ardith's babe, I have been healthy all my days. Tears of gratitude stung her eyes, but she could not stop to shed them, for she must see to this child whose own future was still uncertain.

In the tailor shop, she found some bolts of fine soft linen. She was sure that they had cost Profait a small fortune, but she was equally sure that he would not care if they were ruined to save his son's life. She would make them into diapers and swaddling sheets, a hopeful hedge against any unhappy future.

Surrounded by fur, the child's little face was cunning as a kit's, and she had to smile at it. Then she found a stool and sat with him and held him and sang a song to him. Esther appeared at the front door and hurried in, looking sheepish.

"I am sorry. I was not at home. But Natan found me," she said breathlessly. "How is the child?"

"Jacob," Berthe called from Ardith's bedside in the other room, "that is his name. And now his mother wants to see him."

Fagim peered out from behind the curtain. "Finally, you are here," she said to Esther. "I was beginning to think you had left town."

When Fagim's face disappeared behind the curtain, Esther sent Achtriel a worried glance.

"She does not seem very angry with you," she told her reassuringly, guessing her thoughts.

"Miraculous." Esther breathed and bent to take the child from Achtriel. Together, they came into the bedroom. Berthe was tidying the clean sheets, and Fagim sat at the head of the bed, her hand on Ardith's forehead.

"Shall I see him now?" Ardith asked nervously. When Esther handed her the fur-wrapped boy, she looked at its little face and wept.

"He is hardy," Esther told her. "And I have seen many an early birth."

"His breathing is quite strong," Fagim said. "Now if we can keep him warm and fed…"

"But my milk has not come," Ardith cried. "How will I feed him?"

"It will come soon," Berthe said. "Until then, put him to your breast and give him suck."

Ardith looked again at the baby and, opening her nightshirt, put its little face close to her nipple. The boy's head turned hungrily, and after a few attempts, he got the nipple in his mouth.

"That is the best sign of all," Berthe said delightedly. "He is not only clever, but he has a will to live." But no one replied to her, for they stood enrapt, gazing, like the Magi, at the quiet sanctity of motherhood.

When Esther and Achtriel had finished cleaning the kitchen, Fagim came to them.

"One of us must be here at all times," she said. "At least this week."

"We can take turns. I will stay tomorrow," Esther offered.

"I can stay today and tonight," Achtriel said.

Berthe gave her a long assessing look. "Good," she said at last.

After the sisters left, Profait hurried in, looking pale.

"I am to stay for a few days to help…" Achtriel told him.

"Thank you, thank you," he seemed distracted as he glanced toward the curtain.

"Your son is strong, and he will live," Achtriel told him. "Jacob is a fine boy." To her surprise, Profait began to weep. She had never seen an adult cry before. It was unsettling.

"He is small but hardy," she repeated.

"Yes, thank you," he said absently and approached the curtain to the bedroom like a man confronting doom.

But in the other room, their murmured conversation was subdued and calm. The new parents talked politely till it seemed there was no more to say, and they fell silent. She reheated some soup and when it was warm, she pulled politely on the curtain. "Shall I bring you both some food?" she asked.

Profait pulled the cloth aside. "You are a good child," he said. "Yes, please bring food to my wife. I am going out. To Tahto's house," he added. "I shall tell him of your kindness."

"It is not kindness," Achtriel told him cheerfully. "I am happy to do it." But he did not answer her and quickly left the house.

Achtriel filled a bowl with soup for Ardith. She carried it into the bedroom and placed it on a little bed stand. Ardith was staring at her in the strangest way. "Shall I feed you?" Achtriel offered.

"No. No, you are a good child. Here, please hold the…Jacob while I eat." Achtriel took the baby. Ardith did not talk for several minutes as she ate her soup. Then she looked up at Achtriel, the strange look returning. "You…"

"Yes?"

"You are different…than others. Your infirmity…"

"I can do almost anything now," she said brightly. "Macha helped to strengthen my arm and leg, and Tirzah is teaching me to walk better."

"No. I know that. What I mean is…you are different…that others look at you…differently.

"Yes. They always have."

"If my son were to have a similar…"

Although she felt both angry and embarrassed, Achtriel remained polite. The woman was fearful for her child and could not help herself.

"It is not easy," she said. "Sometimes, it makes me want to hide. But there are so many blessings in my life… I try not to think about it." They did not speak for a while. Achtriel found a stool and sat down on it with the boy. She gazed at him and rocked him in her arms. "I do not think Jacob will be like me," she told Ardith.

"You don't?"

"No. When I was born, I was already different…in my arm and leg. It was not caused after I came into the world."

Ardith breathed an enormous sigh of relief. "It was not because…"

"No." Jacob was asleep now. If angel's faces could be seen, they would look like this. "He is a beautiful child. There is nothing wrong with him. We only must make sure he eats and does not get cold. Shall I bring some more soup for you?"

"Yes," Ardith answered quietly. "Yes, that will bring my milk in."

Carrying Jacob, Achtriel went to the outer room and found a wide soft bench to lay him on. Surrounding him with bolts of cloth, she made a place from which he could not fall. They are both wary of having me here, she thought. Do they think that I will drop him or infect him like a leper?

She cursed her infirmities then, as she had cursed them every morning of her life. For in her dreams, she was not crippled but ran and jumped. So each awakening was to disappointment. "But not again," she told herself. "I will only think of what is lovely in my life. For I have Tahto."

"Do you have a cradle for him?" she asked when she returned to the bedroom.

"No. Yes…" Ardith said. "The hostler's boy was making one, but it is not finished."

"Then we must think what best to lay him in," she said and looked around the room.

"There is a shipping box in the larder. It is sturdy."

Achtriel found the box filled with dried peas that she poured into a nearby bowl. The box was solid and well balanced. It smelled like growing things. His ark of bulrushes, she thought happily and went outside to clean it. As she knelt, washing it, beside the well, she saw Profait returning home. She would not disturb them now. She poured the water out of the box and set it in the sun to dry. The day was going to be sunny.

She watched the sun climb slowly to its highest perch. A flock of ravens, raucous in a nearby tree, took turns chasing one another from their perches. Their cries seemed to be those of pride. I am alive they were bragging. It was indeed a thing to brag about, she supposed, in the animal world. And in her own.

She began to wonder what it would be like to be a mother. To be responsible for the very life of a child. To have a little person so close to you, so easy to love. She spun a pleasant daydream of it as she waited to return. But when she came into the tailor shop, Profait was pacing by the bedroom curtain, scowling.

"Is something wrong?" she asked, but he began to shout.

"Please find someone else to watch my child," he said coldly.

So they do think I am a leper, she thought. Now she was so angry she could not contain it. "I can do anything anyone else can do!" she said. "I can cook and clean, fetch water. Look, I've made a bed for him! But do you think that I will hurt him? You suppose because I am damaged that I will ruin him? That is not true. My infirmities cannot be shared with anyone. They are mine and will always be."

She felt the tears she had not cried earlier come to her eyes. She put down the box and turned away, so he would not see them. "I will fetch Esther," she said.

"No, no. I am sorry," Profait said, touching her shoulder. "You do not understand me."

"You want me to leave. I understand that."

"No, no, child. I am sorry I lost my temper. It has been a harrowing day. The boy is so very small and…"

"You think that I will drop him."

"No, no. I think having someone capable with Ardith is the best thing for us now. I must leave for Rodom tomorrow for several days, and I am just a little fearful. You see, you left him on that bench and went outside." He pointed to the sleeping child. "I did not know you went to get the bed. I thought you had forgotten him."

"Forgotten him?"

"You are still a child."

Achtriel felt her face turn red. "It was not because of my... deformity?"

"Whatever gave you such an idea? I well know you are as capable as any. But I thought you had left him and gone to play. And then when you did not return promptly, it was your youth I was unsure of, not your body."

"I stayed away because I thought you wanted time alone," she said.

"Yes, of course. I should have known it. Can you forgive me?"

"Yes," she said. She knew she also should apologize for her outburst but could not bring herself to do it. "I am not like others my age. I have never been," she said quietly.

"What a silly pair we are, you and I. Arguing at cross purposes," he shook his head.

"Here is the bed," she said pointing to the box. "I have cleaned it."

He picked up the box from her and examined it. "Yes. He may well fit in this till the hostler's boy is done with his," he said. "It is not elegant, but my son seems to be a sanguine fellow." He smiled ruefully. "Here we were shouting at one another, and he was imperturbable." Just then, Jacob made a delightful coo. They went to look at him. In his sleep, he was making the funniest of faces. Then he stretched and yawned in a leisurely fashion. They could not help but laugh.

"Let us pad his bed, young nursemaid," Profait said. "And let us make his diapers from something soft. I can tell he is a creature who likes his comforts."

When they had lined the bed with down and covered it with the linen, Achtriel returned to check on Jacob. He yawned and woke briefly from his sleep. Then his little face began to frown, and he opened his mouth and rooted.

"You will see your mama soon, my friend," she told him. "But first, I must check your other end." Luckily, the calfskin was still clean. She wrapped his bottom in a diaper and knotted it gently to hold it in place.

"Profait!" They heard a cry. Grabbing the baby and hurrying to the bedroom, they found Ardith, sitting up in the bed and gesturing excitedly. "My milk will be coming soon I can feel it!"

"That is good for this fellow is hungry," Achtriel said and handed him gently to his mother. Jacob attached himself to her breast with so little difficulty that Achtriel wondered aloud. "How do they know how to do that?"

"The same way all God's creatures know their purpose," Profait said. "The angels give them their instruction before they are born."

"Well, he has learned well." She laughed, for the little boy was sucking hungrily.

That night, she slept on the floor beside Ardith's bed. Profait had gone to spend the night with Tahto.

Ardith had fallen quickly into slumber and so had Jacob in his ark. She, however, lay awake. She kept sitting up to check on the baby to make sure he was alive. Once she thought for sure that he had ceased to breathe. She was horrified until she saw his stomach moving gently. He is small, she told herself, and he has subtle breaths. But after that, she sat up all the night to ensure the continuation of each one.

After several hours, Jacob began to stir. He raised his little arms and tried to put his hands into his mouth. Then he screwed up his face and began to cry.

"Oh, you are hungry," she said delightedly. "Let us wake your mother. She will see to that." She touched Ardith gently upon the shoulder, but the young woman sprang up as if chased by wolves.

"Is he dead?" she asked Achtriel.

"Not at all." She laughed. And as if to confirm this, the boy let out a vigorous wail. "He is hungry."

Ardith looked over at her son. "I have naught yet to give him," she said fretfully. "But look, perhaps I do!" She examined the wetness on her shirt front. "I have milk! Thank the lord!" she cried happily.

Achtriel lifted the boy and handed him to his mother. He latched onto her breast and began to gulp in liquid like a drunkard.

"I think he knows that he is small and wants to remedy it quickly," Achtriel said. "And I do not think that that will be a problem."

Ardith gave her a grateful look and stared down at the nursing child. "I believe you are right," she said cautiously. The child nursed avidly and then, just as purposefully, fell asleep. Ardith handed him to Achtriel who lay him in his bed.

"I need to get up," Ardith said, struggling to a sitting position. "Can you help me?" she asked uncertainly. Achtriel came to the bed and braced herself against it so that Ardith could lean on her. Ardith put her feet on the floor and pulled herself to a standing position. She swayed for a moment, but Achtriel steadied her.

"Thank you. I am strong now," Ardith said, taking a feeble step.

"I will go with you to the outhouse," Achtriel said, holding Ardith's arm.

"But the boy...?"

"He is in the arms of Morpheus," Achtriel assured her. "He will not notice."

"What a character you are," Ardith said, "If I had spoken as cleverly and boldly, my mother would have slapped me."

"Why?" Achtriel asked, helping Ardith to the little door that led out to the backyard.

"She would say a girl like that will never get a husband." Ardith lowered her foot carefully onto the grass.

"I do not think I will get one anyway," Achtriel said. "So I can say what I will."

"I did not mean..." Ardith turned to look at her.

"I am not sad about it," Achtriel said, taking her arm to steady her. "Husbands seem to need a lot of looking after. But it would be nice to have a baby."

"I hope you know," Ardith said archly, sitting on the pot. "That girls who think such things are headed for disaster."

Achtriel thought about this as she waited. What was disaster to one kind of person might be simply life to others, she reasoned. And besides, what further harm might disaster bestow than that which life had given her at birth?

On the way back to the house, Ardith insisted on walking without help. "Are you in any pain?" Achtriel asked.

"Not a great deal," she answered. "Nothing so bad as yesterday."

"I wonder why God should ordain that suffering must be the lot of women," Achtriel mused. "It doesn't seem fair."

"The Pentateuch explains it."

"I know, but all Eve did was try to learn the truth. Why must we be punished for it?"

"That Tahto has put such ideas in your head." Ardith sighed, opening the door. "I do not like Profait to visit him."

"Tahto is the most educated man in Neustria," Achtriel said, trying not to sound angry. "It is not dangerous to have ideas. It is dangerous not to think."

"He is an educated man, it's true," Ardith agreed settling herself on her bed, "My village did not have a teacher. I was lucky to have learned to read."

"Who taught you?" Achtriel asked as she held the blanket for Ardith.

"My father," she replied. "With the aid of birch withes."

"Have you read anything besides the Torah?"

"No," she replied and turned over and went to sleep.

Achtriel went to check the fire and renew its wood supply. The night was warm, and hopefully, the day would be so too. She opened the front door and stepped outside. In moonlight, the little houses on the commerce row seemed charmed. They could have been the huts of elves.

This reminded her of her woodland fancies. How different were her thoughts now than in the previous autumn. Then, she had stayed almost entirely away from town for fear of taunts, or worse, attacks by village ruffians. But in this year, she had come to know so many friendly souls. And as her circle of acquaintances had widened, so had her comfort with the world.

And she had more responsibilities. Not only must she see to Tahto's health, but to the lives of others who seemed somehow in her care. She was surprised to notice that she numbered Tirzah in this lot, although the older girl no doubt would have scoffed at such a notion. But in a way, the reticent and strange beauty did seem fragile and to need tending.

And now, there was Ardith, a vituperative sort, and poorly educated. And Jacob, who needed vigilance in spite of his apparent hardiness. She shivered in the night air and went inside to see to him. He was sleeping soundly in his box. Achtriel sat down on the floor and leaned her cheek against a stool, watching the sleeping baby. In order to stay awake, she silently recited psalms, envisioning pictures to go with them, lively illustrations to the timeless words. Thus, although she stayed awake until the morning, it did not seem tedious.

Just watching Jacob sleep was thrilling. A sense of lightness, of newness seemed to hover over him. Even the stuffy air lightened with it. When dawn approached and the birds began their chorus, he moved his mouth and stirred. Soon, he was awake and complaining of hunger. She woke Ardith who fed him sleepily. "Thank you, Achtriel," she mumbled when the feeding was over and slipped back into sleep. The boy slept also on Ardith's chest. What poetry there was in their simple pose. Of what significance were ceremony, riches, pomp beside such elegance? Achtriel rose carefully, so as not to waken them.

She went into the pantry to see what there was to cook. Profait was cautious with his money; it was common knowledge. But he had seen the pantry stocked well for his wife's confinement. There were pulse and barley cakes, fruits and honey. There was a root cellar too, with turnips, parsnips and leeks. A rooster crowed, announcing, perhaps, that one of his wives had born eggs. She went to the henhouse and found that this was true. The hen clucked nonchalantly as Achtriel removed the egg. "I will give you extra feed today," she told the chicken, "for your generosity."

The sun was climbing in an orange sky. Its beams, touching the clouds from underneath, seemed to illuminate them. "Like the bright steeds of Helios," she thought as she returned to the quiet house. Cautiously, she gathered flour and yeast and set about making bread. It would be nice to visit the bakers today to report on Jacob's progress, but she dared not leave the house. Even though Margit had come for Berthe, it was unusual for Gentiles to come inside a Jewish home. But perhaps, as they were now friends, it would no longer be uncomfortable.

Chapter 25

When the smell of baking bread began to fill the rooms, Ardith awoke. Achtriel could hear her rising from her bed and making her way out the back door to the outhouse. Pulling aside the curtain, she looked in at Jacob. He seemed to have grown fatter overnight. His formerly callow cheeks were round and pink. She sent a prayer heavenward for his continued health and as if he heard this he awoke.

His expression was puckish now and comical. When she bent close to him, he looked about as if to find his bearings. "Hello, my friend," she said, lifting him carefully. He smelled of milk and also of the freshness of another realm. She nuzzled his soft head and kissed it.

He seemed contented for a moment but then began to squirm. Soon, he was crying. She walked about the room to try to quiet him. "Your mother will be here soon," she told him. "Patience is a goodly trait." But he was not chagrined by her admonishments and only cried louder. By the time Ardith returned, he was screaming.

"What is wrong?" she asked testily, as if the fault were Achtriel's.

"He is hungry," she replied.

"Well, give him to me," she said sitting on her bed. "You should have let him sleep."

"I did not awaken him," she protested.

"I will not have enough milk," she fussed, "if he feeds every hour."

"The more you feed him, the more milk you will make," she said, handing her the baby. "Fagim will tell you."

"I suppose I must believe you, though you are but a child." She attached the child to her breast. "Though how you came to learn so much about these things I do not know."

"I have helped Fagim and Esther many times. They are well skilled in all ways of nursing."

"What a different life you have had than most children." She sighed. "At your age, I ran about the village with my friends."

"None of my friends are children," she explained. Ardith looked at her.

"I suppose that is true. What of that girl, Tirzah. She is not so many years older than you. Well, her life must needs be different than our own, she is a beauty after all. Astonishingly so. Her skin is very dark though. Is she an African?"

"Apparently."

"I have seen Africans. There is a whole village of them near my town. Runaway slaves they say. But you must stay away from them, they eat children."

"They say that about Jews as well."

"Yes, but that is nothing but ignorance."

Achtriel opened her mouth to respond, but then closed it. If Ardith was too stupid to recognize her own twisted logic, there did not seem to be much point.

"Most men," Ardith said, raising her eyebrows, "Would only take a girl like that as a concubine. But she is so extraordinary that it only makes her more exotic. The suitors will arrive ere long."

Remembering the tragedy of Bonda's life, Achtriel said, "I hope not."

"Envy is sinful," Ardith said.

"I'm not envious," she insisted, but she could see by Ardith's smug expression that she did not believe her.

"I myself was lucky to have made a match," she continued, lying back on the pillows. "I had twelve sisters, and no dowry to speak of. But my father told me of Profait, an older man but kind. With a good business and a house. Not my ideal husband but fair enough. I have been content."

"Why do you never come to our Sabbaths?" Achtriel asked.

"I was taught a wife's position," she said. "A wife does not run about like a goose. My mother beat that sensibility into us."

"But there is no one to scold you for it now," Achtriel reasoned. "Your mother cannot reach you here."

"How little you know of the world," she said. "Rumor and gossip fly from town to town with the merchant's wives. Sooner or later, word of my conduct would reach her."

"What can she do to you? You are a married woman now."

"Send me letters to upset me so I cannot sleep. I cannot be so troubled, I will lose my milk." She looked down anxiously at Jacob.

"But letters take so long to travel with the merchants. By the time they got here, he would be a fat and healthy boy."

"I hope so," she said doubtfully. They heard a knock on the front door, and Achtriel went to open it. It was Tirzah. In the rosy dawn, she could have been a dryad or a nymph, except for the expression on her face.

"Is he alive?" she asked furtively. "They sent me to enquire. Profait would not come home unless he knew."

"He is fine," she said. "You can tell him that the boy is strong and nursing well. Would you like to see him?"

"No," she said, already leaving.

"Will you tell Margit?" Achtriel called after her. "I would not want her to be worried." Tirzah made a gesture with her hand as she slipped between the houses. It could have meant dismissal or assent. It was hard to tell. Profait returned as she was taking the bread out of the oven.

"What a delicious smell!" he said. "And how is my family?"

"They are both well. Jacob has grown fatter overnight."

"Hello, hello," Profait said, pulling the bedroom curtain aside.

"Good morning, husband," Ardith said. "Come and see the boy." He let the curtain fall behind him, but she could hear their polite discussion. What trouble a husband seemed to be. It appeared one must be deferential to them at every moment.

Ardith's voice was completely changed. The crossness and irritation, even her authoritative tone, were much subdued. In their place was an exaggerated pleasantness, as if, by virtue of his maleness,

Profait required cajoling. He too sounded formal. How burdensome to have to cloak one's feelings all day long. It would be like living at a synagogue.

But Profait, emerging from the bedroom, did not seem at all perturbed. He was beaming. He came and sniffed the bread like an actor in a pantomime.

"Well, well!" he said, patting her on the shoulder. "In spite of all your education, you have learned the homely skills. We may see you married off one day."

"I doubt it," she replied, breaking the bread into pieces. But he did not seem to have heard this for he was striding royally about his tailor shop.

"My customers can now return here. I have gone to them these past few weeks, so Ardith could rest."

"Perhaps she has been too much undisturbed," Achtriel said. "I think she must be bored in there alone."

"True, true," he smiled. "That is why I have just told her my surprise. Several months ago, I invited her mother to come for a visit. She will be here in a few days' time."

Achtriel did not know how to respond. "I do not think..."

"It will be delightful!" Ardith called from the bedroom. "Thank you, dear husband, for always considering me."

"And now I shall serve my lovely wife some breakfast," he said, putting some bread and cooked eggs on a plate. He returned with it to the other room.

Achtriel took a piece of bread for herself. "I will never get married," she decided, "I could not live such a pretense." Poor Ardith having to endure her horrid mother just because she could not tell her husband how she felt. Being an adult seemed fraught with affliction.

"You may run along and play now," Profait said, sticking his head out through the curtain, "We shall not need you till the noon."

"But what if Jacob needs tending?" she began.

"He will be fine," Profait assured her. "He is asleep."

"Do not let him get cold or cry too long if he awakens," she said anxiously. "He will exhaust himself. And he must be fed as often as possible."

"Yes, thank you," Ardith called, sounding more like her ordinary irritated self. "I can see to him now. I am his mother after all."

Achtriel left the house reluctantly. She was not convinced that Ardith, mother or no, was capable of tending such a fragile soul. She went to the well and sat beside it. I will wait where I can hear if he is left to cry, she told herself. I will not lose him to their obduracy. Later, when the sun was fully risen, she was delighted to see Margit and Tirzah coming toward her.

"Hello!" she cried happily as she stood to greet them.

"Good morning to you," Margit said, smiling. "Thanks to Tirzah, I've heard that all is well with the tailor's wife. My aunt was fretting for her half the night."

"We have come to help you if you need something," Tirzah said, seeming oddly friendly.

"Thank you. But Profait has bid me leave. I think he feels the boy is out of danger."

"Do you think so?" Margit asked.

"Not truly, no," she said. "He seems quite strong, but I have heard of even full-grown babes to take sickly."

"Shall I send for Esther and Fagim?" Tirzah asked.

"That might be wise," Achtriel agreed.

"You are a thoughtful one," Margit said to Tirzah. "I'll go on with you to fetch them. My customers have had their morning fare, and I will not be missed till noontime." They went off, holding hands, and whispering like conspirators.

Achtriel watched them go. How nice to have companions one's own age, she thought. She must admit that she had wished, despite their differences, to have become a friend to Tirzah. But at least the older girl behaved less coolly to her when Margit was there. That was the best she could hope for, it would seem. And yet this did not alter her earlier opinion, that Tirzah needed her, if only to have someone to command.

Soon, the sunlight grew hot, and she moved into the shade beside the well. All was silent at Profait's house, but she was not at peace. She stole closer and crept behind the house to listen. She could hear Ardith and Profait talking—business she surmised by Ardith's coy and stealthy questions. She heard Profait reply to her, with some irritation, "It is too late to cancel the order. I shall have to order more from Rodom if I do not have enough."

"Indeed, with the wedding, demand will increase," Ardith said sweetly. She could not hear Profait's mumbled reply. Then Ardith called out after him. "Hire that poor lame girl till then. I am told she designs dresses very cheaply."

Achtriel recoiled at this unwelcome image of herself. I could say evil things of her, she reasoned, if I chose to. But Tahto would not like for her to have such thoughts. He always made it clear that, to him, most people must be overlooked, like children. But such discipline was almost impossible for her, and she walked back to the well imagining the cruel things she might say to Ardith.

"What are you doing out here?" Fagim's insistent voice broke through her thoughts. Achtriel looked up to see Fagim and Esther walking toward her. They were bearing baskets full of cheeses and fruits.

"They felt that I was not needed till the noontime."

"That woman does not know what is required to keep a babe like that alive," Fagim said darkly.

"I tried to stay but..."

"Don't worry, Achtriel," Esther insisted. "I will speak with her. She is somewhat awed by me, but why I cannot fathom. She will do as I say."

"She is awed by you for you are beautiful, and in her eyes, that is the highest good," Fagim replied dismissively. "But whether she will heed my words or no, I shall make something clear to her. That child requires constant vigilance." Esther and Achtriel followed Fagim to the tailor's door, upon which she knocked impatiently.

Profait appeared and bowed his head politely. "How kind of you to come," he said.

"Kindness is not my intention," Fagim said, handing Esther her fruit basket, and brushed past him into Ardith's room. Esther placed both baskets in Profait's arms and followed Fagim resolutely.

"What is the matter?" he asked Achtriel.

"I'm not quite sure," she said politely and went to watch the confrontation.

"Why is he not wrapped in the fur?" Fagim was almost shouting. "Did I not make it clear to you that he must be kept warm?"

"I was only looking to his cleanliness," Ardith answered testily.

"His cleanliness will hardly matter if he does not live," Fagim said, picking up the boy and wrapping him inside the fur.

"But I need to change his…"

"You will do that in a manner which does not allow him to be chilled," Fagim insisted. "If you had heeded my instructions, you would have seen to this. Leave his upper body wrapped while you attend his diapering." She opened the shawl carefully at the bottom while keeping his torso well swaddled. "Two things, I told you. Only two are paramount. He must be warm, and he must feed as much as possible. If he dies, it will be because you have ignored this." Ardith could not withstand such castigation and dissolved in tears.

"I only tried to do what I thought best," she wept.

"You have been blessed, "Fagim said, "with a healthy child. But he is small and before his time. That is why I told you to keep Achtriel about. She is not incautious like yourself." Ardith's face as it glanced at Achtriel was chagrined and resentful.

"I will stay with you today," Esther offered soothingly. "Achtriel must rest now and have some refreshment. She will come to you at evening."

"I can stay…" Achtriel protested, but Esther waved her away.

"Go home now and sleep," Fagim told her.

On the way home, Achtriel realized that she was indeed quite tired. The thought of a nap in her bed, perhaps with Sachela for company, seemed very inviting. But when she arrived at her room, she was surprised to see Tirzah and Margit there. They had taken out the contents of the clothing trunk and were examining them.

"Oh, Achtriel," Tirzah addressed her in the overtly friendly way she used when they were not alone. "I have told Margit that she can have some of your dresses. You never wear them."

"You are welcome to them," Achtriel said, yawning. "I do not like to think that they will go to waste. I would have given them away, but Macha said the mothers would be angry if I did not show appreciation for their gifts."

"Well, we will say that you have sold them. They will approve of that."

"You're right," she said. "They all know Tahto has been ill."

"I can pay you ought for them," Margit said brightly. "I will bring you rolls and bread when they are left. You'll have much less baking then."

"Yes," Tirzah replied. "And I shall put a bug in Macha's ear that Achtriel is growing and needs more new clothes. Then it will spread to the mothers at the synagogue."

"I know other... Gentile girls who might would love these clothes," Margit said cautiously.

"Fine. We shall sell them at a decent price. We will have a good business before long."

"But...won't the mothers mind?" Achtriel worried.

"What if they do? There is nothing they can say. They have given you the clothes, and that is that."

"But..."

"Don't fret so, Achtriel," Tirzah said sourly. "It is not as if the Jewish wives will get any the less benefit from their charity. The Almighty will approve of their intentions.

"I suppose."

"How fare the tailor's wife and child?" Margit inquired.

"They are well so far."

"Stand up and let me see this color on you," she instructed Margit.

"Yes. The green lining brings out your eyes and hair."

"Duggin will be pleased. She laments on about not affording to dress me well."

"Does she want you to marry then?" Tirzah asked.

Such was the extent of Achtriel's exhaustion that, although she dearly wished to listen to the older girls, her eyes closed of themselves, and soon, she was asleep. When she awoke, the day was waning. It was very strange to rise into late afternoon with a ghost moon in the sky. Tirzah and Margit were gone, and Achtriel could hear Berthe and Nimrode talking as they set the evening table. Suddenly, Sechela bounded onto the bed, and with her pleasant rumbling nudged her face into Achtriel's neck.

"You make that sound when you are happy," she said. "Now I can learn what other things you like. It is a shame that people were not given that ability." Sechela's purrings grew louder as Achtriel stroked her fur.

"Child? Are you well?" Berthe called into the room.

"Yes. Very well, thank you, Berthe," she replied.

"Then come and help with dinner. Tirzah has gone to the tailor's house, and there is much to do."

"Why is she there?" Achtriel asked, sitting up and thus rousing Sechela who jumped away.

"The tailor's wife has asked for her. She wants her help."

"But I was meant to help them…"

"Yes, I know. But the…the family feels you are too…"

"I am not too young! I was doing…"

"You were indeed," Nimrode, appearing behind Berthe, interjected. "Fagim was here and told us what a marvelous job you did with the babe."

"It is only that Ardith does not like me."

"I'm afraid it's true," Berthe admitted.

"But I'll be quiet and polite. I need to be there!"

"Now, now." Nimrode looked sympathetic but useless.

"I know what to do! I've worked with Fagim many times…"

"Yes. We understand," Berthe said, glancing at her and then looking at Nimrode. "But it is the tailor's wife's decision, and she is the mother."

"But Jacob needs me!"

"He will be well."

"How do you know that?" Achtriel cried, feeling tears begin to gather in her eyes.

"Esther will be there tonight to make sure all goes smoothly. So you see there is nothing to fret about. Now come and make those lovely rolls you girls learned from the baker. Tahto has guests tonight, and we must do them credit. "Come along now," Berthe repeated. "Tahto's guests will come out soon, and we must feed them. You have work to do."

"The baby was my work," she complained.

"Your elders have decided differently, and now you must obey them." Berthe arched her brows in such a way that it was clear no succor would ensue from her. Reluctantly, Achtriel rose and went to wash herself.

As she prepared the salad, though, her thoughts were anything but obedient. It was unfair! The baby Jacob needed her! Certainly, Tirzah could not care for him as deeply. She was not the kind or mothering sort, a category into which, until two days ago, Achtriel would not have included herself. But Tirzah did not really notice anything that would not bring some advantage to herself. She might be sweet and pleasant with Ardeth, and she would probably do a creditable job caring for Jacob. But he needed more than that. He needed someone who could concentrate only on him, at least until he was stronger. And neither Tirzah, nor Ardith, was fully capable of that.

"Hurry with the salad, child, the men are coming from their study," Berthe called. "As we have a special guest, I do not wish us to seem tardy."

"It's done," Achtriel said, none too enthusiastically, and brought the salad into the dining room. There, to her surprise was the blond man who had, it seemed now years ago, given her the vellum as a gift.

"Well, hello, wise one," he said to her, smiling.

"Hello," she said.

"And how have you fared since last we met?"

"Quite well," she told him. "I used your gift to draw people at the fair and made enough money by it to help Tahto when he was taken ill. I must thank you again." She bowed her head politely and went to put the salad on the table.

"You seem a bit disheartened? Nothing dire I would hope?" His tone was teasing and thus somewhat irritating, but she answered him.

"I was caring for a baby who was born early and is weak, and because the mother did not like my…my looks, I was dismissed."

"I see," he said, his amused tone softening. "So you have been the subject of unfair judgment."

"I suppose you could call it that." She straightened the dishes on the table and adjusted the cloth over the rolls to keep the heat in.

"Alas, it is the way of the world, child. If folk cannot despise thee for one attribute, then they shall find another."

Achtriel looked up at him curiously. "Did anyone despise you in your life?" she asked him. "I find it hard to fathom as you are a man and handsome and well bred."

He stifled an amused smile and answered, "Ah, but there are those who hate me for refusing to accept the privilege that comes with such gifts. And one of them, I hate to say it, is my mother."

"Your mother?"

"Yes. You see I was to have been made wealthy landowner, through marriage, and I was not so inclined."

"But surely she could not have hated you, her own son?"

"Oh yes, and very much so. She will not allow me to return home, and so I have wandered many years and thus spent my youth in tolerable freedom."

"But don't you miss her? If I had a mother, I should want to be there always."

"I suppose I do, that is the sting of it. And yet I do not regret my choice for I have met so many fascinating souls, here and abroad. Of which your grandfather is by far the cleverest. Although there are holy men and women in Hibernia who could come close. But they are but copyists not enlightened thinkers as he is. So you see although the fates have dealt you several blows, they have also placed you in a very blessed home."

She sighed. "I know I am the most fortunate of girls. I have been allowed to study and to learn great things."

"Indeed! I have met young ladies endowed with beauty, riches, and intelligence who would exchange places with you in an instant."

"With me? To have my arm and leg into the bargain?" she glanced up at him briefly.

275

"To be confined and hampered in one's very soul is a more crippling way of life."

She was quiet for a moment. Then she said softly, "But if they have beauty and wealth, they may exchange them for a life of ease and thereby find time for scholarship, I would suppose."

"Then you would suppose falsely. It is hard to understand the woes of those who seem so different from you. But I can tell you that I know such girls and women, my own sister being the chief example, who would take your infirmities and count them as a trifle to be allowed such freedom to learn." Achtriel looked at him and then back at the dinner table.

"Of course you are right. I must try harder to remember it."

"My sister is just as quick as I am and as avid a scholar in her youth. But now she has grown old before her time, bearing and caring for children. She has eight already with the ninth on the way. Such is the fate of women."

"That is so," Achtriel agreed. "But doubtless, I shall never have children and so suffer an opposite sadness."

"Come now." He smiled at her, his blue eyes sparkling. "You are a fine girl."

"That is not what others say."

"Never listen to the prognostications of inferior folk," he said. "For life itself is never sure, more so the future."

"Ah, Antonus, so you have met our little scholar," Nimrode said jovially, striding in from the study room.

"But we have met before!" the man said.

"Indeed! So this is not your first visit to my brother's house."

"No, nor will it be the last, if the Good Lord shields my steps."

"Well, well," Nimrode said. "We shall be fortunate in that; shall we not, Achtriel?"

"Yes," Achtriel replied, stealing another glance at the handsome man. His height and breadth bespoke a man of rugged means, and yet his golden hair and vibrant skin crowned these like a flower on a stalk.

After their pleasant dinner, which was only briefly upset by the insistence of Sachela on sharing the table with their food, the men once again retired to the study. Achtriel began to see to the dinner things and the storage of food. Then she washed the dishes and prepared to dry them.

"She is not as she seems," a voice spoke behind her. It was Berthe.

"Who?" asked Achtriel, although she knew.

"Tirzah." Berthe sighed. She came into the kitchen and picked up a dishcloth.

"When first she came to us…" Berthe took the stew pot and began to dry it. Then, as if suddenly recollecting where she was, turned her attention to the task at hand and fell silent.

"When did she first come?" Achtriel asked, attempting to sound dispassionate, though her interest was keen.

"Oh, it is nothing. It is nothing," Berthe answered, turning to carry the pot to the kitchen cupboard. "Well," she said, brushing her hands against her skirt to cleanse them. "Now, let us finish with our work so that we may have a chance to read before retiring."

Achtriel pulled a clean rag from the drawer to dry the spoons. "Was she a child?" she asked, trying to mask her fervent curiosity which, once piqued, could become agonizing if unrequited.

"Why, you are both still children," Berthe said brightly. "Although you, yourself, rarely behave as one."

Perhaps because she was still exhausted from her sleepless night, Achtriel's irritation unexpectedly overcame her. "I am not a child inside my mind!" she said angrily.

"Go and rest now, child. Don't you think you will feel better in the morning?" Berthe said kindly, but Achtriel did not reply. Dragging her less able leg behind her like a stubborn child, she went silently to her room. Since Tirzah had been sharing the bed, it had ceased to offer sanctuary. But now, Tirzah was with Jacob.

Achtriel removed her outer clothes and tossed them in a pile. There was some comfort in having the room to herself. Sachela, who had been outside chasing insects, leapt onto the open windowsill. Seeing Achtriel, she jumped into the room and rubbed against her ankles. Achtriel bent to pick her up.

She went to the bed and deposited the cat and herself on it. Then she lay on her side and curled up. Tonight she could sleep alone as she had used to in a position more comfortable for her limbs. As if sharing her sense of freedom, Sechela settled at Achtriel's feet and began to lick herself. Soon, she was making the whirring sound that signaled her contentment.

Achtriel looked gratefully at her small companion. How simple it was to love animals. They did not deny their need for affection. Perhaps Tirzah would find love in helping a fragile child, she reasoned. But this seemed unlikely. Not that Tirzah was completely without solicitude. She had, in her own way, taken Achtriel and Margit under her wing. There were now three separate piles in the room. One for clothing that Tirzah had chosen, the other, for ones that Tirzah insisted Achtriel wear. The remaining garments, except for Achtriel's unruly pile, were neatly folded.

She reminded herself how fortunate she was to have been raised by Tahto. Without him, she would not have lived a week. As her irritation and anger cooled, she began to feel ashamed. She thought about going to Berthe to apologize, yet, somehow, she could not bring herself to do it. I will tell her tomorrow, she decided, as she pulled the blanket about her and drifted into sleep.

In the morning, she awakened later than she normally did. It was strange not to hear the morning chorus of birds. The house, too, seemed oddly quiet. She rose and dressed and went to investigate. Indeed, Berthe was not at her usual station, hovering about the kitchen like a large bee. Perhaps she had gone to the tailor's house to check on Tirzah's progress.

Vowing never to set foot in Profait's house again, Achtriel gathered bread and cheese and wrapped it in a cloth. She went outside, planning to set out for her neglected forest. From the town came pleasant sounds of industry, the clang of a bronze worker's mace, the shouts of men to their slaves and apprentices. Voices could be heard exchanging greetings. It looked to be another sunny day.

She decided to visit Fagim who might need help in preparing for her wedding.

The thought of spending the day with Fagim was pleasant. Despite her occasional sharpness, Fagim was a comfort. There was nothing of which she was unaware, yet she did not chatter about unnecessary subjects as Berthe was wont to do. In Fagim's presence, one felt understood.

Placing her lunch in her kirtle pocket, Achtriel set off for the high road. As she ascended the rise to Fagim's house, looking down only to step around boulders and smaller stones, the morning raised her spirits. The sky was blue and vast and clean. Below it, the brown earth slumbered, dreaming of spring. The rich color of the hills, the smell of baking from the nearby homes, a trill of birdsong, all these were cheering. In spite of her crooked limbs, she felt strong and lively. Even the climb did not tire her.

When she came to Fagim's house, nestled in a narrow alleyway behind the church, she knocked vigorously on her window.

"Come in," called Fagim's hearty pleasant voice. "Why, it's you," she said when Achtriel came inside. "I hope you have come to help me for I have much to do. I am finishing some tinctures in the drying house and preparing dyes for Profait's cloth."

They spent a pleasant morning making dye and dried herb remedies, the latter a process which Achtriel found endlessly intriguing. Plant properties, combined with solvents, became something which nature had not invented. What was it that the plants contained or were made of that retained their quality? How did the dissolving sharpness reach into the essence of the herbs and magnify them? These and other questions, she sought to understand until Fagim, having exhausted her knowledge, declared that she did not really know. Stirring the bright colors in the comfortable house, quiet except for the cooing of birds which roosted in the overhangs, Achtriel was momentarily at peace.

"And why do people choose to wear dyed garments?" she asked Fagim. "Why not go about in plain and simple cloth. All the trouble we take, the time and interest and expense, must mean we have a need for beauty like that for food."

"Some more than others," Fagim remarked.

"Yes, but why? Why is prettiness a thing which people cherish so? Why is it a necessity to us?"

"A good question," Fagim said.

"Why is it that folk assume that beauty brings superiority? If a girl is born a certain way with a face inspiring admiration, she is reckoned holy. And yet she may be no better to the world than one who is…not so blessed. It is illogical and unfair."

Fagim raised her eyebrows as she ground the herbs and sighed. "Well, you may ask," she said quietly. "Well, you may ask."

They were silent for a time. Achtriel was patient. She knew that Fagim too would tire of this bland monotony. Soon, she would begin to talk of interesting things, if only to amuse herself.

"It is," she said at last, "a mystery indeed. Although we, who are educated and aware of all the great philosophies, should not be snared so easily, it seems we too are vulnerable. I, for one, spent many years inside my own mind that is, envying Esther her loveliness."

"You, Fagim?!"

"Ah yes."

"But you are so wise and very strong…"

"Indeed," Fagim interrupted her. "Alas! These attributes are not admired, or only as an afterthought. It is feminine beauty which makes the mark."

"I am afraid you are right," Achtriel said. "The eyes of people when they look at Tirzah…"

"Yes?"

"They betray a certain fear, a native humility. Noble thoughts are no match for her beauty.'

"Yes. And yet the irony is that beauty brings its own hazards and grief."

"What do you mean?" Achtriel asked, forgetting her stirring. But she would not discover further answers in this morning for the door creaked open, and Esther came in.

"That woman!" Esther exclaimed, removing her headscarf and tossing it on a chair.

"What? Ardith? Is Jacob not well?" Achtriel stammered.

"He is well at present, but in spite of her."

"I must go to him at once!" Achtriel cried, throwing down the sewing and getting to her feet.

"No, I do not think that best either," Esther said, placing a restraining hand on Achtriel's shoulder.

"Why not? I love him better than she does. I love him vastly more than Tirzah could."

"I see you speak the truth. But sometimes we must travel a circuitous route to reach our aim."

"What is Ardith doing?" Fagim asked, as furrows formed between her brows.

"I cannot put my finger on it, that's the irritating thing." Esther shook her head. "She does as I instruct her, at least when I am there. But something in her attitude is just amiss. The baby senses it as well."

"She is afraid he will be crippled. She would rather that he died." Achtriel spoke bluntly. Fagim and Esther turned to stare at her. "It's true!" she said, her lips aquiver with impending tears.

"How horrible. And yet I think you may be right." Fagim nodded.

"Have you some reason to suspect this?" Esther asked.

"Of course. She questioned me at length upon the subject."

"That does not mean…"

"No, I could not prove it," Achtriel said bitterly. "It is just something I know."

The three of them were silent for a while. "The child needs to know that he is wanted. Otherwise, he will not fight to stay alive," Fagim said, voicing their thoughts.

"I want him!" Achtriel said, crying now.

"I know you do, sweet child," Esther said kindly and held Achtriel's head against her chest. "But you are just a babe yourself. You cannot be his mother."

"I can!" she insisted through her tears.

"It's true you are an extraordinary girl," Fagim said kindly. "But there is more to raising children than even you can know."

"Nonetheless you have given me a good idea," Esther said and patted Achtriel.

"What?" she asked, raising her head.

"You will see, my clever one," returned Esther jauntily.

"A mystery!" Fagim exclaimed to Achtriel. "The thing you love best."

"But only when I solve the riddle," Achtriel complained.

Chapter 26

The next morning, Esther appeared at Achtriel's house. Tahto, his family and their guest, were sitting at their morning meal.

"Come in, come in!" Tahto called gaily when he saw her face at the door. The blond man straightened himself and smiled broadly.

Achtriel had been awake all night worrying over Jacob. She had had to stop herself several times from running to his house. She was sitting glumly at the table, although the handsome Antonus had made several attempts to brighten her spirit.

"I have a solution." Esther sat at the table, looking pleased with herself.

"A solution to what?" asked Nimrode.

"The tailor's wife is fearful that her child will be deformed. She does not love him, and he will die," Achtriel said.

"My dear, such extremity, you insult the poor woman surely?" Berthe admonished.

"And you have devised a remedy?" Antonus asked Esther, his eyes twinkling.

"Yes, and I shall need your help, and Achtriel's."

"I should be honored to assist in anything you might devise for me," he said.

Just then, the front door opened, and Frans came in. He was dressed in his courtly clothing, a silken shirt with Persian decorations in which small golden trinkets glimmered in the morning light. "I am here as bidden," he said, "and with accoutrements."

"I am now thoroughly intrigued." Nimrode grinned.

"Well, as we have no time to lose, you will have to wait to learn the outcome," Esther said. "Achtriel come to your room. We must have a planning session."

Later that day, Achtriel stood on a tree stump, peeking in at Ardith's back window. Both she and Tirzah were asleep. Jacob lay in his cot beside the fire. Achtriel was relieved to see that he was wrapped in his fur. An imperious knock sounded on the front shop door. Ardith awoke abruptly and called to Tirzah, "Some custom! Profait has left for Rodom! Quick, we must attend to it."

Tirzah rose reluctantly and went forward to open the door. There stood a regal figure, an elegant and kingly man, attended by Frans.

"I am in need of tailoring," the man said. "I am staying at the Manse and have had a slight mishap. This fellow has been assigned to conduct me and has brought me to your establishment. I hope he is not mistaken in his choice."

"No, no…" Tirzah said uncertainly and looked back for Ardith.

"Who is the proprietor here? I demand attention!" the tall man boomed. Tying up her kirtle, Ardith hurried into the front room and executed a frightened bow.

"My husband is away on business, Your Excellency," she stammered.

"And what of you? Have you no tailoring skills? I am in need of repair on my garments before I attend a fete tonight. I was told this was a decent tailor shop, for such a backward area." He fretfully inspected the rip on his cape then looked about the shop. "Your materials seem acceptable."

"We have only the finest, Your Honor, my husband brings them monthly from Rouen…"

"I don't care where they hail from!" the tall man shouted. "Are you going to attend me or must I report to all the local gentry the inferiority of your services?"

"Of course, of course, sir. What is it you need?"

"Can you repair a seam, woman? Without damaging this gold inlaid cape, which cost me a twenty solildi?"

"Of course!" she answered. "Yes, if you please, sir, please sit down; and I will fix it for you."

At this, Frans tapped on the tall man's side and beckoned him close. He whispered something in his ear at which the regal features dimmed.

"Are you quite capable of this, woman? You do not seem... prepared."

"Of course, of course, sir," Ardith assured him and reached to remove his cloak with trembling hands.

"What is this? Your fingers shake! I cannot let a tosspot touch my cloak!" He stopped her hands and plucked them rudely from his person.

"I, swear, Your Excellency, I am... I can do it very well..." Ardith stuttered, on the point of tears.

"Pfff! I do not care to risk my best cloak to your fuddling. Have you an assistant, woman?"

"I..." Ardith looked pleadingly at Tirzah who only bowed and said, "I was not trained in such things, sir."

"I would so imagine," he said assessing her. Then he turned to Ardith with a sour expression. "Well, worse luck for you and for your husband to have wed a simpleton." He turned toward the front door. "Come, Ambsace, we shall not bring our custom to the Jews in future."

"No. Wait. Please, sir, please. I will repair it well, you'll see," Ardith begged. "If my husband hears I have destroyed his custom, and that of all the Jews, he will divorce me, and I have a little child..." As if on cue, Jacob began to wail. Tirzah looked inquiringly at Ardith who stood frozen.

"So you have produced an additional incompetent?" He smiled coldly at his own joke. "Very well, I have a soft spot for small children. Bring him here to me."

Ardith looked at Tirzah who did not move. "Certainly, sir," Ardith said, bowing, and hurried toward the back room.

"I wager she is just as doddering a mother," the man said loudly and sat himself grandly at the tailor's stool.

When Ardith emerged a moment later with the child in her arms, the tall man rose and went to view the infant.

"Ah, it is a male at least. I would not have thought you capable…" he muttered. "An intelligent fellow by the look of him. Nature is at times inscrutable." Jacob, perhaps sensing his mother's discomfort, began to cry again.

"Well, put him down, Mother. I have decided to give you a chance. But hurry now before I change my mind."

"Oh, thank you, sir, a million times, I shall not disappoint you." Ardith motioned at Tirzah with her head for her to take the child. Tirzah came forward and took the baby stiffly in her arms. At this, the child began to scream, his little face bright red.

"Woman, have you no better sense than to employ an odalisque as nursemaid?" The man guffawed and looked for confirmation to the dwarf. "That girl has never held a child I warrant, nor was bred to. Your poor husband would do well to let you go I say and hire a wet nurse to take your place." Ardith's face betrayed a fierce mixture of shame and nascent anger, which she had the sense to quell.

"Well, come and take my cloak, woman. My hosts await me." But before she could proceed, the baby squealed and in the midst of a terrific yell spewed vomit over Tirzah's chest. The tall man turned away, sweeping the golden cloak over his nose.

"Tirzah, take him in the other room and see to him," Ardith said in an attempt at a commanding tone.

"He has soiled his fur as well, what should I…" Tirzah asked.

"Just do something!" Ardith cried, and Tirzah, holding the child at arm's length, conveyed him to the other room. The sound of his increasing screams were hardly muffled by the curtain that separated the two rooms.

"He will be fine, Your Honor. Just let me attend…"

"Fine? The child is clearly unwell. Have you no notion of your own stupidity?"

"Please, sir, just let me take your cloak," Ardith was nearly crying now.

"A woman with no better sense than to trust the care of a sick child to a concubine? I think not. Come, Ambsace, I've seen enough." He rose to leave. Suddenly, a knock was heard at the front door. Ardith stood frozen, unsure what to do. The door was pushed open, and Esther came into the room, followed by Achtriel.

"What is wrong with Jacob?" Esther asked in some alarm.

"Oh, nothing, see to him, please, Esther, I beg of you…" Ardith pled on the point of tears.

Esther's eyes took in the arch tableau and alit on Achtriel. "I would ask this child," she told Ardith, but I can see you have more need of her in here."

"Please just…do something." Ardith begged. Esther looked at Achtriel before she went off to the bedroom.

"Does your cloak need mending?" Achtriel inquired of the man.

"Indeed, but there is none here who can do it, though it is a tailor shop."

"Please allow me, sir," Achtriel came close to examine the cloak. Ardith blanched alarmingly at Achtriel's twisted forearm, fearing more reproach. But instead, the man bowed deeply to the girl.

"You must be the scholar I have heard about," he said deferentially. "Ambsace, do not they talk of her about the castle"

"Oh yes, with much amazement," Frans agreed. "It is said she can draw better than the royal portraitists, knows five languages, sings and plays tambour, even teaches Latin to the gentry's sons."

"I can sew as well," Achtriel said, examining the hem of the cloak. "This seam is raveled; it requires careful mending."

"Well, none but you shall touch it," the man said, removing his cloak while giving Ardith a sidelong glare.

"Here, Achtriel, here is our gold thread," Ardith said, bringing it. "She can do it well, Your Excellency, she often works for my husband in this capacity. Please sit at Profait's table while you work, dear child. I shall fix our guests some tea."

"Can you boil water?" the man asked doubtfully, not watching her go. "Oh, very well, what further damage can you do?" he indicated with his head for her to prepare the tea. "Ambsace, follow her I beg you to ensure our safety."

Esther came into the tailor shop then, holding Jacob. "We are not sure how to clean the fur," she said to Achtriel. "I do not want it wet lest he chill and take a fever. I have wrapped him in my woolens for the moment, but they are not an able substitute."

"Hold the fur beside the cook stove," Achtriel told her, glancing up briefly from her sewing. "Be careful not to get too close, or it will burn. When the bile is dry, you can clean it with diluted vinegar."

"Ah, I knew you'd have the answer," Esther said.

"Is there nothing which she does not know?" The man said loudly, for Ardith's benefit.

"I do not know my parents," Achtriel said simply. "I was left on my master's doorstep at two days old."

"This only proves the idiocy of the lower classes." The man sighed. "They value all the silly qualities in girls and women and do not recognize intelligence. That is why all kings and high officials of note must prize and foster talents such as yours. We do not want our noblewomen turning out like the tailor's wife," he said this loudly for the benefit of Ardith.

"Your cloak is mended, sir," Achtriel said, rising from the table and presenting it to him.

"Amazing, one would never know it had been stitched," he marveled. "Child, you have preserved the reputation of this Jew, at least he has the sense to hire those who can fill in when he is not at home. Woe to him and his addlepated spouse, if you had not appeared."

"Here is the fur, is it quite dry enough?" Esther returned from the kitchen for Achtriel's inspection. Ardith followed, cowering, behind her.

"Yes, that is fine," Achtriel answered. "All you need to do is take it close by the refuse heap. Then you can brush off the surface with chamomile water and wrap him so he stays warm."

"Here is your tea, sir," Ardith said, meekly, holding a cup to him with quivering hands.

Ignoring it, the man admonished her. "You are fortunate that your business has been saved by this able child. You would do well to heed her words in other areas. Do not destroy your son the way you almost did his father's livelihood. Good day."

"We shall tell our royal friends about this deed," Frans said, taking Achtriel's less able hand and kissing it. Then he and the tall man strode majestically out the shop door.

When they were gone, Esther turned to Ardith. "Well, all's well then. Achtriel, I have need of your keen eyesight, come with me to remove any remaining bile." She and Achtriel went through the bedroom to the refuse heap. "Your room is quite untidy, Ardith," Esther remarked as they went out the back door. "Filth breeds contagion. I would have it cleaned at once, "Cleaning the cloak hurriedly, Esther and Achtriel avoided each other's eyes. Both knew that, otherwise, they would be unable to control their laughter. When they returned, Ardith was lying on her bed, looking very pale, as Tirzah ineffectually attempted to straighten the room.

"Where is Jacob?" Esther demanded.

"In … in his bed, Esther, he is warm enough," Ardith protested weakly.

"No, he is not!" Esther reprimanded her. "Fagim has given you two simple responsibilities. Keep him warm and well fed. If you cannot see to this, perhaps we should employ a wet nurse as the gentleman suggested."

"No, no…" Ardith cried. "We cannot afford one. I can see to him." She lifted herself shakily from the bed and went to retrieve the baby.

"Here, wrap him in this and keep him warm," Esther said, handing her the cleaned fur, "Unless you want to bury him within the week."

Ardith gave Esther a terrified look. "Yes, Esther. I will see to it," she assured her.

"It is imperative that you do," Esther told her. "Come Achtriel, we have work to do. We shall return later in the day to check on him." When she and Achtriel had hurried from the merchant street to the road toward the village, they gave vent, at last, to their laughter. Frans and Antonus, who had been waiting for them there, joined in.

But Achtriel's merriment soon ceased. "Poor Ardith." She said. "She was so afraid. We should not have done this. She feels terrible."

"You are a goodly soul, as the preacher says." Frans smiled. "But the woman will be fine. I have known a good many like her. They do not remain long in self-recrimination."

"But she was only afraid, and now we have made her more so," Achtriel worried.

"There are some things which one needs to fear," Esther said. "The death of a child is one of them. I am sure her suffering would be much greater in that case."

"Still, the child is right," Antonus said. "Perhaps we should go back and admit our prank."

"She will find out soon enough," Esther said. "She is coming to Sabbath. She has never come before. Until now, she has remained all day inside that house. I don't know how she does that. She will see you and Frans there. I say she should remain in fear and ignorance at least a few days more. Elsewise, the lesson may not quite sink home." Achtriel reluctantly agreed, but all the way home, she continued feeling very sad for Ardith.

When they reached Tahto's house, they were surprised to see Tirzah approaching from the other direction.

"You!" she exclaimed when she saw Antonus.

"I beg forgiveness, child," he bowed graciously. "The jest was meant only for Ardith. I am heartily sorry if I offended you," he proffered his gloved hand. "My name is Antone."

Ignoring his gesture, Tirzah swept past him. "No, I am sure you are correct. I am hardly interested in any babes, nor no doubt ever will be."

"But you are too young to know such a thing," Antone protested.

"No," Tirzah said, "I am not."

"One cannot see one's own future so clearly," Esther said quietly. But Tirzah had opened the door and gone inside.

Later that night when they lay together in the interlude before sleep, Achtriel renewed the subject.

"But babies are so especially sweet. When you hold them, it is like nothing else on earth. Surely, when you are married…"

"I will never marry. Nor bear children."

"How can you know?"

"I am quite certain that before I ever consent to such a fate, I will drink poison."

"Tirzah!" Achtriel exclaimed, shocked. But Tirzah merely rolled away from Achtriel and pulled the blanket over her.

A short while later, she added sleepily, "I have suffered enough."

Chapter 27

In the morning, Achtriel found Tirzah in the kitchen, baking. "Are you not going to Ardith's to help with Jacob?" she asked.

"I am not needed," she replied, pulling a bread pan out of the oven.

"But she is not capable of managing alone!"

"She is not alone. Just after you left, her mother arrived."

"Oh, dear." Achtriel felt truly repentant now. "Poor Ardith!"

Tirzah prodded the bread to test its readiness. "You have too much sympathy," she stated flatly. "If I had been such as you, I would not have survived." Then she returned to her cooking and ignored Achtriel who stood watching her for a long time, wondering if this were true.

At the Sabbath dinner that week, Ardith was spared further humiliation for Antonus had departed, and Frans was needed for some entertainment at the castle. Now, overdressed in blue striped wool, Ardith sat between her husband and her mother at the dining table.

"Your color is returning," Fagim complemented her.

"And the boy looks hardy," Nimrode added kindly.

"He is a glutton," the mother remarked, glancing at the babe in her arms with a mixture of pride and disdain. "He would eat all day if she allowed it."

Esther looked astonished, "But that is precisely what he needs!"

"You see, Mother, I was doing right," Ardith said archly.

"If she has her color back," the mother sniffed, "it is due to me. I have taken the child at night so that she can sleep."

"That is a great help, and we see its good result in them both," Fagim said. "But it would not wake her were you to place the child beside her in the night so it can nurse."

"I have never heard of such a thing," the mother said coldly but looked down at the sleeping child. "I suppose I could attempt it," she muttered. "I have only raised thirteen living daughters yet of course I know nothing."

"Yesterday, he smiled at me," Profait said beaming. "At five days old. The child will be a scholar."

"Then perhaps we will have a second prodigy," Esther said, smiling at Achtriel.

"With remarkable children such as these, we are blessed." Berthe smiled, taking in all the young folk. But Natan was not following the conversation, and Tirzah seemed preoccupied.

After dinner, as Achtriel and Tirzah tidied the kitchen, the adults began to talk of Fagim's wedding. Achtriel stopped her scrubbing so she could listen, but Tirzah gave her a sidelong glance of disapproval.

"Is it your wedding?" she asked sarcastically.

"No." Achtriel blushed. "But it will be a great festivity. That will be exciting."

Tirzah returned to work with no further comment. Achtriel, however, still smarted at the exchange. She knew full well what Tirzah must be thinking. How sad it was that Achtriel, who would never have a wedding, was so intrigued.

"And it will be nice for everyone," Achtriel continued. "The whole town will come. Even the Gentiles, for Fagim has doctored them all and saved so many lives." Tirzah did not answer and, in fact, appeared as if she hadn't heard. "All the girls will need new garments," Achtriel added.

"That is true," Tirzah said, looking up. "I had not thought of that. Yes, we must begin at once to measure them. Esther will be too involved to sew for them, and we will do well to take advantage of it."

"What do you mean?"

"Margit and I have begun an alteration business. She is an accomplished seamstress, and I have much design experience. We will need your help too."

"I? But...where will you get the extra cloth?"

"From your collection. I have saved the usable material, and Ardith has agreed to furnish us with remnants. Margit will tell the girls and women, and soon, they will be vying for our services. In such a market, our clothing will fetch a fine price."

"But if you cut up the clothing that the mothers have given me, they will be offended."

"Let them be." She shrugged. "It will not lessen our profits. Their daughters will insist on our more worldly styles." Achtriel thought a moment. It would be good to earn enough to furnish Tahto with extra food this winter. His lungs were still frail, and in the rain and cold, she feared his illness might return. "Has Margit spoken with the Gentile girls?"

"No, but she will do whatever I tell her. And I am improving her as well. She is speaking much more elegantly now. It isn't hard to learn. Hurry with your work, we need to begin planning." And before Achtriel could assemble a reply, Tirzah had departed.

So it was that, throughout the months of preparation for the wedding, Achtriel was kept busy with sewing, designs, and sorting material. The clothes, as Tirzah predicted, were in such demand that loud arguments broke out between the Gentile girls and even among the Jewish ones. So busy did the enterprise keep her that she barely had time to learn the music she was rehearsing with Nadaasya. He was composing two new pieces for the wedding. They both incorporated Mogul scales and Persian poetry and rhythms. At night, she would come home from his house with music careening through her mind, where it collided with images of patterned shawls. As she fell asleep, rows of stitches filled her vision.

As the weeks went on and Naadasya's pieces grew more complex, she began to worry that she never would be able to remember, let alone do justice to his compositions. Fortunately, Frans was in the program too and would go over the new material each evening as he walked her home.

"What if I can't remember anything, right on stage in the middle of the performance?" she asked him.

"Then you will be like every other performer."

"But what do you do?"

"You make it up." He winked.

"That is all well for a storyteller, but I would have to conjure something that fit in with his scales and harmonies. And the rhythm…"

"Don't worry, Achtriel," he assured her, "You will do fine."

"But what if I don't?"

"Haven't you ever…not done well?"

"Not in front of a whole town. I should embarrass Fagim and all her guests!"

"You worry too much," he pronounced. "Now sing me the second part." And Achtriel, to her surprise, would remember what she had learned, although she had no idea how she'd managed it.

But as the weeks went on and the demands from Tirzah and Margit increased: a longer hem for a tall girl which would diminish her; a vertically striped darker robe for a chubby one to hide her girth; an appliqué for the daughter of the largest merchant to adequately indicate her wealth; not to mention the many late nights of sewing during which Tirzah continually urged her to work faster; her ability to keep the music straight began to erode.

Naadasya and Frans cajoled her when she told them she could not perform and pooh-poohed her fears about embarrassing them. But nevertheless, she began to become ever more certain that she was destined to forget her place in the midst of a passage and be utterly dumbstruck.

In the old days, before Tahto's new family arrived, she would have gone to him to ask him what to do. He had always listened and taken her seriously. But now she hated to disturb him. He and Nimrode were working on an important project, cataloguing the ancient texts Nimrode had brought, so that they could be copied and preserved.

She had never seen him so engrossed in work, and at dinner, he seemed far away, as if his mind had stayed in the study. And Nimrode was always at his side, except when they retired. She could not bring herself to bother him before his nightly rest, for she knew that often he could not sleep if he were so disturbed.

So she kept her worries to herself and tried to find time in the early mornings to go over music in her mind. But Tirzah had also begun waking early and would seek her out and make her work. During this time, it was Sechela who seemed to understand her best.

The cat would follow her all day and rest beside her as she sewed. It was a comfort to think that Sechela would hardly care or notice mere musical failure. It seemed she recognized important things far better than most humans, as if she saw into their souls, and though not overly impressed, remained magnanimous.

Certainly, Tirzah was not so circumspect. Her focus had narrowed like the path into the needle's eye. Several times a day, she counted up the money they would be earning; and at night, she counted it again, a furrow set between her brows. She oversaw her "workers" with a Spartan eye and was not loathe to force them to rehem, if robes hung less than perfectly. However, she remained civil all the while, a trick which assured that neither Achtriel nor Margit felt ill used but privileged to be the focus of such vigilant regard.

This must be how they trained men to be soldiers, Achtriel concluded. On the one hand, there was no escape and on the other the illusion of participation in some grand endeavor. Meriting approval from such an exacting taskmaster brought a sense of pride, all the more for its infrequency. And when they surveyed the finished product and the beaming face of its wearer, there was no denying a feeling of accomplishment. At night when Achtriel fell exhausted into bed, beside the already snoring Tirzah, she recounted all the money she had earned for Tahto so that his health would be assured.

One afternoon as she and Margit sat intently sewing, they were surprised by the entrance of Ardith, accompanied by her mother. Achtriel dropped her work and stood to greet them, but Ardith did not seem to care.

"So this is how you now repay our kindness," she said angrily to Achtriel. "By stealing all our business and impoverishing us!"

"I never thought to…" Achtriel began, but Ardith's mother cut her off.

"But we hear that you are so intelligent!" she remarked sarcastically. "You clearly reckoned that your enterprise would cut into our trade."

"It wasn't my…"

"Of course, it wasn't your intention. You never think how your behavior alters things. You interfere and make things more difficult for all of us!"

The mother was practically screaming now. "The boy is so greedy he demands attention all the time. He will not be content to lie in his bed while Ardith works and cries with such a vengeance that I must attend to him or have neighbors at my throat. And meanwhile, you sneak out and steal our custom. I wonder that all the folk about hold you in such a high regard when you are nothing but a thief!"

Achtriel did not know what to say. She knew they had brought their suit to her because she was a child and so least able to defend herself.

"I am sorry. I did not know that these things affected you so dearly," she stammered, hoping Ardith would relent and become reasonable. But the mother launched into a tirade, calling Achtriel a heathen and a gutter trash, and advancing with such menace that the girl began to cower.

"Leave her be!" A plangent voice rang out behind them, and as Ardith and her mother turned, Achtriel caught sight of Tirzah, imperious and pale behind them.

"It is not the girl's doing, she never sought to injure you," Tirzah said, her voice quiet but commanding. "I have chosen to begin this enterprise, and if you find your business suffering, it is because your garments are inferior."

"So you have taken her side too?" the mother turned around to face Tirzah. "What hold has this foundling gained on you, I thought you more clear headed than the rest."

"Indeed I am," Tirzah replied. "And I can see that you and your silly daughter have chosen to harass my helpers rather than take up with me. Do not add cowardice and lack of foresight to your list of faults."

"Our business lessens as your own enlarges," Ardith said somewhat timidly. Her mother nodded, trying to appear menacing but not quite achieving it.

"Yes. And what of it?" Tirzah asked. "It is as likely that your rude unsightly mother has scared off your patronage than that our simple enterprise has hurt you." Ardith's mother opened her mouth to retort, but in the face of Tirzah's coolness, she was rendered speechless.

"Now leave my workroom. Business is business, and you have no legal standing to interfere with ours." The women stood and gaped at Tirzah, like a pair of goats before a lion. No one moved.

"Perhaps we can combine our efforts..." Achtriel began, but Tirzah scoffed.

"I would not trust their workmanship to fashion undergarments."

"My daughter's husband has been making garments since before you were born," the mother objected.

"Then why is he not here?"

"He... does not know that we have come," Ardith admitted, beginning to seem somewhat pitiful.

"Well," Tirzah said as she walked dismissively past them, "as he has not behaved absurdly like his womenfolk, I am happy to negotiate with him. I will come down to the tailor shop after our midday meal, and perhaps we can arrange a compromise. Now, get out of my workroom."

Ardith and her mother looked at each other as if for counsel. Finding none, they left the room, but not without a hostile glance at Achtriel. Tirzah shook her head and muttered something foreign which did not sound complimentary. Then she went to examine her stock of used cloth.

Achtriel remained where she was. The anger, the hurtful words had stung, and because she was so tired, they seemed more penetrating. She did not understand why Ardith, and now her mother, held such loathing for her. True, they had played that trick on Ardith with the nobleman, she supposed that angered her when she found out, but her dislike of Achtriel had predated that.

It had begun when she had talked with Ardith about Jacob's physique. Achtriel could only surmise that Ardith and her mother considered her a peon. It all began to seem quite cruel and very unfair. Why should she become the target of such debasement? What had she ever done or chosen to do that merited their hatred? She had certainly not chosen to be lame. All at once, her life seemed cumbersome, too great a load to bear. To disguise her imminent tears, she hurried to the door.

"Don't be such a goose…" Tirzah began, but Achtriel moved quickly out of earshot, dragging her bad leg behind her like a pike. She went as far from the house as she could manage then sat down on the ground and wept.

Was this the life to which she had been destined? To be a target for no other reason than the way she looked? And as Antonus had clarified, she was in the very luckiest of circumstances. What reception could she hope for in the wider world? No better than a leper's or a mendicant's, to be an object of derision, malice or mere pity. She looked down at her twisted leg. It was intolerable, infuriating, inescapable; she was like a half-dead mutilated hare caught in a trap.

Suddenly, she hated everyone. How easy life would always be for them, Tirzah beautiful and strong, Margit, who spoke now like the gentry, and would no doubt find a husband from the merchant class and have a brood of healthy children, none of whom would limp. Even Nimrode and Berthe, with their dim but pleasant view of life, could stay oblivious. Even Tahto—but at the thought of him—she began to cry in earnest. For he had left her, had tired of her. Content in his scholarly insulation, he was hers no more. And yet she loved him and could never leave him. Would stay beside him whether he noticed or not, forever.

"What is all this?" a bemused adult voice inquired. She looked up to find Nimrode, pail in hand, gazing down at her.

"Nothing," she said, turning to hide her face.

"Sorrow is never nothing," he said, putting down the pail and crouching next to her. "It is the intersection of our lives with truth. Tell me why you cry."

"I am tired, that is all," she said.

"I think I know you well enough by now to know you're not the sort to cry at nothing," he said kindly.

"Yes, I am," she said, wiping her face with her hands.

"What foolish thing has brought you low then?"

"Foolish women," she replied.

"Those two termagants who left just now? The tailor's wife and mother-in-law? Now that is a silly pair." He shook his head. "Why the Holy One sees fit to populate the world with stupid folk I cannot guess. When I was a boy, I would sit dumbfounded by this fact for hours." He crouched beside her.

"What is it makes them dunces? I would ask myself. Is it that they cannot see or cannot hear? But no—this isn't true. They see and hear and smell the same as smart folk. The trouble must be with the way they think, I reasoned. Their thoughts are small and puffed up like a starchy biscuit. As such, they bounce around inside their heads till they become quite stale. It is a shame." Achtriel could not help smiling at this image. "He must have a reason for it. God is perfect in all his acts," Nimrode said. "But I can find no such use. I stay away from them whenever possible."

"But if they come to you…?"

"Oh yes, and they do, don't they, they love to bother people. Well, in that case, I would say the wisest course is to pretend to be one of them, but even stupider. Then they will be satisfied and go away."

"That is hard to do." She sighed.

"Ah yes. But luckily, you will have many opportunities to practice this skill. There are many dunces in the world. The Good Lord has provided." Achtriel glanced up at him, and he began to chuckle. His laughter was rich and silly like Tahto's, and it made her feel better just to hear it. "Try to find the humor in it," he told her. "It is the only recourse."

"What is wrong?" called Berthe approaching them.

"Oh, nothing, wife. I will have your water in a moment."

"But what is it? Why does the girl appear so sad?"

"It is nothing," Achtriel repeated. "Really, I am just tired."

"Has my Tirzah been too hard on you? I know she can be sharp when she has set her mind on something."

"No, not at all," Achtriel replied. "In fact, she sought to help me."

"Did she? That is good!" Berthe seemed surprised. "I was hoping this enterprise would bring her greater patience, and it seems it has."

"Apparently, the tailor's wife and affinate have used the little one to vent their spleen," Nimrode said, patting Achtriel sympathetically.

"Well, of course, they would. They would not stand a chance with Tirzah; and well, they know it." Berthe sniffed. "I shall have words with them."

"No, please," Achtriel implored her. "It is all my fault. I was tired and let their words upset me. I shouldn't have."

"And what did Tirzah do?" Berthe asked.

"She told them to leave me alone. She is going to talk to Profait after midday. I think she has a plan."

Berthe smiled, obviously pleased. "Of course she has, the potentate. That girl was born for conquest."

"But this one here, I fear, is not of the same cloth," said Nimrode, stroking Achtriel's arm.

"Too true," Berthe agreed. "A Brahman like her grandpapa."

"He is not really my grandfather," Achtriel began.

"Indeed?" Berthe looked at her quizzically but did not elaborate.

"But you are very like him nonetheless," Nimrode said with a meaningful glance at Berthe. "He is not a businessman and never will be. And nor shall you."

"How do you know?" Achtriel said, wiping the last of her tears on her palms. "I may learn to be."

"I would not wish it for you," Nimrode said. "It would be a waste of brilliance."

"If only you were born a boy." Berthe sighed. "Your future would have been assured."

"Well, I was not," Achtriel said, brushing dirt off of her legs. "And I must find my way in spite of that."

"I have no fear you will," Berthe told her. "None at all."

"Thank you for your kindness," she told them both, and struggled to her feet.

"It is not that," Nimrode assured her, standing also. "We are a family, and we prosper on the talents of each one. And you a shining star among us, a great blessing, boy or no."

"Thank you," she repeated. "I must go help Tirzah prosper now."

"As I have no doubt you shall." Berthe nodded; Achtriel knew that they were watching as she ambled toward the house. When she reached it and looked back, they were watching still.

Tirzah and Margit glanced briefly from their work as Achtriel came back into the bedroom. Margit seemed sympathetic, but the look on Tirzah's face was hard to read.

"Those women are beastly," Margit said and glanced at Tirzah for approval of her fancy word.

Tirzah frowned. "Curs like that weaken themselves with their own folly," she muttered. "It never pays to let them see that they have troubled you."

"I wish I had as good administration of my sentiments as you," Achtriel said, returning to her seat.

"You must learn it," Tirzah declared, pulling a strand of thread between her teeth and severing it. "Or folk like that will always bark at you."

"Yes. You maunt bark back!" Margit said, reverting to her market vocabulary. "I mean you must."

"I am not good at that," Achtriel picked up the kirtle she was working on and resumed her stitching. They sewed in silence for the rest of the morning until the church bell tolled for noon. Then Tirzah, with a determined frown, set her work down and stood up.

"I'll return this afternoon," she told them as she smoothed her tunic and walked away. Margit and Achtriel glanced at each other, but neither of them spoke.

Later that afternoon, Achtriel heard Tirzah's voice outside the bedroom window. "I do not see why I should," she was saying.

"It is the way of the Jews," Nimrode replied. "It works better in the end."

"Well, I am not a Jew, and I can manage my own way," she muttered.

"Ah, but now you are," Nimrode said gently. "When you came to live with us, you were legally remanded."

"I did not consent to that!"

"It was the only way I could keep you. And I hope you still recall how difficult that was." There was a lengthy silence during which Achtriel put down her work and inched toward the window.

Tirzah and Nimrode, looking up and seeing her, moved away from earshot.

A while later, Tirzah came back to the room and, looking frustrated, set her work upon her lap. Margit and Achtriel exchanged glances but kept sewing. After a while, Tirzah said something they did not understand and left the room. When she returned, she had Ardith with her. The mother followed, with Jacob, much larger now, slung across her hip.

"Oh, he looks so well!" Achtriel said happily and rose. But the mother took a step away and turned, with Jacob, toward the door. "I will wait out here," she said coldly, her eyes on Achtriel.

Tirzah sighed. "Ardith will work with us," she said. "Here Ardith, take the kirtle Achtriel is working on; I'll find her something else to do." Looking smug, Ardith walked up to Achtriel and held her hands out.

"You may have it, and gladly," Achtriel said, handing over her work, "my eyes were getting tired simply looking at it."

"No doubt you're meant for better things," Ardith said rudely and waited until Achtriel had left her seat. Then she sat down with a small flourish and examined the stitching. "I can see your eyes were weak, the hem is sloppy. It will have to be redone." She began to rip the stitches Achtriel had spent all morning doing.

"Stop," Tirzah held Ardith's arm, "I will decide." Narrowing her eyes, she looked over the seams. "They look alright to me. Leave them in."

"Well, I do not know why folk are so enamored of your garments." Ardith shrugged, laying the kirtle on her lap. "The work is poor. Most like they're taken with your fancy ways and do not care if the seams last."

"If yours are better, we shall know it soon," Tirzah said returning to her seat, "When you have completed something."

Ardith, with a sour face, knotted the ends of thread she had ripped and picked up the needle. "I am sure you will," she said half to herself and, feigning concentration, set to work.

"Take these garments out into the sun and look for stains or gaps in workmanship," Tirzah ordered Achtriel, who, without a moment's hesitation, dutifully complied.

Outside, breezes stirred the trees. The boughs, like maidens, tossed their tresses and gloried in the wind's attentions. All around her, moving branches made a dazzling choreography. Achtriel dropped the pile of garments on a chopping block and, like a prisoner set free, entered the dance.

How grand it was to not be working. On an afternoon like this, how evident that the air was designed to delight. Of course, she knew that work was what sustained them, and that this was better employment than most could hope, but still… the smell of leaves, and the sunlight winking through the branches…it fairly gave permission to be idle.

She glanced back at the house where her bondage lay. Perhaps she could just take a minute. After all, Tirzah herself was often gone for hours at a time. And she had not mandated expedience or set a limit on this task. The garments, if they did need fixing, could wait. Besides, their workmanship, despite Ardith's insinuations, was fine.

Taking up the clothing, Achtriel crept toward the house. Once inside, she lay it carefully upon the table, so that the robes should not get wrinkled. No sound came from the bedroom in which the others likely sat discomfited, unspoken insults on their tongues. Margit was humming, no doubt trying to foster harmony. Stepping quietly, Achtriel left the house and, as fast as she could manage, hastened toward the forest.

She did not intend to stay there long, only it had been so long since she had been there. The saplings were taller now, and there were patches of lavender in the clearing. She saw a vixen with four half-grown kits and could not help but watch them play. A group of mother sows emerged from the underbrush with their yearlings, saw Achtriel and ambled off, the young ones trotting behind them.

The air smelled of beech and sycamore, and the sky, between the treetops, was a merry blue. Her old haunts had overgrown, but still, the forest welcomed her like a prodigal child. When she heard the noontime bells, she gasped and had to hurry back, hoping her truancy had not been discovered.

All seemed well as she approached the house. There was no irate Tirzah, scouring the yard for her. Sechela hurried up with a little mew but did not follow her into the house. When Achtriel saw the garments, she understood at once. The cat had found them a soft resting place. Her underfur lay in clots upon the topmost kirtle. And while brushing the tufts away, Achtriel discovered something worse. A blue tassel, which the Gentile butcher's wife had been enamored of, was now a torn and tangled mess.

Looking about quickly, Achtriel picked up the pile of clothes and stole with it out to the yard. Thankfully, the rest of the garments were unblemished, but it took her many minutes to remove the fur from them. There was no remedy for the battered tassel. As if sensing her complicity, the cat rubbed anxiously at Achtriel's leg. The animal's expression, guilt subsumed entirely by self-satisfaction, was so amusing that it was impossible to scold her.

"How do they look?" Startled, Achtriel looked up to see Tirzah approaching.

"Um, they seem well," she replied. "Only I had to take this tassel off, it was discolored."

"It doesn't look discolored," Tirzah said. "It looks destroyed."

"I had some trouble while removing it."

"Indeed." Tirzah raised one eyebrow.

"I am sure the butcher's wife would have been embarrassed to have worn an ornament of such poor quality."

"No doubt."

"Fortunately, I believe there is another one. I saw it yesterday when I was sorting. It is green, but it is better kept."

"Well then, you will have to bring it to Ardith tomorrow morning to be affixed."

"Ardith?"

"Yes. She will be replacing you."

"But I need the payment to help Tahto!"

"Yes, I know," Tirzah said. "That is why I have assigned you to another task."

"What is that?" Achtriel asked apprehensively.

"You will be delivering the finished products to their owners and recording all complaints and the amendments necessary."

"Oh," Achtriel considered this. "That doesn't sound so bad."

"It isn't. Your first customer, in fact, will be the butcher's wife. As soon as Ardith has repaired the dress, you will deliver it. Tomorrow."

"Of course," Achtriel tried to smile.

The next day, after a glorious morning of doing nothing, Achtriel went to the workshop prepared to face an ugly scene. But to her surprise, the three seamstresses sat busily sewing in an empty, but untroubled silence. Ardith looked up when Achtriel entered "Here," she said handing her the dress with its green tassel firmly affixed "I have done my best to mask your damage."

"Thank you," Achtriel told her, meaning it sincerely.

"Let us hope the butcher's wife is not upset," Tirzah said with a meaningful glance at Margit.

"I know her," Margit said. "She can be a virago."

"She can?" Achtriel asked hesitantly.

"Once I saw her throw a shank of lamb at her own daughter," Margit said, smirking at the memory. "Because the butcher had not brought her something fetching from Rouen."

"Oh."

"You had better be prepared to show humility," Ardith said. "If you have any."

Achtriel picked up the kirtle and headed to the door.

"Good luck!" Margit called after her. The others giggled.

Still, the day was so radiant that it seemed nothing could mar it. Achtriel strode cheerfully with her loping gait, along the road to town. In the common fields, she could see slaves and workers sowing the winter wheat. She heard a guttural shout behind her and turned to see Natan who had been following her.

"Hello!" she waved cheerfully at him. "I am going to Armageddon."

He caught up with her and asked, with his quizzical face, what on earth she meant.

"Well," she said resuming her walk beside him, facing him so he could read her lips, "Sechela destroyed a tassel on this lady's dress, and I must hope she doesn't throw a lamb shank at me."

Natan described the circumference of a side of lamb with his hands and made a funny puzzled face.

"It seems she has been known to do so in the past when she is angry."

He nodded, comprehending, and then acted out the scene of someone two handedly wiping meat juice from his face. She laughed.

Then he pantomimed that his cat now was big and sometimes fierce but always friendly. He gave her to understand that he had determined, definitively, that his cat was the male.

"I already knew that," she said, "because Sechela is so superior." They walked in a companionable silence after that until they came to town. When Achtriel turned to go toward the butcher's shop, Natan chuckled behind her. When she turned around, he acted out the part of someone, ducking from an airborne piece of meat.

"If you see me returning all bloody, you will know what happened," she called back at him and went bravely on her way.

The Gentile butcher by town standards was a wealthy man. Not as rich as many merchants but comfortably off. His wife was younger than him by several decades and had a raucous well-fed lot of children. One of them saw Achtriel approaching and ran inside, no doubt to announce her.

She had cherished a faint hope that the woman would be gone, and that the kirtle could be deposited with her husband. But the wife herself came striding out to meet her. She was a handsome woman with a straight sharp nose and a mop of curly hair. Although she seemed no older than a girl, her face was creased with worry or habitual irritation.

"Let me see the garment," she demanded.

"I was responsible…" Achtriel said, handing her the dress. "It is my fault that the tassel is not blue…as you wished." She watched the woman turn the garment over, inside out and backward. Then she gave it a proprietary whisk or two and glared at Achtriel.

"It was my fault…" she repeated. "If you want, I will come work for you to make up for it…after the wedding."

"What happened to the blue one then?" the woman asked. "The green is not the color of my fibula; I wanted them to match. That is why I paid her extra."

"Is it that Roman pin I've seen you wear? The one with engraved birds and little flowers? It is the most elegant object in Briga."

"I know," the butcher's wife said, fingering her collar. "It was a wedding gift from my stepfather; his family is wealthy."

"They must be to afford a luxury like that. How fortunate we are that we can gaze upon it now and then. I hope you will wear it to the wedding."

"But it will not match," she complained.

"That is much the better! "Achtriel said. "The green will make it stand out even more. Everyone will notice it and be green with envy."

"Where is the blue one?" the woman asked, frowning at the green tassel.

Achtriel sighed. "It was my fault."

"So you have said, now please explain. I do not like it when I am disappointed, and I am now, quite unhappy."

"Well, I left the garments on the table and…"

"Yes?" she leaned irately on one hip.

308

"Um, Sechela adored the tassel so, she only wanted to have a look, but somehow…"

"Who?"

"My cat."

The woman's frowning face slackened.

"You see, it was such an unusual color, and so irresistible…that she…"

"A… a cat? You say a cat attacked it?" The woman's pale face turned quite pink.

"Yes, but I made sure that nothing further…"

"A cat?"

"Yes. I'm very sorry," Achtriel, recalling Ardith's warning to show humility, bowed her head. There was a silence, during which she did notice a humbling, even frightened, upset in her stomach.

"And it is a female?"

The direction of the conversation had turned so quickly that Achtriel, looking up at the butcher's wife, was momentarily speechless.

"I don't…"

"The cat, idiot. Is it a female? You do know the difference, do you not?"

"Oh. Yes. And my friend has a male. We got them at the same time."

"You are obviously lying," she sniffed, turning the garment in her hands to reexamine it. "There are no cats in these parts."

"Natan and I, we got them in Rouen," she answered, unsure how best to maintain her humble attitude on this new topic.

The woman looked heavenward. "Holy blessed God!" she cried and took Achtriel roughly by the hand. "Look here. Look at this!" The woman had dragged her onto a small patch of earth which Achtriel thought, for a fearful moment, might contain the gravesites of previous blunderers. "Do you see?"

"I don't…"

"This," she took Achtriel's face and bent it roughly toward the ground, "this is how they've ruined all my husbandry!"

"They?"

"The rats, imbecile." She gave her a shove. "The wretched things."

"Oh."

"A scourge on all god-fearing souls." She kicked at a clod of earth. "They are ruining my crops. We will become paupers having to buy all our food!

"That is a shame."

"I have done everything to no avail. I have set the children out here with sticks for hours. Good-for-nothings! I beat them till they bleed, but still, they do not catch the horrid things."

"It is difficult no doubt…"

"I have tried my hound, but it is as useless in these matters as a log. I am nearly ready to tear it to pieces!"

"That would be cruel!"

"The garden, you stupid child. Not the dog." She knelt on the dirt to gather several half-eaten plants. "Each year, I lose more, and I must go sooner to the market. At this rate, I will soon be forced to sell my valuables."

"Oh, dear. That would be a shame, your lovely pin."

The woman glared at Achtriel, but then she narrowed her eyes. "If you will promise me a male and female from your first litter, I will forget about the tassel."

"You will?! Oh! Thank you! That is wonderfully kind!"

"It isn't kindness," she said with a harsh laugh. "I have never been accused of that," she brushed her hands together to remove the dirt and stood up. "Now you must bring the male cat to your house for several days as soon as possible."

"I have to ask Natan. We were going to…we had some idea of making it a business."

"Nonsense. The cats will soon breed nicely on their own." She surveyed her garden. "But before that, I shall do quite well by them myself. You may keep whatever other cats you get and let them multiply. But mine, since they are the first and finest, shall be touted as more expensive. Is that understood?"

"Yes, thank you," Achtriel stammered, not believing that her doom had been so suddenly remitted.

"And the next time you go to Rouen, you will find me something nicer than that tassel. And you will sew it on for me."

"I will try to find something."

"You had better for I have my heart set on it. Now go away and see to the cats. Go on!" She gestured as if shooing away rodents and returned to her house.

"Thank you," Achtriel called after her.

What a fortunate reprieve! Of course, Natan might have objections on the business end, but he could take those up with her himself. Besides, there were no kittens yet and should not be for quite a while, the cats were still so little. She began to sing as she walked back the way she came. It was a glorious morning.

She took as long as possible returning home. But, she reasoned, she had best not annoy Tirzah. Delivering garments would give her many other stolen moments, so she must keep the job. Whistling an Arabic song that Naddasya had taught her, she walked back into town, taking care to avoid Duggen's stall, lest she mentioned to her niece the lassitude evident in this morning stroll.

When she got back, the seamstresses were intent on some internal disagreement and did not notice her arrival. She sat and waited for Tirzah to tell her what to do.

"I work faster than both of you!" Ardith was protesting loudly. "Why should I be paid the least?"

"You need it less for you are married, and your husband has a business," Tirzah answered. "And you are here only at my behest, so do not rile me."

"Why less? Margit has other business also, and you are still a girl, supported by your parents."

"They are not my parents," Tirzah said. "And I have been the cause of their misfortune, so I am indebted."

"Tosh, when you are married off, they will grow rich by it."

"But that shall never happen," Tirzah said. Ardith and Margit, looking up from their work, stared at her.

"Mayhap it will not be so bad…," Margit said gently.

"Not married? Ridiculous. You will have no choice in that, say what you will," Ardith scoffed. She resumed sewing, albeit with ears piqued with curiosity.

"I think it could be quite lovely, sometimes. When I am with…"

Ardith looked up rapidly, and Margit caught herself in time.

"So, you have a man already," Ardith said. "I do not need to know his name; I can find out easily enough."

"I do not know if he returns my love," Margit said shyly.

"Just watch he does not require that you prove yours," Ardith said. "Or you will have a bastard just as your mother did."

Margit turned bright red and stared so angrily at Ardith it seemed she would soon pommel her.

"You know naught about my mother," she said. "And if you talk of her again, you will see how well a Gentile girl can hurt you."

"Stop this silliness!" Tirzah told them both in an exasperated tone. That was when she noticed Achtriel, and seeing an opportunity for diversion asked if she had fared well with the butcher's wife.

Very well," Achtriel replied with a small grin.

"You are probably lying. Let me check your face for wounds," Ardith scoffed.

"There are none. We are on quite good terms."

"Astonishing," Margit remarked, still glaring at Ardith.

"It took a while, but I was able to convince her that the green was best, and she sends regards and thanks to all of you."

"I sincerely doubt that," Ardith said.

"Well done, Achtriel," Margit said, looking away at last from Ardith's face.

"Oh, my head hurts," Tirzah told them all. "Your caterwauling has undone me. You finish up this hem, Achtriel, I will relieve you after midday."

"God bless all cats." Achtriel smiled, replacing Tirzah at her post. "Including you, my friends." She even smiled at Ardith, for today, she could be cross with no one.

The next morning, Tirzah was not there when Achtriel awoke. Assuming she must be about on business, Achtriel lay luxuriously abed until Margit arrived.

"Where is she?" Margit asked laying down a tray of green cheese and bread she had brought for their lunch.

"I don't know." Achtriel yawned. "Did she say anything yesterday about being away?"

"No." Margit frowned. "And this is not like her."

"I am sure she will be here soon." Achtriel sat up and stretched. "Too soon," she added.

"Well, we had best be working when she does come," Margit admonished. "Have you finished the trim on the miller's linen?"

"Yes, I finished it by candlelight and had little sleep because of it."

"The wedding will be over soon," Margit said cheerfully, taking up her own project, a decorative embroidered sleeve for a wealthy widow. "And we shall be paid and fat."

"We have been paid some already, have we not?" Achtriel sat up reluctantly.

"Oh yes. Tirzah has collected almost half of what we are owed. She has kept the records in her safe box."

"It will likely be some while after the wedding till all our customers have fully reimbursed us," Achtriel reasoned, laying aside her blanket.

"Not at all," Margit replied. "Tirzah has made them each a legal contract, which they have signed, or marked if they cannot write; and it requires all payment to be due before the wedding night."

"So they will not have clothes if they have not paid. That is unusual in this town but clever of her," Achtriel reasoned. "Some of these families are known for holding out years before resolving debt."

"I think she realized that when she was at Ardith's house, those months ago. She told me she explored the tailor's tally books while Ardith was asleep."

Achtriel, irretrievably awake now, got out of bed. "Did Ardith find out? Is that why she is so angry?"

"Oh no. Tirzah is too clever to be discovered. Ardith was furious simply because we had taken her trade. And that is no fault of ours, for there is no law forbidding competition."

"Then why did Ardith come to work with us?"

"What else could she do? Profait still tailors for the men, but all the women have become our customers. With their business cut, she needs the income."

"I suppose that is the way of things," Achtriel said, lifting a tunic from a pile of unfinished clothes. "I think I will not become a businesswoman. It seems mean."

"Well, your sister seems determined to make one of you." Margit laughed, and Achtriel looked up in some surprise. She had not thought of Tirzah as a sister. Nor had she ever considered that Tirzah might reckon herself as such. It was a strange thought, and she was not sure how to feel about it. There was not time to speculate, however, because Tirzah herself strode into the room, looking pale and angry.

"Where have you been?" Achtriel asked.

"Nowhere that you need to know of," Tirzah answered and went to survey the finished work. "Is this the best you could do on the miller's sleeves? The stitches are as gnarled as vines."

"I stayed up half the night to finish them," Achtriel protested.

"And mayhap you fell asleep while you were at it. Fix these stitches." She threw the garment behind her.

Margit stood up and knelt to pick it up. "I think this part is good enough; it is really only the last part you need to redo," she told Achtriel quietly. Feeling all happiness seep out of the morning, like mop water into dirt, Achtriel sat down to fix the stitching.

Chapter 28

After midday, Margit stopped sewing and went to arrange their lunch. Achtriel looked up eagerly, but Tirzah did not seem to notice.

"Are you not hungry?" Margit inquired kindly.

Tirzah did not reply. Achtriel and Margit exchanged glances.

"Are you feeling unwell?" Achtriel asked.

"Yes!" Tirzah shouted, and standing, threw her sewing on the floor. "And if you both keep pestering me, I shall walk out of here and leave the rest of the work to you!" With that, she strode out of the room. They could hear her angry footsteps leaving the house.

"I wonder what's wrong," Margit said.

"She gets angry sometimes. I usually don't know why."

"Yes, but..."

"What?"

"This is different somehow." Margit frowned as she cut the bread.

"You are a good friend to care so much about her."

"She's had a horrid fate," Margit said, unwrapping the cheese. "Would have killed most people."

"What happened to her?" Achtriel asked casually, hoping the information would continue flowing from Margit's lips. But instead, she looked at Achtriel and said sternly, "You don't need to know."

When Tirzah returned after lunch, the girls were careful not to talk to her. They could see, however, that she seemed upset. Finally, after several hours of sewing in which she was clearly in pain, Tirzah rose quickly and went to vomit out the open window.

"I will get Berthe!" Achtriel said, rising.

"NO, you will NOT!" Tirzah said as she wiped her mouth with her hand.

But it was too late. Berthe had heard the retching from the kitchen and come running.

"Here now, lie down," she said soothingly to Tirzah and led her toward the bed.

"No! I have to finish; the wedding is only a week away."

"Ardith will get her mother to help out," Berthe told her, "You will do none a service by worsening."

"I am perfectly well," Tirzah protested but allowed herself to be steered to the bed and fell onto with a groan.

"Achtriel, run and get Ardith. Then fetch Fagim."

"Yes, Berthe," Achtriel said. Hurrying out the front door, she could hear Tirzah's vehement moans of protest.

It was another lovely day. There was no sign of impending rain, and the air was warm in the sunny places. Selfishly, Achtriel was thrilled to be outside in it, although she admonished herself to have concern for Tirzah. Still, their relationship, sisterly or not, so often left her feeling wounded; it was hard to feel enormous sympathy. She kept a steady pace toward town but was not inclined to hurry overmuch.

On the way, she saw Natan and found herself jealous of his leisurely gait. Why was she so hard at work while he idled? Nevertheless, she conveyed the urgency of Tirzah's state to him; and looking shocked, he hurried off to find his mother.

"I should have sent him to get Ardith instead," she reflected apprehensively, as she approached the tailor's house. It would have been a pleasure to spend time with Fagim. No such outcome awaited her at Ardith's; she was certain.

As she knocked on the tailor's door, she could hear Jacob cooing. In spite of herself, she softened toward the family, even the bad-tempered mother. If the boy was happy, they must have something to do with it. She was smiling when Ardith's mother opened up the door.

"What do you want?" she demanded.

"Tirzah is unwell. Berthe asks if you and Ardith can come help us with the sewing."

Ardith's face appeared behind her mother. "Unwell?" she asked.

"She is retching and in pain. We don't know why."

"I have a notion," sniffed the mother, but Ardith pushed her out of the way.

"I will come at once. Mother, see to the boy," she said firmly.

"I do not know why I should be so used," the mother complained. "I have watched him all the morning. I was going for a walk."

"I'll be back as soon as I can," Ardith said.

"That's hardly true," her mother said. "You'll be there till sundown in all likelihood."

"Bring Jacob when it's time to feed him," Ardith called after her as she and Achtriel hurried off.

"I should have gone home e'er now, if not for my kindness," the mother called after them, "Though little you note it!"

"She would set a price on every act of service." Ardith sighed as they approached the road. "And taxes too."

Laughing at this, Achtriel found to her surprise that Ardith's dour wit was a welcome note in an otherwise discordant morning.

When they entered the workshop, they saw Berthe, Esther, and Fagim bent over a reclining Tirzah.

"Thank you for coming," Fagim said, turning to glance at Ardith.

"Is she very ill?" Ardith asked as she removed her cloak.

"I am fine!" Tirzah said. "And do not speak of me as if I am not here."

"She is in a great deal of pain," Esther said, daubing a soft cloth on Tirzah's forehead.

"Yes, and this," Tirzah pushed Esther's hand away. "Is making it worse."

"It hurts to be touched?" Berthe asked. "Does the sunlight worsen your pain?"

"Everything worsens my pain!" Tirzah said, "Including all of your babbling!"

"I have seen this before," Berthe muttered. "One of my bonds-women suffered from it. The Africans had a remedy for it. Perhaps I can find it in my notes."

"I have seen it also." Fagim frowned. "It is more common among noble women. Some of them are quite debilitated by it, but I know no cure."

"I will see what my journals tell me," Berthe said and left the room.

"If you would just leave me alone, I would soon be well," Tirzah insisted but then let out an agonized groan.

"Poor Tirzah!" Achtriel said.

"I am not poor and do not pity me!" Tirzah yelled. "Just go away!"

"Is she in danger?" Margit asked, coming to stand beside Achtriel.

"No, no danger," Fagim said, rising and wiping her hands on her skirt. "The pain will pass. But it can last for several days."

"Then bring me a knife and let me die," Tirzah moaned.

"We will do no such thing, "Esther said, taking Tirzah's hand. "Now calm yourself and wait till your mother returns."

"She is not my mother," Tirzah muttered. "I have never had one, and I do not need one now."

"Hush," Esther admonished. Tirzah grimaced but was silent.

"Margit, kindly show me what needs working on," Ardith said quietly. With a nervous glance at Tirzah, Margit nodded and led Ardith from the bedside.

"Achtriel, don't stand there like a stump," Ardith said as she passed. "You are not a nurse. Come do your work."

Reluctantly, for there was something compelling in the mystery of this illness and its potential remedies, Achtriel returned to sewing.

"Blue balm," Berthe announced, reentering the room with a large bound record book. "The Africans called it Choga, but appar-ently, there is a similar plant that grows around the Mediterranean.

Perhaps there is an equivalent one to be found locally. I have a drawing of it."

In an instant, Achtriel's sewing was abandoned as she hurried to Berthe's side to view the picture. It was a bushy plant with yellow daisy like flowers.

"It looks like something I saw growing in the woods," she said. Berthe turned to look at her.

"Have you seen this growing around here?"

"I think so. There are lots of them in the clearing. I could go see if I could find some."

"No!" Tirzah groaned from the bed. "The wedding is only a week away. We have promised our customers that their dresses will be done. Keep sewing!"

"I can take over for her," Berthe told Tirzah.

"I can help too," Esther offered.

"As can I," Fagim said.

"Tosh! You are the bride!" Berthe admonished.

"How silly," Fagim protested. "I am embarrassed by all this fuss to begin with. Am I to be further ashamed by sitting idle while my friends are in need?"

"I can go to the woods and be back before midday," Achtriel said brightly. They all looked at her with the exception of Tirzah who had turned her face to the wall.

"Go then," Esther said. "But be mindful of wild beasts."

"I like wild beasts!" she called as she headed for the door.

Amid the trees, the midmorning light capered about the forest floor, speckling the foliage. The boundless quiet beckoned all her senses. It was hard to ignore the temptations that every cranny of the undergrowth proffered. Here, a furry spider had cast a web so vast it draped the stalks and branches like a veil. There, a raven sentinel reported her and was echoed by a chorus of proprietary cronks. Rustling branches marked the skulk of creatures she would have dearly loved to see. But it would be selfish now to stop and spend her time in exploration. Tirzah lay in pain, and it would be cruel to dawdle. No one would know it if she did, but God was watching, and she did not need more black marks on her slate.

Yet, she could not help but feel disloyal to the woods. They were her first community, her temple and sanctuary. She had left them for the human world, a choice whose wisdom she could question still. She hoped they had not forgotten her. That would be an orphaning far worse than her first. For although Tahto was her greatest love, and the prospect of his death an unimaginable loss, she knew that human lives, unlike that of the wilderness, would ever be finite.

When she reached the clearing, she found that, in her absence, the canopy had grown above it. What once had been a sunny hollow in the woods was now small and dark. Nevertheless, there was a corner where sun-loving plants had managed to survive. Among them stood the bush whose flowers looked like those that Berthe had in her journal. Unsure which part of the plant was medicinal, she pulled up a section of it by its roots. It smelled pungent and lemony. She hoped it would be helpful to Tirzah.

Tying the plant to her waist with her belt cord, she turned to leave. But there in the clearing stood a red wolf with a torn right ear, eying her intently. Achtriel, perhaps unwisely, felt little fear. She had always longed to see this creature closely and stood enthralled. It was only after it had turned and bounded off that she took account of any danger. She wondered if the animal had truly disappeared or had simply gone to reconnoiter with its hunting fellows. In that case, there was little she could do to save herself. She noticed that her hands were trembling and shook them roughly to stop it. Tahto had told her that wild animals can see fear and be emboldened by it.

She quickly scanned the area for a means of escape should the wolves come for her. The trees were tall and difficult to climb, but she spotted one whose lower branches seemed accessible. Moving slowly, she approached the tree. There were no sounds from the woods, surely a pack of wolves would make some. A hawk squealed overhead, but it did not seem a warning, just a show of pride.

She stood beside the tree for several minutes. No disturbance bothered the surrounding brush. Finally, she decided it was safe to move. Nonetheless, if wolves were watching, it would not do to seem afraid. On her return journey through the woods, she bellowed out Naadasya's bawdy songs like a swaggering sailor.

When she emerged from the woods, she stopped to look down on the village. She had to admit that she was glad to see it. However cruel people were, they seldom ate each other. She added a verse to her song in gratitude for this. It praised the Holy One and thanked Him for His oversight. Despite its savage ways, the human world could boast this meager kindness.

She returned home to a silent house. Startled, she began to fear that Tirzah had worsened, and that they'd moved her to Fagim's for doctoring. Then she heard a moan from the bedroom and, hurrying there, discovered the girl, prone and huddled on the bed. The windows had been decked with blankets blocking light out of the room. It seemed like a catacomb.

"Did you find the plant?" she mumbled.

"Yes!"

"Achtriel, for God's sake, stop your shouting! The noise is pounding at my skull."

"I'm sorry. Where are the others?"

"They said the best thing for me was to be alone. It hasn't helped."

"Where did they go?"

"I don't know. I don't care."

"Well now, I have the plant. What shall I to do with it?"

"Look in Berthe's journal over there." Tirzah made vague motions with her arm. "There are instructions."

Achtriel found the journal on a sewing table and perused it. "It looks like you crush the leaves and stem into a paste," she said, "I'll try it."

"Talk with Berthe first! My God, you'll poison me!"

"At least you would be out of your misery," Achtriel muttered as she left the room and added, "And so would I."

She found Berthe at Profait's shop. Ardith, her mother, Margit, Fagim, and Esther were hard at work completing the remaining tailoring. Jacob, fat and pink now, slept on a cot in the sun.

"Ah, Achtriel. Did you find the herb?" Berthe asked, her eyes fixed on her sewing.

"Something much like it. I have brought it with me."

Fagim rose and came to inspect the plant.

"It is feverfew," she said, fingering the flowers. "How did the Africans prepare it?"

"They crushed the leaves and flowers," Achtriel said. "I read it in the journal."

"Yes, I think that's right," Berthe agreed, glancing up.

"I'll see to it,' Ardith said. "Achtriel, take my sewing."

"I can prepare the tincture," she protested.

"I'm sure you can, but as I am your elder, you will do as I ask you." Ardith took the plant from Achtriel and handed her pointedly the kirtle she had been working on. Achtriel sighed and took the garment.

"How many more garments need finishing?" she inquired, sitting down.

"I think we will be done by the Sabbath," Esther said brightly.

Margit was sent to bring Tirzah her balm, for Ardith could sew more quickly than she. Ardith's mother saw to Jacob, when he cried, and tended him. No one seemed to notice anything amiss in this, but Achtriel felt demeaned. The loss of her post as Jacob's nurse still rankled.

Before the others came, and before Margit had risen from the stalls to join them, the choice would have been clear. Achtriel, once seen as fully competent, was now consigned to servitude. Why had she learned to sew so well? She should have pretended to be as crippled as they thought she was and now have been excused from all this drudgery. But she continued working nonetheless and contented herself by following the women's talk.

"What ails that girl will not be cured by flowers," Ardith's mother opined.

"Hush, Mother," Ardith said, glaring at her.

"What do you mean?" Esther inquired.

"Only that there is much fornication in this town," replied the mother. "I have it from the gentile butcher's wife that…"

"Never heed those tales!" Esther interrupted. "Some folk have nothing more to do than spread false rumors."

"Whether they are false or no will always out. Women cannot long escape the fruits of sin." Ardith's mother fixed Esther with her sharp gaze till Esther turned away.

"What matter if a woman acts upon her will?" Fagim said hotly. "Has she not the right to choose her own companions?"

"If the Holy One had meant for us to do so," the mother stated, "it would be so written. Clearly, He does not."

"How can we know what the Holy One intended?" Achtriel interjected.

"It is in the scriptures, silly girl."

"But I have read so many scriptures. The ones from Greece and Alexandria are particularly…"

"Pooh," Ardith's mother cut her off. "Your grandfather is one of those misguided scholars who insist on studying false doctrine. Our rabbi would soon set him straight."

"Is it more correct to take the word of someone who has not read widely, as Tahto has, or to study whatever texts can be found?" Achtriel asked her. "And what of the ideas of Philo and Eusebius? Philo says that Moses was a Platonist and felt that everyone was free."

"There have been so many different views about the nature of the soul." She continued musing as she sewed. "The man from Ravenna brought us a text an Arab merchant sold him. It is Jesus teachings to Mary. He told her that men and women are equal in the sight of the Lord, and that men are wrong to conquer women and treat them like cattle. And she says He loved her as a woman. And they were not married." Warming to her topic, Achtriel looked up. It was then she noticed that everyone sat frozen, staring at her.

Esther quickly turned to Ardith's mother, like a person set to douse a fire, but it was too late.

"Aphacorsim! Sacrilege and witchcraft! Is this what that old man is teaching hereabouts? I will tell the elders to take all his books and burn them!"

"They are only ideas," Achtriel began, but the mother rose from her chair and pointed to the door.

"Leave at once!" she commanded. "I will not share a room with such as you. And tell your grandfather that he is evil, and his judgment day is nigh!"

"But I only meant…"

"Perhaps you'd better go now, Achtriel," Esther said, helping Achtriel to her feet.

"But what is wrong with speculation?" she asked as Esther moved her toward the door.

"Certain people cannot tolerate it," she said quietly, opening the door. Closing it behind her, Esther whispered "Go home now and tell Tahto to hide all his texts. There may be trouble." When she opened the door to return, the women's voices rose behind it, the loudest, of course, was Ardith's mother's which rang with a note of hysteria. Stunned, Achtriel stood still. What had she done? She had not meant to frighten anyone. And now, Tahto was in danger. She turned and ran as quickly as she could to warn him.

"Where is Tahto?!" she gasped as she came through her front door. Berthe looked up and put her finger to her lips.

"Hush, child," she said quietly. "The balm has helped Tirzah, and she is sleeping. Do not waken her for pity's sake."

"I'm sorry," Achtriel said softly. "But I must speak to Tahto now! Something terrible may happen."

"He's in the study. But don't disturb them with your childish…"

"No! You do not understand," Achtriel said and hurried to the back end of the house.

Tahto and Nimrode were there, surrounded by a sea of scrolls and codices. They were bent over one, examining it with relish.

"Tahto! I have ruined us!" Achtriel cried, running to him and sinking to the floor.

"How can that be? Are fanatics at my gate with torches?" he joked.

"Very nearly, Tahto, I'm afraid. I was just talking about Philo, and that text Antonus brought us and…"

"Oh dear," Nimrode said, looking up from the scroll they were studying. "Let me guess, Ardith's mother is it?"

"Yes. How did you know?"

"There are many like her. Narrow-minded souls who wish to bury any knowledge with which they disagree."

"I'm sorry, Tahto," she said, tears springing to her eyes. "I didn't know!"

"And how could you, little one," he said consolingly and stroked her arm.

"Do not worry, child, your grandpapa and I are well prepared for such circumstances." Nimrode winked.

"But what if they come and burn …"

"They cannot burn what they don't find," he said. "Now go and help Berthe with the dinner. Everything will come out well."

"You know, I haven't looked at you for far too long," Tahto said, touching her face tenderly. "You have grown longer in the face and taller. You begin to look like someone I once knew…"

"Who Tahto?" she asked with desperate curiosity.

"I am not sure…" he pondered, gazing at her.

"A very pretty person, whoever she is, or was," Nimrode said cheerfully. "Now go about your work and do not worry. There has been no harm done yet."

"Nor will there be," Tahto assured her. "I have lived too long among these people to be taken in by them."

"What will you do?"

"I have a cache which none can find where I keep such as might alarm the enemies of thought."

"But what if…"

"They have not the patience nor the fortitude to search as diligently as one would need to locate it. And so we will be safe, as always."

"It's true." Nimrode smiled at her. "By the time we sit down to dinner, the evidence will have disappeared. Come, Tahto. I doubt the woman is a present threat. Nonetheless, we ought to take precautions."

"Do not fret about it," Tahto said, kissing her head. "It is an inconvenience, that is all."

"Perhaps you had better not repeat such conversations outside our home, in future," Nimrode added.

"I see that now," she said. "I'm sorry I was foolish."

"That is something you will never be," Tahto said with a smile.

While they were at dinner, Profait paid them a visit. Tahto offered him a chair.

"She will be gone tomorrow," he told them, sitting down. "Thankfully. I do not like such quarrelsome behavior in my house."

"I imagine Ardith is upset as well?" Berthe asked.

"Oh, not in the least," Profait said. "She has prayed for this day for months. I insisted that her mother stay to help. Ardith would have sent her home after the second week."

"Perhaps Ardith will feel more kindly toward me now," Achtriel mused.

"She does not dislike you," Profait said, taking the piece of oiled bread that Berthe handed him. "She had twelve younger sisters as a girl and had to raise them. The virtuous mother was continually elsewhere."

"So she thinks I am another sister?"

"So she treats you as she thinks apt for little girls. She does not appreciate your skills as do we who know you better."

"And rightly so," Berthe said, looking sideways at Achtriel. "A scholar you may be, but the world will judge you always on your good behavior."

"Nonetheless," Profait said, returning to the previous topic, "I would take precautions with our manuscripts for several months. We do not know the trouble she is capable of brewing."

"We have hidden them already," Nimrode told him.

"In the coming months, we shall revert to our translation into Hebrew of the Persian texts, Tahto said, "They want completion anyway, and we have a buyer for the copies."

"I would much rather help you with that than complete the sewing," Achtriel brightened.

"I am sure you would," said Berthe. "But Tirzah now is making herself ill with worrying about her business."

"But garments are frivolities! The ancient manuscripts are much more important!"

"They have survived for many centuries," Berthe said. "Another few days will scarcely harm them."

Chapter 29

As it turned out, thanks to Ardith's rapid work, the clothes were done before the Sabbath with several days to spare. These Achtriel spent happily working on her music with Frans and Naadasya. They were to perform a piece that Naadasya had composed. It had sections with elements of all the music he had gathered from his travels. The words to the songs were in many languages, and although she did not know what she was saying, which Naadasya said was just as well, she was able to imitate them well enough. She and Frans learned to harmonize both with their voices and their instruments. Naadasya was delighted.

Esther came by every day, ostensibly to see how they were faring but, as anyone could tell, mostly to visit Naadasya. His whole face brightened when he saw her, and he approached her, a bit shyly, like a lad of fifteen. Achtriel knew that they were sweethearts, but what this meant exactly she was not sure. Frans caught Achtriel's eye when Esther led Naadasya outside-to "confer" —and winked.

Preparations for the wedding could be seen about the town. Women and men wore expectant looks on their faces, which, along with their clothes, were kept cleaner than usual. Townsmen addressed one another with a begrudging respect. Girls stood about in little groups, discussing their new clothes. Even the tiny children were more boisterous than usual, no doubt anticipating the abundant food.

The day before the wedding, Achtriel woke to find that she was alone. Bread and cheese had been left on the table for her breakfast along with a basket and a note from Berthe. "Please find as much feverfew as you can today. Tirzah is much better, and it seems to cure her headaches. Join us at Fagim's house later for a ceremonial meal." Practically an open invitation to spend all morning in the woods!

She could tell that it would be glorious outside. One of those late autumn days when the air itself was like a cool drink. In every tree, birds were chatting gaily to their neighbors, like women hanging out the wash. With a sigh of pleasure, she took the basket, a water pouch, and the bread and cheese, and headed for the woods.

As she neared them, the day grew warmer, so that the forest's coolness was welcoming. It was heaven to be in the trees, alone, on such a morning. She felt no need to hasten toward the clearing where the medicine plant grew. Tirzah was out of pain, and everyone else enjoyably occupied. She had not walked unhurried in her favorite environment for far too long. It was almost noon, therefore, when she approached the clearing, singing loudly to intimidate the wolves.

She sat down on a log and unwrapped her lunch, glad she had remembered to carry a sack of water, for she was tired and thirsty. As she chewed, she heard loud clumsy movements in the brush. Alarmed, she sprang up, fearing that an injured wolf or boar might spring out. But instead a child's face, scratched and filthy, appeared over the thicket. It may as well have been an animal's, for its desperate eyes, intent on her food, were huge and savage.

"Hello?" she called. "Do you speak Frankish, are you hungry?" She held her bread out toward the face, which, if such a thing were possible, grew even more voracious. Suddenly, a skinny form lunged past her, pushed her over, and began to fumble with her water sac.

"Wait!" she said. "I'll open it for you," but as she righted herself and prepared to lift the strap over her head, she stopped, astonished. "Sorgen!" she cried. "What are you doing here?"

"Give the water," Sorgen commanded, and Achtriel at once complied. She watched as the slave girl drank thirstily until the sac was empty.

"What are you doing here?" she repeated, but Sorgen said only, "Food!" and reached, with jagged fingernails, to wrest the bread from Achtriel's outstretched hand. When she had eaten the bread and cheese, she eyed Achtriel narrowly and sat down on the log. Neither girl said anything for several minutes.

"You help me," Sorgen uttered at last. It sounded more like a request than anything she'd said so far.

"If I can, I will be glad to," Achtriel told her. "What do you need?"

But before she could answer, the girl turned very pale and fell into a heap beside the log. Alarmed, Achtriel bent down, lifted the girl's head from the dirt, and held it. As she looked down at the small body, to check for injuries, she was first dumbstruck and then horrified.

"You're pregnant!" Achtriel said quietly when Sorgen opened her eyes. "But you are just a child!"

Sorgen seemed to be half asleep, but she raised herself onto her elbows and looked down at her swollen belly. "I be small," she said. "I think I twelve."

"How did you…"

"The master," she narrowed her eyes.

"Monsieur Hildebard?"

"No. He good. The new master, Lady Isobel's."

"Oh!" Achtriel could not think what to say.

"You help me," Sorgen repeated, and this time looked up at Achtriel.

"Of course," she said. "What do you want me to do?"

Sorgen sat up and began to rub her arms.

"You are shivering," Achtriel removed her outer tunic and handed it to the girl.

"Thank," Sorgen said flatly. Then she stared into the middle distance for several moments. "Tomorrow at wedding," she said finally, "you find my sister."

"The woman with the red dress? But I thought she had run away with the nobleman.

"She not run away. She come home. He stay with her."

"So she is your sister."

"No. They all my sister. The nine be at any festival that is law."

"The nine?"

Sorgen looked at her with some of her old contempt. "The nine of the goddess. Bring Selka, she of the red dress."

"What shall I tell her?"

"Nothing. Bring her to me. She take me home. Don't talk any-one else!" Sorgen said fiercely, as if she were, indeed, a wild animal.

"Of course not."

"Or I taken back to Master's. He kill me so ladies not find out."

"I will make sure that no one but your sister learns anything," Achtriel assured her. "Are you well enough to stay here by yourself?"

"Yes." She sighed. "What else I do?"

"You could come back with me, my friends would hide you."

"No. Then they killed if he finds out. Now I have this." She wrapped the tunic around her like a cloak. "I be well."

"I have to get some of these plants," Achtriel said, indicating the feverfew.

"For your sister?"

"Um… yes. She has bad headaches. Only she is not my sister, really. I have no parents," Achtriel said.

"Neither I. But in my hamlet, we all kin."

"That is nice. Is there anyone else I should bring to you?"

"Only Selka."

"I will come back right away and bring you food and water."

"Thank you," Sorgen said again.

"Are you sure you are alright?"

"Yes."

"There are wolves and hungry bears…"

"I know. I crawl through hole in hollow tree, stay inside, too far to reach."

"Good. Go back there now and rest. I will be back soon."

She followed Sorgen to ensure that she was safe inside her tree. Then she handed her the rest of the bread and cheese, and waited till she finished the remaining drops of water in the sac. Stringing this over her shoulders, she hurried to pick the feverfew, making sure to leave enough so the plant could regrow.

When she reached her house, it was, thankfully, still empty. Depositing the plant on the kitchen table, she went through the larder, gleaning food from places it would not be missed.

She found the largest wine flask and filled it up with water from the well. Then she took the smaller sac and poured milk into it. There was an extra blanket in the winter box, and with that and as much food as she could carry, she headed back to the woods.

She did not want to think about what had happened to Sorgen. While it was true that slaves were often poorly used, most people in Briga were kind to them. The synagogue sent committees to all households which kept bondsmen to intercede for slaves and servants and uphold their human rights. Sometimes folk resented it and accused the Jews of trying to convert the slaves, a punishable crime. But usually householders came to understand the logic.

It was more economical to keep healthy slaves, and ones who were contented were reliable. Lady Isobel's husband, no doubt, came from some far Rhinish village, somewhere too harsh to tolerate a Jewish presence. With no one to teach them Godly ways, they must have sunken into evil. Thank God Sorgen had sisters who would care for her. Now she and her baby could have a happy life.

It was hard to grasp that a girl as tiny as Sorgen should be expecting a child. She was only slightly taller than Achtriel herself. In face and body, she resembled someone not much older. How could Isobel's husband have fancied such a little girl? It did not make any sense. Of course it did not follow then that Isobel might be expected to be lenient. In situations such as these, the slaves and servants typically were blamed. And worse, in such circumstances they were subjected to harsh penalties, including death.

But Sorgen was just a child or looked like one. How could anyone imagine that she had enticed a full-grown man? Still, if she were in her position, she would have also taken flight. Where there are no laws in place to shield a human life, it can be taken as freely as an animal's. By the time she reached the clearing, boldly practicing her songs, Sorgen had left her tree and come to wait for her. She was standing in a patch of sunlight, trembling in the leather tunic.

"I have brought enough to eat to keep you comfortable until tomorrow," Achtriel told her, lifting the wine sack from her shoulders and placing the basket on the ground. "And here is a blanket to warm you." Sorgen did not look up as she took the things from Achtriel.

She wrapped herself inside the blanket and peered at the food in the basket.

Finally, she said, "I sorry I bad to you."

"It's not your fault. If I were you, I would be jealous of me too. I have a home and friends, a family of sorts. Although your sisters seem like they will care for you."

Sorgen nodded silently. "Selka say I not to injure you."

"Will you be glad to go home?"

"Yes, home." She looked thoughtful for a few moments then added, "Our place secret. None may tell it. That is why nobleman not return. He must stay now or die."

"Does he want to leave?"

"They say he happy. We have good life."

"I hope you and your child will live well there."

"I never let my child come to the lawless world. I never let her slave."

"Why did you come?"

"My mother steal things. She killed. Some say I should be kill to pay, but Selka say no. Let me work in the dark place, she say. Tell us what the lawless do."

"How do you communicate with them?"

"At moonless time, a sister come to find me. I sneak in night and we go far. She tell me news of home, I tell her...sometimes..."

"Did you tell her about the master, the bad one?"

"No."

"I will tell her then," Achtriel said.

"No," Sorgen said calmly, "then they kill him. Then priests come and kill all us."

"Your sisters would kill him?"

"Yes."

Achtriel sat thoughtfully for a while. Then she rose to go. "Tomorrow at the wedding, I will look for Selka as soon as I can. We will be here to find you as soon as we can. Will you be alright?"

"Yes," she said quietly. "Thank to you." Sorgen rose to her feet, and to Achtriel's surprise gave her a kiss upon each cheek. "Don't let priest see you. He evil too."

333

"I won't," she assured her. "Good luck to you and your child."

Sorgen nodded, then she took the provisions and went back to her hollow tree.

On the way back to town, Achtriel was not inclined to sing. Periodically, she made loud noises with a stick upon a tree trunk or threw a stone against a rock to frighten any animals. But her mind was elsewhere. Why, she pondered, are there laws at all? They do not protect the weaker—children, animals and women—from the strong. A man could always lie about a woman's virtue to excuse himself for any action he might take against her. A child could be sold to slavery simply on a whim. Daughters were routinely used as gifts to make alliances among ambitious men.

Where had the justice come from which allowed these things? The priests touted their Roman laws as bane against the often warring tribes. Christ, they said, would bring men together, and all would live in peace. But peace or war, the safety of dependent souls would never be assured. A slave, a child, an animal, a wife were offered scant assurance by that God's laws.

Again, she thanked the Holy One for watching out for her. YHWH, at least as Tahto and his friends portrayed Him, was caring and forgiving. Any scriptures that reported otherwise, they said, were tainted by ambition, greed, or politics. One had only to look at nature to assess His ways. It was not always mild but could be counted on to follow certain laws. The discovery of YHWH's secrets was the job of those who took the time to listen, watch, and think. And they reported that His love was greater than the mind of man could conceive.

The morning of the wedding day seemed to rush by in a blur. Achtriel was kept continually busy, ordered to tasks here and there by Berthe and Tirzah. There was much cooking to be done as well as other last-minute preparations. Tahto had retired to his study, but Nimrode strode about, inspecting everything for gaffes or imperfections. He and Berthe seemed quite suited to their roles as *baal ha-bayetim*. No doubt, she reasoned, they had overseen much formal entertainment as householders in the lavish east. When the preparations were complete, Tirzah hustled Achtriel into the bedroom. She proceeded to dress her with great circumspection, as if she were a doll.

"There," she said finally, pulling at an errant fold. "You look respectable."

"What are you going to wear?" Achtriel asked.

"The green kirtle and overdress. Berthe gave me some earrings and a necklace to match my pin."

"I'm sure you will look better than respectable."

"I have a business now. If I dress well, it is as advertisement. Otherwise, I would not care."

"I thought you liked rich clothing."

"I am used to it, that is all," she said. "Why is your hair always escaping from its braids? It is impossible." She frowned as she attempted to tuck in the wayward tendrils.

"No one cares about my hair," Achtriel protested, retreating.

"You represent us all at such a ceremony. I will not have your messiness embarrass me."

"Why would it embarrass you, you aren't my mother."

"I'm expected to look after you, whether you realize it or not."

"Why?"

"Because I'm older."

"But…"

"Stop your endless questions, Achtriel. Your hair will have to do. I haven't got the patience to fix it. Now go and tell Berthe that I'll be ready in a minute."

Achtriel did as Tirzah bade her but continued the unfinished conversation in her mind. "Age is accorded more respect than it is due," she retorted silently. "It does not make you my master."

Esther was arranging borrowed spoons in piles upon the dining table. "My goodness, look at you," she remarked. "A perfect young lady!"

"I will never be that," Achtriel said. "And apparently, my hair is equally unfortunate."

"It looks just fine," Esther assured her. "Now come and help me pack these spoons. Natan is coming to transport them."

"When will he be here?" she asked nervously, remembering his merciless teasing of her previous trumpery. But he was in the door before she could escape. To her surprise, he merely nodded at her, an expression of approval on his face. This was quickly superseded by awe when Tirzah entered the room.

Her hair was pulled up tightly from her forehead like a lady's. It made her look much older and incredibly more elegant. The green of the kirtle shone against her amber skin, and when she looked up, one could see that it matched exactly her translucent eyes. The silken overdress draped her body like a Grecian robe.

"Can you help me clasp this necklace?" she asked Esther. Natan hurried forward before Esther could respond. Tirzah looked at him uncomfortably but allowed him to reach behind her to fasten the clasp. He stood there as if transfixed until she walked away.

"Has Margit brought the serving boards?" she asked.

"Yes, indeed," Esther said. "We scarcely needed them though. The entire town came with their own, piled with delicacies."

"How nice," Tirzah said, but her face betrayed a doubtful estimation of these rustic offerings. "But I have paid Margit and her aunt quite well to make sure the food is adequate."

"Everybody loves Fagim," Achtriel said. "They would not lose this opportunity to show it."

"I am sure no matter how much food we have prepared it will be eaten and enjoyed. The feasting will last several days and by then, folk will have consumed whatever can be had." Natan pantomimed a hungry person lifting up a serving dish, pouring all the food in his mouth and then eating the dish. Despite her newfound dignity, Tirzah could not help but smirk at this.

"Perhaps we should retrieve our better dishes before then," she remarked.

Natan, at this encouragement of his comedic skills, began to caper like a drunken peasant.

"Well, I think the preparations are complete." Esther smiled. "Let us hope the townsfolk enjoy our feast. I've never given one before."

Natan, still dancing, made a bumptious face and even Tirzah could not help but laugh at it.

"Look at our esteemed elder!" Nimrode called to them as he led in Tahto from his study.

Tahto's beard and hair were trimmed, and he wore a woolen cape with tassels at the lining. Nimrode stood and fussed over him, straightening the pin on his overshirt and sweeping off what dust he could access with a tiny brush. Tahto submitted to his brother's ministrations with a patient air and smiled appreciatively when Nimrode was finished.

"You are the picture of a proud householder," Nimrode said.

"What is expected from such a person?" Tahto asked bemusedly.

"You will lead us to the village green," Nimrode instructed. "And we shall follow in procession, two by two. Berthe, do we have the candles?"

"Yes," she answered. "I will carry them until we are assembled on the wedding course. Achtriel, as the youngest child, you will hand them out to the *chavara*. Tirzah will come behind you and light them."

"Any household might be more than proud of such lovely young ladies." Nimrode smiled. "Indeed, brother, you now may hold your head up with the foremost families in town."

"I was not aware that my head was in another posture," Tahto said. "But I thank you for the rise in social stature which you now accord it."

"A respected family is a Jew's crowning achievement. The only earthly ornament worth coveting."

"Then I shall wear it proudly," Tahto said and assumed his position at the head of the assemblage with only a hint of drollery.

"You all look perfect," Esther told them. She held the front door open, and they followed Tahto, like a clutch of ducklings, out toward the village road.

"Try to walk with dignity," Tirzah whispered to Achtriel. "You need not sway so much if you place your feet carefully."

"I'll try," Achtriel replied and did attempt to swallow the rebellion which this slight inspired. But as she stepped beside Tirzah, like a dog crossing an icy pond, she could not help but bristle at the comment. Why was it that girls who had been born with everything—beauty, grace and perfect form—were the ones most likely to be critical of those who did not share their luck? Could they not conceive of an existence in which such gifts were absent? If so, their souls must lack the breadth, which even animals evinced, to sense another's feelings.

And we, the lesser creatures, she mused, then must strive to bear such bald insensitivity. If only there were some reward for such forbearance. This did not seem to be forthcoming, however, in human life. The beauties were most often spared the least encounter with the bitterness their attitudes engendered. Instead, the world fell at their feet and lined their path with lilies. But gazing up at Tirzah's lovely profile, Achtriel could almost understand it, although it was unfair. Such perfection was a shard among the refuse, an inkling of the mastery that marked the mind of God.

Indeed, the beauty's presence here, beside the toad-like being Achtriel conceived herself to be, was an amelioration of social standing. Like stones, alight with the reflected glory of a nearby emerald, the entire family seemed to glean respect. Other kinship groups they met along the road nodded at them with marked deference. The men of these clans eyed her own with new humility. This all felt somewhat disconcerting to Achtriel who had, for so many years, seen herself and Tahto as outsiders among both Jews and Gentiles.

As they neared the village green, the scope of wedding revelry became apparent. There were many long tables set up in the middle of the field, which had been cleared and shorn as closely as a monk's tonsure. Men were erecting tall poles decked with festive banners, and long awnings in case of rain. The entire town, from old women to babes in arms, had gathered and was gaily chatting on the grass. Scores of other visitors, drawn by curiosity or the promise of free food, had appeared from the neighboring villages and countryside.

Among them, Achtriel spotted the women from the western woods, the sisters of Sorgen.

When Tahto's party reached the green, folk gave way to let them pass. They were ushered through the crowd to stand beside the huppah, where the other members of the chevara waited. Ardith looked quite happy in a red embroidered kirtle with a white overdress. She held a chubby Jacob on her hip and glanced about proudly at other mothers in the crowd, her earlier fears of his infirmity, it seemed, forgotten. Profait, too, seemed jolly and content. In spite of Tirzah's inroads on his business, he must have made a tidy profit from the wedding trade.

Tirzah, herself, seemed much distracted. Her customary sour expression contained an added sense of irritation. She did not deign to look about the crowd, aside from a quick scanning of her handi-work on those who sported her designs. Her eyes most often sought the middle distance, where some internal occupation claimed her thoughts. Achtriel supposed it was her stated loathing for the married state that was so unsettling. But why should she begrudge Fagim her happiness? And if Tirzah felt some envy was not that living proof that she was not so disaffected as she claimed.

Perhaps all the women present felt a twinge of jealousy, seeing Fagim and Mosse so obviously overjoyed. But Fagim had made herself a valuable friend to all who had suffered illness. Besides, such a fortunate outcome for a woman who had left her husband was encouraging, especially to those who might contemplate such an action. So the townsfolk, now lining up to face each other in two long rows, lifted their tapers for the rabbi to ignite. Soon, there was a cavalcade of little flames held aloft to bless the couple on their marriage walk.

Tahto, Samiel, Profait, and Esther lifted the huppah poles and carried it to its appointed spot, where Naadasya waited with his ude. The rabbi, for once regarding them with something like approval, assumed his place beneath it with a patronizing nod. As instructed, Achtriel gave out the candles to her chevara. Tirzah followed her and lit them. Hushed respectful murmurs could be heard, which Achtriel was certain she, herself, had not inspired. Tirzah was a personage now, thanks to her elevation of the town's sartorial standing. It was ironic that this girl, who had arrived with nothing but a foul disposition, a paucity of education, and a pretty face had gained a respectability which had eluded Tahto his entire life. What further proof was needed of the scant regard accorded rectitude and learning?

But she was not inclined to pursue gloomy thoughts, for Fagim could be seen now, radiantly poised at the far end of the wedding formation. As she walked between the lines, her slim hand encompassed by Mosses' hairy one, kindness and ebullience surrounded her. Loving smiles and bright flames made a gleaming archway for the couple. It was not the ceremonial observances, but the obvious goodwill lighting the faces of the attendees, that made the moment beautiful.

Behind the huppah, Naadasya began to strum his ude. Frans came and stood beside him, and together, they sang a lovely old Semitic melody, a Hebrew song so ancient; it was said it had originated long before the Jews had lived in Babylon. It spoke of the beauty of a woman's body, and the gentle bower it became to soothe and cheer her husband. Clearly, the creator wished a man to wed, go forth, and multiply as commanded in the Pentateuch.

And yet, Achtriel could not but reflect, so many spouses seemed unhappy. Even among the Jews who, of all nations, most prized a loving family, a marriage where partners seemed content was a rare blessing. Fagim would, no doubt, be that fortunate woman who would find what the Creator had intended when He invented matrimony.

Perhaps the secret to a happy union was not such a great mystery. Fagim and Mosse had been friends for many years before they could think of being wed. Wasn't this a better system than the one currently employed? One in which a girl or boy was bartered like a lump of silver, and at an age when both were far too young to have a choice about the matter. At least she did not have to worry about that, Achtriel consoled herself. No matchmaker would advertise her charms. Only a fool or a desperate man would stoop to wed a cripple such as her. And even then, he would not offer much to have her. She would have to be forever thankful to any man who might accept her. It did not seem so different than slavery, where a person's market value dictated their worth.

At this thought, her mind returned to poor Sorgen, alone in the woods like a forgotten lamb. She looked back through the crowd to where the women from the slave girl's village stood. They were talking softly to each other, occasionally laughing as if at some bawdy jest. Throughout the interminable wedding rites, in which the Kettubah was read and endless glasses of wine drunk and speechified over, Achtriel could think of nothing but Sorgen.

Luckily, Sorgen's people had a different set of customs. But still, to have one's future stolen on a lecher's whim, this was a dread circumstance that befell only females, in the "civilized" world. Once again, she questioned the validity of laws, their supposed evenhandedness. The Jewish laws were clear about so many things—property, taxes, business interactions, marriage—but still, a girl could hope for scant protection. Democratic as they were, there was a sharp distinction between a woman's rights and those of men.

The Gentile laws changed constantly. Some well-placed cleric or magistrate would decide that such and such was bad, and make a law. No wonder people tended to ignore them, although in the case of Jews, this laxity was fortunate. Otherwise, each anti-Jewish program would become widespread and choke the narrow strait of tolerance in which they managed to survive.

But protected or not, Fagim was clearly thrilled to be a married woman. She blushed and smiled as Mosse broke the wineglass, amid the raucous cheers of the spectators. Even Achtriel shouted out her wishes for their happiness. The couple, hand in hand, made their way back through the passage of uplifted lights, laughing as they were pelted from both sides by flower buds. Finally, they turned and called for everyone to come and feast.

Achtriel quickly looked about. She did not see Tirzah or Esther, so she slipped unnoticed into the crowd. At the far end of the field, she spotted Sorgen's compatriots dressed in their form-fitting clothing. Each one had a large garland of leaves and flowers encircling her head. They were moving languidly toward the food line, as if hunger never troubled them. The townsfolk offered no such pretense. They rushed to the tables like a gang of churls, albeit with much good-natured raillery. The chance to eat one's fill was a rare, intoxicating event.

The women from the woods observed the hurrying villagers with disdain. Nonetheless, they did increase their pace. They secured a spot in the long line, ignoring what must have been jibes from those nearby, skeptical, no doubt, as to the women's right to be there. The one who had given Achtriel the parchment, the one Sorgen called Selka, looked away from them distractedly, as if such vulgarity did not concern her. Thus, she witnessed Achtriel's approach.

Achtriel discreetly beckoned to her, giving her a meaningful stare, then gazing off as if to assess the crowd. Selka, looking curious, left the line to join her.

"I need to talk to you," Achtriel said quietly, "in private. It's about Sorgen."

Selka raised her eyebrows. She looked back at her sisters and then fixed Achtriel with an incisive stare. Nevertheless, she followed her across the field. When they were far enough to be sure no one was watching them, Achtriel pulled her behind a tree.

"What?" Selka asked.

"I need to take you to her later. She is in the woods."

"Why?" Selka demanded.

"I cannot tell you yet, someone could overhear you if you talk about it."

"When?"

"After the meal, I have to sing in a performance. When I am done, I'll come to you and take you to her."

"Has she be wicked?"

"Not at all. It's not her fault."

"Why she tell you? She no like you." Selka drew her brows together in a suspicious frown.

"I found her. I was in the woods. She is alright now, but we should reach her before evening falls. It will be very hard to come this way through the woods at night. We could get lost."

Selka studied Achtriel for a long minute.

"We not get lost," she told her.

"Still," Achtriel said doubtfully, "we should leave well before it gets dark."

"When you come, I go with you." She turned to leave.

"Wait!" Achtriel cried. "It's very important that no one overhears you, talking to your sisters. It would be very dangerous if..."

"They not know our tongue."

"But there may be some well-traveled folk about. They might have learned it."

Selka laughed. "Then they be one of us."

Achtriel started to say something, but Selka merely waved her hand dismissively and walked away.

Staying hidden to ensure they were not seen together, she worried about Selka's rashness. How could she be certain that no one would understand them? The priest had studied every dialect from here to Paris to sermonize the heathen. Mendicants, performers, and even some herdsmen made it a point to learn a host of different tongues. Although the sisters' odd accent and sentence structure was unusual, local dialects were often mutually comprehensible. Although, Tahto had once told her that these women's language was unique.

She peered out from behind the tree. Selka had rejoined her friends and was speaking furtively to them. From time to time, she would look about the crowd suspiciously. Achtriel wished she had emphasized more fervently the need for secrecy. Although a pregnant slave girl was hardly unusual, the fact that everyone assumed Sorgen to be a child would make the incident a source of gossip. Always eager to assert his legal powers, the priest would make a point of prosecuting her. Isobel's husband, to clear himself, could try the girl for witchcraft, and no doubt, ensure she hanged. Or worse, they'd rouse the gentry to eliminate the women from the western woods forever.

After several minutes, Achtriel emerged and made her way toward the party. The guests were filing past the dinner tables, filling up the bowls and plates they had brought with them for that purpose. She could see Naadasya gathering his instruments and looking up with some concern, no doubt in search of her. She hurried toward him across the field, adopting a cheerful demeanor that she did not feel.

When he saw her, Naadasya looked relieved. "Ah. There you are," he said. "I forgot to tell you that we are ensured a place at the head of the dining line. I worried that you would not get to eat."

"We've waited for you," Frans said cheerfully. "What's wrong? You look so pale."

"You're not ill are you?" Naadasya asked.

"No, not at all," she said heartily. "But I am hungry!"

"Very well then," Naadasya said with relief. "Let us feed our star musician!"

"I am not a star," she protested, following them toward the tables. "I am only learning about music. You and Frans are far starrier than I will ever be."

"A star is brilliant even when obscured." Frans winked at her.

She felt herself becoming nervous then. With everything she needed to remember and with the worrisome distractions caused by her involvement with Sorgen, it would be hard enough to rise to the demands this piece required. If they expected her to shine, she feared, they would be disappointed. It would be terrible to repay Naadasya's tutelage and kindness with a poor performance. As they approached the wedding guests, she tried to clean her mind of everything but music.

Natan stood at the head of the line and ushered them through. The table was so loaded with fancy food, it resembled the dresses in their improbable colors, in which ladies now bedizened the scenery. There were many kinds of animal foods, which Achtriel confessed a curiosity to sample. But she saw the blank dead face of a pregnant goat, whose unworldly eyes seemed even odder in death. She thought of Sorgen, whose own belly would soon swell with that burgeoning of life, a miracle of God so wantonly desecrated, as a rule, by men. Avoiding the goat's blinded eyes, she looked at the countless other dishes to choose from. Cheeses, salads, beans, mushrooms, bread, olives, grapes, and pickled green beans, radishes, cabbage and carrots.

She had not told the truth about her appetite. Her nervous stomach was prevented from such homely pleasures. Her heart was

344

pounding, there was a ringing in her ears. And to make it worse, she knew she must feign anticipation, even joy.

"Take some more," Frans chided her. "We must plumpen that pretty face of yours."

"You are not taking much," she told him.

"A dwarf cannot afford to get too fat," he said. "It weighs upon our bones. Besides, I have the opportunity to eat such fare more often than your neighbors. The duke has brought his cook along from Paris, and she is very good. But you are much too thin. How will you find a husband with those sallow cheeks?"

"I don't think I shall," she said. But to please him, she took a large heaping of beans and a piece of bread so moist and sweet it almost seemed like cake. Remembering Sorgen, she also took dried fruits, hard eggs, and flatbreads. These would keep well and be useful on her journey home.

Sitting with Naadasya, Esther and Frans, she forced herself to eat and to join their jolly conversation. Esther seemed particularly merry. Her rich complexion glowed; and her blue eyes, with their black lashes, shone like sapphires.

"Do you all remember your parts?" Naadasya asked.

"I do," Esther said. "I am to announce you as the Royal Songbirds and step out of the way."

"It seems a pity to waste such an eye-catching element," Naadasya mused, looking at Esther. "Are you sure you don't want to stay on stage with us?"

"I do not play any instrument, nor do I know the songs," she demurred.

"Ah, but none would notice it, nor care. They'd only wish to look at you."

"You could move your mouth like a fish's while we sing." Frans suggested playfully.

"Thank you, no," Esther said. "I think I can forego that display of my talent."

"Ah well." Naadasya sighed, smiling. "In my next production, I will write a part expressly for you. Perhaps it will be a theatrical."

"It had better be" Esther laughed. "I cannot imagine myself singing to an audience."

"But you have a lovely voice," Frans said. "I have heard it."

"When?"

"When you came to visit our rehearsals, you were often humming one of the Hebrew tunes you taught us. And when you left us you did so, singing."

"Because she was so happy," said Naadasya.

"Because I was not sewing." They all laughed at this.

Achtriel thought back to the hours of tedium that the now ubiquitous garments had demanded. And yet, despite the care and expense lavished on these costumes, their owners now feigned indifference toward them. In conversation with their neighbors, they did not, like the little girls, show off the features of their new attire or twirl around to show the back. Rather, they acted as if nothing could be farther from their minds. Their eyes, however, avidly trailed all who passed by, assessing every feature of their ensemble.

Achtriel decided that the realm of clothing, and its fascination for those whose bodies were attractive, was—at best—a vain distraction. She had to admit, though, that the industry involved in its procurement was lifeblood to those, like Esther and Fagim, who plied its wares. It kept the nobles occupied and gave employment to the weaker slaves who, otherwise, might risk their health as laborers. A girl as undergrown and skinny as Sorgen could hardly have survived without it.

Still, she reflected, the time, expense, and effort spent on clothing, if put to better use, might itself obviate the need for slavery. If the nobles and their merchant minions turned their concentration to the problems which persisted around them, the inadequacy of current forms of food production, the burden such continual scarcity imposed upon the poor, they might devise innumerable solutions to the ills which plagued their village and so many like it.

"Look! Natan is waving to us," Naadasya said. "I think we soon will start."

"You have hardly eaten a thing," Frans reprimanded Achtriel.

"I am too nervous," she explained. "I will leave my plate with Esther and come back for it."

"A good idea," Naadasya said. "And you know, a nervous stomach is a boon to singing!"

"Let us go then." Frans rose to his feet. "Come, my butterfly." He smiled and proffered his hand to Achtriel.

"I hope your piece goes well," Esther said and kissed Naadasya on the cheek.

"With comrades such as these it cannot fail," he told her merrily.

Achtriel's unspoken doubts about her own success were laid aside as she took the hand Frans offered her and rose to accompany him. Following him clumsily to the huppah, she could not recall a single line of her song. She dearly hoped her memory would recover when she heard the tune. If not...she could not finish the thought. Soon, they were gathered at the little stage erected before the huppah for the wedding entertainment.

Chapter 30

"Ladies and gentlemen," Esther's lovely voice rang out. "I have for you the Royal Songbirds. Let their music bring joy to your hearts, just as your presence at our celebration brings gladness to us all." She left the stage with an impish nod to Naadasya and went to stand among the audience. Naadasya turned to face Frans and Achtriel. He raised his hand into the air as Frans breathed deeply and prepared to sing.

"YHWH and the local gods and fairies, help me now," Achtriel whispered to him. "I cannot remember one note I am supposed to sing." A wink was all the answer Frans gave her. And then the music started.

To her surprise and great relief, the melody awoke her memory. When she opened her mouth, the song escaped and took to the air. Despite her worries, the tones, like well-trained falcons, soared as they'd been trained to do. The combination of voice and strings, like a latticework, made places that the notes could land, like graceful creatures of the sky.

She tried not to look at the faces of the crowd. It would be too easy to spot Selka, or worse yet, Lady Isobel and her perfidious spouse. Instead, she let the music buoy her, like a sea bird on the wind. Once, however, her concentration momentarily lapsed. At the far reaches of the crowd she saw the priest, gesticulating wildly at Selka. The music deadened in her throat, and she could not revive it.

Frans looked at her quickly and took note of her condition. Without attracting notice, he slipped his hand into her own. An odd sensation emanated from his fingers. Icy cold at first, it became quickly hotter. Soon, she felt a current travel up her arm and gather in her neck. At once, the notes became unstuck and issued forth. She looked at him with great surprise, but he just smiled.

"What did you do?" she asked him later when their piece had finished.

"Oh, nothing," he said. "Bardic trickery. It comes in handy as I've said." Naadasya was bowing to the loud approval of the audience, and now he turned to smile at them.

"I am so sorry," she told him as they left the stage.

"For what?" he asked her.

"I forgot my part. I should have practiced more."

"Nonsense. No one noticed. It was but a momentary lapse. It happens to us all." Nonetheless, she felt she had not done justice to his lovely work and all his kindness to her. But there was nothing to be done. One could not alter time. Much as she wished she could have gone back to correct her error, it was not within the bounds of human capability. And now she saw the priest advancing toward her, like a bull.

Pretending that she had not seen him, she did her best to disappear. From behind the broad back of a carpenter, she saw him question Esther. Scanning the crowd, Esther caught sight of her but looked away and shook her head politely at the priest. Wasting no further time, Achtriel made her way through the guests and found Selka, lying on her side upon the grass.

"What did the priest want?" Achtriel asked her, obscuring herself within the group of Selka's sisters.

"Stupid man," Selka scoffed dismissively.

"Did he ask about Sorgen?"

"No."

"What did he want?"

"Tell everyone what to think."

"Well," she looked back through the crowd and caught sight of him, talking vehemently to a group of villagers. "I think we should go now," she said.

Selka stood up slowly. One of her nearby sisters said something in their curious tongue, and Selka answered her.

"What did she ask you?" Achtriel implored as she and Selka blended cautiously into the throng of wedding guests.

"You not need to know. Ask too much."

"I am worried about Sorgen," she whispered. "If the priest finds her, it could be terrible."

"He no care about Sorgen. He want my baby." She put a protecting hand on her abdomen, although it had hardly even begun to swell. "Put water on it, he say. Baptize or it go to hell." She laughed. "This place be hell."

Achtriel sighed but ceased her questioning. She went to retrieve her food from Esther and, when she returned to Selka, furtively deposited the portable items in her sack. Soon, she could not speak at all. It took all her concentration to keep up with Selka who moved so swiftly through the crowd that it was difficult to follow her. At the far end of the field, where there were no guests, Selka stopped and frowned at the adjoining trees.

"This how you get through forest?" Selka asked when Achtriel caught up to her. She pointed to a nearby thicket.

"No. It's not the way I go, but it is likely safer. I do not want to walk through town across the bridge. We might be seen."

"You know way from here?"

"Not really, but I think it will work. If we head east, we should be at the clearing well before dusk."

Selka did not comment. She merely stepped into the forest and vanished like a sylph. Achtriel hurried after her and finally spotted her standing in a copse, surveying the surrounding wood. With a nod to Achtriel, she moved ahead. Not surprisingly, she seemed accustomed to the art of moving through trees. She would disappear or so it seemed, and just as Achtriel had given up all hope of finding her, would resurface, waiting in a glen.

Soon, they came upon the river, much wider here than Achtriel had anticipated. Selka looked across the waters, as if taking their measure. She glanced back at Achtriel appraisingly. "You move good," she commented.

"I come here a lot."

"You cross river here before?"

"No."

"You hold on me. Come." She gestured for Achtriel to take her arm.

"I will be fine."

"Not if water high. Come here."

Achtriel tied her outer robe about her chest and secured her food sack beneath it. The water was startlingly icy for a summer day. It swooped in frothy eddies over rocks and boulders, and seemed a distant and fearsome cousin to the little stream that danced beneath the bridge. Maintaining a foothold in it, difficult for her even on solid ground, became a monumental task. Even with Selka's steadying arm, the crossing was lengthy and hazardous. When they reached the farther bank, they stopped to wring the wetness from their clothes.

"You strong," Selka said with some surprise.

"Thank you," Achtriel replied, although she would have liked to add. "All cripples are not helpless." But she knew that Sorgen's fate depended on the goodwill of this woman, so she would not risk offending her.

The riverbank was soft and mossy, warmth to her chilled feet. Achtriel stood on it for a moment and looked up at the sun. "That way is east," she said, but Selka shook her head.

"No. We stay by river. Easier walk." Before any objection could be raised, Selka strode upstream, as if she knew precisely where to go.

"Have you been here in this part of the woods before?" Achtriel asked when she reached the river bend where Selka stood awaiting her.

"No."

"Then perhaps we'd better…"

"You follow me."

"How do you know if the way you're going is correct?"

"Tss. The wind!" Selka said, as if the answer were ridiculously obvious.

"The wind can change," Achtriel said, but Selka had marched on ahead. There was no choice but to follow her, or risk becoming stranded. She wished they could have taken her familiar route. Had she been blind as well as lame, she could not have failed to find her way there. This portion of the forest was unknown to her, however, and seemed colder, larger, and more dangerous.

Selka, though, was unconcerned. She could have been out on a pleasure hike, so little did she take note of the landmarks. To make things worse, the sun would set early at this time of year. Even in summer it was hard to spot its glimmer through thick trees. Achtriel began to fear they would get reversed or follow the river too far in the wrong direction. Soon, it would grow dark, and they could lose all sense of reckoning.

"I think we should head east now," she said finally when she reached the spot where Selka waited for her.

"What means east?"

Achtriel felt her stomach sink to her knees. "East. That way, away from the sun. You don't know..."

"I not need to know." Selka said. But even so, she seemed to be at somewhat of a loss. She looked about and scanned the forest canopy. Then she did a curious thing.

She knelt down on the riverbank and closed her eyes. For several minutes, she did not move. The silence of the forest, interrupted only by the wind-tossed branches, surrounded them. Selka's voice, so soft that at first Achtriel could not be sure if she were hearing or imagining it, began to chant in her peculiar language. Among the strange sounds she produced, the word Mari was sung repeatedly. It was as if she were addressing this Mari and asking for her favor. Suddenly, Selka's eyes flew open, and she stood up. She seemed like some kind of golem, as if she were being jerked and tossed by wild internal forces. Then she looked up at the sky. To Achtriel's astonishment, a huge grey owl was circling overhead. Catching sight of it, Selka nodded and seemed instantly to be herself again.

"She say go here," Selka said matter-of-factly and headed off into the trees.

Achtriel did not have time to try to make sense of this strange occurrence. Deftly skirting branches and hopping over fallen trees, swiftly and confidently, Selka bounded forward. Ignoring her infirmities, Achtriel attempted to keep pace with her, but it proved impossible. Nevertheless, Selka could be counted on to reemerge, stepping nonchalantly from the underbrush, whenever Achtriel lost her trail.

They went on this way for what seemed an interminable time. At last, Achtriel glimpsed the welcome sight of her old clearing, although she had not approached it from this angle before. Standing in the center of it was Sorgen, watching Selka's swift approach.

When Achtriel reached them, they were speaking rapidly in their weird tongue. Despite her gift for language acquisition, Achtriel could find no common thread, no parallel to decipher their vocabulary. It was as if their sounds and syntax were unearthly. Nonetheless, she did not need to understand their words. Their gestures, and expressions needed no translation. Selka was furious, and Sorgen was trying to assuage her. Finally, Selka calmed enough to notice Achtriel.

"She say she know the father. This true?" she demanded, turning to face her.

"He run away," Sorgen insisted, looking pleadingly at Achtriel.

"Yes. He ran away," Achtriel said.

"She say she no want to lie with him."

"He force me!" Sorgen cried.

"I have heard that he did that to other girls, everybody says so." Achtriel added.

"What his name?"

"Poppy," Sorgen said.

"Poppy, yes. He was a bad man."

"Then I find him."

"He...it will be very difficult. He had a horse."

"How a slave have horse?"

"He steal it," Sorgen said, looking at Achtriel.

"It was a very fast horse. He has been gone for months. He could be anywhere."

"I find him," Selka said again. Having made this resolution, she seemed to become calmer. After a moment, she took Sorgen in her arms. Soon, they were both weeping.

"You go back now," Selka said when they had dried their eyes. She fumbled in a pouch tied to her waist and offered Achtriel a silver coin.

"No. You keep it for the baby," Achtriel insisted and handed Selka the sack of food. She could feel them watching her as she turned to take the path toward town. The day was waning now. Not sharply as it did later in winter but softly, almost wistfully. The birds were calling to their loved ones, reminding them to hurry homeward.

Now that her objective had been reached she could relax. The forest sounds and smells, like friends, allayed her recent fears. She was beginning to feel almost happy. The wedding was over, there would be no sewing drudgery for quite a while. When Tirzah paid her for her hours of work, she would have enough to furnish Tahto with fresh milk and eggs for months. With the remainder, she could buy him beans and corn to last all winter. She recalled Fagim's laughter and her shining eyes. Perhaps, she thought, she had misjudged the world. Life might not be as grim as she supposed. Even her own future might proffer some happiness.

Just then, she heard a rustling in the trees. Out from the bushes stepped the reddish wolf who had menaced her earlier, recognizable by his bitten right ear. It stood blocking her path and fixed her with its yellow stare. She stood as still as she could. She knew it would have been unwise to run even if she were capable of it. There was no time to climb a tree, and all the ones nearby were short and spindly. There was nothing to be done. She stared back at the wolf, unable to do otherwise.

Then to her surprise it did an astonishing thing. As if it were a well-trained dog, it folded its hind legs and sat. After a moment, it stretched its front legs and lay down, for all the world like an old hound, lazing in the afternoon. Its face regarded hers with what seemed a not unfriendly smile.

"Hello," she said to it. The wolf blinked its eyes and let its tongue hang out of its mouth. She was still trying to decide what next to do when it stood again and ambled off into the forest.

It was miraculous. The whole day had been unusual and somewhat enchanted. First, Frans's Bardic trickery which freed her tongue. Then Selka's unexplainable contact with the owl and now the wolf's comradery. She knew that, if indeed some magic had been used, it would not do to notice or remark on it. Such actions, although she could not recall who told her so, could cause the charm to fade away, like something that had never been. Like so many things in life, there was no choice but to accept its existence and be thankful.

When she came to the edge of the forest, she realized that she was tired and also very hungry. She did not feel like returning to the wedding. Her efforts at pretending to be gay, in the midst of the fear surrounding Sorgen's departure, had left her drained. But there was nothing to eat at home; everything had been set out for the party. Sounds of its music and laughter, adrift on the summer breeze, could be heard even here, high above the village. Reluctantly, she made her way down the hill and toward the festivities.

When she reached the field, she could see Frans and Naadasya, playing lively music for the dancing guests. Spotting her, Frans waved and beckoned. He pointed to the drums beside him and then at her, his message: that she should join them and make music. At another time, she might have found the opportunity to play in such exciting circumstances irresistible. But now, she could not bear it. She smiled and waved to him, pretending she had not perceived his meaning.

The food tables were arrayed with rich and unusual dishes. Thankfully, the goat had been consumed. She found an unused wooden bowl and filled it. She was about to bite into a honeyed barley cake when Tirzah's sour voice prevented her.

"My God, your dress. What have you done to it?"

"I...I went into the woods."

"Look, your tunic is all stained, and it smells like river water."

"Yes, I...I'm sorry. It could not be helped."

"Could not be helped? Do you know how much work I put into that tunic?" She took the wilted cloth between her fingers and shook her head

"Even though my head was hurting, I made sure that you would have a decent dress. I can see my efforts meant nothing to you."

"No. I'm sorry. There was something...it needed to be done."

"You are really such a child, Achtriel. I should have known you were too young to appreciate anything. You care more for your games than any work I have done for you."

"That isn't true. I love the dress!"

"So much that you went off to play and soiled it. And look! The material is scratched and torn. I won't be able to reuse it. Even the ribbons!"

"I'm sorry. I can't explain…"

"I don't need an explanation. The dress is ruined." Tirzah sighed and turned to leave.

"Wait!" Achtriel cried. "I can repay you from my earnings. You can deduct the cost of the dress before you pay me."

"Then you'll have nothing left."

"What do you mean? It's only one dress. I have worked on piles of them since we started. I should have earned at least a follis!"

"If you were a seamstress, and not a mere assistant that would be the case."

"But I did as much as anyone!"

"Yes, but your work was shoddy, Ardith had to fix it many times. And so did Margit. I paid them both accordingly."

"That isn't true!!"

"Look who is talking about truth!"

"What…?"

"Your cat destroyed the blue tassel. You lied about it. If you had been honest, I might have overlooked it, but you weren't. I took the cost out of your wages."

"What will I be paid then?"

"Here," Tirzah reached into her purse and handed Achtriel a pentanummum.

"But this is nowhere near what I have earned!"

"Since I'm the business owner, I determine who earns what. And you, as you've proved today, are but a child. I think it's more than adequate." With that, she turned and walked away.

A baleful fury filled Achtriel's chest. She stood, stunned by rage, and watched her "sister" move across the field. Attentive and approving comments were apparent, even at a distance, in the groups of villagers she passed. Berthe and Nimrode, amidst a cluster of religious Jews, welcomed her to their circle with a beaming pride.

Tirzah glanced dismissively in Achtriel's direction and spoke to Berthe. Although out of earshot, the content of her words was unmistakable. Berthe shook her head and looked at Achtriel reprovingly. The faces that surrounded her reflected similar sentiments. Only Nimrode glanced at Achtriel with kindness and seemed to be defending her. His efforts appeared unsuccessful.

Achtriel's face grew red with shame and anger. When at last she could coax movement from her legs, she turned away. Now she wanted only to be gone from here, from these people who cared more for dresses than the rescue of a slave. Although they did not know of this, and she could never tell them, their censure seemed deliberate, condescending and unfair. Leaving the revelers, who now seemed a vast disapproving throng, she made her way back to the road. To her dismay, she saw Fagim and Mosse, followed by Natan and Violette, approaching her.

"Achtriel!" Fagim said smiling, "I have some wonderful news!" Unable to speak for fear of loosening the bitter tears behind her eyes, Achtriel stopped. "Don't you want to know?" Fagim asked gaily. Achtriel nodded.

"I have sold my house. Natan and I are moving in with Mosse!"

"That's wonderful," Achtriel managed to tell her.

"But that is not the best of it! Can you guess what is?"

"No."

"Now I can afford to educate Natan! He knows his Hebrew letters but has not been able yet to read or write. Just imagine what he can accomplish if he learns these things!"

Natan was looking at her curiously. Since his communication skills thus far were based on gesture and expression, there was little hope that he would fail to grasp her present mood.

"And guess who we have chosen to 'ope the stores of learning' to my son?" Mosse said grandly.

"You!" Fagim embraced her.

"I...I wouldn't know how to..."

"Nonsense!" Mosse said heartily. "If anyone is capable of devising ways to teach him, it is you."

"You are so creative and resourceful; we have no doubt you will accomplish it," Fagim said.

"And we will be able to pay you. You can now support old Tahto in his advancing years."

"Thank you very much," Achtriel said. She tried to imitate their happy faces but knew that she had made a poor attempt. Only Natan seemed to notice this, however, as they kissed her happily and left.

Her house was empty when she got there. Even Tahto was still at the wedding. Its revelry would continue through the night and following day. She could hear the giddy noises from her bedroom window. Sechela, sensing, in the mysterious way she had, that Achtriel was home, jumped onto the windowsill and rubbed her cheek against its frame. Grateful for a kindred soul, and one not overly preoccupied with momentous doings, Achtriel embraced her. The familiar smell of her fur was comforting.

"I hope you have had a nice day," she said, stroking the cat. "Mine has not been." Sechela, her throat rumbling, moved her body against Achtriel's hand. She followed happily when Achtriel removed her wet clothes and lay on her bed. Soon, the two were curled up together. Achtriel had not realized how exhausting the stressful hike had been and felt herself drift instantly to sleep.

When she awoke, the room was dark. Out the window, nascent stars were taking their positions in the sky. Suddenly, she heard a scraping sound and sat up in bed. Tirzah was pulling the trunk of clothes and materials along the floor of the bedroom. She stopped when she saw Achtriel.

"So this is where you've got to," she said. "Everyone has been wondering." Her dismissive tone reignited Achtriel's ire. There were no words to match the bitterness she felt. Tirzah put the trunk down and began to gather things.

"What are you doing?" Achtriel finally asked.

"I am leaving."

"What?"

"Yes. You will be rid of me. I have bought Fagim's old house and Berthe, Nimrode, and I are moving to it. You and your beloved cat will have the bed all to yourselves." Tirzah went about the room, collecting sewing tools, her toiletry, and clothing. A lengthy silence fell. In it, Achtriel's unspoken rage sat like a miasma.

Slowly, however, this began to dissipate. In its place, she was left with a feeling that confused her. It was only after Tirzah had gone, pushing the laden trunk into the common room and then out the door that Achtriel was able to identify it. To her surprise, the emotion closest to the one that now laid claim to her was loneliness.

To be continued...

Glossary of Hebrew/ Hebrew slang words

From The Joys of Yiddish by Leo Kaplan 1968

1. Am ha-aretz : A vulgar, boorish man or woman
2. Apikoros: A Jew who does not observe religious practices
3. Balebos from Hebrew baal ha-bayet : Master of the house.
4. Berriah : A woman of remarkable energy, talent, competence
5. Bet Din : A rabbinical court
6. Chachem : A clever wise or learned man or woman
7. Chuppah/ Huppa : Wedding canopy
8. Dybbuk : evil spirit
9. Golem : An unformed thing, folkloric mythical creature
10. YHVH : Jehovah
11. Kovid : An honor
12. Mitzvah : A meritorious act
13. Nayfish: A person of no consequence
14. Purim : The Feast of Lots, from the Book of Esther
15. Rosh Hashanah : Beginning of the year.
16. Sachel : Native wisdom, common sense
17. Sefer Torah : The scroll containing the Five Books of Moses
18. Shul : A school or study house
19. Torah : The Pentateuch, or Five Books of Moses
20. Tzaddik : A man of surpassing virtue

About the Author

J eannie Troll is a psychotherapist, musician, artist, and writer living in Palo Alto, California. She has combined her long-standing interest in 'child prodigies' and early medieval history to create the series that begins with *A Clever Girl*. Her years as a social worker have given her a lot of insight into the lives of outcasts, trauma survivors, and others who travel the darker currents of human society. Music, the arts, and an incessant curiosity help to keep her afloat.

CPSIA information can be obtained
at www.ICGtesting.com
Printed in the USA
FSOW01n0313010318
44979FS

9 781635 680447